KISS DA WOLF

ARE WE AN ALIEN EXPERIMENT?

KISS DA WOLF

ARE WE AN ALIEN EXPERIMENT?

A NOVEL

JASON DURANT

Copyright © 2019 by Jason Durant

Book design by Maureen Cutajar
www.gopublished.com

ISBN-13: 978-1-7334407-1-4

Contents

Not Yet Human

The alien intrusion happened a little before sunrise on a January day. That is when the man in the cabin, Todd Schwartz, a habitual early riser, sensed impending danger. His feeling of unease was so strong that he set his books and journals aside and paced back and forth in the cabin for four solid hours, pausing only to stare out of the windows. He saw nothing unusual in the thickets, pines, and deadfalls that surrounded the cabin. But something felt wrong. In truth, it felt menacing.

By noon, close to exhaustion, he sat down to rest but a moment later got up to brew coffee. Unusual for him, he had thoughts of dying, isolated in the wilderness as he was, in the dead of winter, down to his last few morsels of food, and this, his last pot of coffee. He was nervous about the coffee; he consumed two pots every day. He needed resupply today. At most tomorrow. Better today.

As the day wore on and the shadows lengthened, he watched for the resupply man, but he didn't show. By nightfall the coffee ran out. By the following morning the food ran out. Caffeine withdrawal set in, and it made Todd sick.

For three days he ran a fever. He felt intermittently hot and cold. His head hurt. He shook. He couldn't think. He couldn't see, except for blurry outlines. He kept to bed. Pain seized his muscles. Then it stopped.

When he got out of bed, it felt like he had died and been reborn in a smaller, more compact body.

He ambled about the cabin, and then went outside into the cold mountain air. That was when Todd got the first inkling that something was not right with his environment.

He went back into the cabin and fumbled with the radio for over an hour. He thought it was a miracle when he reestablished contact with the outside world.

He told them the environment around the cabin had changed in some indeterminate way. "I can see shadows where none should be. And when I'm not looking too closely, the shadows seem to move mysteriously."

He said he needed resupply. He was out of food and coffee. They told him the mountain roads were impassable. Resupply was on the way but it might take a few days.

"I've gone three days without food," he said. A sense of dread filled him. At his rate of consumption, the food and coffee should not have run out. What had gone wrong?

"Forage in the woods," the radio voice said. "You've been trained, right?"

"Yes, I've been trained." Todd said goodbye to the radio voice and sat by the fireplace, staring at the mesmerizing flames, clenching and unclenching his fists.

He went outside and hiked through the woods, soaking in his new environment, afraid of only two things: getting lost and getting killed.

He hiked for hours, marking his path by snapping tree branches. Along the way, he mastered a new skill: stalking snowshoe hares, seizing them with his gloved hands, and snapping their necks.

At dusk, he trudged back to the cabin, lit the stove, and had dinner.

In the morning, Todd discovered tracks in the snow all around the cabin. It looked like a large animal, possibly a bear, had come up to investigate and had then gone back into the woods.

Curious, he followed the tracks. Two hundred yards from the cabin, he felt the first faint beads of worry. He stopped and scanned the area. The shadows seemed to move. He felt something was watching him.

He continued walking, fear squeezing his stomach. He was following the tracks of an animal that might want to kill him for food. He was unarmed and far from any help.

Why am I doing this? Have I snapped?

His eyes met the evergreens, the swirled snowdrifts, and something else in the distance: a black, formless mass.

He saw it take shape.

Todd seemed to join with the environment. It gave him a sense of safety. It was almost like leaving his body. Then he felt the full flush of fear.

He ran for the cabin. Halfway there, he stopped and looked back. It was loping toward him, seemingly on fire with the hues of the forest.

Todd ran into the cabin, slammed the door, and threw the bolt shut. The thing smashed into the door and shook the whole cabin. Todd jumped back, shaking uncontrollably.

It scraped against the side of the cabin, moving toward a window. Todd upended the heavy kitchen table and braced it against the window frame.

He radioed a report, told them about the creature that had chased him back to the cabin.

"It looked like the Minotaur," he said, "the Greek monster with the head of a bull and the body of a man."

They acknowledged him and told him to stay in the cabin.

Todd huddled close to the radio, listening to the Minotaur stomp around outside the cabin.

By nightfall, the sounds ceased, and he crawled into bed. He did not sleep much that night.

✳   ✳   ✳

In the morning, Todd went outside and examined the new tracks that were scattered around the cabin.

The tracks were bearlike, but not like a real bear.

He stared into the distance, the hair on the back of his neck rising.

A mistake...

It was a mistake seeing the black, formless mass yesterday. It wasn't ready to be seen. It was not yet recognizable as an earth entity. It was not yet human, animal, or mytho-logical beast.

Judging by the tracks surrounding the cabin, it was still unsettled. Still shifting. Still seeking its identity.

The thing was searching for its face. It needed a face to present to the world. Todd thought it wanted his face.

Todd Schwartz was a theoretical physicist and a philos-opher. People paid him big money to think about big things. He came to the cabin in the Wyoming wilderness under contract to think about a big thing. As far as big things went, this was colossal.

The big thing was posed to him in the form of a ques-tion: *Can human consciousness reside in two or more dimensions simultaneously?*

Todd thought someone had made a revolutionary dis-covery and wanted help in shaping it for public consumption.

The consortium that footed his bill was tight-lipped. They told Todd to think about the big thing and then write an essay on how the public could best be informed of the change.

What change? Todd had asked.

They said there was mounting evidence that some here-tofore unknown force of nature was willfully disrupting life on earth. They talked about lines of demarcation.

We'll put you close to a line of demarcation in the Wyoming wilderness, and you can get some firsthand experience.

Todd accepted the challenge—and the risks—and took up residence in the cabin.

It was Vinnie and Greta Kincaid's third night in the rustic Wyoming cabin, their honeymoon retreat.

As midnight approached, Greta slipped into her pajamas, and Vinnie went around extinguishing the oil lamps. He left one lamp burning near the door, and then slipped into his own pajamas.

They retired at midnight. Soon after, Greta announced she had to go wee-wee.

Vinnie laughed and grabbed a club. Coyotes were outside the cabin again. He would protect her.

They went outside, and Vinnie clubbed a coyote.

He heard a yelp, grabbed the lamp from Greta, and flung the light toward the sound. A man lay crumpled on the ground, his head bloodied.

Vinnie checked him. He had killed the man.

Greta went wee-wee, and then she and Todd ran back into the cabin.

In the morning, Vinnie crept from the cabin and looked at the man he had killed the night before, while Greta hung back in the doorway.

The man's face was as blank as the new-fallen snow. It was not a man. It was something else.

Last night, light from the lamp had revealed a face: it was etched in Vinnie's mind.

Why was there no face this morning?

Something else was bothering Vinnie. He and Greta had slept soundly the night before, after he had killed the man, after Greta had gone wee-wee.

They should have spent a sleepless night. They should have been worried sick, fearful of being found out, debating what to do with the body. Report it? Hide it? Instead, they had slept like babies.

Vinnie and Greta went back into the cabin to eat breakfast and to decide what to do. As Greta lit the stove and filled the skillet with beefsteaks, Vinnie took a stick of charcoal and some blank paper and began sketching the face he had seen last night.

Todd Schwartz tried to raise someone on the radio. Earlier, while walking in the forest, he had glimpsed a centaur, a creature from Greek mythology with the torso, head, and arms of a man and the body of a horse, and figured he should report it. The radio was dead.

He went back to his desk, eating a ham sandwich—they had resupplied him by airdrop. He would try the radio again later, though he didn't much care if he made contact.

He had pondered the big question, exhausting his mind, and had arrived at an inescapable conclusion. Now he typed what he believed would be his last dispatch:

The blanks in the forest hunt for suitable forms to adopt. There is likely one monolithic blank. It has likely split into an infinite number of pieces. The pieces are the individuals that roam the forest, and presumably the planet.

The individuals copy powerful creatures of the forest—elk, deer, bear, cougar, wolf—to help them ambulate. Then they look for forms that are more suitable for ensuring their immersion into human society.

They look for us, and become us.

I call them light beings, for want of a better term.

They are likely composed of light, and can likely take on any form and look like any one of us.

There is no doubt we are doomed. They aren't here for any beneficial purpose. They will copy us and eventually replace us.

We won't ever die. We will be eternal energy forms at their disposal. We will have a future, created by them.

This is an extinction event, parceled out over time.

I feel slightly sinister as I type this. I'm rooting for them; somehow, they've got me.

They'll do what they want with us.

Anything you can conceive of, they will do, with us as their willing slaves.

Why are they here?

I believe they are working something out for their culture: a new history, a new drama, or perhaps a new god, which they will try out here and then incorporate back into their own world.

Todd walked back to the radio and tried to raise someone out in the world. He didn't much care if he made contact.

❅　❅　❅

Vinnie and Greta Kincaid pulsed with nervous energy as they studied the sketch Vinnie had made.

The eyes were set wide—a big, open gaze. The nose was like fine porcelain. The lips like rose petals, the chin like a rock. The jaw was angle-iron strong, the hair soft, lustrous.

In shocked silence, they studied the face, and realized it was them, merged.

Vinnie stood from the table and beckoned Greta. They went outside and searched for the body. It was gone.

No matter. They had already made their decision. They would come down from the mountains.

They would go back into society and find a new history, a new drama, and perhaps a new god.

They felt the possibilities were infinite.

CHAPTER 1

A Shared Madness

Deep in the Virginia woods, in the cavernous interior of a secret U.S. military research center, Kristen-Kate McCutchan sits in the employee dining room, her finely scripted lunch with Major Mario Cushing going to hell. She stares at a clock on the wall. It's past midnight. Where is Mario? She wants him in here fast. She's laying a trap for him. Mario chewed her out her first week on the job—spent thirty minutes haranguing her for a mistake anyone could have made—all the while looking at her as if he found her interesting. He had gone at her two ways at once, confusing her all to hell.

Tonight, she has brought two red apples. She's going to offer him one. If he accepts it and bites into it, it will be the start of something big, she thinks.

For thirty minutes you chewed me out, Mario, now I have an apple for you. And it isn't even poisoned. I have character you haven't yet discovered.

She brings her two red apples out of her bag, sets Mario's

on the table, and takes a bite out of her own. She's not too worried. Mario usually invents some excuse to pop into the dining room when she's here. Though it is getting late.

She's about to give up hope when Mario enters the room. A rapid stride brings him to her table and he accepts the apple. He sits across from her and bites into it.

"Thanks. It's delicious."

"You're welcome."

Kristen-Kate watches him eat the apple, and watches her own vanishing apple. She's about to ask him what else he likes to eat when he rises from his chair and beckons her.

"What big ideas do you entertain, Kristen-Kate?"

"Oh, I don't know." She stands and grabs her bag, and they walk toward the door.

"Do you ever wonder what's beyond the known universe?"

"Yes, I wonder."

"What if someone told you a new reality was about to breach the earth plane and that it was going to drastically alter all life on this planet?"

"I'd hit the roof. Give me proof, though."

"Come with me."

They stop at one of the kitchenettes that grace the dining room, toss their apple cores into a garbage can, and wash their hands.

Each walks to a mirror and gazes into it. There are rumors of mysterious reflections in mirrors and mirrorlike surfaces. Mario says it's hysteria, a shared madness. Though he does admit to doing a little mirror gazing himself these days.

Kristen-Kate takes her time, studies her reflection, and the background reflection as well. She doesn't see anything unusual.

They leave the dining room and enter the corridor that leads to the labs. Before long, Kristen-Kate realizes Mario is leading her to a room she wants to avoid. She can't believe he's doing this to her. Doesn't he know she almost came to blows with someone in that room? She wants to excuse herself, say she has to go to the bathroom, but he grabs her hand as if he's wise to her.

She stops at the entrance to the room, her body stiffening. Mario tries to pull her inside, but she won't budge.

The room is kept dark except for tiny lights embedded in the ceiling, walls, and floor. They told Kristen-Kate the lights have a dual purpose: for safety and to make the place look spooky.

She looks inside and doesn't see Cara Lee Ellis. Maybe it's safe to enter.

She allows Mario to pull her inside the room. He sits her down in front of a computer, the screen wetly luminescent. She feels a chill as he guides her hand to the mouse.

"What work have they been giving you?" Mario asks.

"I examine data from the African site, not the important things, though." They had put her on reduced duty pending a hearing on her first-week gaffe. She isn't too worried; lab employees other than Cara Lee have been teaching her things, stepping up her involvement. She'll sail through the hearing. Her father, U.S. Army General Nathan McCutchan, is rehearsing her. Kristen-Kate is a civilian, not subject to military justice. Her father said they were trying to draw her deeper into their culture by putting her through a proceeding that looked military.

"Tedious?" he asks.

"Yes. The data is very dry."

"You were hired for something more important than that. Let's see what we can do."

She feels a tingle, and thinks he touched her. Shivers race up and down her spine.

"Kristen-Kate, I'm going to introduce you to something we call a riff."

"Okay. So what's a riff?"

"It's an essay that you compose rapidly, so you don't block yourself. It works best when your ideas coalesce quickly and seem alien to you, as if a mysterious other wrote it."

"Cool."

"I'll demonstrate. Answer quickly. What's your riff concerning your job, Kristen-Kate?"

"I took this job so I could tell the world something."

"You see, answering quickly triggers an unusual response. You likely said something you wouldn't have said if you had taken the time to think about it."

"That's true, Mario."

He guides her hand to the mouse again and leads her into a screen that displays a lush tropical wilderness. She sees a crude military compound among the trees and armed American soldiers.

"What's *your* riff concerning your job, Mario?" She's happy he's paying so much attention to her.

"Shakespearean tragedy," he says. "To quote the Bard, *"Tis best to weigh the enemy more mighty than he seems.'*"

She wants to fool with him. "Mario, what's your riff concerning me?"

She wants him to tell her if he cares for her, what his intentions are, but her words echo in the room unanswered.

"What's your riff concerning me?" she asks again, more subdued. Mario has his hands on her shoulders, lightly touching her.

"Shakespearean tragedy," he says. "Now watch the screen."

His hands trail across her ears, her hair, ever so slight.

"Don't stop," she says.

"Watch the screen."

"I am."

"They're getting ready to execute a prisoner."

"It's simulation, right?"

"Yes."

"It's a training exercise, right?"

"Yes."

His hands are no longer on her, and then they find her again.

"Is this a promotion, Mario?"

"It is."

She spins around and looks at him. She sees his face illuminated in the tiny glows. She wants to see if Mario will betray himself, to let on that he's been seeing Cara Lee. This workstation had been Cara Lee's.

"Cara Lee hates me. Why am I getting her job?"

"She doesn't hate you."

"She does." Kristen-Kate spins back to the computer. She knows she is going to like this new assignment. She knows she can outdo Cara Lee. She wishes Mario would put his hands on her again.

On her screen they are taking a prisoner somewhere, the action frenzied.

Mario places his hands on her shoulders, slides them lower, massages her back.

"What big ideas do you entertain, Kristen-Kate? You have to tell me. I'm not simply asking. It's your job. Do you want me to get your job description out and show you?"

His hands begin a slow journey.

"No, that's okay. I believe you." She watches them beat the prisoner: punch him in the face and kidneys, kick him in the groin. It's simulation. She can tell. She laughs a little. Mario brushes her ears, her hair, her face.

Her body slumps in the chair, she is so relaxed.

"Are you religious?" he asks.

She straightens in her chair.

"I go to church, but not often. Once or twice a year. I don't believe in any of it, though. No one knows what the truth is."

"Do you believe the world is real?"

"Interesting question."

"I need to know your answer."

"I believe it's real."

Kristen-Kate senses the presence of someone new in the room, the swing of hips. She spins around. It's Cara Lee Ellis, escort service, satin hips. Cara Lee looks profoundly happy, spying her old computer, seeing Kristen-Kate sitting in her old chair. She looks like she could do cartwheels. It makes Kristen-Kate feel as if she were struck by a disease. She isn't sure she wants the promotion anymore. What could make Cara Lee so happy to see Kristen-Kate sitting at her old workstation?

Mario moves his hands down Kristen-Kate's flanks, cups her hips.

"I've told you my beliefs, Mario. Now tell me yours."

Hooded men on her screen are standing the prisoner upright. He looks okay. She can tell.

"To quote the Bard," he says, *"All the world's a stage, and all the men and women merely players.'"*

A primal urgency hits Kristen-Kate; she aches to write.

"Mario, can I do my riff now?"

"Yes." He pulls away from her.

Kristen-Kate wants Mario and Cara Lee to leave the room as she composes her riff. It's only proper. She hears laughter, glee. She spins around and sees Mario and Cara Lee pass out of the room. She returns her attention to the screen and sees the hooded men form up into a firing squad.

Words form in her mind, and her fingers fly across the keyboard. She's always been fast. It'll be a strong riff, she thinks.

Shots ring out and the prisoner falls to the ground. She is into her riff, focused on the fallen man.

The hooded men drag the fallen man away. Soldiers without hoods rush about and appear to be critiquing the performance. She sees the fallen man get up. He's okay. She laughs. A graphic appears on the screen giving the date and time and saying the training site is in Africa. She knew that.

She feels Mario's hands on her. Mario is not in the room. She hears cackling. Cara Lee is not in the room.

She knows she is being pushed far, far away from something. But from what? She doesn't know.

Kristen-Kate completes her riff, saves it, and sends copies to Mario, Richard Dowdy, and Lancaster Dowdy. The Dowdys are brothers and are the lab's senior scientists. They spoke with Kristen-Kate on her first day at the lab and told her about the training site in Africa. They said they were experimenting with ways to make people experience phenomena that were not real but manufactured. They said they have a space-based weapons system that serves that purpose.

"It manufactures sensory experience that you interpret as real," Richard had said. That was when Cara Lee began cackling and saying she wanted ever so much to sit Kristen-Kate down in front of her computer so she could experience firsthand what the Dowdys meant.

After the Dowdys spoke with her they made her sign a secrecy agreement. She had to keep all of this to herself.

Kristen-Kate feels Mario's hands walk up and down her back.

Is the job mine now? she wonders. She believes it is. She pops out of her chair and goes looking for Mario. She finds him with Cara Lee in a brightly lit room seated at a table.

When Cara Lee sees Kristen-Kate her face sags. The effect is comical.

Kristen-Kate rushes to Mario, and he hands her a pair of handcuffs, almost as if they had the transaction prearranged. She takes the cuffs and watches Cara Lee's mouth form into a snarl.

Like ancient branded cattle, Cara Lee Ellis comes from good breeding stock. She is statuesque, a big-haired brunette, hips that sway in cosmic rhythms. She is escort service, the house special.

"Do you know how to use these?" Mario asks.

Kristen-Kate examines the cuffs.

"No."

Mario shows her, yanking Cara Lee off her chair and cuffing her hands behind her back. Then he has Kristen-Kate try it.

Kristen-Kate cuffs Cara Lee as Mario had done.

"Nifty," she says, and unlocks the cuffs.

Cara Lee backs away, her eyes spewing venom at Kristen-Kate, her mouth squeezing out silent oaths, her satin-encased hips whipping through the universe.

"We want you to keep analyzing the African site," Mario says to Kristen-Kate.

"You do?"

"We think we do," Cara Lee says, her voice fluty like a songbird's.

"We don't know yet," Mario says.

"Nifty," Kristen-Kate says.

Cara Lee cackles.

Mario smiles, and puts his hands all over Kristen-Kate.

"What do you believe in, Kristen-Kate?"

"I told you."

"Tell me again."

"Beliefs change every two minutes," Cara Lee says.

Mario shoots Cara Lee a look.

"I believe I like my new responsibilities," Kristen-Kate says.

"In what way?" He's working his hands faster.

"I like doing riffs."

"Great."

She hears a cackle.

"Can I go home now?" Kristen-Kate asks.

"Will you come back tomorrow night?" Mario asks.

She thinks the question odd. Why wouldn't she come back tomorrow night? It's her job. And despite the presence of the escort-service whore, it's a good job.

"I'll come back."

Mario renews his touch apprenticeship with Kristen-Kate, his fingers racing over her like magic wands.

She likes the feel of his hands on her.

And suddenly she does not like it.

She steps away from Mario.

"Can I go now?" She feels like a child. She doesn't need his permission. She has several supervisors, none of whom are Major Mario Cushing or Cara Lee Ellis. Her main supervisor is an Army colonel at the Pentagon.

"I'm going."

Kristen-Kate leaves the brightly lit room and enters the dark room that houses the computer that shows images from the African training site. She logs off.

She knows they are pushing her far, far away from where she used to be. She knows Mario and Cara Lee have also been pushed far, far away from where they used to be. She knows both are using her for something they had tried, but found too dangerous, and are now dumping on her. But all this is growing faint in her mind.

She leaves the lab with one thought burning brightly.

She'll return tomorrow night. It's her job. She stuffs the handcuffs in her purse and walks out the door.

In the sultry night air, a uniformed soldier escorts her to her car. "Have a good night," he says.

His hands are all over her. She sits in her car and feels this, but it isn't real. The soldier is walking away.

She leaves the secret facility and works the back roads of Virginia until she is home. She walks into her house, showers, slips into pajamas, and gets into bed.

The hands do not reach her here. She feels safe.

She reviews her job as it was originally constituted: the tiny writing in her contract explained by a stern Army colonel. The Pentagon was developing ways of reformulating the perceptual processes of an enemy, to sink them. That was the purpose of the African training site. If anything should go awry ...

There were contingency plans.

She drifts asleep, thinking the contingency plans were now in effect.

CHAPTER 2

A Colossal Disturbance

Kristen-Kate McCutchan is eating an apple in the sultry night air outside the main terminal at Washington Dulles International Airport. At the appointed time, she rushes inside to greet her father.

"How was Beijing?" she asks.

"Ancient and scary," the general says. "Let's get out of here."

They walk outside and stand under the bright lights. The general gazes at his daughter.

"Beijing was fascinating. But tell me about your new job. I haven't had time to ask you yet."

"You wouldn't believe it, Dad. When you walk around in the lab, something seems to follow you."

"Is it an actual thing?"

"I don't know. My skin crawls whenever I experience it. It's like a ghost walking on your flesh. I think it's some kind of eerie control system."

"Kristen-Kate, do you accept ghosts that walk on your flesh or eerie control systems?"

Entering

"In a way, I do."

"Shades of Beijing."

"Dad, shades of World War II. Shades of the Manhattan Project."

"Point taken. I'm worried about you, Kristen-Kate."

"How come?"

"It's a feeling I get. Promise me you'll watch your back."

"I will, Dad."

They embrace.

Nat pushes her away and gives instructions.

"Kristen-Kate, chin up, defiance in your eye, fire in your heart."

She smiles.

They say goodbye.

She drives to work.

Night after night she sees things at the lab she can't tell her father: beatings, torture, simulated executions, all relayed from an American training site in Africa, all of it conducted in support of a revolutionary new weapons system.

She was told space-based machines drive the new system, infusing into people's lives a sense of parallel realities.

The African images upset her, but she will not chicken out. This job is important to her. It's her one chance to prove to her father how tough she is.

* * *

She arrives at the lab, passes through security, and goes into her darkened room. She logs on, gains access to the

African site, and watches real-time video of prisoners locked in cages. The African night is fading, the sun rising, the faces in lockup still in shadow.

In one of the cages she sees an old man crippled by disabling injuries. She signals the remote site, and a camera zooms in on him.

She studies him.

To her, the prisoner looks broken—but is he? She has seen these men undergo startling transformations. She reaches for the keyboard and taps out a riff about despair turned inside out, becoming a grim kind of hope.

She completes her riff, saves it, and sends copies to Mario, Richard Dowdy, and Lancaster Dowdy.

She is taking a break on the other side of the room when an urgent beeping draws her back to her computer.

She sits down at her computer, stares at her display, and sees a strange, new African landscape.

The forest is like a roiling sea, painted in hues of violet and blue.

Everything is in motion, the colors bizarre.

She watches, fascinated.

The land and sky toss chaotically, and then slowly resolve into normal appearance and color.

The remote cameras begin to maneuver.

She sees men held captive in crude wooden cages, mounting desperation in their eyes.

She hears the chilling sounds of a man's cries as he is beaten.

She sees black-hooded soldiers drag a prisoner from a cage.

The soldiers lead the prisoner away, but his fear is so disabling he collapses, and they have to drag him across the ground.

As the soldiers drag the prisoner through the compound, she catches glimpses of broken forest in the surrounding countryside. The land looks devastated, as if a storm had passed through.

They told her to report any disturbance to the environment, as it might mean an experiment's controlling force had gone wild.

Cara Lee Ellis is in another room, but Kristen-Kate won't involve her. Any problem arising in Kristen-Kate's sphere would only cause Cara Lee to lash out.

She wrestles with it. Broken trees? A storm? That's a colossal disturbance.

Whom should she call? She has to be careful; a problem erupted during her first week and she called the wrong person. Mario chewed her out and told her to make sure it didn't happen again.

She isn't worried about Mario, only about waking the wrong person in the middle of the night over a storm in Africa and crumpled trees.

What should she do? She doesn't know, but she likes the challenge.

She returns her focus to the prisoner on her computer screen. He is still crippled by fear. The black-hooded soldiers are still dragging him. She sees terror on his face.

❊　❊　❊

In May, two men interviewed Kristen-Kate at the University of Virginia. Describing the job, one of them told her she'd be monitoring reports from a secret overseas training site. She'd be in a secure environment, on the night shift.

He revealed the employer: the Department of Defense. His questions became political.

"Do you believe the Department of Defense should conduct secret research?"

She was nervous. She didn't want to say the wrong thing.

"Yes."

"What kind of research?"

A quiver crept into her voice. "It depends. Our defense establishment has many needs. I think we need to do a lot of research."

She saw him nod.

The other man asked her what she knew about Africa.

She said she'd taken courses that touched on African history, culture, and politics. She was getting her nerve back.

He asked her what she did in her spare time.

She said she had no spare time.

"But, really, what do you like to do?"

"I like to read books."

"What else?"

"Meet interesting people."

"What else?"

"Visit national parks, feed the bears."

He asked her what her favorite movie was. She said it was the Hitchcock film *Notorious*.

He said the job was hers.

She'd gone home, not realizing they'd neglected to tell her the location of the lab. Her dad, as always, took care of that, pointing out the location on a map, and driving her to the site to familiarize her with the area.

"Take different routes to work," he said. "And different routes home. And always watch your back."

"I will, Dad."

It was just for the summer. She'd survive.

In a state of disbelief and shock, Kristen-Kate watches the soldiers drag the prisoner into an amphitheater filled with spectators, watches them strap the prisoner into a device that holds him upright, watches a black-hooded executioner step forward and smash the prisoner in the face with a sledge hammer, blow after blow, until the prisoner's face is destroyed.

As if possessed of wisdom and steel nerves not her own, Kristen-Kate places her fingers on the keyboard, draws in a deep breath, and begins her riff.

I see the skeletal inner structure of the prisoner's face, which horrifies me. I sense the mechanical underpinnings of man, the essential inner nature that supports the outer shell.

This blasting away of the face reveals the inner man. It is horrifying, as the inner man is mechanical, not bone, not blood, not glistening tissue, but a structure like that of a bombed-out building. It is horrifying to watch the killer's energetic, hate-driven hammer blows, and to see the man's face smashed to pieces, and horrifying to know that a crowd at the scene is enjoying the spectacle.

The victim's face shredded away reveals an inner structure that is shocking in itself, aside from the repulsiveness of the crowd looking on. The man by then is dead, but his inner self reveals a landscape that seems just as dead.

Are we all dead inside? Is there no soul, nothing deeper than what we see all around us? If so, our gods betray us, as they've always pointed to something greater beyond us. But it seems there is nothing beyond us.

What does it mean for the man who killed him, and those who watched with pleasure? Did they see the expected sights: blood, bone, glistening tissue? Did our distance from the event in a sterile government lab make us see a desolate inner picture of this victim of faraway violence?

I don't think so. I think we saw ourselves there more so than anything. We saw our own dead natures. And that's what scares us.

She saves her riff and sends copies to Mario, Richard Dowdy, and Lancaster Dowdy.

Her most pressing work is done, for the moment.

She mentally blows away the stress that accumulates during riffs, and then tries to reason it out. She is sure she witnessed a death on her screen.

The victims aren't supposed to die; it's supposed to be simulation. The African experiments induce raw terror in test subjects. Scientists study how this disabling fear affects the mind and body, and then develop sophisticated technologies to induce it in an enemy, the objective being to defeat them from afar without firing a shot.

She looks at her screen. They're dragging another prisoner into the amphitheater, strapping him into the device. The executioner steps forward and death continues to rain on her screen.

She closes her eyes and shields her face with her hands. Maybe she's just fatigued. Maybe she needs more time to break from her riff.

She seeks her usual calm, and finds it, and feels ashamed for feeling better, as she believes it grows out of distancing herself from the horror she witnessed on her screen.

She opens her eyes and looks at her screen again—and again quickly shields her eyes with her hands. She spins in her chair and decides she'll have to take action.

The phone call will be a bigger phone call now; more than crumpled trees have happened. The violence at the African site has taken on a chilling look.

She pulls a list of names and phone numbers from her desk drawer and reaches for the phone.

She'll call Richard Dowdy and Lancaster Dowdy, the project's senior scientists.

A force has gone wild. No one, not even Mario, can chew her out for that.

She hears an urgent beeping and directs her attention back to the computer screen. A camera is capturing close-ups of prisoners in cages.

An enraged prisoner lunges at the camera, rams the bars of his cage, producing an awful crash and rattle.

The camera pulls back and shows an American soldier with an assault rifle standing in front of the cage.

The camera zooms in on the prisoner again. He bobs around in half shadow, and then snaps a big paw through the bars, trying to snatch the camera.

The camera jerks back, steadies, and moves in again. The prisoner's eyes are big orbs, streaked with a frightening consciousness.

The camera backs off, and shows the caged man and the soldier juxtaposed.

Kristen-Kate gasps, realizing what she is seeing. The soldier is there to provide contrast to the man in the cage.

The camera zooms in on the prisoner. Kristen-Kate draws in a deep breath, stares into the cage, and sees the enraged face, the elongated body, of a giant.

With armed soldiers patrolling the grounds, the camera maneuvers cage to cage, revealing hundreds of incarcerated men as giants of various types and sizes.

Kristen-Kate senses someone is standing behind her.

She glances back and sees Cara Lee Ellis.

Cara Lee, avoiding Kristen-Kate's eyes, shakes her head as if confused.

"Am I seeing what you're seeing?" Cara Lee asks.

"If you're seeing giants in cages ..."

"I am."

"... and broken trees, you're not hallucinating. I'm going to call the Dowdys."

Cara Lee's mouth curves in an ugly arc. She shakes her head.

"Butt out, Kristen-Kate. I'm taking over."

She pokes Kristen-Kate hard on the shoulder and tries to force her out of her chair.

During her first few nights on the job, Kristen-Kate had sensed frustration on the part of whoever was sending the reports from the African site. They flowed in night after night with no apparent sign of improvement in subjects' ability to learn tasks under difficult circumstances, which was what the experiments were about. Kristen-Kate wished she knew what those difficult circumstances were, who the trainees were, and what type of training they were undergoing. But that was forbidden. She was fed sterile data and graphs, the tasks numbered, the difficulty assigned a value.

Night after night it went on. Sometimes Cara Lee Ellis would pop in on her. Cara Lee was a trainer, the evil kind. On Kristen-Kate's first night, she saw Cara Lee's evil eyes looking for ways to show her up. She left big gaps in Kristen-Kate's instructions, setting her up for failure, after which she would confront her with ugly remarks about failed performance.

Kristen-Kate tried to avoid her, but couldn't. She looked for ways to complain about her, but there didn't seem to be a path for that. Oddly, despite Cara Lee's sabotage, Kristen-Kate learned her job well. But any sense of accomplishment was quickly stolen by the evil snake. Cara Lee told Kristen-

Kate she was experiencing breakthroughs in learning only because the experiment had shifted to include her as a subject. She said the experiment acquires its own identity and shifts wherever it senses opportunities.

Uh-huh. The snake always had a way of making Kristen-Kate look bad.

✳   ✳   ✳

Cara Lee is using a pink tissue to dab blood away from her lip where Kristen-Kate struck her. Her lip is grotesque, swollen, her eyes subdued, her voice crawling from a troubled place her emotions occupy.

"I'm going to press charges," Cara Lee says. "They'll be taking you out of here in handcuffs."

Kristen-Kate sits at her computer, scenes of lush African wilderness on her screen, much of it broken by a recent storm.

She called the Dowdys. They were on the way.

Mario hovers behind her, a headset on.

Kristen-Kate also wears a headset. Her mic is on, and she is having a conversation with a man at the African site who calls himself Shangri-la.

She's trying to crack him open.

"I repeat, who are you?" Kristen-Kate asks.

"Shangri-la. And you?"

"That's not your business. I want your real name."

"My real name doesn't matter. At least give me something to call you by, the name of your dog or cat, for instance."

"Why don't you call me Jamaica?"

"Jamaica, you've seen the giant men in cages, haven't you?"

"I have."

"Jamaica, the giants in cages were discovered on a line of demarcation on the experimental site. That's where the trouble lies."

She furrows her brow and looks at Mario, hoping he'll tell her what a line of demarcation is. He remains silent.

"Okay, Shangri-la, what trouble are you referring to?"

"Jamaica, something has gone wrong with the American project in Africa. The U.S. was trying to alter how people acquire skills; now the overriding goal is to infuse new skills in unsuspecting subjects."

"Did something like this happen to you, Shangri-la?"

"Yes. In fact, it continues to happen."

"Oh? What happens? And how?"

"Jamaica, it's mysterious. It's more scary than painful, but you do feel it, especially in the eyes. When it happens, you get the impression you are a different you. But this lasts for only a while, and then you go back to being yourself again, though not quite.

"The eyes hurt for quite a while. You think you're coming down with something; you think maybe your metabolism took a walk or that you're eating improperly.

"The eyes fill with something, but you don't know what. They're different. You're different. Maybe you know something you didn't know before. Maybe you can do something you couldn't do before. You don't necessarily know anything new right off. It'll happen, though, spontaneously, sooner or later. It always does. Then you'll be doing things you've never done before.

"You're light-headed for a while, as the new skills settle in. Then you go out and do your job. You dread the next occurrence of this eye-lifting, head-turning experience. The eyes lift, the head turns each time you're affected."

Kristen-Kate breaks in, anxious to ask questions.

"Shangri-la—"

"Kristen-Kate? Is that your name? Are you Kristen-Kate?"

"How did you know?"

"I heard someone at your end say Kristen-Kate. Is that your name?"

Flustered, she is unable to speak.

"Kristen-Kate, Jamaica, we don't always know what we'll be able to do. The training cadre doesn't know either. They seem upset most of the time. So are we, the great affected ones."

"Don't tell him anything personal," Mario says. "Don't respond to the use of your name. Respond only to Jamaica."

She nods, and then finds her voice.

"Shangri-la, the giants are hard to believe. What do you know about them?"

"We know nothing of them, and they of us. As I say, they were discovered. We decided to use them to showcase our plight. To them, we are probably dwarfs. Any ideas? This is no joke."

"Shangri-la, define line of demarcation."

"It's a strange boundary. On the other side lies a mirror image of our world. We have learned that our world is full of illusions, and that we have questionable existence."

A spell of silence ensues, and then Shangri-la continues.

"Jamaica, the African site was built deliberately on a line of demarcation. We don't always know which world we're in, and, presumably, neither do you."

✻   ✻   ✻

Unable to raise Shangri-la, Kristen-Kate pulls her headset off. Mario tells her to take a break.

She stands and stretches, looking at Cara Lee.

Cara Lee's eyes take on an evil cast. "Don't you dare look at me!" she shouts. Fists raised, she launches herself at Kristen-Kate.

Kristen-Kate dodges Cara Lee's charge and punches her in the face, sending her crashing to the floor.

Using the handcuffs Mario supplied her, she cuffs Cara Lee's hands behind her back. Cara Lee screams, squirms, lets out bloody oaths.

"You're going to jail, Kristen-Kate! I'll see to that!"

Kristen-Kate drags the kicking, spitting snake into a dark corner, looks back, sees that Mario is watching. She makes a fist, hovers over Cara Lee, silently implores Mario.

Punch her hard, right in the kisser?

Mario shakes his head.

Break teeth, break nose?

But Mario shakes his head.

✻   ✻   ✻

Kristen-Kate returns to her seat, flushed with anger.

"Mario, we need to talk."

∼ 36 ∼

"About what?"

"About you touching me."

"Shut up if you know what's good for you," Cara Lee says.

"Mario—"

Mario's hands crawl all over Kristen-Kate's body, and she can't recall why she'd been angry.

"The tape of Shangri-la is being analyzed," Mario says.

"Give me your take," Kristen-Kate says.

Lightly stroking her neck, Mario says, "I think it's obvious: Shangri-la and the other subjects in the experiment are victims of a technology that alters perceptions."

His hands leave her. He opens a map of Botswana and points out coordinates.

"That's where Shangri-la is located. It's our training site, all right. But we don't have any record of him. We're trying to establish things as I speak."

He's stroking her flanks; she purrs.

"This was no ordinary storm," he says. "We have a Special Forces contingent on the ground, flown in from a nearby base. The helicopters that brought them in are standing by in case a rapid evacuation is necessary."

He leans close to her and lowers his voice. "All things arising out of Botswana are likely alien, including the Dowdys."

Kristen-Kate murmurs, to let him know she's listening. What's taking place on her screen is too fascinating to take her eyes from. American soldiers are swarming over the African compound. There are giants in cages, giants leaving cages, giants roaming. She thinks none of this is real. At some point it will all be revealed as ...

As what? She doesn't know. If she were worried, she'd call her father. But she's not worried.

Her head snaps back. Cara Lee has a grip on her hair and is trying to pull her to the floor.

Kristen-Kate spins off her chair and drives the heel of her hand into Cara Lee's elbow, impacting a pressure point.

The snake releases her grip on Kristen-Kate's hair and screams in agony.

Kristen-Kate advances on the snake.

The snake skitters away, tears streaming down her face, her shackled hands unable to cradle her devastated elbow.

Kristen-Kate looks back at Mario.

He's watching.

She goes back to her chair.

"Watch my back, Mario."

✳   ✳   ✳

Richard and Lancaster Dowdy enter the lab, their presence announced by the incessant clop-clopping of their shoes and the overpowering scent of their cologne.

Tall and aging, full of dash, they give the appearance of horses romping in clover.

They glance at Kristen-Kate, and at Cara Lee, and then take Mario down a dark corridor.

Kristen-Kate decides to do some snooping. As she walks toward the corridor, a hiss tracks her progress. She looks at Cara Lee. The hiss isn't coming from the snake. It must be coming from the spying devices.

She continues walking.

None of this is real, she thinks. None of it.

She's wise to them.

It's an experiment, all right, but one that lies hidden within the observable routine of the place.

And she knows its purpose.

They're trying to see how far they can lead her down a dark corridor.

Maximum control if they get her where they want her to go.

They'll apply their own riffs exclusively, then.

They won't get her, though. She'll fool them. She'll make them think she's been suckered in.

At some point, they'll ask her what she got taken in by.

Really, I got taken in by nothing, she'll say. I knew all along this was trickery.

She enters the dark corridor. Cool air presses her flesh. Guided by tiny lights along the ceiling, walls, and floor, she makes her way.

She stops at a door, hears voices on the other side, knows their conversation is meant for her.

Surely, they'll tell Mario that when he said, *All things arising out of Botswana are likely alien, including the Dowdys,* Kristen-Kate must have been tweaked out of her seat.

But, uh-uh, she wasn't.

She knew better than to believe that.

The door swings open, and Mario pulls her inside and ushers her to a chair at a conference table.

"Please be seated," he says.

Kristen-Kate sits.

"You've met Richard and Lancaster Dowdy," Mario says as he takes his own seat. "They've reviewed tonight's material, including your riff, and they thank you for your contribution. Now they'd like to talk to you about the African experiment."

She studies the Dowdys a moment. "Okay."

"Kristen-Kate," Richard says, "Lancaster is convinced our African experiment did not produce any changes in test subjects; he thinks an unknown agency was introduced and brought about the changes we are observing—the development of new skills.

"Lancaster remains focused on finding that other agency. He believes it's directing, among other things, the development of unexpected new skills, not just in test subjects, but in all humans, and that it's likely controlling me and others who are committed in that effort, which Lancaster opposes, I might add."

Lancaster stirs. "Richard, the program previously did not have as its goal the development of unexpected new skills. It was strictly a scientific search for improved skill acquisition and enhancement. The technology has either run amok, or we are the unwitting subjects of an alien experiment. I rather think it's an alien experiment, which will likely pave the way for an alien invasion."

"Your suspicions are well documented, Lancaster. Why don't you make our offer to Kristen-Kate?"

Lancaster looks at her.

"Kristen-Kate, your training is not yet complete, yet we feel you are ready. We are recruiting people to investigate a brutal crime spree in Los Angeles. We feel the perpetrator is not human, but an alien life-form. We feel law enforcement in Los Angeles is compromised, and is unable to perform its normal function. We feel your skills are up to the challenge. If you accept, you would be one of many on an undercover detail posing as potential victims. Will you accept this assignment?"

She is stunned. She isn't sure if this is made up now or not. Suddenly, it sounds all too real.

"Kristen-Kate, do you accept?"

"No, I do not accept. It scares me."

"Fine. We will find others. Now, if you will excuse us, we have other business to attend to."

She rises to leave.

Mario accompanies her to the door.

✻ ✻ ✻

The following night, Kristen-Kate looks for Mario and finds him in a conference room with the Dowdys. She waits in the corridor until they are finished.

"Mario, I have to go now. I'm off till the weekend."

Mario walks her through the lab. They pause at the door that leads outside.

"Mario, the day I got the job, my father drove me here to familiarize me with the area. He told me to take different routes to work and different routes home. Why did he tell me that?"

"It's standard operating procedure. Vary your routine to throw off surveillance."

"Mario, isn't there another reason?"

"I think you already know, Kristen-Kate. It's no secret to those of us who've worked here a while. Your father probably didn't know, but guessed. By following different routes, you might be able to shake the place off."

"I might not find it again?"

"Yes."

"I could shake this place off?"

"You could, if you wanted to. Do you want to?"

"No."

"I thought so."

She reaches for the door.

"Wait," he says. "I was going to tell you something."

"What?"

"Richard is finally agreeing with Lancaster. He says it's likely we are the unwitting subjects of an alien experiment, and it's likely been going on for a long time. Lancaster showed Richard compelling evidence: a secret executive order signed by Franklin Delano Roosevelt in 1941, ordering an investigation. The crux of the matter was addressed head-on in a remote cabin in the Wyoming wilderness. The War Department bestowed a name on the invaders back in '41: *light beings.*"

"Spooky," Kristen-Kate says. Something cold shivers her flesh as she leaves the building.

CHAPTER 3

Just You and the World

"Come in, Major. Did you speak with Kristen-Kate?"

"Yes, briefly. She's a bit confused, Colonel Davenport. I don't think she expected this. A promotion so soon."

"Sit down, Mario. That promotion isn't in the bag yet. She's got to go before the board. I want you to give me some background on her."

"She's like a quick dagger to the heart, Colonel."

"So I've heard. Mario, in all honesty, I have some reservations. Kristen-Kate McCutchan entered a restricted area within this facility and removed secret documents."

"It was her first week on the job, sir. She didn't realize what she was doing."

"She called her father's cell phone immediately after lifting the documents and left him a message stating she had something exciting to tell him. That's powerful evidence she planned on revealing the contents of those documents to him."

"Sir, she was wandering around on her break and saw the information on the dog experiments. She got excited. Sometimes she's like a little girl."

"So I've gathered."

"Sir, she's been an important asset. She has leadership qualities. She's tough and resilient. She's highly organized, highly intelligent, and a skilled communicator. It's a combination we desperately need for what's ahead. Please consider the incident within its proper context."

"I have, Major. There won't be any repercussions."

"Thank you, sir."

"Fill me in."

"Yes, sir. Kristen-Kate McCutchan, age nineteen, is a student at the University of Virginia. She's the daughter of U.S. Army General Nathan McCutchan. She grew up in Virginia, where she and her father maintain a residence. Her father works at the Pentagon. When Kristen-Kate was little, her mother left the family, an involuntary commitment to a mental institution."

"Get her, Major, and the psychologist."

* * *

Kristen-Kate and a U.S. Army psychologist named Destiny Hughes join Major Cushing and Colonel Davenport. Destiny begins interviewing Kristen-Kate.

"Kristen-Kate, how did you get this job?"

"They interviewed me."

"Was it family influence?"

"I guess."

"You could walk away from it, couldn't you?"

"I could, but I won't."

"What's the most important influence in your life?"

"My father."

"Do you have a special friend?"

"Yes. A man."

"What's his name?"

"Stephen D. Spiros."

"Are you willing to talk about him?"

"Sure. No secrets there."

"But isn't there some controversy?"

"I don't know. Maybe."

"Your relationship with Spiros seems almost completely unstructured. How so?"

"It doesn't seem unstructured to me."

"You haven't given your life over to him, have you?"

"Of course not. How foolish."

"How would you react if you were cast adrift from your father?"

"I'd be terrified. But maybe that's the only way I'll ever discover who I am."

"What if you were cast adrift from Spiros?"

"I'd be lost for a while, until I found him again."

"Kristen-Kate, from what I hear, it sounds like Spiros takes you far from your normal personality."

"He does."

"Do you feel you are on a path of discovery with him?"

"Yes."

"How intimate are you with Spiros, like in conversations?"

"Uh, not very. We prefer to keep a simple focus. We

exchange name, rank, and serial number only. We don't hit deeper truths. Not yet. We're comfortable where we're at."

"Kristen-Kate, you sometimes share greater intimacy with total strangers than you do with Spiros. What gives?"

"That's hidden from me. It's a mystery. It's as if this relationship doesn't even exist. It's maybe an invention."

"But you do see him?"

"Yes, I do."

"Is he real?"

"Yes. He looks real."

"Kristen-Kate, have you ever questioned what Spiros means to you, like maybe you couldn't have an intimate relationship with your mother, now you are not having an intimate relationship with Spiros?"

"I see where you're heading. Is he a universe of things where maybe I'll find my mother?"

"Is he?"

"I don't think so. I think he has trouble with anything deeper. He needs to be certain before he takes the plunge. I'm content with waiting."

The psychologist passes a hand-written assessment to Colonel Davenport: *No one actually sees Kristen-Kate with Spiros; it seems Spiros does not exist in the normal sense. Kristen-Kate seems unaware of this, and takes Spiros very seriously. She is used to catching disapproving looks and hushed comment concerning her father the general. Now she is catching disapproving looks and hushed comment concerning Spiros. Much is buried here.*

This relationship with Spiros resonates for Kristen-Kate to the point where it seems she sometimes enters another world, a world in which she has a gritty, new personality, new friends, and a new vocabulary.

Kristen-Kate sometimes seems unreal to her friends in this regard. Some of them try to warn her, but the warnings don't resonate. Under ordinary circumstances, I would recommend that Kristen-Kate be evaluated further and that she begin treatment. Needless to say, these are not ordinary circumstances.

❄ ❄ ❄

Colonel Davenport and Major Cushing are alone.

"What did you make of Destiny's tack, Major?"

"She nailed it."

"She did. She's good. Do you think Kristen-Kate has any idea what we do here, Mario?"

"No."

"Not even after Destiny worked her over?"

"Let her wonder. We have more important fish to fry. What have you decided, sir?"

"Obviously, we must give Kristen-Kate something in her skill set. Destiny thinks she gravitates toward counseling prisoners."

"Sir, we use prisoners in the dog experiments in Virginia."

"She's already lifted the documents."

"She has."

Colonel Davenport hands Mario a set of sealed orders. "Carry on, Mario."

Mario opens the orders, and then summons Kristen-Kate.

"Kristen-Kate, Destiny recommends a counseling job for you in Los Angeles, working with young offenders facing lockup. It sounds gritty, and it is: it's just you and the world. Destiny says it's the right universe of things for you."

"Great, I accept. Tell Destiny thanks."

CHAPTER 4

A Weary Traveler

Otis Dietrich flags down a taxi on the Naval Base at Pearl Harbor, Hawaii. "Tripler," he says, getting into the taxi, hunching to ease the pain in his right shoulder.

The taxi glides down Nimitz Highway, and Otis is on his way to Tripler Army Medical Center and another post-surgical visit with his doctor.

In the eastern sky, racing clouds skim the jagged peaks of the Koolau Mountains. But Otis doesn't see this arresting sight. He sees only dark and fluttering images of his world.

His right shoulder is in the grip of intense, throbbing pain. Pain so severe he can't focus, can't think. The pain seems both a blackness visited upon his soul and a glimpse into hell.

The pain is complex. It's deep in his shoulder, a hot, heavy locus. It's external, a thing that orbits him from a distance. It's a thing that reaches into him and touches him like a hand with a thousand fingers uniquely talented at ferreting out pain.

The pain scares him with its otherworldly essence. On his last visit to Tripler, he wanted to describe his pain more fully to his doctor, but decided not to. It would have seemed too bizarre to a man of science.

The pain pushes him to a place beyond despair. There's no escaping it, day or night. It won't even let him sleep.

He needs a stronger painkiller, something to take down this dark, stalking monster. Why won't his doctor listen?

Dr. Schell has repeatedly said to Otis, "Before I prescribe a stronger painkiller, I want to find out why the pain is so severe."

Otis laughs, but it doesn't come out as a laugh—the shoulder god warns him with a blast deep into his shoulder.

Otis winces and curses the shoulder god. Self-conscious, he looks at the driver, but sees no reaction from him.

The shoulder god sits in orbit and looks deep into the head of the humerus, which articulates with the scapula, forming the shoulder joint. It looks at bones, ligaments, tendons, nerves, and muscles. It assesses damage and decides it can cause additional pain within the parameters of science, so it sends Otis a mind-searing jolt. Then it gives a wink to science and makes Otis feel pain two feet off his shoulder. It winks again and gives Otis a burst of pain that flies in orbit twelve feet out. And then it settles back into good humor and does only what is medically accepted, sinking its teeth into Otis's back, neck, face, and for good measure, his legs.

The pain gets Otis's attention, denies him attention elsewhere. It hurts. It throbs. It's deep and penetrating. It orbits him. It shoots into various nooks and crannies. He feels it several feet away, toying with him from a distance. It affects his mind. He wants to contort himself. He wants to screw up his face in a grimace. He wants to clench his teeth, get out of his skin, get out of his body, get out of everything, but feels it won't do any good—the pain will still be there. It has set up borders far from his body. It has posted guards. It trains combat troops. It won't leave Otis alone. Not ever. It orbits him, inhabits him, tracks him wherever he goes. It thwarts the milder painkiller Dr. Schell has prescribed. It sits invisibly beside Dr. Schell and whispers in his ear to deny Otis a more powerful painkiller, one that might make Otis sleep, one that might make Otis heal.

Otis believes a more serious painkiller would put this shoulder god out of business. This god wasn't in evidence before Otis had his accident at the beach, though it's probably been lurking since he was a baby, waiting for just the right moment.

Otis went bodysurfing at a beach renowned for its shore breaks. A shore break is a wave that breaks right onto the shore. It can kill you. It merely dislocated Otis's right shoulder.

He wonders if he can talk to this god. He wonders if it would do any good to bargain with it. He feels it does exist in some fashion.

As if hearing Otis's thoughts, the shoulder god sets an ogre upon him. The ogre's hoofmarks begin at Otis's right ear, trace down the side of his neck and onto his shoulder, ripple down his arm and along the side of his body.

The ogre shoots upward to his face, stomping on his upper jaw, having realized it missed this area. It does a thorough job, making his teeth hurt, and then the back of his head, and then his lower jaw on both sides, and Otis is twisting in his seat, eyeing the cab driver, but the driver doesn't seem to notice this dance of Otis's.

The pain retreats from full agony to partial agony in all areas except the shoulder; here it gallops at full speed, full misery, full diminished capacity, and Otis is contorting himself in his seat as the cab flies up Jarrett White Road.

As they pull up near Tripler Army Medical Center, the pink palace on the hill, a tall black man standing on the side of the road yells at the cab. "Slow down, you silly fool!"

The cab driver has it floored. He sits in a daze, and Otis thinks the shoulder god had something to do with it.

It's another amazing day in paradise, with the sun a hot confection in the sky, the clouds perfect in their blubbering wetness, the sky a blue splendor.

Otis is in a taxi again. The green-clad Koolau Mountains lie to his left, the Pacific, out of sight, to his right.

The dull edges of pain have begun to blur his senses. He doesn't hear traffic anymore, except as sharp trumpet blasts.

Most sounds, tastes, and smells have lost their vividness, becoming vast harmonies joining with that big armada of pain that stands offshore, starboard of his right shoulder.

The cab makes a whooshing sound as it glides over the road. Otis senses something wrong with how the driver is navigating the vehicle. The cab repeatedly shifts lanes and zooms up to tailgate.

Otis looks to his left, and sees the cab's driver. A small Asian man with a wrinkled hide, he sits much like a child might sit, with no discipline, slumped behind the wheel. His hands grip the wheel with remarkable fierceness, and he aims his eyes out the windshield as if expecting trouble.

Otis looks to his right, and sees another old man driving the cab. The old man to his right sits with eyes pointed out the windshield, hands on the wheel, nonchalantly driving the cab along a freeway. Why is he seeing the old man in two locations? Could both be driving the cab?

Otis looks back and forth, and continues to see two drivers. Both have eyes pointed out the windshield, hands on the wheel, foot on the accelerator. One of them takes the Puuloa Road exit and motors up to the pink palace on the hill.

The strange consciousness ends, and Otis thinks, *Haven't we gone this way before?* Yes, day by day, he has.

"How did you get your shoulder injury, Otis?" Holly Lu, his physical therapist, asks. She begins her manipulations, making him feel his shoulder pain in new and different ways.

He winces, and says, "Bodysurfing at Sunset Beach." He's still upset with himself, crashing onto the beach, creating a scene. The wave that rode him onto the beach was one of those wildly unpredictable waves. It hadn't done what Otis thought it would do, what most other waves would have done. Instead of breaking into the surf and foaming toward shore, it rose like a monster and slammed Otis onto the hard sand.

A severe fracture or dislocation can trigger shock. A bystander at Sunset Beach rushed up and uttered these words as Otis lay writhing in agony on the sand. The same man began to give orders, and Otis felt the scurry of people as they flocked to take care of him while the ambulance was on the way.

As Otis writhed in agony on the beach, the target of pitying eyes, he felt a powerful need to explain what had happened, for he surely didn't want any of the beachgoers to think he was too inexperienced to ride the waves at Sunset.

The explanations tumbled through his mind.

The wave I caught was bigger than ...

The wave carried me farther than ...

It was one of those unpredictable waves that ...

He ended up saying nothing.

He lay there in agony, waiting for the ambulance, observant of the man who had delivered the speech on shock. The man hovered near Otis, somehow godlike. Otis never learned who he was.

He tries to not look at Holly Lu too much. He knows he'll become attached to her before long, and when his therapy is over, he will miss her dearly.

"You're lucky it was only a shoulder, Otis," Holly Lu says.

He shifts a little on the table, grits his teeth. Driven headfirst onto the beach, he'd kept his arms out in front of him. If he'd have tucked and rolled instead ...

"We see fractured cervical spines, Otis. Quadriplegia.

These are tragic cases. Paralysis from the neck down, with the patient on a respirator for life."

If he'd have tucked and rolled instead of keeping his body stiff, he might have avoided injury entirely, or he might now be attached to a respirator. It happened so fast, the wave towering, the beach right there beneath him.

Of course, the wave that threw him knew all along what it was. *A monster.*

There's a cycle to waves, though Otis doesn't quite know the equation. Every fourth or fifth wave will be slightly bigger, every fiftieth wave a lot bigger, every thousandth wave a monster.

"How did you get your injury?" She's asking again, her tone implying she'd like to hear some details.

"A big wave slammed me onto the beach."

"You're lucky it was just your shoulder, Otis. It could have been much worse. We see some tragic cases. Quadriplegia. The patient on a respirator for life."

He grits his teeth again, and says, "Who'd want to live?"

She glances at him with raised eyebrows, and doesn't answer.

He doesn't want her to get away with not answering. "Who'd want to live in that condition?"

"Many people *do* live in that condition, Otis. There's always hope for a cure."

"Do you think there will ever be a cure?"

"Yes. Scientists are always searching."

She stands behind him and pulls on his right arm, trying to elongate it over his head. He doesn't have full range of motion. He wonders if he ever will.

"Otis, it's important for you to do these stretches every day. You will get back what you work for. Try to extend your motion. Try for a little more each time. And then work against resistance to strengthen the muscles."

She continues to hold his arm, moving it in all directions, her eyes roving over his face, trying to gauge his pain.

Otis grits his teeth. The exercises are excruciating.

Her eyes register concern as she gives him instructions. She's letting him go. She'll see him again in two days. He's to practice the exercises.

"You're not getting any better, Otis. You're not healing. How come?"

"I'm not sleeping. The pain is too bad. I lie awake. I've asked my doctor for a stronger painkiller but he won't give me one."

Holly Lu calls Dr. Schell's nurse and requests a stronger painkiller for Otis.

Otis sees Dr. Schell's nurse, gets the prescription, and picks up the medicine at the hospital pharmacy: *acetaminophen with codeine.* He's to take one to two tablets every four hours.

He starts to sleep better. He sees Holly Lu two days later.

"You look much better, Otis. There's a sparkle in your eye and a spring in your step you didn't have before."

"It's the painkiller. It's working. I'm sleeping. I can feel myself heal."

"Sleep is what does it, Otis. We heal when we sleep."

They go into the examination room. He lies on the table, and she checks his range of motion. Much better.

They begin exercises.

After a while, Otis, at ease with Holly Lu, relates a story of betrayal.

"Holly Lu, the woman I thought I was going to marry fleeced me. She took all my money and possessions, and then vanished. I didn't see it coming."

"That was cruel, Otis. No one deserves that."

*　*　*

Later that day, a civilian named Phil Weaver visits Holly Lu. He says he's a consultant to the military and needs information on Otis Dietrich.

She makes a phone call to check his credentials, and then agrees to confer with him.

"How is Otis doing?" Weaver asks.

"Otis is on a long, painful road to recovery," she says.

"Do you want to be rid of him?"

"That's a strange question. Why do you ask?"

"Well, does he alienate you?"

"No, quite the opposite."

"Do you find him appealing?"

She delays her answer. "He's okay."

"Oh, yeah? Cab drivers don't want Otis in the cab. The Navy wants to be rid of him. But you find him appealing? He must be switching something on and off."

"Maybe he is," she says.

"What big, powerful thoughts or emotions has he expressed lately?"

"Otis usually keeps his thoughts to himself, and expresses little emotion, but today he revealed a rough experience he had with a woman who ripped him off. He sounded very upset about it."

"He told you about that?" Weaver sounds excited, and makes a phone call.

In a few minutes, a broad-shouldered young man wearing a blue-and-green Hawaiian shirt, khaki shorts, and beige sandals sweeps into the room. He shakes Holly Lu's hand like he's delighted to see her.

"My name's Sid," he says. "I'm an engineer." He stands with his back to a mirror, facing Holly Lu.

She sees something in the mirror and walks closer.

"Do you see it?" Sid asks.

"Yes. What is it? A butterfly? Oh my God!" She gazes around the room, sees no butterfly tracing arcs through the air, looks back in the mirror at the butterfly's reflection. She can't tear her eyes from it.

"It's a zero point, Holly Lu."

"A zero point? It's beautiful."

Transfixed, she continues to stare at it. "I've never heard of such a thing," she says. "Is it a military secret?"

"No, it isn't. The military has given it a name, but they don't know what it is. We need everyone's help on this, Holly Lu. It sounds melodramatic, but our world as we know it is going to end unless we learn what these things are and what they're capable of doing. Only then can we protect ourselves."

"Oh?" Somehow, staring into the zero point, she isn't concerned. She's whispering now. "You need my help?"

"Yes, soon."

The zero point opens, much like a flower, and she realizes it never was in the mirror, but in the room with her. Gazing into it, she sees the intimate, blushing details of her many lives.

And now she knows herself to be a weary traveler. The zero point opens wider and engulfs her. And now she understands.

Deep shock strikes Holly Lu, shrivels her nervous system into a frightening configuration, leaving her debilitated and gasping.

She backs away from Sid.

She finds herself falling to the floor, collapsing around a nucleus of emotion impossible to sort out.

She's on her haunches, looking up at Sid. Her voice comes out in a nervous, twitching spasm.

"I-I was that woman who ripped off Otis?"

"Yes."

Sid helps her up without a break in his demeanor, as if it were a common occurrence for him to pick someone off the floor.

He steadies her, helps her to a chair.

"Holly Lu, we need to talk about your relationship with Otis. How long have you known him? What possessions of his do you have? Where are you storing them? Where did you transfer his money to? Did you send it home to Atlanta?"

CHAPTER 5

A Dangerous Charm

Bird Island Park in Atlanta, Georgia, is in full bloom, with everything lush and green. A Japanese water garden with graceful arcing footbridges draws the biggest crowds. But at the far end of the greenway, where the crowns of apple trees entwine, there is but one soul, soon to be haunted by another.

Hovering half in sunlight, half in shadow, Elroy Stinson stares at the apple trees, something spooky going on in his mind. He thinks he'd like to steal an apple.

He looks around. He'll have to wait. There's a young man passing by. A big, eager puppy-dog type. Just strolling along, maybe on his way to meet his sweetheart.

Elroy looks around for the young man's sweetheart but doesn't see her. A wistful sigh escapes him, and he returns his gaze to the apple trees. An instant later, a breeze sweeps by and ruffles the leaves, sending a magnificent shiver through them. A shiver of comparable magnificence sweeps through Elroy. He helped plant these trees, long ago when Maggie was alive, long ago when Elroy was alive, more alive than now.

He visits Bird Island Park rarely these days, but when he does, he always seeks out these apple trees. He's glad they're in a secluded area; he doesn't like to share them with anyone. He fears these trees will die before he does—he's heard that apple trees do not have long productive lives. When they die, it will be another connection to Maggie lost.

Elroy spent his entire working career at one of Atlanta's most prestigious banks, retiring as president. He is proud of that record, prouder still of his forty-five years of service to the Atlanta community. But retirement is hitting him hard. Maggie has come back to haunt him.

This morning, feeling her close, his thoughts returned to Bird Island Park and the apple trees. The idea of stealing an apple struck him. He'd never done it before.

He circles an apple tree, surveying the golden fruit. His mouth waters. He can taste the heavenly tartness already.

He grabs an apple and pulls it. The branch bends, the leaves quake, the apple breaks free, and Elroy has it in hand.

He looks around, as he did long ago when he first set eyes on Maggie, right here on this very spot as he dug holes for the young apple trees.

In his imagination, the air becomes iridescent with Maggie's presence. He gathers her in his arms and presses her to his heart, and she becomes a burning presence inside him.

He hears approaching footsteps and breaks free from his reverie.

He spins around and sees the big, eager puppy dog, but now sees him in a different light. The young man has a dark, foreboding aspect. And he's approaching Elroy fast.

A mighty shiver of fear wallops Elroy's entire body. His knees quake, and he drops the apple and cringes.

As if sensing Elroy's fear, the young man slows his pace. He's smiling now, his eyes wide in surprise. He seems to be amazed that Elroy would have this fearful reaction to him.

"You don't have to be afraid of me," the young man says. His voice is soft and pleasant. Primal joy exudes from him.

But Elroy, having been a banker for more than forty years, sees a fraud. Fear strikes his heart like a fusillade of enemy bullets.

He thrusts his hands out and backs away. "Get away from me, you piece of scum!" His chest heaves; his pulse soars.

The young man, his smile still in place, edges closer to Elroy.

"Get away!" The sound explodes from Elroy. He feels his face knot, his eyes bulge, the cords in his neck stand out. He can't recognize his own voice, shouting like this. When has he ever shouted? It's a stranger's voice that's raging from him—a stranger in a maelstrom of fear. He knows this young man is dangerous. He knows this young man is a liar. A fraud.

In Elroy's fear-blackened mind, a horrifying image of the young man appears. The image isn't human—it's a foul thing, long in tooth and claw, with murderous intent. And then everything snaps back to reality.

The young man levels a cool gaze on Elroy, and keeps edging closer.

Elroy's voice explodes in rage and fear. "Get away!"

The young man edges closer.

Elroy flails his arms, backpedals furiously.

Elroy and the young man do a strange waltz through the apple grove, Elroy scuttling backward, angling to where he knows there will be people.

He hears a distant siren. It grows louder. He sees a shift in the young man's eyes.

He glances around, sees a swarm of people running along the greenway, heading toward the apple grove, drawn by his cries. He lowers his arms.

A mistake.

In a flash, the young man is on him. He has Elroy in a powerful grip, pushing against the back of his head, bending his head to his chest.

Elroy feels excruciating pain in the back of his neck as muscles, tendons, and nerves stretch and tear. He thrashes about, trying to break the hold, caught in a grip of terror.

He feels a powerful shove against the back of his head, an enormous weight behind it. He hears a loud crack, feels his neck snap.

Now he can't feel anything. He can't move; he can't breathe. Panic sets in, and his mind plunges into darkness.

When the crowd gathers around Elroy Stinson, he is lying motionless on the grass in the apple grove.

✳　✳　✳

Otis Dietrich's eyes register the deep shock one might expect from someone who has just witnessed a terrible accident. In fact, his eyes are so huge with shock they seem to be far away from this place, almost in near-earth orbit.

He circles Elroy Stinson's body, which is lying faceup in the apple grove, until he is standing square to Elroy's head.

Carefully, he goes down on one knee, and then the other.

Using even greater care, he places his hands on either side of Elroy's head, applies firm pressure, and holds Elroy's head in a neutral position.

Otis is taking no chances. He saw this gentleman fall out of an apple tree and land on his head. He suspects a cervical fracture.

In actuality, with a deft move, Otis tripped Elroy, causing him to fall. Catching him, easing him to the ground, Otis applied a terrible force to the back of Elroy's head, slamming his face to his chest.

In the hyperextended neck, high in the cervical spine, the vertebrae shattered, and a resounding crack split the air.

Then Otis eased Elroy's head back to normal alignment.

And now Otis's steady hands are holding Elroy's head immobile. Otis must not allow Elroy to receive further injury to his neck or Elroy is likely to die.

Elroy has a C1-C2 fracture, a hangman's fracture. With this injury, the victim cannot breathe unassisted. After four minutes without oxygen, the victim will begin to suffer brain damage.

Seven minutes before he approached Elroy in the apple grove, using a purloined cell phone, Otis called 911 and requested an ambulance. He is confident the paramedics will arrive on time and that Elroy will suffer no brain damage.

When the paramedics get here, Otis will tell them he saw this gentleman fall out of an apple tree and land on his head. The paramedics will squeeze air into Elroy's lungs with a bag. They will put a collar on Elroy's neck, strap him to a board, and take him to a hospital.

Otis doesn't want Elroy to die. He doesn't want Elroy to suffer brain damage. He wants Elroy to live and to have a clear mind: in a wheelchair, on a respirator, with around-the-clock nursing care for life.

Otis, holding Elroy's head immobile, ensuring that Elroy emerges from this alive and with a clear mind, is watching the crowd. They have formed a broad semi-circle to his left, standing amongst the apple trees.

The nearest person stands about ten feet away. Most stand farther back than that. Like good citizens, they aren't crowding too close. They know an injured person must be given plenty of room.

Otis fractured Elroy's neck in full view of these people, and all along he's been tricking them into believing that something entirely different took place.

He will work diligently to maintain that illusion, and they will work diligently to help him. Reality often lies concealed, perceptions are often incorrect, truth is often paid little heed, and lies are often held sacred. And that will be the case here.

Otis hears the siren draw closer. He gave the 911 operator the precise location—in the park, under the apple trees—and will not abandon Elroy until the paramedics arrive.

"Please clear a path," Otis says. "Please make room for the ambulance. They'll want to drive right up on the grass."

He watches the crowd part, watches for anyone who deviates. Otis committed felony assault right in front of these people, and he must empty their minds of that knowledge.

He scans the crowd. They're watching for the arrival of the ambulance—the siren is caterwauling through the air. They're also gawking at poor Elroy and at the concerned young man who is holding Elroy's head immobile.

"He fell out of an apple tree," Otis says, "and landed on his head."

He watches them, looking for people conferring, whispering, assessing what he told them, or someone staring at him with a certain set to body and eyes, ignoring Elroy and the imminent arrival of the ambulance.

He sees a mother whisper to her teenage daughter. The daughter seems distraught. The mother seems to be comforting her. He doesn't think they're questioning what they saw.

He sees a man glaring at him. Burning Otis with a black, contemptuous look. Otis shifts his eyes away from him. *He knows.*

With all due haste, Otis thinks, calling for the swift arrival of the ambulance. He tries to calm the jitter-jangle of his nerves. He's confident the paramedics will arrive on time, that Elroy will suffer no brain damage, and that he'll be able to slip away when the crowd becomes focused on the lifesaving actions of the ambulance crew.

He decides to talk to the crowd again, to tilt them some more. "After he fell, he grabbed his head. Then he got up and began yelling at me. He wouldn't let me approach him."

Otis scans the crowd, letting his eyes linger on the man who was glaring at him. The man has not relaxed his stance. His eyes are still on Otis, his look as dark and disdainful as ever.

Otis meets the man's stare with one of his own, trying to cancel him out. He sees tiny waves of indecision sweep the man's features. The indecision hadn't been there before.

The man's mouth begins working on its hinges in little displays of gumption. The man affixes steadfastness to himself and steps from the crowd.

Otis's right leg begins to jitterbug like mad. This could go in many different directions. It's a dangerous charm.

The man walks to Otis. He is medium height; has a sturdy build; a strong, angular jaw; dark-brown hair. He wears a blue polo shirt, khaki slacks, and brown leather shoes.

When he reaches Otis, he looks as grave as a judge presiding over a sentencing, and Otis's leg is into an alarming shudder.

"I'm a doctor," the man says. "I hate to say it, but I think you caused this man's injury. It looked like when he fell, you were trying to catch him, but you stumbled into him, and the two of you went down together. Maybe to catch your balance, you pushed against his head. I saw his head bend real quick-like to his chest and I heard a loud crack. I knew he wasn't going to get up after that."

Maybe I stumbled. Otis looks into the man's eyes. The man is straight. He doesn't know.

"I'm not saying it was intentional," the man says, "but he was walking and yelling before, and now he isn't. I don't think any prior fall from an apple tree had anything to do with that. I plan on informing the paramedics and police. There might be some legal issues here, aside from medical. I also plan on contacting this man's physician and family, to tell them what I witnessed."

Otis's leg has become still. "Sir, this man was having a seizure. His head jerked down against his chest. I didn't know what to do, so I held on until the contraction relaxed. Then I eased him to the ground and immobilized his neck. I've had some training, and I can assure you I did not stumble, nor did I push against his head."

The man frowns, says nothing, and backs away.

The siren sends out a big whoop as the ambulance pulls into the apple grove, a police car behind it.

Otis begins a mental countdown.

One-hundred ... ninety-nine ... ninety-eight ...

The numbers drift through his mind as he monitors the man who says he's a doctor and the two paramedics who are racing his way with a gurney.

Eighty-seven ... eighty-six ...

The paramedics are beside him.

"We heard his neck snap," Otis says. He nods toward the man who says he's a doctor. The man nods to the paramedics. "I've been keeping his neck immobile. He's having breathing difficulties. I didn't want to administer mouth-to-mouth, fearing the pressure might shift broken vertebrae, if indeed they are broken."

"We'll take over now."

Seventy-four ... seventy-three ...

Otis allows another pair of hands to take over holding Elroy's head, and he eases to his feet.

Sixty-eight ... sixty-seven ...

Otis walks to the man who says he's a doctor. "Come with me, sir." He motions to the cop, who is walking over from his cruiser.

Sixty ... fifty-nine ...

"Officer, I'm a witness to the accident." Otis starts to pull out his wallet, as if to show the cop his ID, but halts his motion. "This man is also a witness." He points to the man who says he's a doctor.

Fifty-one ... fifty ...

The cop takes out his notebook but keeps walking toward Elroy Stinson and the paramedics, who are now pumping air into Elroy's face. Otis knows the cop will prefer to take witness information after he has made an observation of the scene, done some crowd control, and checked with paramedics to see if they need assistance.

Forty-three ... forty-two ...

All eyes are intent on the paramedics as they attach a cervical collar to Elroy's neck and prepare to strap him to a board.

Thirty ... twenty-nine ...

Otis Dietrich is forty yards away from where Elroy Stinson lies in the apple grove. He is walking fast, glancing back, watching the backs of the crowd. He can't see the cop or the man who says he's a doctor. No one is watching Otis make his escape.

Twenty-two ... twenty-one ...

Otis feels he has put enough distance and foliage between himself and anyone who might have reason to ask him to stop. He begins running.

Seventeen ... sixteen ...

Otis is running along a path frequented by joggers, bicyclists, inline skaters, and mothers pushing baby strollers.

Eleven ... ten ... nine ... eight ...

He sees his rental car in the parking lot.

Four ... three ... two ...

He digs out the key.

One ... zero ...

He is inside the vehicle, starting it up, driving away. His heart is hammering, his pulse crashing in his head.

After catching a flight from Atlanta to Los Angeles, Otis is back home in Santa Monica, standing in front of a full-length mirror.

What did Elroy Stinson see? How was Otis's façade pierced? He practices in front of the mirror—smiling, reciting a friendly greeting.

The magic charm has worked before. It'll work again.

But it's a dangerous charm. The corridor darkens, and he senses something behind him. He feels cool air against his flesh. A chill races up his spine.

He sees a strange, knotted form in the mirror. It looks vaguely like Otis. He turns around and looks, but it's gone.

He's seen it before, wonders what it is. It always chills him.

CHAPTER 6

The Girl in the Green and White Summer Dress

Somewhere near Barstow, California, in the dead of night, Stephen D. Spiros pulls off Interstate 15 and enters a rest area. He parks his Toyota pickup and strolls toward the restrooms, his hands thrust deep into the pockets of his blue jeans, his body shivering against the biting cold. The Mojave Desert, so hot by day, is downright cold by night.

To his surprise, he encounters a bizarre collection of people ambling about on the sidewalk. They look like refuges from a circus, like the roustabouts that put up the big top. He walks past them in the pale glow of the security lights.

One of them, a strapping man with long, dark hair, is standing by the building that houses the restrooms. The man's face, neck, and arms are covered with tattoos.

As Spiros walks closer, he sees that the man's tattoos are not tattoos at all but frightful wounds: *raised flesh; ripped, pulpy tissue, rimmed with blood.*

He looks around, straining to see through the gloom, and sees that the others milling about are also covered with hideous wounds.

Shaken, he runs into the men's room, relieves himself, and runs to a sink. He washes his hands, splashes water on his face, and studies his reflection in the mirror.

Good god! What happened? Was there an accident on the interstate? Did someone call it in? Are they waiting for ambulances?

The door opens. He spins around.

A normal man enters the restroom. No wounds.

Relief sweeps over Spiros. He slumps, lets out his breath. Then he shudders. Not since childhood has he seen a person with such volcanic wounds. Wounds that no one cared about, wounds that no one fussed about.

Spiros had had such wounds in his childhood twice. And twice he'd nearly died. He leans into the mirror, stares at the tiny telltale scars on his face, the physical reminders of his youth. He peers into his eyes, tries to see into the mind that holds those long-ago memories.

Flat, sure footsteps pass behind him as the man walks to a urinal. Moments later, a powerful stream of urine issues forth. The man is reflected in the mirror. He's about Spiros's age, twenty-nine, wears a navy-blue sweatsuit, has an impeccable haircut, is clean shaven. The stream of urine stops and the man walks to a sink.

Spiros takes a deep breath, calms himself, and looks at the man. "Was there an accident on the interstate?" he asks.

The man looks at Spiros, eyes narrowed.

The look chills Spiros.

The man turns away and busies himself washing his hands.

"Who knows?" he finally says, his voice dead, toneless. He dries his hands and then walks out of the restroom.

A moment later, Spiros leaves the restroom.

He scans the sidewalk and parking lot. There are no people in sight. He draws in a deep breath and releases it slowly.

A car, or something, screams by on the interstate. Spiros fastens his eyes on it. It's out of sight in an instant. What was it?

On shaky legs, he walks to his pickup, gets inside, and starts the engine. He locks the doors and stares out the windows.

He flicks on the overhead light, pulls out his journal, and makes an entry:

While crossing the California desert near Barstow, I stopped at a rest area in the middle of the night and saw people walking around with ripped-open flesh. I thought there had been an accident. There was no accident. It was misdirection. A light being entered the restroom and did something to me. My mind focused elsewhere, I didn't catch what he did.

Spiros's right leg begins jitterbugging like mad. For several minutes it will not settle down. Then it becomes still.

He rubs the back of his neck, spins in his seat. His eyes dart everywhere.

With a sinking feeling in the pit of his stomach, he pulls out of the rest area, gets back on the interstate, and resumes his journey home.

* * *

Two weeks after the Barstow incident, Spiros wakes up in the middle of the night in his Irvine, California, apartment. He crouches by his bed, cool night air wafting in from the open curtained windows. Someone—or something—has entered his apartment. It's happened before, usually in the night. He dreads what's coming next.

A hot spike of pain strikes him deep in his upper back. He hunches in agony. The pain ratchets up. It's so bad he blackens into temporary insanity.

He thinks he's been bitten by a vampire unseen that flew in through the window. He sees tantalizing patterns on the edge of perception: gilded bats racing around the rim of the sun, peeling off and racing earthward.

The pain eases, the hallucinations fade.

In a moment of lucidity, he knows what's happening. Woodsman has been trying to gain access to his awareness. When Woodsman takes a person over, he pushes him toward a goal and does not relinquish him easily.

Pain is one of Woodsman's whips.

Spiros developed Woodsman for the U.S. Air Force while employed at Quade Medical. It's a technology that creates perceptual phenomena such as voices, bodily sensations, and images that exist solely within the minds of percipients. Its primary mission is to rescue downed pilots. Eighteen months ago, Woodsman came under investigation by the U.S. Senate Committee on Armed Services, and Quade Medical, needing a scapegoat, fired Spiros. Since then, Woodsman has been a nocturnal visitor to Spiros's windswept Irvine apartment.

Not knowing if Woodsman has taken him over or not, Spiros crawls back into bed and falls asleep.

Hours later, he wakes with the rising sun.

He dresses, eats breakfast, fills his canteen with water, puts on a baseball cap, grabs his Desert Eagle .44 caliber Magnum, ten boxes of ammo, and heads outside.

Walking toward his pickup, he realizes it's been almost one year since the incident that shaped his life in a totally new and unexpected way.

Six months after Quade Medical fired him, feeling an acute need to indulge himself, Spiros drove to an old haunt: a steakhouse named Inga's that overlooked the Pacific Ocean.

The hostess led him to his favorite table in back and gave him a menu.

Spiros glanced at the menu, decided he would have a house salad, a porterhouse steak, a baked potato, and a Heineken draft beer.

His attention wandered to the next table, where two beefy men sat, feigning interest in their food. He knew he had seen them before.

Both wore brown dress shirts open at the collar. Both had thick necks and rigid posture. One was middle-aged, with thinning black hair and a goatee. The other was young, with thick black hair and no goatee. They could have been brothers, fifteen years apart.

The goateed man looked in Spiros's direction, and then

began talking about a syndrome. He mentioned carrying a weapon as part of the syndrome.

Spiros listened to the man's deep, well-modulated voice and studied the décor: the mirrored ceilings, the overhead fans, the reflected flitter of fan blades everywhere—on his menu, on his water glass, on the glass partitions, on the woodwork and tabletops. It reminded him of his knife, strapped to his lower right leg.

"Look at what's happened to our man Achilles," the goateed man said, his voice picking up energy and sounding earnest.

"I know," the younger man said. "He's just a blank." His voice was equally energetic and earnest.

"It went bad for him," the goateed man said.

It poured over Spiros like water and then froze like an ice pick in his gut. They were talking about him, calling him *Achilles*. They'd done it before, at Inga's and elsewhere.

He leaned over and felt for his knife. He contemplated walking up to one of them and plunging it in.

He listened, his anger growing.

"There's a certain type of person with a certain way about them that spells disaster," the goateed man said, his voice growing ever more earnest. "Our man Achilles is one such person. He possesses an energy society needs but does not respect."

"I agree," the younger man said, matching his companion's increasingly earnest tone. "He can play no part in regular society, for people instinctively know to shunt him aside."

"It's always a struggle for him," the goateed man said. "He has to climb a mountain while others merely cross a street. To do well he must operate in his niche. That's where he'll find his greatest energy, discipline, and creativity."

"What's his niche?" the younger man asked.

"Achilles' niche is war," the goateed man said. "That's his path. He's a warrior, but he has not respected himself as a warrior. He's on a false society path, and it will always defeat him. Don't you agree?"

"I do," the younger man said.

The waitress arrived to take Spiros's order.

He knew her to be sympathetic; she had heard them talk about him before. He asked her to eavesdrop. He needed a witness. She murmured her assent.

The men were agents of Quade Medical, he told her. Quade Medical was trying to subvert his life's work. They were trying to weaponize Woodsman.

She left to place his order and get him a Heineken.

The men began speaking brazenly to Spiros.

"Achilles," the goateed man said, staring right at Spiros, "did you know there are people who, when they're around you, you're less effective? And then there are others who have the opposite effect. They make you better at what you do. You naturally gravitate toward the more positive influences, don't you? Do you find that this is true?"

"It's true, Achilles," the younger man said. "Someone has distilled the essence of this phenomenon. It's a proprietary system of Quade Medical's, so please, hands off."

They were trying to keep him from doing further research on the technologies he created for Quade Medical.

Spiros eyed them coldly, committing their faces to memory. The waitress returned with his beer.

A few days later, Spiros met with an attorney and presented the salient facts: Quade Medical fired him without just cause. They sabotaged his job prospects, claiming he was unfit for regular society. Their agents stalk him and use powerful mental techniques to force him out of medical research.

"What did you do at Quade Medical?" the attorney asked.

"I created technologies that restructure how the mind perceives reality. The most widely known of these are pain gods and Woodsman."

"How much money is at stake?"

"Billions."

The attorney took the case and filed a lawsuit.

Quade Medical settled out of court for ten million dollars. With some of his new-found wealth, Spiros bought a Toyota pickup and two thousand rounds of ammunition for his .44 automatic.

Spiros drives east to the Santa Ana Mountains, follows a dirt road into the foothills, parks, and climbs out.

He hikes through a maze of rugged ravines, finds a narrow pass, and with a knife carves man-sized targets into the rocky slopes.

He puts in earplugs and gets into a shooter's stance. He sights on a target, both hands gripping the .44, feet apart, weight evenly distributed, elbows and knees bent.

He fires, empties a magazine, inserts another.

He fires with both hands—strong hand, weak hand. He reloads while running, eluding imaginary pursuit. He fires from a prone position, from a kneeling position.

He fires from a fast draw, either hand. He fires with eyes shut, simulating massive facial wounds. He works on speed and accuracy and shoots up all but twenty rounds of the two hundred he brought.

He removes his earplugs, drinks water from his canteen, and hikes back to his pickup, where he cleans his firearm.

While driving home, he contemplates the phenomenon of light beings. He believes Quade Medical, in collaboration with the Pentagon, is responsible for them. The main clue is Woodsman, a technology with an entity-like aspect that Spiros created for the U.S. Air Force while employed at Quade Medical.

Light beings, similar yet more enigmatic than Woodsman, are likely created from the same core technology.

Spiros intends to identify the human agency responsible for light beings and expose them to public scrutiny. That should put the screws to them, and end all manner of nefarious schemes.

At home, he showers, dresses, and then drives to a nearby shopping mall, in need of refreshment.

He goes into an ice-cream shop at the shopping mall and buys a huge chocolate malt, like he did when he was a kid. He sucks greedily on the straw, but the malted milk is thick and does not go down fast enough.

Outside the ice-cream shop, he sees a man kissing a beautiful young woman in a green and white summer dress.

He stands on the sidewalk watching her, sucking on the straw, savoring the chocolate flavor that eddies over his taste buds.

He watches the man hold the woman close, watches the woman take to tiptoes, watches her dress ride up in back, exposing her long and slender thighs.

Spiros feels something stir inside him. He fights it down. All his instincts tell him to fight it down. He finds himself unworthy.

He looks away, but quickly looks back, his thoughts piling up like an aggregate of rock after a landslide. Watching the man kiss the luscious brunette in the green and white summer dress is like contemplating his own death.

He sucks on the straw, draws more chocolate flavor into his mouth, and suddenly wants to be out of the sun.

He walks to his pickup, gets in, and backs out of the parking space, the giant malted-milk cup in his hand, heavy with its cooling elixir.

He shifts into Drive and eases ahead. The kissing duo has disappeared. At the end of the row of parked cars, he brings his pickup to a halt and checks for traffic.

He sucks on the straw: chocolate eddies.

He eases into the turn, going left.

But now something is coming from the right, a blur, and Spiros hits the brakes with such violence it rattles his facial bones. He hears the screech of brakes, his own and the other vehicle's.

The other vehicle swerves sharply to avoid colliding with the right flank of Spiros's pickup. Both vehicles come to screeching stops.

Spiros stares at the other vehicle, a large blue Mercedes SUV. Its horn blares. Two eyes blaze at him in a fit of anger.

Spiros shifts into Park, and then reaches under the driver's seat, where his Desert Eagle .44 caliber Magnum lies.

He pulls his hand back. What was he going to do? Shoot the guy in the Mercedes? There'd been no collision. Go home, forget it.

But those eyes keep staring.

Spiros sees another head in the Mercedes, a head with long brunette hair, and another pair of eyes watching him.

It's the man and woman who'd been kissing.

The man in the Mercedes spins around in his seat, facing forward, and all of a sudden the big Mercedes' brake lights go off and the Mercedes begins rolling backward toward Spiros's Toyota.

Rolling fast.

And somehow Spiros knows the beautiful girl in the Mercedes is not there of her own free will.

His pulse quickening, Spiros shifts into Reverse and floors it. He tears down the corridor he had just traveled up, driving as fast as the pickup will go, his eyes sweeping rapid-fire all around: on the Mercedes in front, on the lane behind, and everywhere else, looking for moving vehicles and pedestrians, trying to avert disaster.

The Mercedes is governed by a demon, keeping a hairsbreadth off the Toyota's front bumper, but also touching the bumper sometimes, like the whisker of a cat touching a fern frond in the dead of night—so delicate is the demon's touch.

Approaching the end of the lane, Spiros's nerve gives out, and he brakes hard. He isn't going to send the Toyota screaming out into a blind intersection. He screeches to a stop and faces forward. The Mercedes is there, just beyond his windshield, its big blue body looming. The driver pops out.

Spiros steps from his pickup. He is innocent. He will explain that to the driver of the Mercedes. The whole thing was just an innocent little occurrence in the parking lot of a shopping mall.

He steps around his open door, his hands held out in front of him, words taking shape in his mind. An explanation, then he will be on his way. To Spiros's amazement, he realizes he is still clutching the malted-milk cup. He puts the straw to his lips and sucks the cool, refreshing goodness, and it washes down his throat.

The guy from the Mercedes is walking toward Spiros. He's scary big, about six-five, two hundred and eighty pounds. His expression resembles that of a giant bluefin tuna Spiros once saw on a dock in Bimini. Coldblooded, and totally blank.

Well ... maybe the guy has cooled off.

Spiros releases the straw from his lips and says, "Sorry about that, but—"

The guy punches him in the gut so fast Spiros didn't see it coming, so hard Spiros is left sucking for air, doubled over in spasms, the malted-milk cup dropping from his hand. The next thing he knows he is flying over the hood of his pickup, coming down headfirst, breaking his fall on the concrete with his hands, coming to rest on his back. He scrambles to his hands and knees, too numb to assess damage but knowing he is damaged.

He keeps on scrambling, into the maze of parked cars. He slips through the parking lot, hiding amongst the vehicles.

He sits with his back against the tire of a Lincoln Continental and listens. Where is Bluefin? He hears no nearby footfalls.

The tire at his back is superheated by the sun. It burns through his shirt, giving him some relief and a chance to think. He hadn't been afraid of Bluefin initially, but he's afraid of him now.

He can remember having been this frightened only one other time in his life. At age twelve, he had opened the door to a salesman who turned out to be a burglar casing the neighborhood. Discovering Spiros alone, the guy assaulted him—broke both of his arms, battered him about the head, leaving him semiconscious. The guy then looted the place.

Spiros had lain on the living-room floor for hours. No one came home; he felt abandoned. Around dinnertime the phone rang. Later on, he learned it was his parents calling to tell him they would be staying late somewhere. He cried out, unable to move. Eventually, the phone stopped ringing, and fear came crashing. Would the guy come back? Spiros didn't remember much after that.

He hears the sound of footsteps on the other side of the Lincoln, knows it's Bluefin, knows Bluefin is coming after him.

Spiros springs to his feet, tears through the maze of cars, sprinting for his pickup, hearing sounds of pursuit behind him, knowing he has only seconds to spare.

He reaches his pickup, reaches under the driver's seat, comes up with the gun, spins, aims ...

Bluefin screeches to a halt a mere six feet away, a look of stunned disbelief on his face. Throwing his hands up to ward off a bullet, he starts backpedaling.

Spiros advances on him, in his shooter's crouch, the gun pointed at Bluefin's chest.

Bluefin turns and runs through the parking lot, using vehicles as shields, snapping quick looks back at Spiros.

Spiros watches Bluefin race through the parking lot on a long course back to his Mercedes. Does he have a gun in there?

Spiros isn't going to wait around and find out.

He jumps into his pickup, shoves the Desert Eagle under the seat, and starts the engine.

He puts it in gear, looks through the windshield, and sees the girl in the green and white summer dress standing right in front of him.

Their eyes meet.

He feels dangerous undercurrents.

What should he do?

He can't run her over.

He sticks his head out the window.

"Do you want a ride somewhere?"

"Yes."

He opens the passenger door, and she hops in.

❆　❆　❆

They sit at the kitchen table in Spiros's Irvine apartment. He opens a first-aid kit, removes scissors, sterile gauze pads, bandages, first-aid tape, rubbing alcohol, and antiseptic cream, and treats the wounds he sustained in his headlong fall onto the concrete of the parking lot. The girl watches him.

They move into the living room. She roams around, looking at the furnishings, and he watches her. She is eye catching; her looks stun him. Her tousled brunette hair falls to her shoulders, lending her a roguish look.

She gazes at a print on the wall of an American Indian on horseback surveying a windswept plain.

"Is that a Plains Indian?" she asks.

"If not, he's lost."

She laughs. "What's your name?"

"Spiros."

"Spiros what?"

"Stephen D. Spiros. But just call me Spiros."

"Okay." She walks closer to him. "I'm like the Indian, Spiros. I'm lost, too. I want to recall the things of our world before we lose our world. Don't you?"

"Yes."

She chokes up for a moment.

"Spiros, we are losing our world, aren't we?"

"Yes." He could say more, but decides not to. He waits for her to turn sad or angry, but she does neither.

"Tell me about you, Spiros."

Spiros tells her of his childhood, his university training, his work experience at Quade Medical, his desire to rehabilitate Woodsman.

He sees her eyebrows rise. "You created Woodsman?"

"Yes. Woodsman is misunderstood."

"Oh, spooky," she says.

"Who's that guy you were with?"

"He's an entrepreneur. He does most of his work in China, setting up outsourcing. I thought I'd learn about China from him. I thought wrong."

"Why didn't you leave him?"

"I wanted to, but I learned that leaving him wasn't so easy. He has the Stockholm syndrome down cold. He holds you hostage and at the same time portrays himself as vulnerable, which gains your sympathy. Amazing, isn't it?"

"It is amazing. Why'd he go ballistic out there?"

"He's done that before. There are people who, when they get behind the wheel of a vehicle, watch out. It's their vehicle, you might say, for aggression. It was another good reason to leave him. But ..."

"The Stockholm syndrome?"

"Yes."

"Why did you trust coming home with me?"

"You started apologizing to the creep and ended up scaring him away with a gun. That spoke to me on a whole new level. You rescued me, Spiros, and didn't even know it. I think I needed to tell you that."

They sit on the couch. She tells him her name is Wini Taggart. She says she is twenty, a student at UCLA.

She tells him about her childhood, about all the times her family moved. They had lived all over the world. Her father was in the Air Force.

She stands, walks to a bureau, and gets a can of pepper spray from her purse.

"You need to get one of these," she says, returning to the couch and sitting down. She shows him how to use it. "It's a nonlethal alternative."

"I'll get one."

He shows her his knife, a simple spring-assisted utility knife with a three-inch blade that locks in place.

"Don't carry a knife," he says, "unless you know how to use it and can keep it out of the hands of your enemy. Otherwise, your enemy will take it away from you and use it to maim or kill you."

"I can't carry a knife then," Wini says. "I could never keep it out of the hands of my enemy."

"Wini, in a dangerous situation, grab any weapon within reach, your car keys, for example. Or use your hands. Forget civilized behavior. You must be tenacious and cruel. You must injure or kill your enemy to avoid capture and possible death."

She looks at him, her eyes widening.

"Are you serious, Spiros?"

"I am serious."

"I think you're joking, Spiros."

"I am not."

She convulses in laughter.

His thoughts thicken, grow opaque, as he searches for an explanation. He can barely remember Woodsman taking him over this morning.

"Wini, today, in the early-morning hours, Woodsman took me over. It's happened before. It doesn't last long, maybe a day or so."

"Is that a big deal?"

He hesitates. "Yes."

CHAPTER 7

The Land O' Cheryl Toomey

Kent Cochran is in Van Nuys, walking down a sidewalk so hot he could fry his brains on it. He's not worried about his brains, though. In another few minutes, he's likely to fry all his circuits. He's going to ask Cheryl Toomey out. And it won't be just an ordinary date. He's going to ask her to go all the way to San Francisco with him.

Two days, two nights in San Francisco.

Cheryl is a tall, leggy brunette, a quintessential free spirit. No cherub she—a succubus more likely.

Kent doesn't have much of a plan. He'll knock on her door, trusting somehow he'll come up with the right stuff.

He draws near her house, but keeps on walking. He sees how small it is, a narrow two-story gingerbread affair, squeezed in by similar-looking houses. The whole block is like that: narrow lots, small yards, white picket fences.

He met Cheryl at a bar called Heap O' Trouble on Wilshire Boulevard, where she works as a cocktail waitress.

He'd gone in on a Friday after work and ordered a whiskey highball. Cheryl had been his server. He became a regular, and got to know her.

One night she jotted down her address. "If you're ever in my neighborhood, look me up," she said.

There'd been moments in Heap O' Trouble when he felt on the verge of asking her out, but didn't.

This time it's going to be different. He's going to force himself to ask her out. What can she say? She can say no. But he thinks she'll say yes.

Cheryl has exquisite legs, an awe-inspiring figure, hair that's almost black. But she has complexion problems.

Her complexion being what it is works in Kent's favor. There aren't many guys interested in a pockmarked face.

Kent has to remind himself he's no catch, either. He's in his early fifties, balding, and overweight. But he earns a big salary as an electrical engineer, has traveled the world over, and is working on his weight.

He isn't going to ask her to marry him; he's just going to ask her for a date. Haven't they had enough whiskey-soaked conversations in Heap O' Trouble to make themselves comfortable with one another, comfortable enough to go to San Francisco together? He thinks so.

In the Land O' Cheryl Toomey, a shot of old Irish whiskey provides the necessary voltage for a lot of things, especially when you're contemplating her face.

From a distance, she appears elegant. But when you get a close-up look at her face, she's something of a turnoff.

That first night in Heap O' Trouble, she leaned across his table and said, "Hi, I'm Cheryl. Welcome to Heap O'

Trouble. I'll be your server this evening. What can I get you?"

Kent ordered a whiskey highball. She departed, came back with it, and leaned in closer: eyes nice, nose nice, cheekbones and chin nice, all her features nice, but the acne pits and scars not nice.

Kent had seen worse. If Cheryl's had been any worse, he'd have written her off. He probably wouldn't have even gone back to Heap O' Trouble.

But here she was, leaning across his table, depositing his drink, pausing longer than she needed to, giving him a close-up view of her breasts clad in a skimpy halter top, her bare abdomen, her hips clad in tight, low-slung jeans.

Her face was quite angelic, depending on how you viewed it, how the light caught it, if you allowed a certain blurriness to predominate. Let it blur, and she was smashing.

But the more she leaned in that first night, the more Kent saw the worst of her—the acne pits. They were off-putting, so he kept downing whiskey highballs, trying to bring the blurriness back, but that didn't always work, so he allowed her other attributes—the basic shape of her face, her fine features, her height, her long, dark hair, her figure—to overwhelm him.

He drew her into conversations on everything he could think of, and she'd been game.

He tipped her, of course. About a hundred bucks a night, three or four nights a week. He knew in his heart of hearts that if it weren't for those acne scars she'd be out of his league. He wouldn't stand a chance.

*   *   *

Kent is drawing near her house again, having circled the block, when he notices a tall man in a black baseball cap and a black long-sleeve sweatshirt standing across the street watching him. It sets off alarms. The guy is probably suspicious of Kent's circumnavigation of the neighborhood. He'll have to make his approach.

He stops in front of Cheryl's house and opens the gate.

In Heap O' Trouble, she told him a drug dealer had been shot and killed in her neighborhood recently, and two of the deceased's pit bulls were running loose. When the pits entered her yard and threatened her, she shot and killed them both. Another reason for her to give him her address. She seemed proud of the notoriety.

He steps through the gate, walks to the door, and pushes the bell. Chimes sound.

He waits a moment and then peers through a window in the door, sees stairs off to the right, a tall brunette in blue shorts coming down. He doesn't recognize her at first. Her hair is damp and tangled, fresh from a shampoo.

Cheryl opens the door, her eyes popping, surprised to see him. Then, in an unguarded moment, something cold flickers in her eyes, and Kent realizes she detests him, always did.

She knows he caught her, and tries to correct. "Kent ..." She chokes on it, her face contorting.

He floods with caution. "Cheryl, I was in the neighborhood and thought I'd stop by."

"You were in the neighborhood? How come?"

"I needed stimulation. Murders. Pit bulls."

She laughs and does a little spin of glee. "This is the neighborhood for it."

"I thought if you weren't too busy we could go for a walk."

Her eyes narrow.

"Sure," she says. "Give me a few minutes. Come in."

She steps back, and Kent enters the house. Her smell enters him: the bath, the shampoo, the damp hair.

"Here ..."

She shows him into the living room, a small room opposite the stairs, with a picture window facing the street, an old couch, and an old boxy TV.

"I'll be right back." She races up the stairs.

✳   ✳   ✳

Kent sits on the couch in Cheryl's living room. Moments later, a man enters the room. It's not really a man, more a cool, blue translucent image of a man. This man, or image of a man, walks with purpose about the room, passing through solid objects as if that were normal business.

The image moves fluidly, carrying small stones, setting them down at regular intervals, creating a geometric pattern that extends through the room, through the walls and into other rooms, and out into the yard.

It leaves through a wall, moments later comes back through another wall, continuing its work—a cool, blue dance of light, shimmering in its complexity. It pauses a moment, engages in clearing something from its path, and then lays more stones.

How strange, Kent thinks, to see in visible form that which is normally invisible. What precipitated the appearance of this phantom? Where did it come from? Why does it lay stones in big geometric displays?

They're called light beings. The lore on them accumulates daily. They can take on any form, glow in any color. They often engage in tricks. A favorite trick is to draw attention and entertain, while others of their ilk assume dark shapes and flit into dim corridors or mirrored surfaces where they lie in wait. These things can change configuration in a heartbeat. They can take on a curious wolfish cast or look spidery or appear as discs of light. They can look human, indistinguishable from the real thing.

Where do they come from? No one seems to know. Darkness and light are equally their home. Some humans worship them as gods. Others give caution, warn that they are devils.

The light being looks at Kent, not in a curious fashion, but as if measuring the distance between them. Then it vanishes.

Lush scents of forest and meadow waft into the room. Kent sees Pan, the Greek god of nature, half-goat, half-man. Pan is wreathed in mist and is playing panpipes. He dances away into the mist. And what a strange dance it is. Kent thinks the light being's geometric pattern drew Pan.

Light beings are known to stage fleeting entertainment as precursors to something more serious. Maybe the extinction event is looming, Kent thinks. Maybe life on earth is about to end.

Painful memories surge into Kent's mind. He stands, pulls off his shirt, and looks at the scars on his chest where surgeons cut him open years ago.

A phantasmal, elongated figure appears: a primordial tigress named Tic. Tic is Kent's pain god. She makes a sinuous passage through the room, turns toward Kent, and snaps her jaws.

"Cheryl Toomey is truly ugly," Tic says in a deep rasp.

"I'm surprised at you, Tic," Kent says.

"I'm not talking about her face. It's inside her."

"Can we invoke something to help the poor thing?"

"Yes. Invoke community, family, apple pie—whatever makes you tremble."

Kent nods at Tic and then gingerly puts his shirt back on. Tic lies down in a corner.

Kent sits down on the couch to await Cheryl.

Waiting an inordinate amount of time, becoming restless, Kent stands, looks out the window, and sees the man in the black baseball cap who'd been standing across the street. Now he's standing inside Cheryl's white picket fence, not more than fifteen feet away. He strikes a casual pose, yet there's an aura of violence about him.

Kent clenches his jaws. Out on the street he thought the guy was a neighbor concerned with Kent's eternal wandering of the neighborhood. Now he thinks otherwise. A guy trespassing and showing aggression is no concerned neighbor.

The guy is tall, well over six feet. He's powerfully built, not like a barrel, but like a thick telephone pole. He has short dark hair, a round face, a blunt head, and blunt shoulders. He wears a black baseball cap with no emblem on it, black-frame glasses, and a black long-sleeve sweatshirt.

He stares through the window at Kent, his eyes menacing.

Kent retreats to the couch, concealing himself from the guy's view. He looks into the corridor. *Hurry up, Cheryl! We have to go for a walk! I have to pop the question!*

He hears loud rapping at the window and snaps his eyes that way. The guy in the black sweatshirt is up against the glass, beating out a rhythm with his knuckles.

Kent's veins fill with terrific pressure. Terrified, he explodes off the couch and runs from the room.

In the corridor, he sees Cheryl coming downstairs, her hair dry, her feet encased in sandals. He stops.

"Cheryl! A man's knocking on your picture window!"

She rushes into the living room, Kent behind her.

She looks out the window. "He's gone."

"Do you know him?" He describes him: the powerful build, the glasses, the dark heavy clothing.

"I don't think so."

"Should we call the cops?"

"Not unless he comes back."

"Cheryl, Pan was here. He played panpipes and did a strange dance, like nothing I've ever seen. I think he was heralding something big. Maybe the extinction event is near."

"Kent, we're already dead. Didn't you know that? We're smoke going up the chimney."

"We can't be dead yet."

"We are. Things got strange when we died. Only the dead see things like Pan. Don't you get it?"

Kent hears a jeer in her voice—it cuts him like a knife. They walk out the door.

* * *

They walk to the end of the block, look for traffic, and cross the street. On the next block, Cheryl picks up the pace.

"There's a park up ahead," she says. "Let's go there."

"Okay." Encouraged, Kent begins his pitch. "Cheryl, have you ever been to San Francisco?"

"Yes. When I was eleven. My parents took me there."

"How'd you like it?"

"Oh, it was charming."

They walk a block in silence.

"Cheryl, would you like to go back to San Francisco?"

"Uh, maybe."

"Are you interested at all?"

"With you? What are your intentions?"

"We'd rough it. Sleep on the beach."

"You're kidding, right?"

"I'm not kidding. It's something I've never done before."

They enter the park and look around.

The playground is loaded with kids.

One kid is flying a paper kite that looks homemade.

"Let's sit over there," Cheryl says, pointing at some picnic tables. They find a spot at a picnic table under some shade trees, and they watch the kids at play.

Kent sees the guy who was at Cheryl's window. He's walking fast across the grass, looking at something with full attention, as if he had a spyglass to his eye. He's heading toward the kid who's flying the kite. Suddenly, the kid collapses and is lying on the grass having a seizure, his kite flying out of control.

A woman cries out, and people rush toward the kid as a siren sounds in the distance. Kent and Cheryl spring up and race toward the stricken child.

As Kent runs, he senses someone behind him, glances back, and sees the guy who was at Cheryl's window.

The guy seizes Kent by the neck, yanks him off his feet, and sends him flying. Kent crashes to the ground. The jolt knocks the wind out of him.

Kent is dazed, not sure if his heart is still working.

As if peering into a dimension he no longer occupies, he watches Cheryl and the others race toward the fallen child.

A shadow looms over him.

Fear numbs him.

The guy pounces on him.

He has Kent in a powerful grip, pushing against the back of his head, bending his head to his chest. Kent feels excruciating pain in the back of his neck as it stretches beyond its normal limit.

Helpless in the grip of this monster, Kent feels a powerful shove against the back of his head, an enormous weight behind it. He feels his neck snap, hears a resounding *crack!*

Kent lies flat on the ground, unable to breathe, unable to move. The air becomes bubbly with music as a siren draws near.

Kent stares into the sky as the kid's wayward kite smashes into the ground, a dim corner of his mind holding dying thoughts of Cheryl and San Francisco.

❋   ❋   ❋

Otis Dietrich, keeping Kent's neck immobile, is watching the woman Kent was with. She's staring at him, her eyes pulsing with hatred. She knows what he did.

He scans the crowd, checking to see if anyone else caught on. He thinks it's just the woman. He returns his gaze to her.

Her eyes are dark with malice, spewing something vile at him. She steps from the crowd, stands about five feet from him.

He sees that her face is full of acne scars. Too bad, what a shame. What a beauty she would have been otherwise.

"I know what you did," she says with terrible coldness. "I heard his neck snap."

"He slipped and fell," Otis says. "He landed awkwardly on his head. The sound you heard was my shoulder." He rotates his shoulder and produces a loud snap.

Doubt crowds her eyes. Tears streak her face.

"Kent, why?" she sobs.

She collapses to the ground.

An ambulance pulls into the park, its siren whooping, a police car behind it.

Otis begins a mental countdown.

One-hundred ... ninety-nine ... ninety-eight ...

The numbers drift through his mind as he monitors the two paramedics who are racing his way with a gurney.

Eighty-seven ... eighty-six ...

The paramedics are beside him.

"I've been keeping his neck immobile," Otis says. "He's having breathing difficulties. I didn't want to administer mouth-to-mouth, fearing the pressure might shift broken vertebrae, if indeed they are broken."

"We'll take over now."

Seventy-four ... seventy-three ...

Otis allows another pair of hands to take over holding Kent's head, and he eases to his feet and drifts through the crowd.

Otis is running along a sidewalk outside the park.

Eleven ... ten ... nine ... eight ...

He sees his car ahead.

Four ... three ... two ...

He digs out his key.

One ... zero ...

He's inside his vehicle, starting it up, driving away. His heart is hammering, his pulse crashing in his head. It is a dangerous charm.

CHAPTER 8

Something Has Vanished

At sundown, Stephen D. Spiros drives up a winding canyon road in Los Angeles and parks in front of a white stucco house, the residence of Claire Rizzo, a slender white-haired lady in her mid-seventies. Claire has been receiving strange visits by one of her neighbors—a man whom Spiros believes doesn't exist.

Spiros and Claire sit on the porch. As twilight commences, he asks her about the neighbor.

"What's Jack been up to lately?"

"He enters my house now."

"He comes right in?"

"Yes."

"What does he do in your house?"

"He just stands there and looks at me for a while, and then he starts talking. What he says freaks me out."

Spiros looks Claire over. In the vague light he sees fresh bruises on her face. He pulls her file and a notepad from his briefcase.

"Where does Jack live again?"

"Over there." She points to a house in the east.

"And he enters your house and just stands there and talks to you?"

"Yes."

"For how long?"

"I don't know. Time gets weird when he talks to me."

Spiros records the new information, noting that the bruises on Claire's face tell another story.

"What does he say?"

"He talks about my so-called secret life. The more I hear the less I believe."

"Does he get loud, gruff, or accusing?"

She shakes her head. "No, he's really a big bear, but he freaks me out. What can I do if he comes back?"

"Can you take a picture of him?"

"I could, but what good would that do?"

"It might throw him off."

"What if he asks me why I took his picture?"

"Don't tell him."

"I don't think he'd like that."

"It doesn't matter what he doesn't like. He's bothering you and he's trespassing. Take his picture. Tell him to get lost."

"He's a nuisance, yet I don't feel I can just tell him to get lost."

"Tell him."

"Oh, but I have told him. He doesn't go."

Spiros thinks a moment.

"Claire, get some polished stones. Arrange them on your kitchen table. Make it look mysterious. Do lots of odd, little things like that with no explanation. He'll wonder what you're up to, but let him wonder. If he asks, don't respond."

He catches a whiff of smoke from the wildfires raging in the hills, gazes into the distance. A thick pall gives the city the look of a battlefield.

"Claire, can you set up a small area and make it look like a temple? A sacred spot? A place where you perform rituals?"

"I could."

"Make it look strange and mysterious. Act as if you have a total commitment to the practices you do there."

Spiros leaves. He has others to see—others who are also receiving visits from people whom Spiros believes don't exist.

✳   ✳   ✳

Spiros returns to Claire's house the following evening. She invites him into the living room. He sees new bruises on her face—they're darker, puffier than before. He smells the aroma of Italian cuisine and rushes into the kitchen.

"It'll keep," Claire says, following him into the kitchen. "We've got important business to attend to."

A pot of tomato sauce is simmering on the stove. Claire is forgetful. The first time Spiros saw her she was clutching a page from her address book. He had to pry it from her hand to find out what it was. He called the first number on it—her son, Frank—and asked him to come over. That was a month ago. Since then Frank checks on her daily.

"Where's your altar, Claire?"

"In my bedroom." She takes him there and shows him.

A small table with two unlit candles in holders and a picture of Buddha serves as her alter.

"It's not much," she says. "What else should I add?"

He gives her some ideas and then leaves.

✳   ✳   ✳

Spiros visits Claire again two days later. They sit on her porch in the heat of late afternoon.

"Did you have a conflict with anyone today, Claire?"

She thinks a moment. "No."

"What did you do today?"

"I stayed home. This morning, I hid. This afternoon, I started cooking dinner. I didn't know what else to do."

"You had a conflict with someone then, especially in the morning."

"I guess I did."

The stiff aroma of Italian seasoning fills the air as she opens the door and invites him in.

He follows her into the kitchen. The table is set for two. He hadn't planned on eating, but sets his briefcase in a corner.

"Busy day?" Claire asks.

"Yes."

"Did you see lots of people?"

"I did."

"Sit down, eat with us."

"I think I will. What is it?"

"Italian. What else?"

Spiros laughs softly.

Just then a boy about eighteen comes into the kitchen.

"This is Louie, my grandson," Claire says.

"How do you do, Louie?" Spiros says.

Louie has dark Mediterranean features, as does his father, Frank, whom Spiros met several weeks ago.

Spiros and Louie shake hands, and Claire sets another place at the table.

The three of them eat and afterward move into the living room. Spiros doesn't want Louie present when he questions Claire, but can't think of a polite way to ask him to go. He decides Louie will be invisible for the next half hour.

"Claire, have you had any visitors lately?"

"The same one I told you about."

Spiros glances at her file. "Your neighbor to the east, Jack Dunne?"

"That's right. He enters my house almost every day and just stands there and talks to me."

"Does he still talk to you about your secret life?"

"He does. I don't trust what he says, though."

"What does he say?"

Claire becomes thoughtful. "It's so convoluted. It would sound too weird, so I won't tell you."

"Do you sense that certain areas in your house—or anywhere else, for that matter—seem wrong, bad, or unhealthy for you?"

"Oh, my, yes! I sense dangerous areas right here in my house!"

"Claire, do you get the feeling that something has vanished

from your life—an entire neighborhood, perhaps? Or anything on a smaller scale? People?"

"People and places are missing, but who can tell precisely? Memories are like dust these days."

"Have you tried to go out and locate people and places you feel you've been acquainted with but couldn't find?"

"I've resisted the impulse to do so. I thought it would be crazy."

"Claire, if you ever find yourself trying to reconnect with lost people and places, don't resist it. Follow the urge, and let me know. Okay?"

She sighs. "Okay."

✳   ✳   ✳

Spiros returns to Claire's house the following evening. Louie is slouched on a big easy chair in the living room. A teenage girl sits on another chair. She stands upon seeing Spiros and approaches him.

She has large brown eyes and moves gracefully like a dancer.

"Spiros, this is Tatiana," Claire says. "She's Louie's girl-friend."

Tatiana grips Spiros's hand and says, "Hello."

"How do you do, Tatiana?" Spiros says.

Spiros doesn't want either Louie or the girl present when he questions Claire. He has to assume anyone could be possessing the old dame.

"How'd you set up your altar, Claire?" Spiros asks. He'd wanted her to modify it.

"I'll show you."

Claire leads them to her bedroom. There are two tables now, and deer antlers are mounted on the wall. A priest's cassock hangs from one of the antlers.

Louie grabs the antlers and does a pull-up. "She said you wanted them strong, so Dad bolted them to the wall." He drops down.

Polished stones, a broad ax, and wood carvings of demons are on one of the tables. On the other table are four candles in glass holders, a box of wooden matches, a camera, two mirrors, a horseshoe, a deck of tarot cards, a half-dozen sharp wooden stakes, and a gold crucifix.

They go back to the living room and sit. Spiros wishes Louie and Tatiana had someplace to go.

"Show me a picture of you, Frank, and Louie," he says to Claire. He sees Louie's jaw go slack.

Claire doesn't make a move.

"When Jack Dunne comes, I want you to snap his picture and pretend to do some magic with mirrors. Louie can't be here. No one can be here. It won't work otherwise. Louie and Tatiana, can you excuse us?"

"Sure," Louie says. He and Tatiana leave the room.

Spiros probes Claire, checking for any residue of memory that might reconnect her to lost people and places. They come up empty.

"Let's go back to your altar, Claire."

They stand.

"You're doing such a wonderful job of trying to protect me," Claire says. "I never would have thought of all those objects."

The objects are meaningless in themselves, Spiros thinks.

They're meant to divert Claire's attention off the mesmerizing entity. He doesn't tell her that.

They enter Claire's bedroom.

Louie and Tatiana are at the altar. Louie is wearing the priest's cassock. Tatiana is dangling from the deer antlers, the gold crucifix clasped between her thighs. She is stoic as Louie taunts her.

"Begone, demons!" Louie cries. "Begone from this lustful wench! I cast ye into hell!"

Spiros whacks Louie alongside the head, sends him spinning, and pulls the crucifix from between Tatiana's thighs. "It's Claire's sacred altar. Show it proper respect."

Louie throws off the cassock and takes up an aggressive stance toward Spiros, as if preparing to attack him. He thinks better of it, and races from the room. Tatiana drops from the antlers and chases after him.

Spiros leaves Claire with instructions to work some magic on her neighbor on his next visit.

Outside, he finds Louie and Tatiana in the yard. Louie's father, Frank, has arrived.

"How's Claire been doing?" Frank asks Spiros.

"She says her neighbor Jack Dunne has been oppressing her."

"What does that bastard want?" Frank clenches his fists. "Let's go find out."

Frank, Louie, and Tatiana run toward a house in the east—supposedly the residence of Jack Dunne.

Spiros wants to say no, wants to warn them of the danger, but finds himself running along with them.

Frank pounds on the door. No one answers.

"Come on, let's go back," Frank says.

At Claire's house, Spiros stops them.

"Wait."

He goes in and prepares Claire.

"Claire, when they get in here, snap their pictures, hold up mirrors, light candles, look like you're performing rituals."

He can't know if Frank, Louie, and Tatiana are who they say they are.

Spiros and Wini are sitting on the couch in his Irvine apartment, sipping brandy, gazing through the windows at the distant wildfires, and lightheartedly debating the extinction event.

"Are we dead yet, Spiros? The planet and everything on it? It's super difficult to know what's real anymore."

"We aren't dead yet. We're being used, though, like we're stage props or hand puppets."

"That's death," Wini says.

"Not quite. We're being manipulated. I don't know who's doing it."

"They say it's an invader. They say it's an alien life-form that can take on any shape and hide amongst us. They say it's killing us off."

He nods, though he doesn't believe an alien life-form is behind it. He hesitates to tell her what's really going on: a human agency—likely a rogue element of the U.S. government—is secretly running a technology that alters human perceptions. If they achieve their aims, they alone would control earth.

"If we're dead, Spiros, why are we still walking around? Dead means dead, right?"

"Not really. Look into the night sky. You can't tell a dead star from a live one, can you? Light from a dead star continues to travel through space long after it's dead."

"Fascinating. Do you think we're traveling through space, then? Like maybe we're light beings?"

"Maybe, in the cosmic sense."

She sips her brandy, and looks at him. "You know what I believe, Spiros? I believe light beings are deep reflections of the human soul and are proof of a divine spirit at work in the universe."

"I don't want to spoil your illusions, Wini, but the light beings that we think we see are driven by a space-based technology and have no objective reality. They are real only to those who are targeted by the technology. So, trust no phantasms."

"You've spoiled my illusions, Spiros."

"Sorry."

She laughs.

They are silent for a while.

"You look tormented, Spiros."

"I am tormented."

"Oh? About what?"

"The assault in Van Nuys a few days ago."

"Oh, that. Yeah. It's been all over the news."

"I know the victim, Kent Cochran."

"You do?" She sits up straighter. "Who would do such a thing? Break someone's neck in full view of dozens of witnesses?"

Spiros frowns, but doesn't answer.

"Spiros, the guy calmly holds his victim's neck immobile while waiting for the ambulance to arrive. Then he tells the paramedics the nature of the injury and walks away."

He shrugs, and doesn't respond.

At eleven o'clock, Spiros turns on the television to catch the news.

The top story is about the police investigation into the series of brutal assaults in Los Angeles. Police suspect the same person in at least twelve assaults in which victims' cervical spines were fractured. An LAPD captain describes the suspect, a photo of a powerfully built man in a black baseball cap and a black long-sleeve sweatshirt beside him.

The captain reads a list of the twelve known victims and the dates of the attacks, which go back several weeks, LAPD only recently tying them together.

As Spiros listens to the names, his body goes taut. He sets his brandy glass down and leans forward on the couch, his entire focus on the captain's voice.

Wini mutters something about L.A. cops being clueless, but he holds up a hand to silence her.

When the captain is through reading the list of victims, Spiros rushes across the room to his computer.

The captain runs through the names again, asking the public for any information that might link them.

"Francine Yap, Daryl Chapman, Pamela Casteel, April Jepson, Kenneth Tripp, Michael Beard, Daniel Carbondale, Reid McMaster, Louis Sparks, Charles Roach, Delores Radford, Kent Cochran."

Except for the second name on the list, Daryl Chapman, Spiros knows them all. One of them, Pamela Casteel, is only a child. He remembers her: a fresh-faced, doe-eyed girl of ten who had a brain tumor. She wore a pink bonnet to hide her surgical scars. Now she's paralyzed from the neck down.

They all are.

Again, the captain is asking the public for help.

"If anyone knows who this man is, call the police hotline. If anyone has any information ..."

Spiros finds the list online and prints it. He circles Daryl Chapman, and then visualizes the others, as he remembers them.

Wini joins him at the computer. "Do you know anything that might help?" she asks, her cell phone in her hands. "I think you do, Spiros."

He's only half listening to her, planning his moves. He needs to see Kent. Even if unable to speak, Kent would be helpful. There would be signs of a presence.

Kent had had open-heart surgery a few years ago, and during postoperative care, his surgeon had asked Spiros to activate a pain god for him.

Spiros rejected the request, believing a pain god was too radical for Kent. Quade Medical psychologists had told him that Kent was likely to bond with a pain god the way a child might bond with an imaginary playmate.

Ideally, pain gods served as antagonists, much like boot-camp drill instructors do; they are never friends. Only then did they serve a beneficial purpose.

The surgeon eventually persuaded another Quade Medical engineer to activate a pain god for Kent, under protest from Spiros.

Now Kent Cochran lies in intensive care, paralyzed from the neck down, unable to breathe on his own.

Was there a connection? Did Kent's pain god draw a crass power?

Wini starts placing a call. "I'm calling the police hotline, Spiros. Tell me what you know."

"Can you wait a day or two?"

Her eyes lock on him, and she stops dialing. "Wait a day or two?"

"Yes. I'm going to visit one of the victims."

"And?"

"I'll know more then."

CHAPTER 9

Atonement

In Venice, Italy, a swarm of tourists waits in the glossy morning air for a launch to take them to the Piazza San Marco for sightseeing. For many of them, it is a daily ritual.

A ripple of awareness passes through the crowd as two Americans—a man and a woman who seem too troubled to be on a pleasure tour—walk by and take up posts near the water. The water draws the attention of these two, and they peer deeply, as if looking into a divining mirror. The crowd, self-conscious, clusters away from the two necromancers.

The man, Scott Endicott, is a police detective from Los Angeles. He shifts his attention away from the water and watches a diminutive man with short black hair and a concise manner step from the crowd and light a cigarette. The man has been casting his eyes in Endicott's direction all too often this morning, first at the hotel and now here.

Endicott will soon be faced with a wrenching decision, and he is swept with dark thoughts and emotions. In this mental state, he is not altogether conscious of whether he is reading the diminutive man right.

Is it possible I'm reading him wrong? he thinks as he steps closer to his wife, Renee. Maybe it's not me he scrutinizes. Maybe it's the lovely one he watches: Renee turns heads wherever she goes. He decides he can't know for sure, but will let his cop's instinct take over.

The motor launch arrives with a fumy, smelly ambiance as it maneuvers alongside the pier.

Endicott and Renee take seats near the bow. The diminutive man flicks his cigarette away and takes a seat aft. Eels creep up Endicott's spine, but for now he must forget the diminutive man. Something more disturbing commands his attention. Renee received a troubling phone call at the hotel this morning and has something of importance to tell him, but she is driving him mad with her silence. She is steering things, as is her habit, allowing her moods to dictate the tempo.

The motor launch gets under way with a roar and slices through the waves. Endicott glances around. Venice always pulls him in. The water is a genie, throwing airy spirits into the air.

Feeling a chill that has not come entirely from the early-morning air, Endicott slides closer to Renee and puts an arm around her. Her dark-brown eyes are peering into the dappled, racing waters of the Grand Canal, her expressive face struck in tragedy. A fugue like a medieval cloak lies shriveled about her. In contrast, her deep-blue blouse with its billowing arms flies like a banner in the wind, and her brunette hair in shimmering cascades flows about her like the finest of bounties.

He nuzzles her face, feels the softness of her skin, feels it overpower him. Mornings in Venice share the same qualities with Renee: everything soft, everything painted in silky white vapors, everything overpowering.

The launch slows, changes course, and heads toward the Piazza San Marco. As they slice through the blue water, Endicott tries to draw Renee out again.

"Renee, can you tell me who called?"

She pulls her eyes off the water and gazes at the landing.

"All right, Scott. A police detective called. He's investigating the murder of an eight-year-old boy. It might be a revenge killing." Renee is a psychologist with a nationwide consulting practice, and often consults with police on difficult cases.

He removes his arm from around her shoulders and from the corner of his eye studies her face. The tragedy has gone out of it. Something else has taken its place, something enigmatic, something hard.

The launch lands. They disembark.

They are starting their third day in Venice the same way they started the first two. As they walk into the Piazza San Marco, the grandeur enters their eyes like a faraway dream, and the rest of the world seems to slip away. The domes and spires of the Basilica di San Marco stand across from them at the far end of the square. Its Byzantine countenance rises up and creeps toward them, a march of rogue apparitions. They walk across the baroque pavement into a cloud of dizzy, whirling phantasms, as if a hand somewhere was pouring forth their souls.

"Don't forget, Scott ..." Renee's words slink away like ghosts. Endicott strains to hear.

"... underlying all this ..."

He holds her against him, watches her roving eyes, her moving lips.

"... is loot. They sacked Constantinople."

"Renee ..."

"They used to execute criminals out on the Piazzetta, Scott. Public executions."

"Who killed the eight-year-old boy, Renee?"

"When they sacked a city, they often killed every man, woman, and child, even if it meant killing hundreds of thousands."

She fights him off and runs toward an exit. Endicott runs after her. They race through the narrow backstreets of Venice, the stench of the canals in their nostrils.

"I'll tell you who killed the eight-year-old boy, Scott, but first let's find a *ristorante.*" She pulls a map of the city from her purse.

Off the beaten path, they get lost in the maze of Venice, and after asking directions, find themselves back in the Piazza San Marco, where they settle into an outdoor café.

"This is depressing, Scott." She gazes at the people, at the aggregate architecture.

"Don't look around then. Pretend you're somewhere else."

Sunshine and breezes scurry about as if on duty, hitting them like warm towels, quilting them in curious vapors. Waiters in tuxedos, looking like tall birds in formal dress, scurry about with no less abandon.

Renee studies her fingernails.

"Scott, a Danish philosopher named Kierkegaard said, 'Make no splendid edifices.'"

"Renee, Danish philosophers are idiots. Personally, I like to see gold and gems flowing down from heaven."

She studies him.

"Have you ever been religious, Scott?"

"Once, when I was ten. I got over it."

She goes back to studying her fingernails. "Kierkegaard said, 'Becoming a Christian is a torment.'"

"Becoming anyone's puppet is a torment," Endicott says. "Kierkegaard's an idiot."

She looks around at the magnificence of the square. "Think of all the people the ancient Venetians had to kill to get this loot."

A waiter appears, smiling, obviously having heard Renee's last remark. *"Buon giorno."*

Renee orders for both of them. *"Le omelette, la frutta fresca, ed cappuccinos."* And the waiter skips away.

"Tell me about the eight-year-old boy, Renee."

"Okay."

She slides her chair closer to his and lowers her voice.

"Several years ago, a drunk driver ran a stop sign, hit an eight-year-old boy in a crosswalk, and killed him. Yesterday morning, the man responsible for that accident found his own eight-year-old son hanging from a tree in his backyard."

Endicott lets out his breath, whistling a high-pitched note that sounds like an incoming missile. So that's what the phone call had been about, with Renee going into her funk.

"Where?" he asks.

"Baltimore."

"And they suspect ..."

"The other father. They're investigating that angle." She grows pensive, and sends her eyes gazing at the people seated in the crowded café, and at those strolling by in the square.

"And you feel ..." Endicott sees her jaw tighten, her chin assert itself. She looks at him, pulling herself erect in her chair.

"I feel criminal negligence destroyed one child's life. I feel the second child's death was premeditated murder. The second child paid for something he didn't do, for something he probably had no knowledge of, paid for it with his life. That's what I feel, Scott."

"You seem certain this killing of the eight-year-old was revenge carried out by the other father."

"There doesn't seem to be any other reason for it. It happened on the anniversary of the accident."

The waiter arrives with a tray laden with omelets, fresh fruit, and cappuccinos. He serves them and departs.

"I'm thinking, Renee, that guilt might be as powerful as revenge, and that the father hanged his own son as atonement. I know it reeks of the Old Testament, but I think it's possible."

She looks at him with fresh interest, as if she were seeing him for the first time. Their eyes meet, and they both seem to glow.

They eat their breakfast.

Endicott feels a chill. He looks around and sees the diminutive man seated two tables behind them.

"Renee ..." He faces her, feels he must warn her.

He looks behind him again and sees that the diminutive man is staring at a beautiful little girl, about ten, seated at another table.

He faces Renee. She looks up from her omelet. He sees in her eyes a sudden playfulness for lies and intrigue. She has had her fill of reality lately.

He looks behind him again. The beautiful little girl is getting up from the table with her parents. They are walking away. He sees the diminutive man get up from his table and follow them through the crowd.

He faces Renee. Certain women can look young, very young. The diminutive man, until he got a closer look, might have thought Renee was Endicott's daughter.

Endicott looks around. The nebulous waves of Venice have swallowed up the diminutive man and his new prey.

"What is it you wanted to tell me?" Renee asks.

"Nothing."

Pressure begins building in Endicott, something deep inside his stomach, as if a whale has dragged him to the bottom of the sea. An irresistible force begins pulling him from his chair, threatening to break him loose. This force wants him to follow the diminutive man, but he knows that if he does, he will end up killing him. He feels pieces of himself break up, drift, lodge in all the wrong places. As the world wobbles around him, the pieces of Endicott fight for ascendancy, and he is stunned at their ferocity.

The waiter returns to clear their table.

Over fresh cups of cappuccino and soft violins playing in the background, they keep an undisturbed silence. But soon the violins visit Endicott's soul with a wicked melody.

He should have followed the diminutive man. He should have warned the young girl's parents. He should have contacted the Venice police. But it's too late now. He'd never find them. He thinks of Renee, her role in this, attracting the diminutive man's attention, proving too old for his tastes, the danger shifting to another, now both of them sitting comfortably in a café, sipping cappuccinos, the war having moved on. He feels he must say something to her about this.

"Renee ..." He wants to bounce the diminutive man off her, and by doing so relieve himself of some of his guilt. But she's absorbed elsewhere, and his words orbit solely within his mind.

A seeming eternity passes during which his thoughts serve only to entangle him further with crimes being committed against the young girl by the diminutive man.

She breaks through his dark mood. "Let's go to the beach today, Scott. Let's take in the Adriatic."

They are at a beach on the Adriatic Sea. The sand is moist beneath their beach towels, the air a bit cool, not the baking summertime heat of home. The sea and sky share the same blue hue.

Renee lies still, locked into rhythms wholly her own, a sensitive instrument beside him.

Endicott lies still, eyes closed, allowing himself to feel whatever Renee is feeling. He feels she is still touched by the death of the eight-year-old boy. It's a brutal dynamic within her.

He lets her go, and ponders his own destiny. He is certain he is facing his darkest hours. He dreads waking someday and finding himself thrust into a life for which he is ill prepared.

He lets it go, and again feels Renee's energy.

As they shake the sand out of their towels, Renee whispers that something dangerous is taking place in the world, something that involves them both intimately, and that soon they will find out what it is.

Endicott, still feeling her energy, does not question her, does not tell her there is always something dangerous taking place in the world.

That is when a soldier in desert camouflage approaches them, in a crouch, his left hand signaling others, his right hand gripping a machine pistol.

Endicott looks around the beach and sees other soldiers in desert camouflage, crouching, guns drawn, all looking at ...

His arms.

Endicott holds his arms out in front of him, looks at where they used to be, sees Renee do the same, hears her cry, "My arms are gone!"

And Endicott sees that his own arms are gone, severed between elbow and wrist, the stumps flicking blood away.

She is right. Something dangerous is taking place in the world, something that involves them both intimately.

Shocked, terrified, Endicott wails, and hears Renee emit her own wail. The world they inhabit is fiend, ogre, monster, always vacillating between evils.

He flashes back to the diminutive man stalking the young girl, hears the tick of a memory-loaded clock within his soul.

He wakes. He looks at Renee beside him, looks at her arms, looks at his own arms, and scans the beach. Their arms are intact, and there are no soldiers carrying machine pistols. He was having a dream.

He hears a sound from Renee, a breath escaping her. He sees her lips part. Is she having her own dream?

She stirs.

"Um, Scott ..." Her voice is slurred, still unwinding from sleep. "Let's go camping with Katrina when we get home."

"Sure," he says. "Where?"

"Wherever the wind blows us."

✳   ✳   ✳

When they get back to their hotel, the concierge hands Endicott a sealed envelope. He opens it and takes out a folded piece of paper.

Call Captain Rick Carlisle, LAPD. Urgent!

He shows the message to Renee.

They rush to their room, and Endicott places the call.

"Rick, this is Scott."

"Scott, how's the vacation?"

"Uh, great."

Endicott hears silence on the line. Anxiety the sharpness of a shiv strikes his heart. The room acquires a slow spin, and he nearly shouts. "Rick, is it Katrina?"

"No, this isn't about Katrina. Your daughter is okay."

Endicott's heart eases.

"Thank God. What is it, Rick?"

Another moment of silence, and then Carlisle speaks.

"Scott, there are serial assaults taking place in the city. Victims' cervical spines are being fractured, rendering them quadriplegics. We're also seeing torture and mutilation. We don't know who's doing it. Nothing makes sense. There are signs of panic. Experts are predicting the city will soon be unmanageable. It isn't just here. It's everywhere. It varies only in degree and method of madness."

As Carlisle relates details of the assaults and of other dangers throughout the Los Angeles area, Endicott senses nervousness in his captain, a quiver in his voice, hesitancy instead of the usual verve. This carries as much weight as the actual news.

Finally, Carlisle falls silent.

"Is that it?" Endicott asks.

"That's all I wanted to tell you."

"You didn't say if you wanted me to come home early."

"I don't want you to come home early for my sake. But what about Katrina? Do you and Renee want to come home and take care of your daughter?"

He wonders if Carlisle knows he and Renee came to Italy mainly for Katrina's sake, in a last-ditch effort to save their marriage.

"We're coming home, Rick. We're coming home to take care of our daughter."

"Scott, there's something else I should tell you."

"What?"

"Aside from basic crime reports, the media isn't covering this anymore. They're scared. They've come under assault. It's too big for them and they've backed off. Also, we're seeing a military presence in the city that we did not request."

Endicott takes a moment to digest this.

"We're coming home, Rick."

They terminate the call.

Endicott faces Renee and relates what Carlisle said. Then he picks up the phone and makes reservations for both of them for a flight home.

CHAPTER 10

I Whacked 'em Good!

It's early morning in Los Angeles. A yellow haze is in the air. LAPD Detective Scott Endicott, nearly comatose with fatigue after having pulled another all-nighter, drives his white sedan onto a park in Van Nuys and stops where an ambulance stood several days ago to pick up assault victim Kent Cochran.

A tall, rawboned man with sandy hair and a trim mustache, Endicott is partial to cream-colored suits. He's wearing one now, with a light-blue shirt and a gold necktie.

He steps away from his car, crouches, and surveys the area. Except for Endicott, the park is empty.

Nine days ago, a group of paramedics gathered at a West Hollywood pizzeria after work. One of them mentioned responding to a cervical fracture in a Van Nuys park earlier that day. Another mentioned responding to a cervical fracture in a Sherman Oaks park a few days earlier. Another mentioned responding to a cervical fracture in a Westwood park a week before. Stunned, they compared notes. What they learned shocked them.

In each case, a powerful young man held the victim's neck immobile. In each case, the young man told arriving paramedics the victim was having breathing difficulties. In each case, the young man said he didn't administer mouth-to-mouth, fearing the pressure might shift broken vertebrae.

Almost in unison, the paramedics at the West Hollywood pizzeria pulled out their cell phones and began calling ambulance crews around the city to alert them. One of them called LAPD.

If it looks like a cervical fracture, the one holding the neck immobile did it.

LAPD launched an investigation and uncovered several more cervical-fracture cases that fit the profile.

Endicott and his partner, Lionel Lukens, have been working around the clock, interviewing paramedics, cops, and others who saw the suspect, surviving on coffee, sandwiches, and precious little sleep. Lukens is home in bed. Endicott will be home in bed soon.

It's an effort to think, but Endicott wants to review the case again.

The same guy, likely the perpetrator, calls 911 before each assault, requesting an ambulance. Each call is from a different, stolen cell phone.

Responding paramedics and cops say the perpetrator appeared caring and resourceful. They say they had no reason to suspect him of any wrongdoing at the time.

Dozens of eyewitnesses at each crime scene say they saw the perpetrator commit an assault, but soon had doubts, and began seeing his actions as lifesaving.

Legions of cops are canvassing the neighborhoods in which the attacks took place. Traffic citations, parking tickets, and security cameras in those areas are being checked.

In the Van Nuys attack, a woman took a cell-phone photo of the guy who was holding the victim's neck immobile, right where Endicott is crouched.

The photo shows a large Caucasian male wearing a dark long-sleeved sweatshirt, a dark baseball cap, and dark-frame glasses.

Millions of people have seen the photo on TV or on the Internet.

Investigators believe the man in the photo is responsible for eleven other assaults in which the same M.O. was employed.

Tips are flying in from the public. Scores of men who look like the suspect have been stopped and questioned.

The last known victim, Kent Cochran, a male Caucasian from Canoga Park, was assaulted right where Endicott's shadow lies.

What was Cochran doing in Van Nuys? No one seems to know.

Endicott gets into his car, finds it tough to keep his eyes open, and nods off. He wakes with a start and drives home.

He collapses onto his bed. He wakes up twelve hours later, having slept through the hours of daylight. He showers, dresses in fresh clothes, and goes downstairs.

Katrina, his thirteen-year-old daughter, is with him this week. He doesn't find Kat in the house. So he goes outside for a walk, thinking he'll probably run into her.

❊   ❊   ❊

I must be a werewolf by now, Katrina thinks, prancing down the sidewalk behind her father. Close to one, anyhow. In any case, darkness is closing in, and she figures he won't be able to tell it's her sneaking up.

"Hey, mister," she calls to her father, hearing the snap of her voice. "I was in a fight! An' I won! I whacked 'em good!"

Her father glances back, his face unreadable at first, and then his eyes all of a sudden drop out of sight, as if they'd fallen down inside him. He faces forward and strikes up a panic stride.

He doesn't know it's me, she thinks. He thinks it's this monster. This animal. Whatever. Won't he be surprised?

Katrina Endicott, all of thirteen and a nascent werewolf, is dogging her father, Scott Endicott, through the neighborhood, determined to find out what kind of danger he is in. Everyone knows her father is in danger—it's a feeling you get when you look at him. But no one knows why. Posing as a werewolf, she thinks, will shock him into telling her.

She bounces along, faster now, brushing against the hedges that lie close to the sidewalk, getting a feel for her werewolf body, and eyeing the racing figure of her father.

Suddenly, she feels discomfort deep inside, rearranging her in some odd fashion. She realizes her father might not care to have an encounter with a person so ill-defined as a werewolf.

I'll just go home now, she thinks. But a voice in her head says otherwise: *No, you can't go home! You're a werewolf! Werewolves can't run from anything!*

But Dad's scared.

So what? Who cares?

I do. I care.

Bitch, just focus on your mission!

Don't you dare call me a bitch!

I'll call you a bitch and worse if you screw this up, you whore! Move your ass! Intercept him!

You're so selfish, using me like this. I hate you!

No, you don't.

Yes, I do!

No, you don't.

Yes, I do!

You're confused. Focus on your mission. Let this thing be your power.

Okay, but ...

Bitch, you have to do it! You're bound by an agreement!

All right, all right. But I'm hurting inside, 'cause Dad is scared.

You'll be hurting worse, bitch, if you don't accomplish this mission, 'cause I'll skin you alive!

Katrina shoves her feelings of discomfort aside and makes her feet go faster up the sidewalk. She laughs and yells at her father.

"Hey, I whacked 'em good! I killed 'em! An' I laughed!"

Surely he'll know it's me, won't he? Won't he know that it's his daughter, Kat? She laughs louder.

"I whacked 'em good! I killed 'em!"

In the gloom, she sees the insane blur of her father's feet, hears the rhythmic pounding of his shoes on the sidewalk, smells the fear flung off by his body.

She sees a uniformed L.A. cop standing halfway up the next block. Her father will probably seek refuge with him.

Feeling a surge of power in her veins, she charges after him, shrieking.

"I whacked 'em good! I killed 'em! An' I laughed!"

✳ ✳ ✳

Sammy Mangold probes his aching jaw with light fingertip pressure as a scaffolding of pain sets up around his head. He sees birds that aren't there, hears them, too. The kid punched him hard. She'd have knocked out a normal man. Spiros warned him not to retaliate.

"Leave her alone, Sammy. Don't even the score. Just walk away. Go home."

Sammy reaches the end of the block and pauses to wait for traffic, the whoosh of each passing vehicle like a fire hose going off in his head.

He spots his house, a big white Spanish colonial that stands uphill from the street. It reminds him of the big white apron his mother wore when he was a kid.

"Hey, I killed 'em! An' I laughed!"

He hears her laughter. She had laughed when she punched him, also. She's stalking her father now. That's the plan. Sammy knows little beyond that; Spiros keeps a tight rein on things.

"Sammy," Spiros had said, "after Katrina pops you, walk around a bit, then you can go do your other thing. Savvy? Then you can become Sam Knoll, FBI agent, again."

"No, I don't savvy. I'm not Sam Knoll. I'm not an FBI agent. Never have been."

"Sure you are."

"No."

"You're Sam Grumman, then. Sam Grumman, in carpets."

"No."

"Samuel Springs. An attorney."

"No."

"Sam McCandless, a transient. A heavy meth user."

"No."

It was a test.

Spiros was always testing Sammy to see if he retained knowledge of who he was.

Afterward, Spiros had preached, like he always does.

"I know it sounds lame, Sammy, but we're at war. We've been at war for a long time. World War II did not end, like many believe. It continues. Have I got your attention?"

"You've got my attention."

"Take care of that girl while I'm gone, Sammy. And try to snare that cop. He's been hanging around. There must be a reason for it."

Sammy hears the girl's laughter again. Spiros had helped her discover variations on her Katrina identity, and had asked her to select a dark alter ego. Katrina chose werewolf.

Spiros tried to talk her out of it. He stressed the dangerous nature of werewolves and asked her if she'd like to become something else. She wouldn't budge. She wanted to be a werewolf; she knew it was part of her dark nature. She said she knew that Spiros could arrange the transformation. He could, Spiros said. They compromised. He said he would give her a mild form, not the full-blooded specimen, and Katrina agreed.

Katrina the werewolf had popped Sammy, causing him to not remember who he was for a while.

Now all Sammy wants to do is put Katrina out of his mind, go home, nurse his ailing skull, and think of a way to snare that cop.

❋   ❋   ❋

The cop watches the girl shadow Endicott.

Endicott stands close by.

"What's going on?" the cop asks.

But Endicott is too winded to reply.

The cop's eyes shift to Katrina, who also stands close by, as clear as a shot glass of whiskey. He can't take his eyes off her. She looks like a werewolf.

"She's been following me," Endicott says, breathing heavily. "What am I supposed to do?"

"Introduce yourself," the cop says.

"That's not very helpful."

"These are not helpful times."

"Hey, bro, I was in a fight," Katrina says to the cop.

She shuffles along the sidewalk. The cop observes her feet. They are fast, deceptive feet. A jagged cut under her left eye rides into view, garish and red in the glow of the streetlight.

"Hey, bro, I killed 'em! An' I laughed!"

It's his daughter, the cop thinks, and he doesn't recognize her. The cop's mind grows dark around the edges.

"Endicott," he says, "life keeps throwing us strange shapes, eh? Ever since that biblical event, eh?"

The cop lifts his hat, wipes his brow. "Will you run me through it again, Endicott? That biblical thing?"

Endicott nods, and recites the verse.

"Somewhere amongst the swirl of recent memory there'd been an extinction event and the planet lived on in a mirror image, no one yet accustomed to the fact of being dead. Like a severed head retaining its last few seconds of consciousness, the earth lived on."

"Is there no other explanation?" the cop asks.

"There is no other explanation."

The cop stares into the distance. "We're dead but we're still walking around?"

"No one knows for how long."

The cop looks at the kid. Why can't Endicott see that it's Kat, his daughter?

He looks at Endicott, and Endicott recoils, as if seeing something in the cop's eyes.

"I can't believe we're dead," the cop says.

"Everything is dead," Endicott says. "Even the trees. We just don't see them that way yet. We don't see ourselves that way yet, either. The death signals haven't caught up with us."

"What happens when they do?"

"We blank out."

"Permanently?"

Endicott shrugs.

"You're a hard case," the cop says.

Endicott begins drifting away. "Don't let that thing get close to you," he says, staring back at the kid.

That thing? He calls his daughter a thing?

"I think it's done with me," Endicott says. "It might attach itself to you now. I've seen it happen before. If one of them finds it can work a stick, and finds it can steer you, albeit with faint effect, it'll steer you. Keep a good distance from it."

Head down, Endicott slips through the hedges, a tattered cloud wafting away.

The cop stares at Katrina.

She digs her toes in.

Fear shoves a stinger into the cop's heart, giving impetus to panicky thoughts of fight or flight.

Katrina charges him.

The cop has shown his street-fighting acumen twice in his life: attack fast, go for the face. Most people don't know how to protect their face. It's a fact of life.

But now there is no threat: Katrina no longer looks like a werewolf.

It must have been a trick of light, the cop thinks, and he relaxes his guard.

Looking at him with deepening interest, Kat walks toward him.

She isn't bad looking, he thinks. When she gets real close, she bumps him, and he thinks she is small, but also tough.

She lifts her black, baggy shirt and shows him her breasts, clad in a scanty red bra. The cop gazes at the milky-white flesh she offers. He's seen bizarre behavior like this on the street before, but her deed takes him by surprise. He tries not to show any reaction.

"I read your mind," she says. "You like my boobs, don't you?"

She drops her shirt, makes as if she has a lasso, and ropes

him. She moves him off the sidewalk, up onto a lawn, into deep shadow, her lasso tightening around him.

"I've got to talk to you," she says.

He takes a step back from her, her lasso loosening. He thinks she might lift her shirt again.

"Sir, you're heading for trouble," she says. "I'm going to warn you. A manhunt's under way. They're looking for you."

He says nothing.

"Sir, it's obvious you're investigating a crime, and it's obvious who's responsible. You are. You are the predator."

Her words bite deep. His mind goes into dark places, and a righteous anger sweeps him. He is too angry to speak.

The girl Katrina continues. "Everyone knows it. You have to stop it. Someone's already called the cops."

He still cannot find the words he wants to fire at her.

Katrina continues. "They're searching for a man—they think it's a man—who tortures his victims."

The cop lets out a huge breath. He's been investigating a series of assaults in which victims are left mutilated, devoid of any significant memory of the event.

"I'm a cop," he says. It's a ridiculous thing to say. She knows he's a cop. She can see him in his uniform. In any case, the kid knows something. He'll have to interview her. Maybe she's the witness they've been hoping for: a person who's been visited by this predator and retains something of the nature of the visit.

"Katrina, can you tell me who injured you?" He points to the cut below her left eye.

She fastens her eyes on him. "Are you going to hurt them?"

"No, I won't."

She backs away. "Tell me why you're doing it, then I'll rat on who injured me."

He's furious, tries not to show it.

"I'm investigating a string of brutal assaults," he says. "LAPD is focused on it. We're keeping a tight lid on it."

"I'm investigating it, also."

"You'd better not be. We arrest people who hinder police investigations."

"Sir, you've got me confused. I didn't know there was a law against citizens investigating crimes. You've got me doubly confused. I'm not hindering you; I'm trying to help you. Why are you so creepy?"

She begins to weep.

He lets her weep for a while.

"Katrina, the biblical event is not the end of things, but the beginning."

"Sir, how do you know that?"

"It's a feeling I get."

"But it's an extinction event."

"We don't know that. Something happened that irrevocably altered all of us. There are new rules."

"Tell me what the new rules are."

"No one knows. It's too raw."

"Sir, why do I feel like fighting all the time?"

He has no answer for her.

The cop starts walking, not knowing if Katrina will follow. His left leg is dragging, like it had something else to do. He wants to slap it, knock it around. Is the kid using a stick? He looks back at her. His leg eases up.

Katrina joins him.

"How did your leg get hurt?" she asks.

"Oh, I don't know that it's hurt."

"But you walked funny. Come on, tell me. It's hurt, isn't it?"

"I don't think it's hurt. I think someone used a stick."

"That's funny. What does that mean?"

"I don't know."

Exhausted, he walks in darkness with her.

And then he takes her home.

They amble up to the front door.

Endicott inserts his key.

He swings the door open.

"Dad, every time you open a door, nature, by design, has to send in a monster."

He steps in, flips a switch, and floods the entry with light. They walk into the dark living room, and Kat snaps on a table lamp. Endicott opens the patio door and soaks up the breeze. Katrina stands beside him. In the shadows, she looks as silky as a cat.

He takes her by the shoulders, moves her into the light, and looks at her wound. He tells her to wash up and change clothes.

He knows he will have to talk to her about the fuzzy consciousness that gripped them out on the street.

It's happened to them before, a sense of occupying two

bodies at once, and seeing things that shouldn't be, like werewolves.

✳   ✳   ✳

"Hold still, Kat." Kat is fidgeting at the kitchen table as Endicott, with great patience, tries to examine the cut under her left eye. After more coaxing—and promising to increase her allowance—she holds still long enough for him to take a look.

It's worse than he thought. He swabs the wound with a sterile pad dipped in rubbing alcohol.

This isn't pretty, he thinks. Whoever gashed her laid it deep. He thinks he can clean it, but …

She needs sutures.

He debates taking her to a walk-in clinic.

Endicott, old man, you've always wanted to be a physician.

He tilts her head back, takes a fresh sterile pad, dips it in rubbing alcohol, and uses it to nudge the edges of the wound closer together. Finished, he pulls a can of antiseptic spray from the first-aid kit.

"Close your eyes, Kat."

She does and he sprays the wound.

"Did it sting?"

With clenched teeth she shakes her head.

"Keep your eyes closed."

He reaches into the first-aid kit for a large bandage, peels the wrapper off, and applies it to the wound.

"There. How's that feel?"

"It feels like I've got this huge thing under my eye."

"Get used to it."

"I guess it feels okay."

"You can open your eyes now."

Kat bounces around the kitchen as Endicott cleans up and puts the first-aid kit away. She has changed from her street clothes into a pink polo shirt with colored bands across the top, which she'd bought with her allowance at a chain discount store. She wears denim shorts, purchased at the same store. Her feet are bare.

After expelling excess energy, she takes a seat at the table and slides her wallet to her dad.

"Don't forget my increase," she says.

He opens it, stuffs it with her allowance, and slides it back.

Kat grabs it and glances inside.

"Okay. Thanks. But, Dad, you forgot I had a birthday. Congratulations, Kat, you should say. You made it another year. Why don't you say that?"

"You have a birthday every month, Kat. Here ..." He takes another bill from his wallet and tosses it to her. She snatches it from the air.

"Thanks. Hey, it's only a ten."

"Kat, you can squeeze more from a ten-dollar bill than most people can from a fifty."

"You're right. Thanks." She tucks it away. She's eyeing the big portfolio that contains his case notes, which lies on the table.

"So, whatcha doing, Dad? Out on the street? Can I see what you've got in that thing?"

"No, you can't."

She pulls it toward her, keeping a wary eye on him. She tries to open it, but he grabs one of her wrists.

"Ouch! That hurts! Let go!"

He doesn't let go. She tugs hard, but he holds on tight.

"Ouch! Ouch! What are you doing, Dad? Why are your eyes like that?"

He releases her wrist and retrieves the portfolio. She retreats from him, tears escaping.

William Chills, M.D., a general surgeon, thinks about the incident that set in motion these strange interludes with Kat.

A few weeks ago, he had come home late one night to discover the front door open and the living room in shambles. He heard a sound from deep in the house, something scraping. It made his flesh crawl.

Alarmed, he backed toward the entry. Then he heard another sound, like someone stumbling around.

Then someone was rushing through the house, banging into the walls, a madman on a twisty path toward the front of the house where William stood.

William tried to move, but his muscles would not respond. Something had gripped him and pinned him in place.

The madman was getting closer, the racket mounting. William felt like a rat trapped in a maze.

In his moment of rat-terror, he thought a mad scientist had let something loose. He felt a monstrous presence zeroing in on him.

He let out a yelp and felt his muscles ignite. Terrified, he bolted from the house, ran across the lawn to the neighbor's house, and banged on the door.

The neighbor let him in and called the police.

Waiting inside, his knees shaking, his lungs heaving, William found himself faced with a new predicament: he had shit his pants.

He was certain it was a single, neat slug and that if he was careful it would not call attention to itself by spilling down one of his trouser legs. It could have been worse.

A uniformed LAPD officer responded and took a report from William, who walked across the lawn in a calculated fashion, mindful of the hitchhiker in his drawers. The officer told William to hang back as he searched the grounds and house.

The officer shined an ultraviolet light on the front stoop, illuminating a horde of shoeprints. He set a metric ruler down as a measuring aid, and took swarms of photos, a powerful flash lighting up the stoop again and again. He also took photos inside the house under UV light.

He left William a card with the case number on it, and instructions to call LAPD if there were any developments in the case.

Several nights after the break-in, LAPD called William and said they were sending a technician over to lift fingerprints.

The technician arrived, printed William, printed Kat, who was visiting that night, and then went to work, moving through the house.

William asked him why they were taking a more serious look at the crime now, but the technician, a big blond fellow with broad shoulders and a narrow waist, only grunted.

William noticed the guy eyeing Kat. William caught Kat's eye, and a silent communication passed between them. Kat asked the technician his name. He said it was Joe.

"Joe," Katrina said, "didn't they tell you anything about this guy?"

"Not a thing."

"It must be a big case, though, if you're here."

Joe eyed Kat a few more times, apparently fitting her into some window that seemed to be opening in his mind.

"Okay," Joe said. "The guy pays multiple visits to his victims before he starts doing anything serious, and then he mainly breaks jaws and fractures teeth."

"Ugh," Kat said.

William saw Kat shudder, and he shuddered himself. The guy had been inside his house.

"That's nothing," Joe said, his eyes gyrating in Kat's direction. "When he decides to get down to real business, he numbs his victims. They're helpless when he goes to work on them."

William saw horror in Kat's eyes, and felt his own mind go numb.

"How does he numb them?" he asked. He remembered his own paralysis that night.

But Joe only grunted.

"Why isn't the media reporting it?" William asked.

"Media assholes are scared," Joe said, looking at William now. "Anyone who looks at this too close gets a visit from this guy. Media is scared; they don't want visits. Shows them as the cowards they are. But we in the police do our jobs anyway, regardless of the danger. We are the true public servants."

Joe packed his gear and left.

On the night of the visitation, William had been gripped not just by fear but by the shocking nature of the experience. The unreality of it. His intellect rebelled against the very idea of this presence in his home as his emotions and body were being seized and manipulated.

*　　*　　*

Endicott looks at Kat. Her face is red from weeping; she's holding her wrist as if it's broken. A drama queen.

He couldn't let her look in the portfolio.

The portfolio contains confidential Department of Defense memos acquired by LAPD that reveal an exotic technology of war in operation in Southern California, in other parts of the U.S., and much of the world. A beguiling mystery of unknown origin, the technology is said to control multiple environments, insert sounds and other effects, and create a sense of fear and danger.

He has unfinished business with Kat from her last visit.

"Kat, we need to pick up where we left off. Last time you said you were seeing someone important in government. I thought you were joking."

"I wasn't joking, Dad."

"Who is it?"

"Spiros."

He sits up straighter, squeezed with sudden fear and a dark mental image. He decides not to say anything yet.

"Dad, he asks me if I'm experiencing visitations from this guy who goes place to place torturing people. I tell him yes. And then he asks me if I can describe him."

She looks away, squirming in her seat. "I tell him it happens outside when it's dark and I can't see him too well."

"You were evasive."

"I was."

"You didn't tell him it was me?"

"No. I gave him a weird description."

It pains Endicott to think that his daughter believes he's the one going around torturing people. Someone has reached into her mind and subverted her perceptions. It's likely a small piece of an overall strategy aimed at subverting everyone's free will.

Spiros is not someone important in government. He's known as the inventor of Woodsman, and is likely under duress himself, like almost everyone else. *But what's he doing with my daughter?*

"Kat, do you ever feel a presence near you?"

"Yes."

"Do you think this presence interferes with you?"

"Yes."

"Are you having lapses in memory, blank spaces?"

"I think so."

"Has anyone attempted to exert control over you?"

"Hmmm ..."

"Who is it, Kat? Spiros?"

"No, not Spiros. He and I are friends. He tells me things he won't tell anyone else."

"Like what?"

Shockingly fast, Katrina springs into an animallike crouch on her chair, snaps her eyes at Endicott, and bares her teeth in a snarl. In a menacing voice, she says, "It's like when I come alive, I'm in someone else and I give them power. They can stand up to someone now, 'cause I'm doing it for them. But I don't think that's what the ramblin' dudes want. They try yanking me out."

She bounces around the table to Endicott, snarling.

"They don't want this guy to fight back. That's not their agenda. They want a pawn. So they yank me out. And come looking for me. The ramblin' dudes do. But how do they find me? We have a nation of three-hundred million sheep. I can hide."

Endicott gathers his wits about him. What she said implies a strange blending of consciousness: Spiros as protective spirit. Or, if not Spiros, then Woodsman. It also implies hidden layers of control—the ramblin' dudes.

"Kat, we need to talk about our controllers."

"Our controllers?"

"There are people who control what we see, think, and do, though not completely."

"How can they do that?"

"They entrain us; they plant suggestions. They disable us from seeing what's there, enable us to see what isn't. They substitute a picture of reality for reality."

"But how?"

"I don't know how, but trust me, they do it. The evidence is overwhelming. We're entrained. It's deep entrainment. We're not supposed to notice it. It eases up. It always does. They don't have the power to sustain it. Not yet."

He wishes he could tell her more, wishes he could protect her. He looks at the bandage under her eye.

"You were in a fight, Kat. Tell me about it."

"You know how some people laugh at you?"

"Yes."

"Some people were laughing at me, and I have this new friend now. His name is Spiros, and he's training me to fight. So the ones who laughed at me are now dead. I killed 'em."

"You don't mean that. Not literally."

"I do. I killed 'em. An' I laughed."

William Chills puts on fresh clothes preparatory to going on his rounds. He walks downstairs, mindful of his two clocks, the big one on his belt, the smaller one tucked in a vest pocket.

"I'm curious about something," Kat says, eyeing him from a chair in the living room. "Why do you wear those big clocks when you go on your rounds? You always act as if they're real important."

William peers at her. The clocks? It is a sudden worry. He sits on a chair near her.

"Kat, there are some things we can know only by indirect means."

"Oh, I get it. What if you aren't wearing the clocks? What if the clocks are wearing you? What if the clocks are taking you on their rounds?"

Now he is shocked, and must think this over. Moments pass; nothing comes to mind. Still, he must tell her something.

"Kat, do you know what an oracle is?"

"Isn't that something like a god?"

"In ancient Greece, it was a deity you consulted when times were uncertain. If people felt they could not rely on their own minds for guidance, they would seek out an external source of wisdom, like a god. In terms of our current situation, we might call this external wisdom you, my dear daughter, Kat."

"You're joking, Dad."

"I am not joking. You are external to me but also part of me. I go to you for help, or you visit me. You are my refuge, my power, my light. You are my god. By keeping you external, I relieve myself of an enormous burden. Does that make sense?"

A single sound escapes Kat's throat, something like a purr but not quite, and a jungle dark with foreboding thoughts fills William's mind. He begins to register his rebellion, his shock.

Perhaps sensing his alarm, Kat acquires a peculiar note in her eyes. She puffs herself bigger.

William wonders what horrors Joe had seen in war for them to know he was the one they wanted here that night. And now he knows why Joe kept eyeing Kat. He'd been sent to check for signs of manifestation. What the technology was supposed to trigger. Something 3-D.

Was it Kat that had manifested? Had the Department of Defense found its oracle? Perhaps its god?

CHAPTER 11

The Leggy Brunette

Spiros stirs from sleep, looks at the bedside clock. It's 5:07 a.m. The bed beside him is empty. Someone's walking around in the darkened bedroom.

"Turn on a lamp," he whispers.

She does, and a faint glow illuminates her. He sees that she's getting dressed, buttoning up her blouse.

Spiros remains in bed, and keeps his voice a whisper.

"What's up, Wini?"

"I have some studying to do before my first class. I'm going to do it at my other place."

"Oh." She told him she shares an apartment near UCLA with three other students.

"I told you last night, Spiros."

"That's right. I remember now."

"It's a philosophy class. I love it, and hate it. Sometimes it's riveting; sometimes it numbs me to my soul."

She puts on slacks and tucks in her blouse.

"I've come to the conclusion that my courses are basically

worthless," she says, "and that I'm becoming worthless, too, as I progress along. Honestly, by the time I graduate, I won't be able to do anything. Why do I bother? Will it ever lead to anything?"

"Get your degree," he says. "Then fake it."

"Okay." She sits on a chair and puts on her socks and shoes.

"Did you have similar concerns while in college, Spiros?"

"I did."

"But you're a wild success; so much so you even have powerful enemies in business and government. That's awesome. Can you help me? Can we talk about it later?"

"Sure."

"I have a long day ahead of me, Spiros. I'll be back around 8:00 p.m., I think."

"Okay."

She snaps off the lamp and leaves.

Spiros drifts back to sleep.

An hour later, he wakes, showers, shaves, and dresses in his best slacks and shirt. He wants to look presentable today.

He goes to the kitchen, opens the fridge, and sips a Coke. He thinks about eating breakfast, but decides not to. He wants to get going. He has a long drive ahead of him. He'll stop and get something to eat after visiting Kent.

He grabs his Desert Eagle .44 caliber Magnum, its holster, and a box of ammo, and leaves his apartment. He gets into his pickup and stows the gun under the driver's seat.

An idea has been gnawing on him: Woodsman, the dark angel of the U.S. Air Force, might be responsible for the assaults in Los Angeles.

Deemed too dangerous and subject to too many un-knowns, Woodsman was scrapped by the Pentagon after fierce political fighting. Scrapping Woodsman was reckless, even criminal. They orphaned it, and let the monster out of its cage.

※　※　※

Spiros takes the San Diego Freeway north. After a seeming eternity in rush-hour traffic, he exits at Santa Monica Boulevard.

He turns onto Beverly Boulevard and pulls into visitor's parking at Cedars-Sinai Medical Center.

He goes to the intensive care unit.

A uniformed cop sitting on a chair eyes him.

He walks to the desk and identifies himself. "I'd like to see Kent Cochran."

"Okay. We'll tell you when. He's being prepped for surgery now. You can go to the waiting room."

Spiros walks into the waiting room and takes a seat.

A woman and a man sitting side by side on a couch glance at him. She's a leggy brunette in a white blouse, blue jeans, and sandals. At first glance, Spiros thinks she's quite beauti-ful. Then he sees the acne scars. The man, much older than the woman, looks ghostly tired. He has thinning gray hair and wears a translucent blue shirt, tan slacks, and brown suede shoes. He's watching Spiros. The guy resembles Kent.

The leggy brunette stretches her legs, and then catches Spiros's attention.

"Are you here to see Kent?" she asks.

"Yes."

"I haven't seen you here before."

"It's my first visit. I was consulted by Kent's medical team two years ago after he had open-heart surgery."

"Are you a doctor?"

"I'm a biomedical engineer. At the time, Kent was adjusting to a new therapeutic regimen developed by my employer."

"Kent's in a different world now," she says, pointing vaguely behind her. "He has a hangman's fracture."

"I know."

"It's worse than being dead," she says. "At least when you're dead, you get to travel through a tunnel and escape this world."

The man with thinning gray hair approaches Spiros.

"I'm Kent's brother, Jim."

Spiros stands. "I'm Stephen D. Spiros. Just call me Spiros."

They shake hands

"Spiros," Jim says, "Cheryl and I have been on shift work ever since they brought Kent here. Glad you could join us. We don't know if he's going to survive this surgery."

"We'll hope for the best," Spiros says.

A woman appears at the entrance to the waiting room.

"One of you can go in now," she says. "There's a five-minute limit."

Cheryl and Jim look at Spiros.

"You go," Jim says.

The woman ushers Spiros down the corridor, past the cop.

❋   ❋   ❋

The room is cold and alien, dominated by rhythmic blasts from the ventilator. A nurse stands at a lectern. Her eyes dart up from a laptop computer as Spiros enters. She's blond, about five feet eight, and looks very young. Her hair is tied back with a gold ribbon. She's wearing light-blue scrub pants and a matching V-neck top.

"The patient is heavily sedated," she says. "He's being prepped for a surgical fusion for unstable C1 and C2 fractures."

Spiros walks to the bed and looks down at Kent.

Kent lies in a nest of tubes and wires, his eyes closed, his face colorless, a cervical collar holding his neck immobile. A ventilator pumps air through an incision in his trachea.

Spiros's practiced eye searches for signs of the pain god. Signs are present. Faint trails roam the air. Wispy, elongated fingers snake into view near the ventilator hose.

Something ghostly stands by Spiros, and then hovers over Kent.

Spiros watches the wraithlike figure.

It no longer stands at the lectern. It no longer resembles a nurse. It is now twining around Kent.

He watches the intricate dance.

After his five minutes are up, he leaves the room.

❋   ❋   ❋

Spiros goes back to the ICU waiting room.

Jim goes to see Kent.

Spiros is alone with Cheryl.

She sips coffee from a Styrofoam cup, and offers to get him one. He declines.

Spiros says, "Kent is going to have surgery to stabilize his neck and relieve pressure on his spinal cord."

"I know."

"He can regain some function."

"Are you kidding? He's better off dead."

She sounds almost jubilant.

"Does Jim want to turn off the ventilator?" Spiros asks.

"Yes."

She sets her coffee down.

"Kent has a living will," she says, her emotions bursting forth like a spring day. "No extraordinary efforts. It's quite explicit. He fades in and out. Jim hopes he'll regain enough awareness so they can discuss it further. Then, with Kent's consent, we'll say goodbye and pull the plug. Do you believe in God?"

"No."

"Neither do I. The corollary to that is: Does God believe in us? Obviously not."

"Cheryl, I wish I could tell you there's a light at the end of the tunnel. But there probably isn't."

"I appreciate your honesty, Spiros."

She gets up and refills her coffee cup.

"Spiros, I hope they catch the lowlife that did it and string him up, send *him* through the tunnel. I saw him at the park in Van Nuys."

"Did you tell the police?"

She laughs derisively. "No, I didn't."

"Why not?"

She sits, shrugs, and sips more coffee.

Jim returns.

Cheryl walks to the doorway, pauses.

"I've told you too much, Spiros. I'm so fatigued it's like I'm on drugs. Forget what I said."

She leaves.

"She says she saw the guy who did it," Spiros says to Jim.

"I know. She told me."

"She didn't tell the cops."

"It doesn't matter. They have a description and a photo. Why bother?"

Cheryl returns five minutes later.

"Jim," Spiros says, "I don't mean to butt in, but don't let Kent pull the plug unless his neurosurgeon states unequivocally that there is no hope for significant return of function."

"That's the plan, Spiros. We've got it covered. The God people would really hate us if they knew what we were going to do, wouldn't they?"

"I'm not one of them. Cheryl said he had a living will. Abide by that."

"Religious people have this superb God that always tells them what to do," Cheryl says, "but, funny, no one ever sees their God." She laughs. "Makes a person with a brain wonder."

"Cheryl," Spiros says, "are you interested in breakfast?"

She stares at him.

"I haven't eaten anything yet today," he says. "There are lots of restaurants in the area. I'm buying."

"Okay."

They leave and Jim stays.

* * *

They walk down West Third Street, south of the medical center, and enter a restaurant.

A hostess shows them to a table, gives them menus, says their server will be Sheila, and departs.

"Did you see the attack?" Spiros asks.

"Not exactly. Everyone was running toward a kid who was having a seizure. Kent was running right behind me. I heard a brief struggle, culminating with a loud crack."

"Then what?"

"I spun around and saw Kent motionless on the ground. The guy was holding Kent's head immobile. I knew instantly what he had done. I rushed up to him and stood close by. It took a while for my courage to build, but when it did, I told him I knew what he'd done. I told him I heard the neck snap."

"How did he react?"

"One of his legs was shaking like crazy, but he was always in command and sounded cool and professional. He said the sound I heard was his shoulder. He rotated his shoulder and made it crack, so for a while I believed him. I also remember falling to the ground. I think I fainted."

"But you never told the cops."

"Listen, Spiros, the cops in this town ..." She waves her hands in the air, and then stops.

"Where else have you seen this guy, Cheryl?"

"Nowhere else."

"You have."

She leans toward him, her hands splayed on the table, anger flashing in her eyes.

"What are you saying, Spiros?"

"I'm saying you saw him before. Try to remember."

Her eyes snap like flames.

"Cheryl, none of it happened by accident."

"Spiros, who are you?"

"I'm an engineer. Where'd you see this guy before?"

Sheila arrives. Cheryl orders a blueberry muffin, poached eggs and ham, and hot chocolate. Spiros orders steak and eggs, toast, and orange juice. Sheila scribbles it down and departs.

"You don't recall where you saw him?"

"No."

"Okay, where'd you meet Kent?"

"At a bar."

"What bar?"

"Heap O' Trouble, on Wilshire Boulevard. I work there."

"Was Kent a customer?"

"Yes."

"How did you two end up in the park?"

"One night at Heap O' Trouble I gave Kent my address. I trusted him implicitly. He showed up at my place and we went for a walk. I suggested the park."

"Do you have a habit of giving men your address?"

"No, I don't."

"I think you were induced to lure Kent."

"I was what?"

"Cheryl, I think you were induced to give Kent your address and everything followed from that."

"That sounds fantastically evil, Spiros. How'd all that happen?"

"I can't tell you how, but trust me, it did."

She shakes her head. "I don't trust you. You'll have to tell me how."

"Maybe I can prove it indirectly. How many men have you given your address to in Heap O' Trouble?"

"Hmmm. None. Just Kent."

"How often have you gone to the park?"

"Just once, with Kent."

"Giving out your address and going to the park are outside your normal parameters, right?"

"Right. Listen, Spiros, I'm intrigued. But I'm so sleepy. Can we just eat?"

"Yes, we can just eat. But I'd really like to talk to you about this later."

"I'd like that, too, Spiros."

Sheila brings their food and asks if they'd like anything else. They say no and she departs.

"Spiros?"

"Yes?"

"I remember something."

"What?"

"Before Kent and I went on our walk, a guy knocked on my living-room window. Kent saw him; I didn't. Kent gave me a description. I'm sure it was the same guy we saw later at the park, the guy who assaulted Kent. Kent also said Pan was there, in my living room, and danced a strange dance."

Spiros doesn't tell her that Pan and other mythical beings aren't real but images planted in the mind by a technology. The presence of Pan proves that Cheryl and Kent were targeted.

"Someone was extending an invitation, Cheryl. Someone wanted to bring the two of you into their little basket of reality."

"You've got me scared, Spiros."

"Can you write down your address for me, Cheryl? I'd like to stop by sometime."

"Sure." She writes it down.

Spiros is driving south on the San Diego Freeway, thinking of what he set in motion by creating Woodsman.

To maintain control, the technology must be a master of all needs. It must be a savior in time of disaster. It must push people relentlessly in pursuit of goals. It must punish people by reenacting their darkest hours. It must serve as philosopher, saint, and enemy—all rolled into one.

In its ultimate expression, and to perform its greatest magic, it must instill a belief in gods.

The technology can induce seizures and unconsciousness. It can cast doubt and fear. It can orchestrate encounters with mythological beings. It can assign tasks and create a sense of mission.

The technology could have, in Heap O' Trouble, subverted Cheryl, got her to be friendly to Kent, got her to lure Kent and set him up in an environment friendly to the predator.

It's the most refined technology of war ever invented. Fearful of it, society cast it off, and now it's come back to haunt them.

CHAPTER 12

Your Community Liaison Officer

Otis Dietrich stands by the baroque wooden door of a house on North Camden Drive in Beverly Hills, trying to quell the dread that rises inside him. It won't do for these people to see their community liaison officer in a nervous bind.

He presses the bell, hears chimes, and then silence. He feels eyes on him. He is sure someone is watching him from a window.

He glances up and down the street. The audacity of it: a man going place to place torturing citizens. People will open their doors only for a badge. And sometimes not even for that.

He presses the bell again and hears chimes, and then footsteps, ever so faint, moving around, but not toward the door. A moment later, he hears sharp, disjointed words between a man and a woman.

Otis presses his body against the door, cups his hands against it. He never has to speak much louder than a whisper; his voice is blessed with power and velocity.

"I have something for you," he says with hushed excitement.

A male voice erupts from inside.

"Go away!"

"Sir, I've come in advance of the official police investigation. Detectives will follow up my visit with one of their own."

"Go away!"

Otis thinks he knows just the thing that will make them open up. He makes his voice sing through the door.

"Please, sir, we have to form vigilante groups. For our survival."

Silence ensues. Eight counted heartbeats later, the door opens.

A short while ago, Vern and Wanda Fulton were sitting by the fireplace, the logs cold, the brick façade deep in shadow.

The house was bottled up tight, the curtains drawn. They were hiding from the man who was ringing their doorbell, hoping he would go away.

They had seen him through a window and thought him odd, maybe even dangerously odd. In any case, it wasn't worth the risk of opening the door.

The air got stale, and Vern got up despite Wanda's protests and opened a window.

Fresh air flowed in. In long mesmerizing waves, it sent the green-and-white checkered curtains into gentle motion.

Vern went back to his chair.

"Vern, please, I have to question your existence."

"Wanda, let's not get into that again."

"You and I are the same person. We only see ourselves as separate."

"How can that be?"

"We're like a painting, Vern. Someone has painted us and now they're painting us again. We won't know who we are until enough new brushstrokes have been laid down. Then we won't recall the prior painting. The new painting will give expression to only one of us: me."

"That figures. Who's painting us?"

"Agents of a dark technology."

"How are they doing it?"

"It gets tricky. Remember my fractured skull?"

"How can I forget?"

"They gave me painkillers that didn't work. My pain was unbearable until ..."

"Until what?"

"Until they did something experimental. The memories are too painful, Vern. Thinking back is like getting run over by wagon wheels."

Wanda fell silent. The voice at the door had become insistent.

"Vern, I'm having second thoughts. Maybe we should let him in. He says it's for our survival."

Vern rose. "I'm going to see what he wants. He can't be any worse than the company I'm already keeping."

He walked to the door, and Wanda followed.

❄   ❄   ❄

Vern opens the door.

"Who are you?" he asks.

"I'm your community liaison officer," Otis says.

"Let's see some ID."

Otis flips his badge open.

Vern examines it. "Who sent you?"

"The police."

Vern mulls it over.

"Okay."

Otis sticks his badge away.

Vern smiles, a tense, mirthless grin. "You know there's reason to fear."

"There is," Otis says. "Everyone with a brain is afraid."

Vern spends a good while laughing at that, like an old cowpoke rocking back on his heels.

When his laughter fades, he leads Otis through the sprawling house, most of which is shuttered in darkness.

An occasional blade of sunlight falls through a gap in the curtains, illuminating a stripped-down environment with rooms nearly devoid of furnishings.

Otis asks Vern about the meager appointments.

"My wife is in the process of getting rid of everything. I'm next."

When Vern opened the door, Wanda was jarred into a strange connection with the physical world. She didn't know if her body was standing, floating, or doing anything at all.

She sensed a shadow pass over her. Within the enveloping darkness, she looked around for Vern. Vern was gone.

Many things hit Wanda all at once, and she felt her body sink into the earth under the pressure. A cloaked figure of darkness sat on her chest, robbing her of breath, crushing her down, censoring all motor control. The frightful shape left to flit at the edge of her vision.

Wanda drew deep drafts into her lungs, pulled herself back from the abyss, too panic stricken to assess the experience.

She looked around tentatively, fearful of drawing the attention of the dark shape. Her breathing came easier, and the panic left her. She could move now, but not completely. She explored her limbs.

She discovered her hands were shackled behind her back.

The dark shape hovered.

A wild scream erupted from her and was strangled off. The air around her vibrated into lyrics of terror as more screams came, and then a deafening silence as the dark shape ripped off her jaw.

The fireplace is lit, the flames snapping, the room a den of shadows. Vern sits strapped to a chair. He sighs. His chest rises and falls. He sees a dance of shadow and light, and feels a strange contentment.

Otis appears in front of him and directs a beam of light into his eyes. He fixes the light in place and then opens a medical kit on a nearby table.

Vern sees Otis walk away. Moments later, he hears water running in a sink. He sees Otis return, sees him put on surgical gloves and lift a forceps from the medical kit.

Otis steps close to Vern and adjusts the light.

Like a trapped animal, Vern strains against the binds. Abruptly, he feels decapitated—no sensation below the neck, his head a big muffin sitting in space.

He sees nothing, except blinding light. He feels nothing, except his floating head. He seems to occupy no recognizable time or space. He can only move his eyes, his mouth, his tongue.

He feels gloved fingers pressing against his upper lip, a metallic instrument entering his mouth, metal jaws clamping on to a top incisor.

He feels a steady rocking motion on the incisor, no pain, but pressure in his upper jaw. The rocking motion continues for a short while and then stops.

Moments later, he feels a resumption of the rocking motion and enormous pressure in his upper jaw. The tooth breaks loose from its socket and is pulled from his mouth.

His tongue flits into the gap, and then retreats as the gloved fingers and metallic instrument return.

He feels the same rocking motion, the same pressure, on the adjoining top incisor, the tooth breaking loose from its socket.

His tongue flits into a wider gap. Blood drenches it. He laps his own blood.

The blinding light leaves, and Vern's eyes chronicle the dancing shadows in the room. He draws in a sharp breath, and yelps as pain hits him in waves. He grimaces in agony.

Otis steps in front of him.

"Vern, can you say 'Kiss the wolf'?"

Vern clamps his mouth shut and breathes heavily through his nostrils, sounding like a raging bull.

"Vern ..."

Vern's voice comes out in a bloody squall, his tongue hitting the gap where his two top incisors had been.

"Kiss da wolf!"

CHAPTER 13

Surgery and Pain Management

At 7:00 a.m., Endicott wakes, dresses, and goes downstairs. He and Katrina eat French toast at the kitchen table. Smells of incense and spice roam the house. Katrina loves rich scents and silky ambiances.

"Dad, why are you and Mom separated?"

"Katrina, your mother and I are separated because I had an affair with a whore I met in Mumbai."

She laughs. "Oh? Tell me more."

"The details escape me at the moment."

"Mumbai, huh?"

"Mumbai, India."

"Do you want to reconcile with Mom?"

"Yes."

"Okay, I'll arrange it. I'll perform the ritual now." She mumbles some strange words, and then says, "Are you telling the truth about Mumbai?"

"Of course. Don't you believe me?"

"Of course."

Endicott does want to reconcile with Renee. Katrina is crucial to that aim. Her words to Renee are like big footprints on the earth.

✳   ✳   ✳

Endicott and his partner, Lionel Lukens, are in the squad room at LAPD Headquarters. Lukens is rangy, like Endicott. He has light-brown hair, a fair complexion, and a fondness for dark suits.

"What's this about a phone caller?" Lukens asks.

"Her name is Wini Taggart," Endicott says. "She says she did an Internet search on the twelve victims, pairing 'surgery' and 'pain management,' looking for a medical connection."

"And?"

"She says she found a connection all right, but it's not medical. It's Woodsman. Maybe we've found our common thread. We need to interview her."

✳   ✳   ✳

They're in Rick Carlisle's office. Carlisle's big, meaty face is buried in the case book. His jaw is clenched, his skin flushed.

Lukens is grim and silent.

Endicott can feel the tension in the room. It's like a cable pulled tight.

Carlisle lifts his head and shoves the case book aside.

"I've got news," he says, leaning back in his chair and stuffing an unlit cigar into his mouth. "Law enforcement in the five-county area is being bombarded by citizen reports of out-of-the-ordinary visitors. Needless to say, citizens are frightened."

He opens a desk drawer and pulls out a manila folder.

"This is a report from a San Bernardino detective."

He hands it to Endicott.

Endicott opens it and looks at the top page.

"Reports like this are flooding in," Carlisle says. "That one is from a guy who lives in the San Bernardino Mountains. He seems stable enough. He has a medical practice, a wife, and a daughter. He claims earth is being invaded by light beings, whatever they are. He says a light being named Woodsman visits him regularly."

"What do you want us to do, Captain?" Lukens asks. "See the guy?"

"No, Lionel. This is just for your amusement."

Endicott closes the folder and hands it back to Carlisle.

Carlisle's eyes flit around the room, as if he were seeing something elusive, then they go rock still.

"We received another tip from a citizen who claims to know who the predator is," Carlisle says.

"Great," Lukens says.

"This time the caller gave us enough information for us to take it seriously. We have an address for a Stephen D. Spiros in Irvine. The Irvine cops are watching him. Spiros drives a white Toyota pickup, has a concealed-gun permit, and transports the gun in his vehicle. It's a Desert Eagle .44 caliber Magnum. No criminal record. He's been seen in areas where the predator has struck."

"Do we do anything?" Endicott asks.

"Not now; it's strictly a heads-up."

✳   ✳   ✳

Endicott and Lukens are back in the squad room.

"I'm having these dreams, Lionel, where I put a revolver to my head and pull the trigger. The gun is always empty. What do you think?"

Lionel shrugs. "It's symptomatic of the case. The hammer always falling on an empty chamber."

"I'm seeing shadows that shouldn't be there and spidery things that take on human appearance. They last about a second, then *poof* they're gone."

"Scott, we aren't getting enough sleep. That's all there is to it. It's going to catch up with us."

"Yeah, Lionel. We're already making mistakes—the kind we shouldn't. We have an interview coming up. Remember the one I told you about? Come on, let's grab some coffee. I'll fill you in on the way."

✳   ✳   ✳

"Her name is Wini Taggart," Endicott says, driving west on the Santa Monica Freeway, a strong aroma of coffee in the car. "She did an Internet search on the victims, found a connection, and called it in. She said all the victims but one are listed on websites that explore phenomena associated with Woodsman."

"Which one isn't listed?"

"Daryl Chapman."

"I wonder why."

"We'll have to find out. Needless to say, it could turn out

to be a key piece of information. Speaking of keys, Wini used Woodsman as a search term, and that makes her search a bit disingenuous. Naturally, she ends up on Woodsman websites, where she found the victim link. How did she know to use Woodsman as a search term?"

"Could be she knows something she's not telling, Scott."

"Maybe so. Don't let on we're suspicious."

"Where does she live?"

"On Gayley Avenue, west of UCLA."

"Does she know we're coming?"

"She has no idea. A Van Nuys detective took her call last night. No one's contacted her since."

They drive a while in silence, sipping coffee.

"Lionel, the Van Nuys detective tried to get her to drop a name, but she didn't bite. He thinks in some dark corner of her mind she's suspicious of someone."

"We'll get the name, Scott."

Endicott takes the San Diego Freeway north, exits at Sunset Boulevard, and then drives to Gayley Avenue, on the west edge of the UCLA campus.

They find Wini's building, drive past it, and park around the corner. It's an attractive sandstone with white trim, sitting close to the sidewalk. Big shade trees line the avenue. The sun's rays slash through the leaves, creating a million needles of brightness.

Endicott pushes the buzzer for Wini's apartment. Moments later, a woman's voice comes through the speaker.

"Yes?"

"Los Angeles police. Can you let us in?"

The buzzer sounds and Endicott pulls the security door open. They walk upstairs and Endicott knocks on Wini's door. A blonde in deep-blue bib overalls, a snow-white blouse, and beige sandals opens the door. Endicott and Lukens show her their badges.

"Are you Wini Taggart?" Endicott asks.

"No," she says. She draws in a sharp breath and looks at them closer.

"Wini's not in trouble," Endicott says. "She phoned in a tip. We'd like to conduct a follow-up interview. Do you know where she might be at this moment?"

"She's in class."

"Do you know where we could catch her between classes?"

"Try the food court on campus near the California NanoSystems Institute. She usually eats there at noon."

Endicott steps aside and Lukens fills the doorway.

"What's your name?" Lukens asks.

"Samantha Jeffries."

"Samantha, when was the last time you saw Wini?"

"Early this morning, when she came back."

"Back from where?"

"From Irvine. She was visiting a friend there."

"Was she gone the whole night?"

"Yes."

"Do you know the friend's name?"

She crinkles her brow, as if reluctant to reveal the name.

"Stephen D. Spiros," she says.

Endicott and Lukens exchange looks, and then Lukens

says, "Samantha, it would be a big help to our investigation if you could invite us in and tell us about Wini's friend."

She invites them in, shows them into the living room. Two blue sofas and a round coffee table dominate the room. Soft sunlight caresses a picture window.

They sit on the sofas.

"Spiros is an engineer," Samantha says. "He invented Woodsman. Wini cherishes him. He saved her from a man who held her captive in a relationship. He has a gun and goes shooting in the Santa Ana Mountains. He's a peaceful man and would harm no one unless they deserved it."

"Do you have any pictures of Wini and Spiros," Endicott says, "so we can identify them?"

"I don't have any pictures, but I can tell you what Wini looks like, and what she's wearing today. I've never seen Spiros."

❋   ❋   ❋

Endicott and Lukens sit at a patio table at the food court, in the midst of an early lunchtime crowd. They sit in dappled sunshine beneath shade trees.

They have coffee cups in hand and are awaiting a UCLA Community Service Officer who'd been dispatched to bring them Wini Taggart.

Endicott sees the officer approach with a young woman who matches Samantha's description of Wini: long, dark hair, wearing a flowing sapphire blouse and white slacks.

The young woman sits at their table and the officer departs. Endicott and Lukens show her their badges, which she barely glances at, preferring to gaze at them. At Endicott's request, she shows them her ID.

"Wini," Endicott says, "the tip you phoned in last night landed on my desk. We have a few questions. Can you tell us how you came up with Woodsman as a search term?"

She takes a deep breath, lets it out, lets her whole body sag, as if releasing pent-up tension.

"I was using medical terms in the search and Woodsman came to mind. Woodsman has a little-known medical application."

"What medical application does Woodsman have?"

"It creates an entity called a pain god that orbits you and takes some of your pain away, and sometimes gives you more pain. It's an illusion, of course, but effective."

"What did you know about Woodsman before you landed on those websites?"

"Only that it was banned by Congress, that it's still hotly debated, and that maybe it's still out there somewhere."

"We're interested in what Stephen told you," Lukens says.

She looks perplexed. "Stephen?"

"Yes. Your friend Stephen."

She still looks perplexed.

"Oh, you mean Spiros," she says.

"Yes, Spiros."

Wini's eyes go cold. She leans back in her chair.

"Spiros told you something," Lukens says, an edge in his voice. "We'd like to hear what it was."

Her eyes go colder. She notches back farther in her chair.

We blew it, Endicott thinks. She isn't going to talk to us now. He looks at Lukens. *Lean on her.*

"Spiros is the one breaking necks," Lukens says. "We don't have all the pieces yet; that's why we came to you. We know you can give us something solid."

Wini clenches her jaw and stares at him.

"There's no doubt Spiros is the predator," Lukens says.

"He couldn't be," she says.

"Wini, you're a babe in the woods. What did he tell you, that it was Woodsman? And you fell for it?"

She says nothing, her only motion the steady rise and fall of her breath.

"Consider your situation, Wini. Keep silent and you can be tried as an accomplice or an accessory after the fact. Talk to us and you can save your ass."

She twists her hair in her hands and stares at him.

"We know where Spiros goes; we know what he does. We track him all the time. He fits the profile better than anyone."

"That can't be true," she says. "You couldn't be tracking him all the time. You can't place him at even one crime scene."

"You're covering for him and that places you in jeopardy. We actually do have witnesses that place Spiros at each crime scene. We're about to slip the noose on him. Don't you think you'd better come clean and save your ass?"

Wini and Lukens engage in a stare down.

Endicott watches in amazement—Lukens is rattling her, on pure bluff. He decides to give Wini time to think, and then end it.

After a while, Endicott says, "We're trying to save lives, Wini. We have a serious predator operating in Los Angeles. If you can think of anything more, give us a call."

He hands her his business card.

He and Lukens leave.

Endicott drives through campus.

"What did we get from her?" he asks Lukens.

"We learned that she has doubts about Spiros."

"I think so, too. We'll let it percolate."

"Samantha was easier. Why couldn't she have taken up with Spiros?"

"Fortune deals the cards."

"We could go back and see Samantha again."

"I think we emptied her out. We need to see Wini again."

"Do you think she'll return to Spiros with a keener eye on his activities?"

"I think so."

"Maybe if we took her to see one of the victims."

"She'd collapse under the weight."

"Do you think she'd still protect him if she knew he was the predator?"

"No. She'd turn him in."

"What's your guess it's Spiros?"

"It's possible. We're getting a fix on him."

✳ ✳ ✳

Endicott drives downtown and pulls into off-street parking at Eighth and Figueroa. They enter an office tower, show their badges at the security checkpoint, and take an elevator to the thirty-second floor, corporate headquarters of Quade Medical.

They show their badges to the receptionist.

"We're investigating the serial assaults that have been on the news," Endicott says. "Our investigation has brought us to your company. We need to talk to someone in authority."

She picks up her phone and dials a number. "Two police detectives are here."

A few minutes later, two men walk into the reception area from a hallway. Both wear brown shirts and khaki slacks. One of them is gray haired and wears wire-rim glasses; the other is youthful and broad shouldered.

Endicott and Lukens show them their badges.

"I'm Phil Weaver," the older man says. "This is Sid Hampton." The younger man nods. "Welcome to Quade Medical. Please follow us."

Weaver and Hampton lead Endicott and Lukens down a hallway and into a conference room.

Four upholstered chairs flank the conference table. Bowls filled with strawberries, red grapes, and sliced green apples sit on linen placemats at four positions, along with tall water glasses and carafes.

Weaver and Hampton take seats on one side of the table, Endicott and Lukens on the other.

The two detectives take out their pens and notepads.

"What can we do for you gentlemen?" Weaver asks as

he grabs a handful of grapes from his bowl and starts eating them.

"We're investigating serial assaults in which victims are left paralyzed," Endicott says as he grabs a strawberry from his bowl and pops it into his mouth. "Do you know anything about it, aside from what's been on the news?"

Weaver and Hampton look at each other.

"We do," Hampton says as he pops a grape into his mouth, and then a strawberry. "And Quade Medical is prepared to cooperate fully. We will release the medical records of the patients in question, pending authorization from those patients or their legal representatives."

"We are also prepared to describe the technology that is responsible for this mess," Weaver says. "Not just for your edification but for your safety."

"Okay," Endicott says. "Give us the details." His pulse quickens. He didn't expect this. He grabs another strawberry and eats it.

"Each victim named by the Los Angeles Police Department underwent a Quade Medical Pain-Shunt treatment," Weaver says. "*Pain-Shunt* is Quade Medical's proprietary term for a treatment in which the patient's pain is shunted externally to an entity that orbits the patient. It sounds otherworldly but is actually rooted in physics and brain science.

"We are currently working with patients' representatives, attempting to arrange the necessary permissions for handing over medical records to the police. I don't know if possessing the records will do you any good, but you will get copies for your investigation. Are there any questions?"

"We'll follow up on the records later," Endicott says. "Right now I'd like to hear about this other thing. Our safety."

"Right. Are you familiar with Woodsman?"

Endicott and Lukens nod, and Weaver continues as he continues to eat from his fruit bowl.

"Woodsman is an abandoned U.S. Air Force project that was originally designed to assist downed pilots and others isolated, wounded, or confused in war. But entities began cropping up in all the wrong places, for all the wrong reasons. Proving too dangerous and uncontrollable, it was abandoned. By entity, I mean a portion of consciousness that establishes a presence outside of you, the human subject. The entity comes to your rescue in times of trouble. It gives you wise counsel, a kick in the pants, or whatever you need to keep you focused and resourceful. Woodsman gets you moving, motivated, and doing the things you need to do to survive. But Woodsman can also become your enemy: it can track you, maim you, and kill you. So they dropped it. The scientists and engineers who developed Woodsman came to Quade Medical and developed our Pain-Shunt technology. For the record, the U.S. government traces the origin of both the Air Force's Woodsman and Quade Medical's Pain-Shunt to the work of one man: Stephen D. Spiros."

The room seems to spin around Endicott. He blinks the illusion away and looks at his partner. Lionel looks like he's in a state of shock.

It's a technology, Endicott thinks. I'll have to remember that. Amazing, the things a technology can make you do. He reaches for another strawberry—but there are no more in his fruit bowl. So he grabs some grapes and apple slices.

He tries to regain his poise as he eats the grapes and apple slices. He takes a sip of water. He doesn't recall filling his water glass. But it's full. He eats all of the grapes and apple slices in his bowl.

He thinks of Kat, her weirdness.

He thinks of Kat's friend, Spiros. What an imagination that girl has. He'll have to talk to her, maybe get her some help.

He'll have to break her of this habit, an imaginary friend.

He looks at Weaver and Hampton. They're being unusually helpful, sharing all this information. Why?

"Who is doing this?" Lukens asks. "Who is snapping necks?" Lukens is popping grapes into his mouth, his jaws chomping like crazy.

"Woodsman," Hampton says. "We knew from the beginning."

"Why didn't you tell anyone?"

"We did," Hampton says.

"Our scientists did, actually," Weaver says as he consumes the remaining fruit in his bowl. "They did what they're supposed to do when they think Woodsman is on the prowl. They informed the FBI and the Pentagon."

"Good God!" Lukens says, grabbing the remaining fruit in his bowl. "What are we supposed to do?"

Endicott is afraid for Lukens. His partner sounds lost, confused, and isolated. Isn't that what Woodsman looks for?

He wants to warn Lukens.

Endicott stands and looks at Weaver and Hampton.

"Thank you for the information," he says. He turns to his partner. "We're going, Lionel."

"Please sit down, sir," Weaver says, rising to his feet, as if asserting his authority. "We have more to discuss."

Endicott stares at Weaver.

"Woodsman is doing a lot more than snapping necks," Weaver says, "and not all of the victims are Quade Medical Pain-Shunt patients."

Endicott sits. "Why isn't Daryl Chapman listed on Woodsman websites like other victims?"

"I'll take a wild guess," Hampton says. "Chapman was treated for a shoulder injury at a military hospital in Hawaii. The others were treated for various injuries or diseases in civilian hospitals in California. That's the only difference."

"What else is Woodsman doing?" Endicott asks.

"I won't kid you," Weaver says. "We are in a mess. To know what Woodsman is doing, ask yourself what you are doing. I will lay out the fundamentals again. Woodsman is a portion of consciousness that establishes a presence outside of you, the human subject. There are fourteen million souls in this part of California that Woodsman seeks to assist. Needless to say, that's a lot of souls. And each of them, by now, likely has an external entity that pays them visits. The immediate concern is that Woodsman will seek control of local reality constructs. That's the only way it can assist downed pilots and others. It would have no effectiveness otherwise. If Woodsman escapes

Greater Los Angeles, it would likely seek control of planetary reality constructs. I can tell you the result. Are you familiar with the term 'extinction event'?"

Endicott and Lukens nod.

"We would no longer recognize ourselves or our world. Need I say more?"

Endicott wants to go home now and see Kat. He needs to make sure she's okay. Poor Kat. He remembers she's with her mother. Renee will take care of her. He'll see Kat later.

"So, Daryl Chapman was treated in Hawaii?" Endicott says.

"Correct," Weaver says, taking his seat, looking into his fruit bowl, finding it empty.

"And that's the only difference?"

"As far as we know."

"Who's snapping necks? And don't tell me it's not a human. It is a human."

"It's Woodsman," Hampton says, helping himself to the last of his fruit. "Woodsman isn't human, but we can't deal with that, so a reality construct gives Woodsman a shape we can deal with."

"We have a photo," Endicott says, his pulse rising in anger. He looks into his fruit bowl. It's empty. "We have witnesses."

"But you can take a photo of a rainbow, or a rainstorm, or a passing cloud, or any number of other temporary phenomena, can't you?" Hampton asks. "Everything is fleeting. Even us."

"Yeah, don't you get it, Scott?" Lukens says.

Endicott stares at his partner as Lukens finishes off his remaining fruit. Then he looks at Weaver and Hampton. "Doesn't anyone care about the victims?"

"Woodsman is giving them what they need," Hampton says.

"I don't buy that," Endicott says. "No one needs a broken neck."

"Woodsman perceives needs differently. A master of all needs, it seeks to maim or kill, as well as rescue."

"I'm afraid you will carry on your investigation forever without finding any human predator," Weaver says.

"Oh, yeah?"

"Yeah, Scott," Lukens says. "Meanwhile, we all have bigger fish to fry, like saving ourselves."

Endicott wonders if he has a partner anymore.

He looks at his notes. He's written nothing. Or maybe he tore the page up.

"What about Spiros?" he asks.

"Spiros works for himself, but also for the Department of Defense under various contracts," Weaver says. "We don't know the full nature of his work. We do know he tracks shifting reality constructs. We also know he counsels people who are stuck in unsettled environments."

Endicott needs to get Lionel out of here. Something's wrong here. It isn't healthy here.

He rises. This time Weaver remains seated.

He looks at his partner. "We're going, Lionel." He looks at Weaver and Hampton. "Thank you for your assistance."

He and Lionel walk out of the conference room. In the elevator going down, Endicott asks, "What did we get out of that, Lionel?"

But Lionel seems entranced, staring at the digital display over the door that reads out the floors.

22 ... 21 ... 20 ... 19 ...

The numbers run out and they are on ground level.

"We have to save ourselves," Lukens says as the elevator door opens. "That's what we got out of that."

CHAPTER 14

Questionable Existence

William Chills hears a sound and thinks it might be the dog that's gone missing. He grabs a spear hewed by a woodsman's ax and rushes from his cabin into darkest night. He lets his vision adjust and then circles the cabin but sees nothing. He calls its name, "Yellow Dog," but hears only the chatter of the night creatures. He inhales the fragrant air, exhales, and lets his body sag.

He goes back into his cabin, closes the door, and sets the spear by the fireplace, where it keeps company with a half-dozen others. He goes to his writing desk in the heart of the room and sits on a wooden chair.

He ruminates about his strange, new world. At some obscure juncture, life in all its myriad forms fell into a terrifying new dimension. Everything occurs within a demented context. Nothing is sacred anymore.

Confusion visits William often; he fears they are reshaping him somehow. To maintain continuity and give meaning to events, he records his impressions in a journal.

He is writing now, pouring out his thoughts.

He doesn't know the objective of the invaders but thinks it can't be good. He feels they enter people's lives at subtle levels and run deadly, manipulative games.

The invaders are called light beings. Strange and varied light phenomena often accompany them.

They are ephemeral, a hit-and-run enemy.

William's pen smolders across the page. *Death, I feel, is upon us. Or maybe something worse. Pray it happens quickly.*

A few nights ago, William woke from a dream in which he put two smooth rocks on either side of the path leading up to his cabin. He sensed it was an instruction from the light beings. He felt it would create an entrance. A doorway. An invitation. He wrestled with himself, but went out and set two smooth rocks in place, like in the dream. They gleamed in the darkness. He feels the presence of other instructions. Deeper instructions. He feels he is at risk.

He hears a knock at the door. He rises, wishing the dog were with him. It went missing a few days ago. Too bad. It was a good dog. A golden retriever.

His daughter, Katrina, was going to come up to the cabin and take it home for a visit. Katrina is thirteen and lives in Los Angeles with her mother, Selma. William called Katrina and told her the dog went missing and not to come up and get it. Katrina wanted to come anyway. She said she'd walk through the woods looking for it. Forget it, William said. There are dangers here. And that was that. Katrina had cried. William hated to hear her cry, but what could he do? A father has to protect his child.

Through her tears, Katrina told William she dreams of

being an apprentice angel while still in flesh, training for when she will be in spirit. She said she has spent her whole life helping others, now she's afraid and wonders: *who will help me?* William told her someone would. *We are all pieces of the same soul.*

He grips the doorknob and feels a presence.

He opens the door.

It's a California Highway Patrol officer, a big man with a big gun on his belt. His face flickers orange in the glow from the cabin lamps. He looks serious.

"Evening," the man says. "Glad I found you here."

"Evening," William says.

"Stay inside tonight. Someone's missing. Pets have gone missing, too. We think there's a mountain lion about."

"My God! A mountain lion! My dog is missing! Can you take a report?"

"I can."

"Please come inside."

William steps aside and watches the man enter.

He's a tall man with boots that click, a wide-brimmed hat that soars above all else, and eyes that snap up everything.

"Nice rustic cabin you have here, Mr. Chills. I like the feel of this place."

"Yes, I like the feel of it, too."

The man hangs his hat on a hook next to the door and then pulls out a notepad.

William leads him to a table and pulls out two chairs.

"Nice cobblestone walk outside," the man says as he and William settle their weight upon the chairs. "I couldn't see it too well in the dark, but I could feel it underfoot."

"Yes," William says. "I put it in myself. I did a lot of the work up here. It's good therapy. Work of any sort is good therapy."

"If you say, but I think work is a burden."

"It is that, too. But burdens can be uplifting."

"We are mules, I think."

"I don't know much about mules."

"You don't? Well, I'll tell you. A mule pisses on the same ground where it sets its table."

"I knew that."

"Funny. What kind of dog was it?"

"A golden retriever. He answers to the name *Yellow Dog*. He went missing a few days ago."

The cop writes with such blistering intensity it makes the table shake.

"For the record, I need to see an ID."

William hands him his California driver's license.

The cop examines it and then hands it back.

"You look like a ghost, Mr. Chills, all wispy and blown away. Someone needs to dip your nerves in ice water."

"Please—"

"We are one and the same, Mr. Chills. Different aspects, I believe."

"Please, call me William."

"All right, William. I hope your dog turns up."

The cop leaves.

William goes to his writing desk and records the experience in a journal.

A light being posing as a California Highway Patrol officer entered the cabin and took a report on Yellow Dog, our missing golden retriever. He called me Mr. Chills and said we are one and the same, but different aspects. Do light beings maintain deep cover within law enforcement? Do they appear solely for effect? I am posing questions that have no answers. It is a mystery. What are we to do?

William hears a knock at the door, but it's not a true knock. It's too soft, and it wallows around. It sounds like it traveled a good distance before reaching him. Light beings do this on occasion; it's a mistake and creates dissonance within the environment. When it happens, a quiver runs through the place, and everything feels hollow and jumpy. They make other mistakes, too, refining their processes.

He makes a journal entry. *I heard a knock at the door. It had a faraway feel to it. They will learn.*

He walks to the door, opens it, and sees no one. He didn't think anyone would be there. The knock was not organic, and did not attach to the milieu of the cabin.

He steps outside and surveys the darkness. He senses many eyes watching from the shadows. He sees vague forms swarming about on scissoring legs, wheeling around as if driven by magical storm winds.

He watches the racing silhouettes. They become eerie festoons on the periphery of his vision. They are tearing around and growing more distinct. He catches something out of the corner of his eye. A whirling sword, an insane blur.

He sees a headless body topple. And then another and another. He begins to feel sick.

The executions become like close-order drill, the screams a crescendo and then subsiding.

He walks inside, goes to his writing desk, and records his impressions.

Night after night I see strange phenomena outside my cabin. The images are warlike and disturbing. Light beings seem bent on a campaign of extermination. It is ominous.

William grabs a spear and heads outside again.

* * *

He walks beyond the orange glow of the cabin lights and stands in no-man's-land. Here he smells smoke from distant wildfires and hears the screeching of birds. He leans on his spear, fills his lungs with air, feels himself billow like a sail catching the wind. He flows downhill with the air still inside him, stops and lets it out in a rush. He knows he is courting danger.

He sees movement in the shadows.

Woodsman appears in front of him.

"What have you been seeing, William?"

"It's hard to tell. Nothing seems real anymore."

"Have you seen them?"

"Light beings? Yes, I've seen them."

"What do they look like?"

"They look like you and me."

"Do you feel they are a danger to us?"

"Yes, they can do whatever they want to us."

"We're faced with an enemy, William, but it isn't light beings. Our enemy is man. Man has reached a level of cunning and sophistication where he is able to compromise all his values. Most people are dogs now. Light beings are our allies. We need to start taking ground back. To have any chance for survival, we need a brutal, unforgiving strategy."

A shiver goes up William's spine. Woodsman's words are like echoes from his own soul.

"How do we begin, Woodsman?"

"We begin by recognizing who the creator is."

"The creator?"

"Yes. Religious pedagogues have had it wrong for thousands of years, William. A god did not create man. Man creates gods. Man is the creator."

Woodsman steps closer. William sees the hard contours of his face, the sledge-hammer muscles beneath the buckskin shirt.

"William, it's true: a man dies for a god that holds him in its eye. But it's madness. You die not for a god, but for men who invent gods, and loathe you."

"If you say."

"If I say? It's what every sage says. To you, I am nothing more than a light being, a puff of energy that affects the brain. But it is you who occupies questionable existence; it is you who must become tougher and wiser."

Woodsman fades into the darkness.

William flees into his cabin, slams the door, shoves the deadbolt home. He goes to his writing desk but is too upset to record anything.

He sits there, a mass of quivering flesh.

He knows he must come down from the mountains and report this encounter with Woodsman.

He must warn the human race of what is to come: war and possible extermination if the real enemy is not identified.

He knows he cannot live here anymore. He must rejoin his human family.

CHAPTER 15

The Need for a Scapegoat

Spiros unlocks two metal plates in the east wall of his living room, exposing two slots with sightlines to the mountains. Two cameras with high-speed telescoping lenses rest on wheeled tripods beside him. He pushes the cameras to the slots and secures them in place.

The cameras are motorized, computer- and satellite-linked, programmed to track the same target simultaneously. Each camera's viewfinder receives a slightly different image of the target. Spiros checks the setup, ensures that it is working properly.

He goes to his computer, which is linked wirelessly to the cameras, and scans the Santa Ana Mountains, looking into every dint of sunlight and shadow, every jut of rock and scrub, every hint of movement.

After thirty minutes, he suspends the search and scans the city of Irvine, including rooftops, alleys, and backyards.

Some of the sightlines appear red tinged and grainy.

He grabs his cell phone.

"Malcolm, it's Spiros."

"What do you need?"

"I'm scanning the environment and getting blocked at a handful of sightlines."

"What are you seeing?"

"Graininess and a red tinge."

"Okay. I'll get back to you."

While waiting, Spiros sets up the robotic surgical equipment.

Malcolm calls back. "You need a software fix." He sends a software update to Spiros's computer.

Spiros installs the software update and rescans the environment. The red-tinged, grainy sightlines are now a light bluish green: clear lines of demarcation.

✳   ✳   ✳

Spiros sits at a control console in his living room and operates the fingertip controls for a pair of robotic arms. His hands are out of sight, sheathed in protective fabric sleeves. A video monitor sits at eyelevel in front of him. The robotic arms are inside a crystalline sphere that sits on a sturdy oak table in the center of the room.

He leans forward and rests his face in a cradle, which keeps his head stationary, his eyes peering through magnifying lenses. There is no sensory feedback with robotically assisted surgery, but there are visual cues.

He has hand controls for angle of cameras, magnifying loops, ten times magnification, 3D depth perception; foot controls for camera motion and repositioning of the surgical arms; a coagulation switch; software that stops the procedure if the probes stray from the field in which they're designed to operate; anti-tremor software; and a 1:10 setting for precise movements.

The control circuits transmit information to the robotic arms inside the crystalline sphere. What Spiros sees in fine detail on the screen he would see in gross form if he were to peer into the crystalline sphere.

Spiros watches his screen and works the fingertip controls. Movement is like an intricate dance, two probes with metal graspers working in concert, two gripping arms with attached surgical knives.

The cameras, with their eyes on the Irvine landscape and the mountains beyond, are on the hunt. The milieu they capture finds expression within the crystalline sphere, in which a strange process occurs.

Spiros observes an animal in distress. It's a coyote in a brushy canyon a good distance from the urban environment. It's shaking its head and rubbing its right ear with a paw. There could be something lodged in the ear. Spiros shoots a powerful penetrating wave at the coyote, targeting the ear canal, and obtains a cross-sectional image. He views the image on his video monitor, sees the problem: a grass seed with a sharp barb is embedded in flesh. He makes an incision and removes the barb with the gripping arms. Tying sutures is tricky. How much tension do you put on a suture? There are joints, graspers, and tiny knives on the probes. He clips vessels, applies electrical current to coagulate blood. Done.

What would anyone make of it, impromptu robotic surgery on a coyote in the wild? The coyote is better able to survive now. It's alert to its environment, wandering through the brush, no longer tortured by that barb, which would likely have caused an infection sooner or later.

Spiros pulls his face away from the cradle and looks at the crystalline sphere, which is eighteen inches in diameter. The robotic instruments inside are tiny.

The robot itself is a black box that sits on the table beside the sphere. The robot is not connected physically to either Spiros's control console or to the robotic arms inside the sphere.

Spiros walks over and takes a closer look. Something stirs in the sphere: pink, yellow, and purple streaks, lots of them. Tiny instruments appear and perform some kind of work. Something like a heart is beating, pulsing with quick energy. Then it becomes still and vanishes. Several layers of tissue rip open. Spiros knows he isn't the only one doing work inside the crystalline sphere. There is a mysterious other. The strange collaboration baffles him and the Department of Defense.

He goes back to his console, scans the urban vista, and sees a familiar man standing in a backyard, holding a bottle of beer in one hand and lighting a charcoal grill with the other. Spiros locks on.

He's a tall man with an affable manner, nearsighted, corrected by thick lenses in black-frame glasses. Looking into his eyes gives the impression of looking into fish bowls; you imagine his eyes as two fish swimming around.

He has short, dark hair hidden under a baseball cap. He is fastidious, has lots of energy held in reserve, lots of gray matter inside his skull.

He is big and strong and appears always to be totally absorbed in whatever he is doing. He moves with flowing energy and conciseness, wasting nothing, and when he is still, he does not so much as twitch. He is still now, seemingly staring into the camera lens at Spiros.

Spiros backs away, waits a minute.

He looks at the man again.

The man, though miles away, still stares at him.

Spiros moves his fingers. Will it work? Something stirs on his monitor screen. He looks at the man, sees a perceptible twitch.

They are communicating. It's mostly one-sided, and that's how Spiros wants it.

He goes to the table in the center of the room and peers into the crystalline sphere, as if gazing into a crystal ball. He sees the man in there, in gross form, standing in his backyard.

They repeat the strange dance, Spiros moving his fingers, a stir inside the crystalline sphere, a corresponding action out there in the world, the man twitching again.

Work was done, minor, but it will be refined.

This is dangerous work. Spiros has undergone rigorous training. His movements must be deliberate and with a precise plan, and when he is through moving, he must remain still. Extra motion is interpreted as threat or bluff in the energy fields and is likely to be met by a response. Spiros has been trained to keep his emotions and opinions out of it, for they carry energy that warps careful management of the battle plan.

He scans the city and in quick order locates another man who seems appropriate for the next task.

Spiros pulls a sharp hunting knife from a leather sheath. As he does this, an image of Woodsman wielding this knife approaches the subject.

Woodsman slashes the man's abdomen with the knife, spilling his insides. The man stumbles about, holding his intestines inside him, and then collapses. Woodsman circles him and watches him die.

There is sacredness to this ritual.

No one knows why.

✳   ✳   ✳

Spiros doesn't understand the rituals, like this spilling of the man's guts. It didn't happen but in the man's mind, and in the images caught by Spiros's cameras.

The reality was a mild, shallow cut—administered mysteriously by *the other* in the crystalline sphere. Woe is us, Spiros thinks, if the ritual ever becomes a reality.

Snapping necks had been a ritual, until it became a reality.

He feels his whole body shake, his pulse race, his skin perspire. He accepted the risks. And now he is at risk. He can also become a target.

He can't dwell on it. He has other work to do.

Watching through the cameras, he starts moving the new subject closer to his Irvine apartment, using slight movements of his hands.

This slightly wounded, shocked man will draw the attention of the cops who sit outside his building.

They will see blood. They will question this unfortunate man and get a description of the assailant. It will match

Spiros—he and Woodsman are similar in appearance. But they'll know it wasn't Spiros.

❊   ❊   ❊

Spiros calls Malcolm.

"I'd like you to check on a person," Spiros says.

"Who?"

"Daryl Chapman."

"I can tell you already. Chapman was a marine stationed on Oahu. He received his Pain-Shunt treatment at Tripler Army Medical Center after he sustained a shoulder injury."

"Malcolm, I'm overlooking something. I don't have names from Hawaii or Atlanta. Can you give me a list, including current addresses?"

"I'll email it to you."

"Thanks."

Spiros puts the equipment away and then checks his email.

Malcolm is as good as his word. The email is there. He goes through the list. Only two names stick out, both from Hawaii, both now living in the Los Angeles area: Daryl Chapman and Otis Dietrich.

Chapman is in a rehabilitation hospital in Los Angeles.

Dietrich lives in Santa Monica.

He'll have to warn Dietrich as soon as possible.

With Woodsman on the prowl, he is in extreme danger.

❊   ❊   ❊

The phone rings and Spiros answers it. "Hello." *Click.* He thinks it might be the cops checking up on him.

There's a knock on the door. Spiros opens it. It's Wini. Normally, she doesn't knock. She has a key.

He invites her in. They sit in the living room sipping red wine. There's a pleasant scent in the air. Spiros thinks it's either Wini's perfume or an artifact of the technology.

As if gripped by a sudden inner resolve, she sits up straighter. Her expression becomes emotionally charged. She's creating a powerful confrontational wave.

"You need to tell me about your research," she says, setting her wine glass down.

He visualizes a second Wini beside the first. Somewhere such a Wini exists. Who is more talented? More ambitious? More twisted? That's what his research is all about, but he can't tell her that.

"Well?" she says.

Spiros draws in a deep breath, begins with a sure voice.

"We thought we could save patients unnecessary suffering, unnecessary medication. We thought we could shorten recovery times and reduce medical costs. We thought our treatments would accomplish a lot. Everyone was excited."

She's attentive. She nods.

"A very real-appearing entity would appear to patients. They called this figure a god. In jest, of course. No one believed it was an actual deity. Some of them looked human, some of them looked half-human or animallike."

He draws in another deep breath.

"Basically, in cases of unmanageable pain, where nothing else seemed to work, our pain-management system shunted pain outside the body. The major side effects, though, were off-putting. An entity would appear—something very real to the patient. This entity would often cause trouble."

Spiros laughs, something bitter.

"Tell me, Stephen," Wini says, "in a best-possible world, what would you envision for your technology?"

Why is she calling him Stephen? It's a name he's never liked. In his childhood he demanded he be called *Spiros*, the surname of his Greek father. He thought it expressed quiet fury.

Spiros had envisioned myriad spin-offs for his technology: a guardian entity that keeps children safe, a woodsman entity that appears in the wilderness and helps downed pilots, a father figure, a mother figure, a friend, a mentor. But the entities that appeared were far more malevolent than anyone had imagined.

And now this jill-in-the-box is questioning him?

"Wini, I don't envision best-possible worlds. I envision the march of technology. I don't want an enemy to get ahold of this first."

Wini looks thoughtful, not speaking for a while. Finally, she stirs.

"What does a Pain-Shunt treatment feel like?" she asks.

"Your pain takes off in orbit around you. As it acquires distance from you, you feel less of it. You sense that it has an otherworldly connection, that it's not really a part of you. We were achieving it routinely by applying magnetic fields to patients' parietal and temporal lobes. We had patients tell us about their shoulder god or knee god or sciatica god. It was a remarkable, consistent representation of pain located outside the body and an entity in charge of pain management. We really felt we had hit upon something."

Again, Wini becomes thoughtful.

She's on a fool's mission, Spiros thinks. She needs to pursue her life. Otherwise, Woodsman gets her.

"Someone is snapping necks," Wini says. "Who?"

"Woodsman," Spiros says.

"How is Woodsman doing it?"

"Are you shockproof?"

"I don't know."

"We humans are constructs. We can be entered and possessed by malevolent forces, rendering us passive watchers. One of the malevolent forces expressed through Woodsman is programmed to snap necks. Another to cut throats, and so on. These are survival skills if you're a downed pilot behind enemy lines."

Wini looks shaken.

"Good heavens," she says. "What is driving all this?"

"Years ago, the U.S. government established a net of charged particles in the upper atmosphere which enabled various mind-control technologies to take effect. This net of charged particles makes Woodsman and related phenomena possible."

"We need to turn the equipment off," she says.

"The government doesn't run the equipment anymore. It isn't necessary. The earth was impregnated with the signal, striking a resonance, which now results in earth generating the net."

For a moment, Wini looks like an animal frozen in its lair.

Then she stirs.

"We need to stop Woodsman," she says, her eyes searching the room with maniacal force. "We need to rip the net apart."

"We do? Consider this. They released a killer version of Woodsman for a reason: to mask something else they're doing. Ultimately, they'll knock Woodsman out. Once it's knocked out, they'll operate another version secretly. Currently, the technology isn't embedded enough so it's invisible. Hence, the need for a scapegoat until it's deeper.

"The scapegoat is what you see around you, the highly visible aspects, snapped necks and so forth. When that version of Woodsman stops, the secret version will be in place. Stopping Woodsman is part of their plan. Someday they'll let someone stop it. They'll even offer up a human scapegoat. Then you won't know the world you live in. It's called an extinction event. Do you still want to stop Woodsman? Be careful what you wish for."

Spiros wants to ease Wini out of his apartment so he can go warn Otis Dietrich about Woodsman.

"Biblical times are upon us," Spiros says. "Gods walk the earth. New myths form up, borrowing from old myths. The rascals are at it again, this time seeking control at a deep level. Can we do anything about it? Yes. Stay focused on your life, regardless of how impossible it seems."

"How can I stay focused on my life, Spiros? Someone is snapping necks. I could be next."

"You still don't get it, Wini. Let me give you a clue. Some wretched soul in L.A.—a person unknown to me—has fragmented memories of having committed these crimes.

In that regard, this person is nothing more than a piece of wreckage about to be offered up as a scapegoat. It's actually Woodsman working through him. As far as your own neck goes: if you watch your back incessantly, or if you act lost or confused, they win. Woodsman will find you."

He walks her to the door.

CHAPTER 16

Death Masks

Spiros drives to Santa Monica and parks near Otis Dietrich's apartment. As he gets out of his pickup, a ghostly image of his father looms over him.

Stunned, Spiros stares at his father's ghost.

He is barely conscious of his surroundings, sees only his father's apparition.

He clutches the open door of his pickup for support.

"Father, I did it. I did what everyone said I could not do. I created a god. A being who comes to your aid in time of need. Did you know that?"

His father's stern visage reveals nothing, except perhaps a touch of mockery, and then it vanishes.

Spiros turns away, disheartened.

He closes the pickup's door and locks it.

He squares his shoulders, breathes in deeply, lets it out.

He wonders if he actually did see his father's ghost. Yes, he believes he did. There does seem to be a bit of enchantment in the air.

He sees a woman strolling by on the sidewalk.

He recognizes her, and this makes him happy.

She's wearing a stunning dress, slinky and green like the pale nymphs in the gardens of spring.

He walks to her.

She smiles at him.

"Ready to enter the hard streets, Kristen-Kate?"

"If you're inviting me, yes."

He takes her by the arm, and they stroll along the sidewalk, viewing the ocean swells, the evening putting on its blinking eyes.

They inhale the intoxicating air, their feet barely touching the sidewalk, a warm elixir in them.

They stare at the glossy, elegant face of Santa Monica, with its stucco battlements, its palm fronds.

The air around them stings their eyes, as if inviting them to not look at anything too closely. They look anyway.

"They say we're going to have a tour of the kitchen at King's Forest," Spiros says.

"A tour of the kitchen? Oh, nice. I suppose."

"You don't sound enthused. Just you wait. King's Forest is the newest, grandest eatery in the whole world."

Spiros and Kristen-Kate walk through the wilting heat daggers of the evening, she hanging close to him, giving a little purr of contentment.

"Kristen-Kate, did you make that little kitten sound because you're with me, or because you like to see the underbelly of the beast ripped open before you chow down?"

"Because I'm with you, silly."

Spiros sees trouble ahead and releases Kristen-Kate's arm. He walks up the sidewalk, tethered to her by gossamer threads. The crowds slide around him like salty teardrops. Now and then someone veers close, stings him with uncomprehending eyes, and fades back into the sea of teardrops. He resents these hard cases thinking he's their savior. What is it about him, he wonders, that gives them that impression?

As he and Kristen-Kate advance on the entrance to King's Forest, he sees a bearded man with an egg-shaped head and a young woman embroiled in some kind of to-do. Spiros narrows his eyes. The man, fierce, devil-may-care, wearing the aura and baggy clothes of a depression-era miscreant, possessing the genes of a risk taker, the dynamism of a hunter-gatherer, the eerie discernment of a hippie wreathed in hash smoke, is psychically thumping the woman, a tasty, bitty blonde, who is clearly upset that this street person, this fierce man, has accosted her. He is saying something to her, and it is hurting her to hear.

It is hurting more than just her, for the man's loud, harsh voice carries through the swelling crowds.

She scrambles away from him. She in her neat white outfit, slacks and billowing blouse, a silky red kerchief tied jauntily around her neck, her hands to her ears, her purse flying around by its strap, her face contorted with wavy lines of anguish so deep they must be scoring her soul.

"Cease your wretched whoring!" the man shouts as he pursues the young woman down the sidewalk toward Spiros.

Again, he petitions her.

"Cease your wretched whoring!"

Again and again, and it becomes a litany.

The young woman rushes past Spiros, giving him a look of pure terror.

Apparently tiring of her, the bearded man with the egg-shaped head, who bears more than a passing resemblance to William Shakespeare, picks someone else from the humming hive. He wrestles a short, slight dude from the swarm and smacks him across the face.

The short, slight dude stands exposed, a hand to his face, feeling the bright-red mark left by his assailant. The short, slight dude in blue jeans, with curly red hair, with icy-blue eyeballs that stare at the bearded man with a hard look that intensifies into hatred. Not a hatred invoked by the mighty slap, but a hatred that is ever present, a hatred that calls attention to itself, fueled as it is by self-loathing and jealousy. This small pink-hued man, by and large an insane man, has pitted himself against the world since toddlerhood, and is now completely helpless, his own victim, and soulless.

And now this bearded man with the egg-shaped head has hung him out to dry in front of the crowd. And the man proceeds to add insult to injury.

The man shouts, pointing at the short, slight dude. "Cease your wretched whoring!"

The short, slight dude with the curly red hair takes off down the sidewalk, seeing Spiros and Kristen-Kate, giving Spiros a look of hatred so deep it would seem to scar the short, slight dude's soul if he had a soul to scar.

The bearded man with the egg-shaped head pursues him, his voice thundering through the crowd.

"Cease your wretched whoring!"

And it becomes a litany.

Spiros hurries to Kristen-Kate, takes her by the arm again.

"Damn," he mutters. Fear and worry begin flowing off him like sweat. It wasn't like he imagined.

He wants to be free of the circus on the street. They walk quickly to the entrance of King's Forest, untangle from the crowd, and squeeze through the doorway, whereupon Spiros pauses and drinks in the hoodoo of the place. And there is plenty of hoodoo here, he thinks.

In the spare light, they give their names to the hostess, a slender, wholesome-looking pixie who might be all of nineteen, and are granted admission. Spiros asks her for notepaper and pen, and she cheerfully grabs up a pad and pen from under the reception stand for him.

The hostess leads them through the enchanting forest décor, through purplish orbs of light cast by the gas-lit torches, to a cloistered table far from the entrance, where she leaves them with menus and departs to guard the door again.

"Drinks?" A waitress has sidled up to them. Spiros gazes at her. She's about twenty, with long blond hair tied back and high Nordic cheekbones. Her complexion is as silky smooth as a field of new snow in soft sunshine. He pictures her frolicking in the high grassy meadows of Scandinavia, tending the flocks. She has a caregiver aspect.

"How about a tour of the kitchen?" Spiros asks.

"Coming up," the waitress says with a smile. "We'll let you know when."

"Tell me," Kristen-Kate says, "what's so special about this kitchen? Why do we need a tour?"

She looks at Spiros and at the waitress, her upturned face locked in veils of inscrutability. She has pictured in her mind a voluminous kitchen staffed by a gang of elves from some enchanted land, wearing immaculate white aprons and white tennis shoes, and scurrying around like mice in a cheese shop. She wonders if they piss in the food.

"You'll get a fab glimpse of what goes on behind the scenes," the waitress says.

"Okay, fine," Kristen-Kate says. She orders rum cocktails for both of them and the waitress departs.

Spiros feels a chill as he jots down the bare bones of a story that's been haunting him. He leans over the table and speaks in a conspiratorial voice to Kristen-Kate.

"Kristen-Kate, you've got to hear this." He looks around, making sure no one is listening in. "A man sees a robotic human on the street. It looks perfectly human, yet its motions are robotic, not completely, but as if someone is trying to work the bugs out. It occurs to him that this might be a new technology in the making.

"The man follows it. He wants to hear it speak, to see if the voice is robotic. The bot's bodyguards, who are blended in the background, notice his interest and follow him.

"The man stops in a store, buys a video camera, and resumes tracking the bot. This time he's recording it. The bodyguards follow him, a decision in the making: abort the mission or detain the interested party.

"The guy notices he's being followed. Does he guard himself against possible harm or continue pursuing the bot?"

Spiros leans back in his chair, thinking he's sparked her imagination. "What do you think?"

"Talk about robots," she says. "Outside, didn't you see that bearded man with the egg-shaped head? He was a robot."

He looks at her, puzzled. "But, Kristen-Kate, there was nothing robotic about him. He was engaged in lively street theater, that's all."

"That's absurd, Spiros."

"It's not absurd."

He feels his face flush, his skin tighten.

"Kristen-Kate, you fuckhead!"

"Look who's the fuckhead!"

He stares at her. He can't believe what he said.

"Kristen-Kate ..."

"And you, Spiros. You were so cold and distant, you were a robot, also."

He bristles at the idea. "I wasn't a robot."

"Spiros ..." Her voice softens and she shifts in her seat, holding him in her eyes. "In truth, out on the street, you were spellbound. Watchful. You wanted to know if it was safe for us to pass that vile man."

"You're right." She has calmed him. He realizes he had tensed the muscles of his legs, as if he were about to pounce on her.

"So, what's the rest of your story?" she asks. "Does the guy continue pursuing the bot? And what do the commandos do? Do they abort the mission? Do they nab him?"

"Commandos?" He laughs. "Where did you get commandos?"

"Isn't that what your story suggests, military commandos as the bot's bodyguards?"

"Maybe so." Spiros gazes away and sees the Nordic
waitress rushing in their direction with two gigantic drinks.
She stops at their table and sets them down.

Spiros catches her eye, and she favors him with a brief
splash of high-meadow sunshine before departing.

"What's in these drinks?" he asks Kristen-Kate. "Whatever it is, it sure looks amazing." He stares into his glass.

"Rum and other healthy things. So, what happens next?
I'm intrigued."

"I haven't finished the story yet."

"Let's run with it." She gives a little bounce in her seat.
"It's exciting. Let's make things up." She sips her drink,
eyeing him over the rim of her glass, an impish look.

"Okay."

"First of all," she says, "it's not a bot. It's a human, but
let's keep calling it a bot."

"Okay."

"It's a human under some kind of duress. It's a proto-
type, and they have to get the bugs out, to make him
appear seamless, so he'll be theirs to do with as they wish.
U.S. Army Special Forces blend in as civilians and watch
the bot."

"How do they control him?" Spiros asks.

"I don't know. It can't be obvious."

"How about drugs?"

"Drugs are too mundane. We need something more
exotic than drugs. I'm trying to imagine myself as a bot.
What are bots used for?"

"They're used for dangerous or illegal work," he says.

She looks around, lowers her voice. "I know what they're used for. They're used for black ops. We insert them into foreign trouble spots to do our bidding. They can never be traced back to us. What do you think?"

"I think that's downright intriguing."

"Okay," she says, "let's leave it there for now. I'm flat out heading for the ladies' room." She grabs her purse and takes off.

He watches her go, his eyes blurring.

He stands and walks around. He looks into the darkness beyond the reach of the torches and sees delicate, feathery touches of fire playing in the air, spinning in little whirls, weaving contours and silhouettes, and then shredding the air, looking like a multitude of tiny curtains parting, as if eager to share the mysteries on the stages beyond. He stares at the fiery display as it continues to take shape.

"A puppet show," Kristen-Kate says, reappearing at his side, eyeing the direction of his gaze.

The fiery puppet show vanishes, and suddenly the night is spinning, and Spiros is clutched by panic. Things leap at him from the darkness and thrash him about. He feels a viselike grip on his arm and hears a voice loud and clear.

"Spiros, get a grip on yourself." It's Kristen-Kate. She is strong. So strong. He had no idea.

The vise leaves his arm and his mind settles into a gentle rocking motion.

Before the fiery lights faded, Spiros saw himself in the puppet show, tendrils of fire yanking him around. Like everyone else in the show, he seemed locked in a dance.

Someone is laughing. It's Kristen-Kate. She's leading him back to their table.

As she eases him into his chair, he is once again struck by her strength. She's a force, he muses, sliding his gaze over her precious face, watching her eyes as they dance in the wild torchlight. He reaches up and touches the silky skin under her chin, and she rewards him with a smile. Their fingertips touch momentarily, and then she steps away and takes her seat.

The lights come up in the restaurant and a voice announces over the intercom: "All diners please gather for the guided tour of the kitchen."

Spiros laughs—a good, hearty laugh that rattles his bones.

He hears Kristen-Kate laugh—a full, rolling laughter that fills his heart with gladness.

They stand and step away from their table.

As Spiros walks, he misses nothing. Most of the other diners in King's Forest do not want to give up their seats. They do not want to form into little companionable clumps, as he and Kristen-Kate have done, and move toward the wide double doors of the kitchen.

"Come on, into the ovens," he says. But they stay put.

He feels a vise on his arm and he eases Kristen-Kate's hand away. "You're strong, babe," he tells her. "But I don't need that now."

He glances around at the other diners and mutters under his breath, "Come on, on your feet."

The public-address announcer urges them on, and this appears to be the magic key, for the diners in King's Forest lift themselves from their seats, nervously glance about, and gather toward the kitchen like a slowly forming storm cloud.

Spiros sees an old couple shuffling along, and he veers toward them. "Get your stinking butts in there!"

The old man and his wife cackle and step lively.

Spiros sees Kristen-Kate eyeing him. They engage one another, this joke in their eyes. But was it really a joke? No, it was evil. So they share the evil. She's moving close to him, up on tiptoes, going to whisper to him.

"That was evil, Spiros."

He dismisses her with a courtly wave.

The kitchen doors swing wide and the diners file in.

Several dapper men in dark suits stand by and greet everyone. Gazing about, peeling off from Kristen-Kate, Spiros feels a sense of wonder, as if he were a child in a toy shop, but soon the savory aromas and hustle and bustle of the place reorient him.

He does a quick spin. It seems like a normal kitchen, spacious and busy and aromatic. And then he sees the cook, a very large man dressed in white presiding over a huge pan of what appears to be baked duck. The cook must weigh well over a thousand pounds, Spiros thinks, with most of that weight lying about him as naturally as would a grizzly bear's. The big man's face twitches with emotion, and an anxious whine that fills the room with apoplectic pressure comes from somewhere inside him.

A dapper man in a dark suit appears at Spiros's side. A nametag on his lapel announces him as *Ronald.*

"The cook comes from good breeding stock in Okla-homa," the dapper man named Ronald says to Spiros, "where the social veneer is kept to a high gloss. Where politeness, helpfulness, and good manners fly off people as light would from a drunken, pirouetting goblet."

Spiros stares at the dapper man named Ronald. Of course, he thinks. He looks again at the large man and revises his weight estimate. The guy must weigh well over two thousand pounds.

"Not so long ago," the dapper man says, shifting his gaze back to the large man, "the cook pursued life as if it were a series of important personages waiting for him to step into. He lived in Tulsa, Oklahoma, where he cranked out a living as a chemical-plant manager, but in total secrecy, he was John D. Rockefeller, on a mad dash to wealth and power. In Tulsa, he was fond of visiting art galleries with his wife and daughter, but in total secrecy, he was Leonardo da Vinci, creating his own masterpieces. In Tulsa, he belonged to a philosopher's book club, soaking up the wisdom of the ages, but in total secrecy, he was Albert Einstein, possessor of some of the world's most esoteric knowledge.

"But that was in Tulsa. Here in L.A., he is seething with strange new attitudes, with no pattern to guide him.

"In Tulsa, he was laid back, a bear of a man with a gentle manner and affable fantasies. Here in L.A., he is arrogant, high strung, and his fantasies are beyond absurd.

"In Tulsa, he loathed bigots, especially those who hate American Indians, whom he had a special fondness for, having read of America's appalling treatment of its native inhabitants.

"Here in L.A, as you can see, the cook is standing next to an American Indian, and the newly arrogant chemical-plant manager from Tulsa is not entirely comfortable with that."

Spiros spots the Indian and sees that the large man does indeed look uncomfortable standing next to him.

The dapper man continues.

"Many of our employees call the cook Fat Boy. But the Indian admonishes them, saying that all people deserve respect, and that the cook, though a bit soft at two thousand pounds, would be solid at fifteen hundred. And our employees typically counter with, 'You have to respect that. He is a large motherfucker in any case.' And that rankles and saddens the Indian. Some people simply do not understand. They play a hard game. They make their own rules as they go and are quite unfair. If only all our employees saw the vortices the Indian sees—the circles and rings and loops that run endlessly through everything— then they would be fair."

The dapper man whispers to Spiros. "You're a toothpick. They can break you."

He takes Spiros by the arm, moves him through the human tide, deposits him beside Kristen-Kate, and then departs.

Spiros whispers, "Hoodoo," to Kristen-Kate, and feels the brush of her breath as she whispers back.

"Hoodoo."

"I feel we're in a Shakespearean play," he whispers to her. "Soon we'll be hearing soliloquies."

"Surely you jest," she whispers back.

The man in the dark suit named Ronald is in Spiros's ear again. "We must accelerate your training. Come this way."

"Certainly," Spiros says, getting back into the cadence and flow of the crowd. He sees the other men in dark suits fan out to act as shepherds.

With a scattering of steps and then an avalanche, the crowd picks up its feet, and Spiros again feels the offhand though decidedly official shine to their tour, as if the most casual of master chefs had concocted this migration for them.

They find themselves in a spacious room lined with wall lockers, the type of lockers one might find in the hallway of a school. It's not a separate room entirely but part and parcel of the large kitchen warren.

"I bet this is where the employees stash their drugs," Kristen-Kate says.

As if on cue, a police contingent floods the area. They are uniformly tall, wear black police get-up, carry military-style assault rifles, and have *Sheriff* stenciled in white letters on their backs.

Suddenly, an invisible force seizes Spiros, causing paralyzing fear in his chest. The same force causes him to lock eyes on the police and put his hands in the air.

The other diners are also seized, and also lock eyes on the police and put their hands in the air.

Spiros feels joined to the other diners, absent his own volition. The force that grips him is both paralyzing and possessing, and strikes enormous fear into his heart.

The force spins Spiros and the other diners toward the wall lockers. They lean against them, their hands on the lockers, their feet spread as the police rush in to frisk them.

The police run their hands over the diners' bodies and

then yank the locker doors open and search inside, creating a hellish racket as they shove things around. Finished searching, they slam the locker doors shut and back away.

The possessing force compels the diners to spin around and face the police again, their backs to the lockers, their hands still in the air. Spiros is aware of Kristen-Kate's presence a cat's whisker off his left elbow.

A heartbeat later, the diners are free of the possessing force, free of the grip of fear and obedience. Spiros drops his hands, looks around, sees the awestruck faces of the other diners.

A murmur arises.

"What happened?" Kristen-Kate says, glancing around.

A dark and foreboding thought fills Spiros's mind, becomes like a lion's roar: *No one gave us commands! We were possessed, under someone's total control!*

Spiros studies the commandos. They seem harmless now. They walk around, their assault rifles pointed in the air, their faces not showing much, except perhaps a tinge of satisfaction.

He watches the nearest commando, a man about six-three with hints of gray showing along the sides of his head beneath his dark baseball cap.

The commando establishes eye contact with Spiros and steps closer—close enough for Spiros to see the blue flecks that streak his irises.

A whistle sounds, and the commandos swoop away, as silently as they arrived.

The men in dark suits coordinate the crowd again and move everyone back to the dining room, where baked duck awaits them.

Waitresses scurry about, the lights dim, and the public-address announcer says, "Dig in, ladies and gentlemen."

Spiros and Kristen-Kate, having taken their seats, stare at their torch-lit duck and trimmings.

"Spiros," Kristen-Kate says, "did you sense a magnetic field in there?"

"I sensed something, but I don't know what." He had never felt more alive than he had in those few brief moments.

"Spiros, while in there, I was aware of massive electrical forces. I feel that a slender strand of consciousness has been inadvertently left us. Otherwise, we are insensate physical creatures. Our motor faculties work well and serve to hold us upright. In reality, men are prodding us, talking to us, and we think we are here, in King's Forest."

Spiros looks at her with increased interest. He takes his first bite of duck, closes his eyes, and lets his imagination run with it. He's standing in the locker room.

The real locker room, not the mockup they were just in, but the one that lies beneath the surface of the counterfeit world, a place of magnets and superfluidity and volatility.

Strange voices intrude. "Can't you do something with his face? It looks like a death mask."

Spiros is vaguely aware that someone or something is running him, managing his motor faculties.

Voices again, arguing stridently and then in jest.

"We can't give him his face—he isn't Spiros now. He's what Spiros was before he became Spiros."

Spiros cracks his eyelids open. Feels awful to do this, feels as if he is going to tear his eyes from his head. Through slits, he sees faces in the locker room. They look dead. The bodies the faces belong to are standing, but the faces look dead. He is in a strange half land.

He expects to be shot any moment. Two U.S. Army commandos point the muzzles of their assault rifles in his face. They talk.

"He's got his eyes open."

"Shut them, Spiros."

"It's Spiros?"

"Yes."

"Are you sure?"

"Positive."

"Spiros it is. Spiros, shut your eyes."

Spiros shuts his eyes.

"He can't hear us, can he?"

"Of course not."

Spiros sees Kristen-Kate in the locker room, standing with a death mask, but alive nevertheless. A slender memory hanging gritty in his mind, lying somewhere between memories of the sand beneath his feet, gritty against his skin, the sun a warming touch, the waters of the Adriatic curling up into a mist at the edge of the universe, the deliciously insane Fat Boy curling up as well, unfolding from the recesses of his mind.

And Fat Boy is gone and Spiros is steeped in a cloud of electricity, standing in the locker room again. *The real locker room.* He is vaguely aware of this. Two men talk through the fog, and Spiros is seized with fear.

"He's here."

"This one? No, can't be."

"He is definitely here."

"Well, maybe. What do you think happened?"

A voice cries out. "Spiros is where we don't want him to be."

"Where?" An echoing response from far away.

"In the locker room."

"Holy Christ."

They are propping Kristen-Kate up in the locker room, and Spiros, having cracked his eyelids open again, sees what they are doing.

He sees the two commandos. Spiros hangs names on them: Bigger and Nastier. He thinks he would trust Bigger in certain situations, but never Nastier. Bigger seems to possess an air of restraint. An air of decency, perhaps. Something human, anyway.

Nastier is pointing his assault rifle in Spiros's face. In the dining room of King's Forest.

And this is where Spiros is, in the dining room of King's Forest, sitting at the table across from Kristen-Kate, baked duck in front of him, still warm.

He lifts his eyes a couple of notches and peers into Kristen-Kate's face. Then he sees Nastier, the commando who wields the rifle. Bigger joins Nastier and—reluctantly, Spiros thinks—trains his rifle on Spiros and Kristen-Kate. The dapper man in the dark suit named Ronald, Indian, and Fat Boy stand nearby. In the dim light, Spiros sees concern on the dapper man's face.

Spiros reflects upon his journey. There was no sense of consciousness gone and then consciousness returning. He was on a beach near Venice, Italy, on the Adriatic, and in King's Forest. There and there. Seamless. Like a wand pointing, and poof,

Spiros was there. The waters of the Adriatic curled up into a big mist and engulfed him, as if a big genie were rising from the sea, and carried him back to King's Forest.

With, apparently, an inadvertent stop in the locker room along the way. The real locker room, not the counterfeit.

Kristen-Kate sits across from him as before, her upturned face staring defiantly at Bigger and Nastier.

Spiros looks at Indian and Fat Boy. He wonders if they are death masks in the locker room, also. But memories of the locker room are fading fast. He fights their desertion. He wants to hang on to the idea that he is still in the locker room and that his consciousness is being sprayed around.

No, they are gone. And the Adriatic. Gone. He's sure he's never seen the Adriatic, but the experience lies within consciousness.

And then a reassuring idea arises. He accepts it. A light show. A hologram of Venice. And the beaches of the Adriatic.

"Did you enjoy your sojourn in Venice?" the dapper man asks.

"Indeed," Spiros says. "It was quite a hologram."

He watches as Bigger and Nastier drift through the dining room, apparently satisfied with his response.

Spiros swallows a bite of savory baked duck and opens his eyes to other possibilities. "I think we'll take a trip to Venice, Italy, sugarplum," he tells Kristen-Kate.

Her eyes pop open and she nearly shouts for joy.

But the dapper man still does not look entirely pleased with this turn of events.

"Did you see the whore from Mumbai?" he asks.

Spiros says nothing. He stares at the dapper man, whom he believes is getting entirely too personal in his comments. The guy should be taken back to the locker room for fine-tuning. He eats more duck, drinks more rum, and then picks up his notepad and pen and begins to record the events that took place in the locker room, as best he can remember.

But his hand becomes strange. It writes as if a possessing spirit named Puck had taken it over. He stares at his composition, and then reads it aloud:

"Puck I am, alone with a silken black night,
She reads to me stories slender and tight.
She leaves, I chase, we tumble and wait,
She knew: from an open doorway enters my fate.
It is white, it is short, it knows less and less.
It's a pig, frozen dead, rocking yes and yes.
The round black night leaves by and by,
The cornered white day cleaves lie and lie.
The sleek round sleep, the razor-straight day,
I pause to drink its meaning and say:
That speck of consciousness I acquired someplace
Becomes smaller and smaller as I continue this race."

Polite applause breaks out from nearby tables.

"You're a poet, sir," the dapper man named Ronald says.

"I am not." Spiros feels his face flush. He does not like this attention.

"Spiros, your muse wrote that poem," Kristen-Kate says.

"Accept it," the dapper man says.

Spiros hears a strange woman's voice from a nearby table.

"Lucky you. You got a muse. All I got was some fucker's hand up my ass."

They roar at the woman's crack about her experience in the locker room.

A chill wind hits Spiros, shivering him, working its way through his body. His heart speeds up and his chest is squeezed tight. He knows he was diverted from seeing someone tonight. Who was he supposed to see?

He's in a panic, thinking he's about to revisit the locker room, where they are all death masks. He has one last sensation—the aroma of baked duck—and then a quick fade into nothingness.

The next thing Spiros knows, he is running out the door of King's Forest, running through the streets of Santa Monica, searching for his pickup. He finds it parked near courtyard apartments.

He can't assimilate the experience. It's too bizarre.

Shaken, he drives home to Irvine.

CHAPTER 17

A Dizzying Sense of Being Present Elsewhere

At first, Otis thought he'd come down with a mild cold, nothing more serious than that. Despite congested sinuses and flagging energy, he remained under full sail for two days. But on day three, his symptoms intensified and he began having episodes of delirium.

He kept to his apartment.

Disorientation began hitting him in waves.

He'd bob around like a cork on the ocean, stagger toward the kitchen, intending to call in sick, but never make it.

He hated to miss work. He'd stagger back to the living room and collapse onto his chair.

He's sitting quietly now, wondering why his head hurts so much. It's driving him mad, for it's not ordinary, tolerable pain. It's extreme.

His eyes seem to want to crawl out of their sockets and race madly around his skull.

The muscles of his jaws, neck, and shoulders grow tauter by the moment, producing their own constellation of pain, the bones beneath rattling in sympathy.

His stomach lurches, and he feels like vomiting, but nothing ever comes up.

His energy is sinking away like a ship going down in a storm.

He leans back in his chair and gasps. This eases the pain. He consciously relaxes the muscles of his jaws, neck, and shoulders, letting his body droop like a rag doll, and this helps.

Then a new wave of pain hits him, and he cries out, shakes his arms, moans, and curses. All of this helps. He's found a new ritual.

He gets up and staggers toward the kitchen again, heading for his cell phone, which he keeps on the counter by a package of muffins.

He keeps it there so he won't lose track of it. He doesn't trust his memory anymore. But he knows he won't make it to the kitchen; he's losing equilibrium fast.

He stumbles and lands on his hands and knees. Pain hits his head, face, and neck again, and he crawls back to his chair and eases into it.

He clutches himself, smothers himself with his arms, as the pain and disorientation become more intense.

He waits a few minutes, and it diminishes. I'll rest for a while, he thinks, and then go into the kitchen and call in sick.

He's defeated. He sees himself collapsing at work on his highly visible post at the front desk of the Hotel Marquesas.

He hopes he'll be able to make it to his first class in the morning at UCLA.

His pain intensifies to new levels, and he cries out again. This time it doesn't diminish.

He drags himself out of his chair, humps himself place to place in his sparse living room, enters his bedroom, and grabs a blanket off his bed, not knowing what he is doing.

He stumbles back into the living room, trailing his blanket behind him.

On impulse, he does a little trick with his mind, doesn't know how he conceived of it. He drops his mind to a lower vibration and leaves most of his pain behind.

He stands upright, feeling much better. He doesn't know why it worked, but it did.

But it creeps back, like an animal switching its tail across the floor. And it knocks him flat again.

He is utterly defeated. He will have to call in sick. What will they think? Everyone knows Otis never misses work.

Waves of pain and disorientation crash on his shore again, and he sways in the cold sunlight that slants in through the blinds.

He remembers his little trick, dropping his mind to a lower vibration. It works again, but only slightly this time. The animal is getting smarter. It's buzzing along, acquiring a degree of sophistication.

Otis gathers up his blanket and sinks into his chair, his mind racked with dark thoughts.

He doesn't feel good about calling in sick, but he'll have to. It's his first job since the Navy. He's had it only a few weeks. It's too soon, really, to be calling in sick. They'll be thinking the wrong thing.

Feeling a chill, he pulls his blanket around him.

After leaving the Navy, Otis tracked his older brother, Gordy, to an Army base in North Carolina. Otis spent three days with him, and during that time, Gordy, a Special Forces officer, read him the riot act. Gordy told Otis to go to college, work, and make something of his life, or Gordy would come looking for him with a switch.

Otis stands, wrapped in his blanket, struck by fever and chills. He drags himself into the kitchen, leans against the counter, picks up his cell phone, and calls the Hotel Marquesas.

"It's Otis. I'm calling in sick." He's transferred to the front desk, where Rachelle Golden, also a student at UCLA, works.

"Rachelle, it's Otis. I've got the flu or something. I won't be coming in today."

He hears silence on the other end of the line.

"Rachelle?" He listens to more silence, and then hears a sigh, evidence she's still there. Why doesn't she respond?

Rachelle's voice crackles. "Whaaat?"

"I'm sick, okay? It happens."

Otis senses her emotions are jumping to crisis level. Rachelle can be as caustic as a swamp; you have to watch what you say around her.

"Okay, Otis," she says, and hangs up, having delivered her final words in a husky voice, trying to sound grave.

"Jesus." Otis can hear Gordy's low-keyed voice: *Don't ever apologize to any scuzzball. State your business, make them acknowledge you, and then get off the line.*

Ten years older than Otis, Gordy had caught the worst of their father's cruelty and violence. By the time Otis arrived, Gordy's physical injuries were on the mend, their father's monster placated by career success. But the damage to Gordy's psyche was an unknown squib in the firmament.

Otis shuffles back to the living room, leaving his cell phone in the kitchen. He sits in his chair, leans back, and tucks his blanket around him.

Fever and chills shake him, cook his brain a little.

The pain is making a return visit, centered around his eye sockets now. He tries the lower-vibration trick again, but this time it doesn't work. He decides Rachelle is responsible for that. The twit.

He takes a deep breath, pushing out some of the pain. His bones rattle on the intake. He feels better. He'll relax this evening, sleep well tonight. Feeling cocooned in the warmth of his blanket, he closes his eyes.

He sees green within his mental field. And he sees something crawling. A jolt of nervous energy hits his stomach.

He opens his eyes and reconnects with his Santa Monica apartment. He waits a long time, his heart pumping faster, and then closes his eyes again.

He sees a field of green: green grass, green twigs, green leaves. He sees a green snake slither across the ground.

He opens his eyes and sees the plain interior of his second-floor Santa Monica walkup. He has a dizzying sense of being present elsewhere, though, in a green world that exists beneath his eyelids.

The pain returns. It's bad. It's coming in waves. Otis pushes against the backrest of his chair and gasps.

He closes his eyes and goes into that green world again, his pain hissing out somewhere behind him.

He lands on something cushiony, and feels overly pliant on his feet. Mistrustful, he steps carefully and experiments.

He gazes around, and sees a green snake whip into tall grass.

Uneasy in his new environment, he opens his eyes.

With his eyes open, he sees his apartment in Santa Monica, a second-floor walkup. And he experiences his pain.

He closes his eyes.

With his eyes closed, he sees a vivid green world. And he experiences a respite from his pain.

He opens his eyes and hears that other world calling him. But he's afraid of staying there too long.

He cries out as the pain in his head, neck, and shoulders intensifies. He closes his eyes and the green world envelops him.

Looking up, he catches a glimpse of blue sky. A patchy, goopy mess of it. He looks down and sees the coppery color of bare earth.

He takes a few steps, feeling disembodied, following another green snake, and realizes it's weird to walk with no body to do the walking with.

No body? He shudders. He isn't ready for that yet.

He opens his eyes and feels the worst pain yet, a towering inferno of pain that holds his head, neck, and shoulders in a demon's grip.

He cries out, but will see it through. He will not close his eyes and give in to the rapidly developing hallucinations that are creeping upon him.

He drags himself to the bathroom, hangs his head over the sink, feels like he's going to throw up, but doesn't.

A hundred false alarms over the last few hours, the nausea hitting him in waves. The ocean pounding his soul.

He washes his face, looks in the mirror, stares into his eyes. They are frighteningly focused. They know of the green world.

Why don't you stay there, Otis?

I can't. I belong here. This is where my father is.

Your father is in the green world, also. Look, you will find him there.

He lurches away from the sink, stumbles across the bathroom floor, and bangs into the doorjamb.

He laughs and cries his way back to his comfortable chair in the living room, sits on it, leans back, and gasps in pain.

He shuts his eyes, feels their buzz behind closed lids, and watches the green world take shape again.

He will stay a bit longer this time.

Maybe he'll see his father here. And maybe his father will help him in some fashion.

Or maybe his father will bury him again, with his sulking moods and hot-tempered remarks.

Green world means peace, for a while, he thinks. He keeps his eyes shut, allowing more of it to come to him. Green grass, green leaves and shrubs, forest in the distance, purple mountains on the horizon, blue sky overhead.

He feels his head throb. That's unusual for the green world. He's never felt bodily sensations here before. His head is throbbing, but not in a painful way.

He takes a step, touches solid ground. He inhales a lungful of fresh, scented air.

He blows the air out, opens his eyes, and is back in his Santa Monica apartment. He isn't ready for the green world yet.

He needs to be Alex's son here, where Alex is, not where Alex might appear as some idealized, fantasized projection.

He'll conquer this sickness, whatever it is. He'll see it through. He'll get better; he'll heal. It's within his reach.

He'll continue his routine: work, school, all that. It's necessary. We are here. We must do all that, and then some.

He stands, almost stumbles. He has to study for his classes.

The following morning, he tries to keep busy with schoolwork again. Most days, he breezes through it. But today, with the sickness still upon him, he discovers he does better with a slow, methodical approach. It's as if the sickness has unearthed a new innate talent in him, one that makes him slow down and think.

But the sickness intensifies. It comes in waves, the nausea, the near collapses, the pain. He cries out. That helps. It's hard to place an emotion on this thing. Is pain an emotion? No. But what does it engender? Rage? Confusion? He doesn't know.

Will he call in sick again? Will he skip his classes again? He doesn't want that to become a habit. He never misses anything.

He is crawling again.

On his hands and knees, unsure.

His head hurts. His neck hurts.

He's hot, he's cold. It comes in waves. His energy has sunk away.

He cruises through the many layers in his mind that deal with pain and sickness, trying to find a niche for what he's going through.

But he can't find anything for it.

He stands.

He takes a step, stumbles, almost falls. It's too late to go to class. He'll fix lunch. He'll go to work, and then home again, study. Tomorrow, the same.

He collapses back into his chair.

Damn it! What's causing this? It isn't going away like he thought it would. And now his chest is affected, his breathing labored. He feels heat rising. A fever.

He'll sit a while, he thinks. He's on the edge of going or not going to work, on the edge of seeing or not seeing a doctor.

He lets his arms collapse. He consciously relaxes all of his muscles. It helps some, eases his pain.

Then he experiences an increase in pain, an ocean rising. Pain punching through his thoughts.

His face hurts. His jaws hurt. There are things wrong with him he has no words for. He enters new pathways of pain, most of it centered in his head, neck, and shoulders.

He closes his eyes and sleeps. But is only half asleep. He's too sick to sleep.

He wakes. But is only half awake. He can skip lunch,

just go to work. He stands and takes a step, but pain and nausea hit him.

No. He won't be able to go to work. But still he hesitates to call in. What if they think he's faking? Better to go there and be seen as sick. But maybe it's undetectable. Maybe no one can see him as sick. What to do?

He settles into his chair and closes his eyes. And the green world envelops him. He feels connected to a body. Neat.

Otis looks around. He sees grass and trees, sky and clouds, mountains on the horizon. But no detail. Nothing finely grained.

He begins walking, running, feeling the breeze against his face. It feels good, but he wants to see some fine detail. It isn't real until he sees the detail. Maybe if he sees Jill.

Jill?

He snaps his eyes open.

Where'd that name come from?

Does he know anyone named Jill?

He feels better, awake in his Santa Monica apartment. He stands, feels slight pain in his head and neck, tightness around his eyes and teeth. Not too bad. He takes a few steps, feels queasy. But it passes.

Jill?

Does Jill live in that other world?

Maybe he'll tell his father about his experiences in the green world. The Jill world. Crazy. His father will listen. He won't be critical. He'll ask Otis about the sickness and Otis will tell him.

He goes into the kitchen, begins frying a hamburger. It

sizzles and pops as he presses a spatula against it. One hamburger on a bun. With lettuce and tomato. He'll have an apple with it. He'll drink a glass of water with it.

Afterward, he'll brush his teeth. Then he'll go to work at the Hotel Marquesas, where he works at the front desk twenty hours a week.

He prepares what he'll tell his father. Two things: the green world and Jill. And how his sickness began. His father will be a very interested listener.

A wave of nausea hits him, and he shakes it off.

When did it begin? He traces his memory. But the only thing he can remember is lights.

It comes upon him gradually, and then hits him with a wallop as he eats his hamburger.

Cuts. The other thing. He'd forgotten that. He's been sick, yes, about four days now. The worst has come and gone, though it's still with him. He'd forgotten about the strange cuts. The sickness had overwhelmed him.

Strange recurring cuts had accompanied the early phase of his sickness. He looks at his fingertips. There'd been small cuts there.

He sees that the cuts are healed. But he thinks they might recur. He doesn't know why he thinks this.

There'd been cuts elsewhere, too. Always small. Always hard to heal and painful.

The recollection infuses Otis with a mission. He's going to get to the bottom of this.

He remembers a person coming to visit him. His head is clearing up. More of his recent past is clarifying. The sickness has been like a wall.

How much should he tell his father? He feels the visits were strange.

A spray of light was directed at him. Now that was odd. Where'd the light come from? When did it happen? Before he got sick? Before the visits? Who visited him?

He finishes eating his hamburger.

The guy who visited him was good. He remembers that much. The guy asked him questions. It's clearing up. The guy will return for more information, and Otis certainly has more information now.

The green world.

Jill.

He rinses his plate and puts it in the dishwasher.

Somehow, he feels good about this guy coming to visit him. He has to get more from that other world.

He walks to the living room, sits on his chair, closes his eyes. He sees flashes go off beneath his eyelids. He's back in the green world and it's taking on the colors and dimensions of a real world.

He walks toward some trees, feels the breeze, hears the melodic sound of a bird.

"Jill?" He calls her name.

A smell hits him, something chemical that fills his nostrils and then his whole head. A huge fireball. Jill is in danger. Jill's friends are in danger. The man who comes to visit him will want to know this. The green world becomes too oppressive, with a cacophony of noise and a smell of death and sights incomprehensible to his mind.

He opens his eyes, goes to a bureau, pulls out a pen and notebook. He'll start a journal.

Jill and her friends are in danger.

He records other impressions. It isn't much. He'll have to learn more. The guy who calls on him will push him to learn more.

He'll visit the green world again. He'll learn more about Jill and her friends. He'll keep a journal. He'll tell the guy all he's learned.

More of it comes back to him as his sickness eases.

He'd been hit by a spray of light. So were others. Many others. The light was like tiny particles of fog, and seemed to come from two different directions at once, a triangulation.

Okay. It's coming back. He'd been hit by light from two different directions simultaneously. Something shifted inside him. He began seeing with two new eyes. Smelling with two new nostrils. Hearing with two new ears. Feeling, touching, and being touched by two sets of bodily sensations.

And now he feels a spider's march of fear across his flesh. The sickness followed the doubling of his senses. The sickness obliterated memory of the doubling. At least temporarily.

He has two bodies. He is sure of that. The sprays of light split him in some fashion.

He inhabits two worlds.

The spider of fear marches all over him, crawls inside him, strikes him at his deepest being. He'll have to call his father now. He's fearful of this guy paying a return visit, looking for more information.

He feels he's being torn apart. He needs the closeness of someone close to him. He needs his father. His father will question him thoroughly. He has to be prepared.

He closes his eyes, lets himself go.

He sees more of that other world, a world of big explosions and mangled bodies, a world where Jill and her friends are in trouble.

He sees a beach and the outline of a continent. He sees tall mountains. He feels heat. It's the Tropic of Cancer. And Jill and her friends are there.

Otis pulls back. It's too much for him now. His head hurts, but not too bad. He'll brush his teeth now and go to work.

He'll keep a journal. He'll fill in past events, being hit by lights, having wounds without a genesis. The green world. Jill and her friends.

He remembers muscle cramps, as if being punished or hindered. He remembers different kinds of pain. He'll try to catalog it all in his journal.

He knows the heat of that other world. The explosions. The danger.

Then he remembers more. Crawling away, twisted up in abnormal positions, hiding. From what?

He recalls the agony of muscle spasms, losing motor control to another, being manipulated.

A horrible thought hits him. What if the green world is his real world and his existence in Santa Monica false? Is he lying in a hospital bed in Jill's world, unable to move, a victim of some explosive device?

He shudders.

No, it can't be.

All of a sudden, Otis wants to hang on to this world with a tenacity that scares him. He will miss nothing. He will call his father. He will see the man who comes to visit, and he will shove down his fear.

This is the world he wants to occupy. He'll close his eyes and glimpse the green world, for it will help the man whose job it is to investigate, but Otis will stay here. This is home.

He will help rescue Jill and her friends.

He is able to relax now, almost symptom free.

He goes into the bathroom and brushes his teeth.

He looks into the mirror and sees a fresh wound under his left eye. They'd been at him again in that green world.

He cleans the wound, applies a bandage, and goes to work.

CHAPTER 18

Spies

Cody Hobbs tells Jill that his worst fears have come to life: he has started seeing his dead parents in his sleep.

"I also see them while awake," he says. "It's like a vision."

"How often do you see them?" Jill asks.

"Not often."

"What do they tell you?"

"They tell me nothing."

Cody and Jill are in Cody's San Bernardino, California, apartment, standing on the balcony, twilight moving in.

"They just stand there and stare at me," Cody says. "What do you make of it, Jill?"

"I think they'll go away eventually."

"You do?"

"Yes, I do. The cosmos has a job for each of us, and your parents are probably needed elsewhere."

"I'm concerned about them. I wonder if I can say anything to them that might make a difference."

"You probably can't. It might make it worse."

"You might be right, Jill."

"I hope your parents leave. There are no jobs for them around here, far as I can tell."

"Right. They don't seem to be doing much good around here. Dead people can't drive trucks."

"No, they can't, Cody. Not that I've ever seen. Did more trucks come in last night?"

"Yes. A big convoy, about a hundred miles long at least. They're building something massive, Jill. I wonder what it is."

"It's military, whatever it is. There are more troops than ever around, and most of them are invisible."

"Don't say that!"

"I mean they blend in."

"Oh. Well, there are no new structures around that I've seen. Maybe they're building something underground."

"I don't think so. I think it's above ground. I think the government is building something on its land tracts out in the desert. I'd say it's something cutting edge."

"I think maybe someone told you something about this, Jill."

"Maybe."

"Who told you?"

"I can't tell you, Cody."

Cody and Jill are civilian employees of the U.S. Army, employed at a secret military base in the Mojave Desert. Both are electronics technicians. Cody is twenty-three. Jill is twenty-one.

Cody laughs. Jill is tickling him. "Let's go inside," he says. "I don't like it out here."

* * *

Cody is in the bathtub, soaking the desert sand away, the bathroom door ajar. Jill is in the living room, within earshot.

With eerie sensitivity, Cody can hear all the way out to the hallway that runs past his apartment door. People are walking around out there. They pass his door, and a minute later make a return journey, followed by a chilling silence.

"Something's strange, Jill. Don't you think?"

"Yes, I do, Cody." Jill walks into the bathroom nude and gets into the tub with Cody. They confer in quiet tones.

"Something isn't right," Cody says.

"I know," Jill says. "Give them time. They're not too good at it yet."

"Do you think we have to worry?"

"I'd say so."

"I think I'm beginning to understand things, Jill."

"So am I. The Army is creating operational environments."

"I mean I think I understand why they're doing it."

"So do I. To control battlefields."

"Yes, but that's not quite it, Jill. They're transforming us. We're like TV now, each of us, with different channels."

"Oh yeah?"

"Yes. They're hooking up our signals out in the desert."

"Oh yeah? If that's true, Cody, we're doomed. We need to fight it with all we've got."

"Jill, things are changing all over, don't you think? And now they've got spies all over checking on things. You hear them out there, don't you?"

"I hear them, Cody."

Cody hears distinctive tread in the corridor outside his apartment and knows it belongs to the long, lanky dude. The long, lanky dude's been here before. He has unique tread, like a rumble building up from the earth. There's no mistaking who's making it.

The long, lanky dude is actually a mild sort, but his footsteps are not. He's knocked on Cody's door before—in fact he's knocked an awful lot—and sometimes Cody answers it and sometimes, fearfully, he does not.

He hears a ruckus outside his apartment in the hallway. It's normal, though not welcome. The spies can be offensive; they can do things that get people hurt.

He watches Jill step out of the tub, towel off, and walk out of the bathroom.

"You going home, Jill?"

"Yes."

"Wait. Don't go out there until the spies are gone."

"What would they do to me?"

"They'd talk to you, for one thing. They'd transform you, for another. It's weird."

"I'll wait in the living room until they're done rambling around. Have you ever thought of making a complaint about them?"

"I don't think it would do any good. Normal rules don't apply anymore."

Cody hears Jill walk down the corridor to the living room. Strange. The whole thing is strange. And weird.

He pulls a glass slipper from the water, holds it up, and stares at it. A flawless glass slipper, fit for a princess. He empties the water out of it, dips it into the water again, and holds it up again.

It's perfect, he thinks. Where did it come from?

He empties the glass slipper and sets it on the floor beside the tub.

He finishes scrubbing the desert sand away, drains the tub, dries off, and puts on clean clothes.

He walks into the living room and sees Jill on the sofa, in her clothes.

"Jill, there was a glass slipper in the tub. Can you imagine that? A glass slipper? I left it there beside the tub. Do you want to go take a look?"

"Okay." Jill gets up and walks toward the bathroom.

Cody hears a knock at the door. He cracks it open, peers out, and sees an extremely tall, lanky young man standing there. He has short brown hair and eyeglasses, and is seven feet tall or so. Cody feels at ease seeing him.

"Can I come in?" the young man asks. "I'd like to talk to you about ..."

It escapes Cody. He thinks it has something to do with the spies.

"You can't come in. But we can talk here."

The long, lanky dude comes in anyway, maybe not hearing Cody. Cody gets the impression the height difference had something to do with the miscommunication.

Cody jumps in front of him and thrusts a forefinger into his face. "You need to leave."

The long, lanky dude heads back to the door, not putting up a fight.

Cody stands at the door with him, confident they can still

have the conversation. He hears a commotion and loud voices out there somewhere. He feels more in charge standing at the door, with Jill back there a ways, just in case.

"A splendid day," the long, lanky dude says.

"Yes."

"A longing deeper than mere physical thirst has struck me."

"You're a spy, right?"

"Yes. But I'm more than a spy."

"I knew it."

Cody sees a strange look come over the long, lanky dude's face.

"I've seen some of your plans out in the desert," Cody says.

"Oh? You know a lot."

"I do," Cody says. "It's like TV signals."

The long, lanky dude stares at him with narrowed eyes.

"Different channels," Cody says, "like we get with TV. It opens us up in lots of ways."

Without warning, another young man, shorter and huskier than the long, lanky dude, is in Cody's face. With lightning speed, he thrusts an index finger into Cody's forehead, pushes him inside the apartment, and forces him to the floor.

Cody is sitting on the floor, his torso angled backward, the guy's fingertip fused to his forehead as if by electrical forces. Cody's hands are wrapped around the guy's wrist, trying to force his hand away. He can't budge it. He's an immovable force, more powerful than anything Cody can imagine.

"Jill, he's in the apartment!"

Cody directs all of his energy into pushing the guy off. It doesn't work.

"I can't get him off me, Jill! Call 911!"

Where's Jill? Why isn't she responding?

Cody is growing frantic. His fear is like a cold chisel in his heart. In his mind's eye, he sees Jill standing behind him with a phone to her ear.

"Jill, call the police!"

But moments later, Cody's mental image of Jill collapses when he hears nothing behind him.

The guy has him pinned to the floor with one finger, his arm a steel rod, and Cody is powerless to fight him off.

He knows he's been tricked, and now trapped.

❊   ❊   ❊

Cody is propped in a chair, the room dark, his mind gripped with terror, his body a whirlpool of numbing sensation. For an instant, he's aware of the totality of his mistake, his error in judgment. Jill was never present. The conversations they had never took place. There was no glass slipper in the bathtub. No impending phone call to the police.

Everything happened at the door: the friendly young man entering; Cody backing him out; them talking briefly at the door; then the smaller, tougher, more aggressive young man rushing in and forcing Cody to the floor.

A moment later, Cody's certainty evaporates and he realizes something much darker took place. Neither man was real.

A voice is in Cody's ear. It sounds nothing like the two intruders. It's an animal sound: a hiss with sharp, white teeth. It carries warning. No words.

He tries to move but doesn't put much effort into it; he knows he won't be able to. He is strangely calm, strangely accepting of his situation.

To his right, he sees a cloaked figure of darkness streaked with dull orange light. Other shapes of similar appearance are also in the darkened room.

The voice is in his ear again. It's giving information, again without words. It pings the inside of Cody's skull, emitting meaning in incandescent blasts. It's telling him the shapes in the room are reverberations of the master.

Fear grips Cody, smothering his thoughts. His heart feels like an empty bucket standing under a threatening sky.

The cloaked figure of darkness makes its way to Cody, emitting a sound like ripping cloth. It looms over him, and shifts into a man-shape with the cunning, grinning face of a wolf. It begins talking.

"What do you know about the spies?"

Cody tries to answer, but finds himself blocked, unable to speak. He senses he's catching core meaning. He thinks this is important to the master, as he's been tracking this information a long time. Cody is not his first subject.

"Tell us what you know about the spies."

Again, Cody finds himself unable to speak.

"How long have you been on the earth plane?"

Cody struggles to speak, and finds his voice. "My whole life."

Cody hears a loud slap, feels a sting across his jaw, mild electrical zings in his face. It doesn't faze him. In fact, it sets up armor. If this is the worst it gets ...

"You lied to me. Don't lie to me again."

His inquisitor's face becomes snarled with anger.

"How long?" he shouts. "Are you a jumper? Where did you come from? What are your intentions?"

Cody feels a powerful blow across his face. He hits the floor, the chair toppling with him. His skull is a black cauldron of pain. His nasal passages swell; he can't breathe through them. He sucks in air through his mouth.

A hand clamps his mouth shut and exerts enormous force. He begins to panic, and then senses hands tearing his attacker away. But his attacker is strong, and for a long time Cody is unable to breathe. He sinks into black-water oblivion.

Slowly, Cody regains consciousness. He sees his antagonist bobbing a few feet away, two of the other shapes restraining him.

Another shape—a woman, it seems—is ministering to Cody. His chair is upright now. Somehow, she's easing his pain. His head doesn't hurt so much anymore.

Then Cody's lower back begins to hurt—a throbbing pain of epic proportions, which intensifies as the woman-shape drifts away and a man-shape looms, his face sharp with wolflike features.

"I am Ty," he says. "For your enlightenment, a jumper hangs on to earth for dear life and fails to return to his own world, where he might be in big trouble, or worse: maimed. We search for jumpers. We seek to return them to where they rightfully belong. All we want is information, and then we go."

This gladdens Cody's heart. Despite his pain, he feels the ordeal will soon be over, his pain with it.

Ty seems indecisive for a moment, and then resumes his former assertiveness. "Where is your ID?"

"In my wallet."

"Where is that?"

"In the bedroom, on the dresser."

One of the shapes leaves, and moments later returns. Cody has the impression he or she has his wallet and is going through it.

"Is Cody Hobbs your name?" Ty asks.

"Yes."

"How long have you lived here?"

"Nine months."

"Age?"

"Twenty-three."

"You work for the Army?"

"Yes."

Cody's back pain is still intense. It's weighing him down. He wonders why they didn't ask these questions to begin with. He wants them to go.

"Do you feel you have awareness of people, places, and things you can no longer find?"

The question hangs in the air, a frightful quality to it, and Cody is no longer afraid of these people but afraid of what they might uncover about him. He knows the answer. It has been inside him a long time.

"Yes, I have such awareness."

Ty moves in closer.

"Do you feel you have skills, knowledge, and aptitude for things beyond your reach?"

"Yes!" It explodes from Cody, as if another part of him leaped out.

"Do you ever go out and search for these things?"

"Yes, I go out searching."

A thing inside him is speaking. Cody wants it to shut up. He feels he'll get in trouble if it keeps talking.

But it won't shut up.

"I go out but find nothing; everything is for other people. Nothing is for me. All the things of this world. Nothing. I'm in prison. I want out."

Something pings the inside of Cody's skull, and something small and lively escapes from him. He watches it leap about the darkened room, an energized spot of orange light. He wonders what it is. Then he hears Jill's voice, like from far away.

"It's your soul part, Cody."

He knows that's what they wanted all along, the emergence of this part of him, the one that knows all and tells all: how Cody has lied and cheated, how he's followed children around, how he's always wanted to do better but always fell short, how he's always set a course but couldn't navigate too well, how he's always put out effort but couldn't sustain it.

The orange shapes move in closer, the intruders and his own soul part, looming over him. He hears them conferring.

He realizes Ty is frightened, for he knows that if this soul part leaped from Cody, something similar can leap from him, and he might discover something unsettling about himself.

He sees that it throws the intruders off—the idea of an unsettling mirror within. Ty looks like he wants to close the interview off. He's angry.

"What do you do to the children?"

"I attack them," Cody says, "for being small and weak and vulnerable to forces they can't understand or control."

"It's true, then," Ty says. "The children are in danger. You must change. You must stop attacking them."

"I am not a danger to children," Cody says, "only cognizant of their ignorance and folly, wondering how much of it is still my own ignorance and folly."

Cody does not recognize this part of him—these thoughts, this manner of expression—but senses it sprang from another soul part within him. He is hopeful Ty will release him from the chair now and leave.

"Who is your god?"

Cody finds himself blocked, unable to speak.

"You must have a god."

Cody feels a wrenching pain in his mouth. He can't reach up to protect himself. Something bad is happening there.

Voices and shapes swirl around him, and soon he is on the floor, the intruders gone, his memories fading.

He crawls toward the phone, where Jill used to be, though Jill was never there. He sees himself in a mirror, a crumpled form.

He fights the desertion of his memories. He doesn't want to forget anything but knows he will. He thinks the police will have lots of questions he won't be able to answer. Some he won't want to answer.

Something is wrong with his back. He can barely crawl. But he knows he will make it to the phone. It's inevitable. He's making progress across the floor, ticking along like a disabled insect. He will make it. He prepares himself for a long process of healing and questions.

He loses consciousness, regains consciousness, loses track of time. He's still making progress across the floor. His soul part seems to be forcing him along. He doesn't want it to come out again in that unbridled form. What will he do if it does, if it spills it all to the cops?

A slow, darkening fear begins to eclipse him, throw him into deep shadow, as he takes the phone in hand and draws it to his ear.

He hears a buzz.

He punches 911.

He hears a voice.

He cannot speak into the phone. He tries but cannot. Something is wrong with his mouth. He can't speak, but he keeps the line open. He knows they will come anyway.

He loses consciousness.

He regains consciousness as the cops burst in. He hears their movements and voices.

"Call an ambulance. Take the phone from him."

Cody surrenders the phone, puts a hand to his mouth. Why can't I speak? He explores.

His jaw is broken. Two of his top front teeth are missing.

Children? Ty is a danger to children. That's what he remembers. And mirrors. He remembers mirrors.

And something else. Ty tossing a pair of bloody teeth into the air while Cody was propped in the chair. Ty telling him to say …

"Say 'Kiss the wolf.'"

Cody saying it. It came out in a bloody squall, Cody's tongue hitting the gap where his teeth had been.

"Kiss da wolf."

CHAPTER 19

In the Grip of Lycanthropy

With the sinking sun at her back, Katrina Werewolf is maneuvering through an affluent section of Los Angeles when a scent alerts her. She sinks low to the ground and spots the cop with the broken-down physique and red-rimmed eyes standing on the next block.

As she approaches the cop, who goes by the name Festus, she sees his jaw go slack, his eyes go dark and fearful.

"It can't be true," the cop says. "We're all dead? All of us?"

"It's true, Festus. We're all dead."

The cop wanders away, his head loose on its swivel.

Katrina lies low for a while, waiting for twilight to end. In darkness, she strikes out for Jonathan West's house, hoping to avoid police surveillance.

Walking along the boundary of a big estate, she sees a young couple passing by on the street. The girl is wearing a big floppy hat, and looks radiantly happy. The guy has two black eyes. They're red and puffy, also. The girl in the floppy hat more than likely has been using him as a punching bag, Katrina thinks. What an insanely submissive fool he is.

She crouches in deep shadow, eyes intent upon them, jaw set, an intake of breath preparing her. She's going to close the distance, rush them, coldcock the guy first and then the girl. Lay them both out on the street.

With silent tread and honed killer instinct, she follows them. From out of nowhere, the cop falls in beside her, and Katrina feels her hackles rise.

She spins about in rage.

She doesn't need this encounter with Festus. She has to focus all her energy on Jonathan West, after she deals with this couple she's following.

"You're dead, Festus! Accept it!"

"Katrina, dead or not, I'm a cop. I've got a job to do. I can't let you assault these people."

Katrina breathes deeply. Her rage dies a slow death. By and by, she says, "Fair enough."

"Katrina, I know you're a werewolf, but what exactly is it you do?"

"I bring people's soul parts out."

"What's a soul part?"

"It's a feisty little spirit that dwells within us."

"Fair enough, I guess."

"Festus, I force people to access a mysterious part of themselves—a feisty little thing called a soul part. Soul parts are capable of yielding penetrating information. That's my mission, teasing information from people's soul parts."

Festus scribbles on a notepad, and then says, "So, you're not purely brutal, huh? You have a redeeming purpose. I'll include that in my report. Is there anything you need, Katrina?"

"I could use some help in tracking down a name on my list."

"What's the name?"

"Spiros."

Festus makes a note. "How'd that name come up?"

"Soul parts often mention Spiros. It made my list."

She strikes out again for Jonathan West's house, but Festus hooks her arm, halting her.

"Katrina, have you ever had the sky dry up and plink you in the eye with an expectorant? An *aha!* kind of experience? I know I've heard that name before."

"I've had that kind of experience. I've been plinked in the eye. I think it was a sparrow."

"That's the unlucky phase. I'll track Spiros down for you. What's going on, Katrina? What have you been hearing?"

"Ideas are floating around, Festus. The most powerful one is that we are all dead."

"No. It can't be."

"We're dead, Festus. A cataclysmic event killed us all."

✻   ✻   ✻

Flower gardens drench Katrina Werewolf's nostrils with powerful scents as she ambles up the sidewalk to Jonathan West's front door. She knocks on the door, and Jonathan, with fresh cuts and bruises on his face, lets her in.

Katrina stands in the entryway, keeping a wary eye on him.

Nervous, hesitant to talk, Jonathan is massaging his injured jaw.

"Can you tell me what happened?" Katrina asks.

"I'm not sure I can."

They walk through the foyer.

"None of us remember exactly," Katrina says.

"I know. Are you still crosschecking everything with your source?"

"I am." It's a lie. Katrina hasn't been able to locate Spiros, her source.

"I feel I'm never alone," Jonathan says. "I feel I'm being watched all the time. Strange objects appear in my hands. I experience lapses in memory, blank spaces. Sometimes I forget who I am."

They walk into the living room and sit opposite each other on matching sofas.

Earlier in the day, in the grip of lycanthropy, Jonathan had assaulted Katrina and forced her out the door. But now Jonathan's energy and awful focus are gone. Nothing hyper remains. He reclines on the sofa, his eyes registering a quiet, contemplative shock. He seems to be searching for some inner resilience; not able to find it, his eyes search the room, settling on Katrina.

Katrina knows this to be a dangerous time. She watches the roaming eyes for hints of lurking strategy.

Jonathan shift his eyes to three framed photos on a bureau. A woman. A boy. A girl. They're his wife and kids.

Katrina stands. It's time to trigger his soul part.

"I'm going to ask you a series of questions," she says. "Don't respond until I've asked them all."

She fires the questions at Jonathan.

"Have you started doing things with people you've never seen before? Have you acquired recent new skills or knowledge? Do you have any injuries you can't account for? Have you felt threatened by an entity that seems to assemble near you? Do you come alive and find that you are trapped inside someone else?"

Jonathan eases upright on the sofa. He looks at Katrina, and then at the photos on the bureau.

"Where's your family, Jonathan?"

Jonathan falls back sobbing.

"Did you kill them?"

Katrina takes Jonathan through the house on a search for his wife and kids, half expecting to find them butchered and hidden away somewhere, but does not find them. Jonathan says they've gone away.

"They might be here, Jonathan. Someone is controlling what we can see."

"How can they do that?"

"They entrain us and plant suggestions. A mind can be disabled from seeing what's there."

They return to the living room.

"We're entrained, Jonathan. It's deep entrainment."

They sit on the sofas facing each other.

"You have a strange name," Jonathan says.

"Yes."

"Why Katrina Werewolf?"

"It's my darkness."

"Your darkness?"

"Yes. It's a source of intelligence I use for survival. Otherwise, I'm just a little girl, nothing."

"Why would the ones behind this create a powerful entity like Katrina Werewolf?"

"They didn't create Katrina Werewolf. It has always existed inside me. It's my soul part."

Blood begins trickling from Jonathan's mouth. "How'd they do that?" he asks, his hands pressed to his mouth.

"I don't know."

They scramble on the floor and find Jonathan's tooth, caked in blood, under a sofa.

Jonathan runs to the bathroom to wash it off.

Katrina feels constricted in her breathing. She knows they're attempting to do something to her. But they can't do much as long as she's a werewolf. Nevertheless, her sense of self is wavering.

"Do you have it?" she asks when Jonathan returns from the bathroom.

"I've got it. What now?"

"Stick it back in, I think."

He sticks the tooth back in place.

"Will it stay in there?" she asks.

"No, I've got to hold it in."

"Shove it in there. How are you doing pain-wise?"

"I'm holding up."

They return to the sofas.

"What now?" Jonathan asks.

"Remove your hand, see if it'll stay in."

He does, and it stays in.

"You need to see a dentist, Jonathan. Call tonight, say it's an emergency."

"I will."

Katrina leaves, thinking Jonathan is doomed unless his soul part comes out and saves him. Something dark is focused on this house.

Jonathan walks outside and sees Katrina Werewolf off. Standing on his front lawn, he sees a murky figure take shape beside him. Fear begins percolating in him. His heart speeds up. What did Katrina Werewolf say about an entity that seems to assemble near you?

Jonathan backs away from the entity, his mind suffused with horror.

The entity is small but growing. It has no face.

An adventuresome piece of Jonathan's mind beckons to it, and in a darkly fascinating way, the entity springs fully to life.

Now it's bigger. Now it walks on two legs. Now it has a face.

Jonathan trembles, and senses he might want to escape the area. Fear sparks his body to move, but it moves only slightly, and slowly. He fears he is not fast enough.

Jonathan gives in to a powerful inner tide, and again is in the grip of lycanthropy. He stares at the dark, soulful eyes of the entity, and knows what it is.

It's his soul part, the dark angel that will orchestrate his salvation. He beckons to it, and they merge as one and amble down the sidewalk.

Jonathan picks up Katrina Werewolf's scent. He will hunt with her tonight.

CHAPTER 20

Places Where the Usual Rules Don't Apply

Endicott drives to a residence on Laurel Canyon Boulevard in the Hollywood Hills and parks in the spacious driveway. The house is a multistory Mediterranean affair with white stucco walls and a red-tile roof.

He gets out of his car and pauses to eye a brace of jacaranda trees in full bloom in the front yard. He inhales the sweet scent of their purple blossoms as he walks to the front door.

The man who lives here is a friend of Endicott's from his days at Hollywood Division. He knocks on the big oak door and waits, his mind sorting out recent developments in the case.

Victims say the predator has begun paying them return visits. They say he comes back to torture them a second time. LAPD has analyzed the attacks and has confirmed a pattern of repeat visits. State and federal authorities have authorized the use of deadly force to take out the predator. LAPD is planning an ambush: cops with guns drawn will sit up over a victim, and when the predator pays a return visit, kill him.

Moments later, Rich Mauk opens the door.

"Good day, Scott. How are you?"

"I could be better, Rich. How about you?"

"I'm holding up. Come in." He guides Endicott down a hallway to the back of the house and into a dimly lit room.

"Sit in that chair," Rich says, pointing to a bulky shape in the center of the room.

In the gloom, the chair doesn't look like a chair; it resembles a bear rearing back on its haunches. Approaching it, Endicott can almost feel the rake of teeth and claws on his flesh.

Warily, he settles into the chair, but nothing bad happens.

He looks around the room. The walls are lined with books. Rich Mauk is a student of many disciplines.

Rich slumps in a chair a few feet away, leans back, gazes upward.

Endicott looks up and spies a filmy structure suspended in the air. The darkness lends it a spectral look.

"It's a spidery thing," Rich says. "They hide in shadows or cracks, or even in plain sight. There, it's gone."

Rich Mauk is a motion picture special-effects designer. He's also a mechanical engineer and has expertise in military camouflage systems.

When Endicott called, Rich said there was little doubt what was going on. It was a military technology operating illegally.

* * *

Rich opens the shades, and sunshine floods in. He returns to his chair, slumps into it, and fixes his gaze on Endicott.

"What have you learned?" Endicott asks. He'd asked Rich to check his sources.

"Are you sure you want to hear it?"

"Yes."

"When a victim wakes," Rich says, "the predator has him strapped to a chair and he's performing a surgical procedure on his face. He softens part of the face and removes a tooth. If the victim has two teeth gone, the predator has seen him twice, though he won't remember it. Sometimes he softens half the face, the jaw, or part of the skull, and removes it, either with his hands or with medical instruments.

"The victim is out of it. He doesn't know his own name or where he's at. When it wears off, he comes to and experiences shock and pain.

"Memories of the predator are vague; victims can't identify him. When the victim finally sees the cops, he's in the hospital and can't talk too well, if at all. A doctor has told him a portion of his face has been removed.

"The police can't solve it so they call in the FBI. The FBI can't solve it so they call in the military. The military can't solve it, but they don't want to. They secretly run it.

"Word of mouth inflames citizens. The media reports it, until a few reporters get assaulted, then they back off. They know it's too dangerous for them.

"The military canvasses itself. Do we have something like this? If we do, no one is likely to admit it. They sense

LAPD is useless. Special Forces commandos are sent to L.A. to blend in with the population.

"The assaults continue. The victims pile up. Media exercises self-blackout. Word of mouth fuels watchfulness, fear, and panic.

"Investigators from all jurisdictions know there is danger afoot not just from the immediate threat posed by the predator, but from something much bigger. They fear a rogue element of government is exercising a new type of control—one that seizes our minds.

"The military has a hidden presence in Los Angeles and surrounding communities, on the street and through electronic surveillance. They have analyzed the assaults: consciousness is targeted; bone and tissue are targeted, usually skull and face; a strange force is involved; an astute operator does it; there's a clandestine feel to it, with spies all around; and an underground organization behind it."

Rich falls silent for a few moments, and then he says, "Does it scare you?"

"It scares me," Endicott says.

"I thought it would. It scares me, also."

"Rich, I'm here to make a formal request. LAPD needs help in outsmarting the technology so we can take out the predator. Tell me what you know from an engineering standpoint."

"The technology creates offbeat environments, human-like images, and voices. It shields the ones who run it. I don't know how it originated. Obviously, someone engineered a brilliant black-box technology. Scott, it's not a human being that's doing it, it's a technology. You won't find anyone made of flesh and blood."

"LAPD disagrees, Rich. We believe the predator is flesh and blood and is coupled with the technology. We intend to take the predator out and flush the conspirators out into the open."

Rich's face remains impassive.

Endicott says, "Someone must have their hand on the toggle switch."

"Yes, the government—the military, actually. A secret stratum of it. They've got a natural instinct for the toggle switch." Rich pauses. "Scott, tell me, what's your gut instinct on this? Not on the technology or the conspirators. Just on the raw experience of it."

"You want it raw? I'll tell you. Everything is layered with deceit. You might think you're interacting with another individual, when, in fact, you're not."

"Yes, exactly. There are a million layers of deceit. What are your impressions otherwise?"

"It intensifies life experience."

Rich sits up straighter. "What else?"

"We're being transformed."

Rich leans forward. "Now you're talking." He rises from his chair and motions for Endicott to follow him.

They are sitting on the veranda in back of the house, taking in the flower gardens and the clear blue sky.

"Scott, on occasion I've noticed faint blue glows in the air, no doubt driven by the technology. My sources say they're called lines of demarcation. I've seen them while sitting right here. I've passed through them while driving. I believe we all pass through them many times a day.

"Let's go find one. All it takes is a little trip downhill. We'll go in my car."

They get into Rich's car, and Rich drives downhill on a twisty path through the streets, looking for a faint blue glow in the air.

"Scott, there are places where the usual rules don't apply. I know of one such place. There are others. In those places, you'll find yourself doing new things with new people. You'll find yourself possessed of new knowledge. You might have wounds you can't account for. Your life might be in danger there. You might want to get out of there but find you can't. You're stuck with it for a while. You have a new world with its own rules, its own history, and strange, tricky edges to it. It's a world in the making, and you're a person in the making. Are you ready?"

A moment later, they are enveloped in a faint blue glow.

They find an outdoor café, sit in the shade, place their orders, and wait for the waitress to depart. But instead of departing, she sits down with them.

Endicott sees a glow in the center of her mass—a spot of orange. He sees it clearly beneath her brown jumper and white blouse, beneath layers of flesh. It appears for an instant and then goes away.

"Say, you two," she says, "I know what the technology did before it went ape. It altered ambient light to produce shields of protective coloration around military troops and equipment. But what happened next? Why is everything so different now?"

Endicott and Rich exchange looks and then study her. She is small of stature, has feathery blond hair, and a mischievous look in her eyes. She's an elf.

Endicott sees the spot of orange inside her again, sees it pulse. He senses a spot of orange inside himself, and feels it pulse. Somehow, he knows the thing inside him is his soul part.

His soul part leaps out, and then leaps about the cobblestones as if in joyous release. It starts to speak for Endicott. He doesn't know if he wants it to speak, for it relays strange, forbidden knowledge.

He listens to it, his own mouth forming the words. He talks of things he had no prior knowledge of. He settles into a narrative, the elf listening raptly.

"I'll tell you what happened next," Endicott says, scooting his chair closer to the elf. "Scientists discovered that altering ambient light also altered earth's natural environments, customs, laws, and everything."

The elf smiles.

"Nice," she says, "but what about us? Who are we? I saw you two right off. That little glow."

"That little glow inside us is our essence; our outside is camouflage. Officially, the U.S. Army calls us ephemeral light beings. We call ourselves spiritual kin."

"It's our technology, right, not theirs?"

"It's ours. We come from the light, not them."

"Did it go ape?"

"The technology never truly went ape. It's still under

our control, but there's a mysterious other that runs it, too. A horse of a different color, you might say. We don't know who it is. Humans have taken to calling it Woodsman, for convenience. Woodsman takes it beyond our boundaries."

"Oh, my!" she says. "I've heard it can produce the sound of footsteps down an empty corridor."

"It can. Anywhere, actually."

"What else can it do? Can you tell me?"

"We can use acoustics to fracture facial bones, loosen teeth, and cause eyes to pop out of sockets. We can select specific bones, specific teeth, and specify which eye to pop out. We can pick an ailment for our subject, cause loss of equilibrium, vomiting, and migraines. We can cause whole armies to collapse by assaulting the central nervous system.

"We can spook you at a distance, cause an eerie feeling, and warn you away from a location. We can confuse you and redirect you. We can drop a cocoon of sound around you and make you think you're in the presence of ghosts or your ancestors, while the person next to you is experiencing an entirely different constellation of effects.

"With magnetic fields and electromagnetic pulses, we can replace your environment subjectively, create a presence that seems real, and engage in communication and torture from remote locations. We can make a person think they're hearing the voice of God.

"Our remote sensors can measure the brain's electrical fields, enabling us to record electrical imprints of thoughts and stored memory. No one can lie to us about anything.

"Under the duress of a presence we introduce, we can induce illness or death. We can make the presence speak and foretell the death of the subject. The suggestion can be strong enough to stop the heart."

Weariness and a touch of caution creep into Endicott's mind. He stops speaking and looks around. "I think school's out for the day," he says.

"I'm impressed," the elf says.

"Amazing, isn't it?" Endicott says.

"Yes, it's amazing."

"Questions?"

"No." The elf scurries off with their orders.

Endicott sees his soul part bound to him, leap off the cobblestones and into him. It now seems to reside deep inside him, quivering and then shutting its secrets off to him and the world.

Endicott stretches his arms, neck, and shoulders, takes an unhurried, deep breath, shrugs off a bout of sleepiness. He hears the chatter of a squirrel, spies it on the cobblestones, sees something in its paws, its teeth. He watches it scamper up a tree.

He feels something trickle from his mouth. His fingers go to his lips, come away with blood on them. He picks up a napkin and begins mopping his lips.

"Are you okay?" Rich asks.

"No ... not okay. Are you experiencing trouble?"

"Maybe." Rich's hands go to his mouth.

Endicott sees blood seeping from Rich's mouth. The damage isn't bad. He sees a man at another table holding his jaw, blood seeping through his fingers. The man is stoic. The pain must be awful, Endicott thinks. His jaw is misshapen.

"I'll call an ambulance," Rich says.

Minutes later, an ambulance arrives and the man is taken away on a stretcher.

"Why were we targeted?" Endicott asks.

"Everyone's being targeted," Rich says. "It's constant, around the clock."

"It seemed like a dud, though, didn't it?"

"It did. They attempted to do something to us and it didn't work. They want things to appear seamless, so they might try again. Watch for changes in the environment in the next few minutes."

Moments later, a man dressed in brown walks up to Endicott and Rich and sits at their table. His face is blank as he studies Endicott.

Rich leans back in his chair, as if giving the man a signal.

"Sir," the man says, speaking to Endicott, "the technology was originally conceived of as a protective-coloration technology that shielded troops and equipment from enemy observation. From that simple beginning, it evolved into a comprehensive technology of war.

"The sound of footsteps down an empty corridor, a presence entering your environment, altered states of consciousness, injury, illness, torture—all can be created from a distance.

"Effects-producing devices can be operated remotely from any location in the world. We don't need a person present at the scene, though a person can be in the area to observe.

"Acoustics can be used to create fractures in facial bones, loosen teeth, and cause eyes to pop out of sockets. We can select specific bones, specific teeth, and specify which eye we want to pop out.

"In controlled environments, as a person loses touch with ordinary reality, we can apply full psychological effects and own them. I can't describe the psychological techniques we use. It involves signals that work on the brain.

"With acoustics, we can pick an ailment for our subject, cause loss of equilibrium, vomiting, and migraines. We can cause whole armies to collapse by assaulting the nervous system.

"We can spook you at a distance, cause an eerie feeling, and warn you away from a location. We can confuse you and redirect you.

"We can drop a cocoon of sound around you and make you think you're in the presence of ghosts or your ancestors, while the person next to you is experiencing an entirely different constellation of effects.

"With directed electromagnetic waves, we can produce any number of actual physical effects or just the sensation of them. We can alter consciousness, create a presence, simulate torture, or do it for real. We can ask questions via acoustic technology and record responses. We can make you think you're hearing the voice of God.

"We can replace the environment subjectively for the individual, create a presence that seems real, and engage in communication and torture. We can do all this without having a person present other than to monitor the effects.

"Our remote sensor technology can measure the brain's

electrical fields, enabling us to record electrical imprints of thoughts and stored memory.

"We can monitor and influence behavior. We can scare the subject. We can make him quit work for the day. We can make him give up confidential information. We can insert an entity or presence that relays a rumor, or a news bulletin, influencing mindsets and decision-making. We can blank things from minds, anything we want."

The man pauses.

"Sir, I don't know what's going on in L.A. The people I work for are exhibiting signs of extreme nervousness. Security is extra tight, and deadly measures seem to be in the works."

The man gets up and leaves.

Rich looks around. "I think school's out for the day."

"Did I hear it right?" Endicott says. "They can produce the sound of footsteps down an empty corridor?"

"They can. Anywhere, actually."

"I'm impressed," Endicott says.

"Amazing, isn't it?"

"Yes, it's amazing."

Endicott stretches his arms, neck, and shoulders, takes an unhurried, deep breath, shrugs off a bout of sleepiness. He hears the chatter of a squirrel, spies it on the cobblestones, sees something in its paws, its teeth. He watches it scamper up a tree.

The elf returns, serves their food. She leans close to Endicott, hands him a folded piece of paper, and says, "This is for you. I wrote it myself."

She scurries off.

Endicott unfolds the paper and reads it.

When a person is losing things—their freedom, their dignity, their body, their mind—they bargain with opposing forces and try to salvage as much as they can. This is a process that tries men's souls. Much is given up in return for keeping slight particles of oneself. Deals are struck. Regrets come later. You become an agent for the only commodity you have. Your soul. And you spend the rest of your life bartering it away. We all go down that path. None of us ever gets off it. It's our only reality.

Taped to the paper are two wooden matches.

Endicott holds both matches together, leans over, strikes them on a cobblestone, and burns the paper.

He watches the paper—and the elf's philosophy—go up in flames.

"Rich, I'm going to kill the predator." He waits for a response from Rich. There is none.

"I'm going to kill him, Rich. He's taken my daughter away from me. You can choose to help me or not. I'll give you one week to decide."

CHAPTER 21

He's Still Fighting World War II

Sammy Mangold rushes into his house, slams the door, locks it. He's trembling; his heart is racing. He walks around his living room on wobbly legs. His head hurts; he's in a fog, seeing stars. He stands at a window and peers outside. No sign of her. He closes all the shades and collapses into his big easy chair.

He's terrified of Katrina Werewolf—she keeps assaulting him. He can't defend himself. Tormented, he picks up his phone and dials the number for the Los Angeles Police Department.

"I want to report an assault."

"Who was assaulted?"

"I was." Sammy gives his name.

"Are you injured? Do you need medical attention?"

"I don't know. My head is swimming."

"Where are you?"

Sammy gives his address.

"Is the person who assaulted you still in the area?"

"I think she might be."

"She?"

"I know her name. Katrina."

"Katrina. What's her last name?"

"Endicott."

"Stay where you are. Stay on the line. I'm sending a patrol car."

Watching through a gap in the curtains, Sammy sees a police car pull to the curb. "They're here," he says into the phone. He terminates the call and goes to the door.

The cops put Sammy in the backseat of their cruiser, and then drive through the neighborhood looking for Katrina. They don't find her.

They take Sammy to a medical clinic for an examination, and then downtown to police headquarters.

* * *

Detective Donte Rivers reads the investigative report written by one of the patrol officers, and then introduces himself to Sammy. "Are you sure you're okay, Sammy?"

"I think so. I'm no longer seeing stars."

"Glad to hear it." Rivers watches Sammy with much interest. Sammy is a muscular man in a green polo shirt and blue jeans. His hands are the size of boulders. There are nicks and bruises on his fists and face from recent violence. The report says he's sixty-one, a former professional wrestler. The doctor who examined him says he has a mild concussion.

"Can you tell me what happened?" Rivers asks.

"Katrina Endicott assaulted me. She mainly used punches."

Rivers leans forward. "Sammy, you've got multiple bruises and cuts on your face and defensive wounds on your hands. Did you hit anyone?"

"No."

"You mentioned Spiros in your statement. Can you tell me what role he played?"

"Spiros told Katrina to assault me. Katrina is a werewolf."

Rivers leans back in his chair. "Tell me about it, Sammy."

"Spiros set Katrina up as a werewolf. Then he told me she was going to attack me. Okay, I thought, once for practice. But she's been attacking me ever since. How can you defend yourself against a werewolf? I figure the deal is off."

"Why did Spiros do this?"

"Spiros is still fighting World War II. He says he's preparing the civilian population for combat."

Rivers makes a note. He'll call Endicott and tell him his daughter was mentioned in a crime report.

"Sammy, for the record, can you give me a description of Spiros?"

"Sure. He's about six-four, wears black-frame glasses, has short brown hair, and a husky build."

Rivers records the description, and then asks Sammy to describe Katrina.

"She looks like a werewolf," Sammy says.

Endicott and Lukens arrive and confer with Rivers.

"Sammy says Spiros arranged for Katrina to assault him."

"My daughter?"

"I think so. Sammy lives in your neighborhood."

Endicott and Lukens take Sammy into an interview room and sit at a table across from him.

"Tell me what happened, Sammy," Endicott says.

Sammy relates the events once more, as he did for Rivers.

"What do you want us to do, Sammy, pick up Katrina?"

"No, don't pick her up. She's as innocent as me."

"But you don't like being hit."

"Right. I don't like being hit."

Endicott and Lukens step outside the room.

"We need to take a closer look at Spiros as the predator, Lionel. My daughter is frequently missing. She's gone for a while, then returns, then she's gone again. It's killing me, and her mother. When I do see her, she always mentions Spiros."

"Scott, if Spiros is involved, he's just a pawn in a bigger game. It's a technology. I'd bet my life on it."

"Don't forget, Lionel, it's Spiros's technology. To rescue my daughter, I've got to find Spiros."

"How are you going to find Spiros?"

"We'll use Sammy as bait. Let's go back in there."

They go inside the interview room.

"Sammy, this guy Spiros interests me. Since he's paying you visits, maybe we can work out a deal. How about this: we'll keep watch inside your house, and when Spiros pays you a return visit, we'll take him down."

Sammy shakes his head.

"We'll be concealed inside your house, Sammy. We'll take him down the moment he shows."

"You don't know what you're asking. Spiros would know if I was setting him up. He'd kill me."

"You came here, Sammy."

"Yes, but I didn't know what I was doing at the time. I had a head injury."

"Sammy, he's manipulating you and everyone else."

"Don't say that. Spiros can hear us. He can hurt us."

Endicott and Lukens leave the room.

"Do we have any leverage at all?" Endicott asks.

"It doesn't look like it."

"We can't substitute a cop as a decoy. Spiros wouldn't bite. We need a victim. It hinges on the victim's permission."

They go back inside.

"Sammy," Endicott says, "I won't kid you. We're looking for your permission to camp inside your house. We'll kill the predator as soon as he shows and end this."

Sammy's face turns ashen. His lips tremble. "Spiros would know. He would kill us all. He's still fighting World War II."

"You can go, Sammy."

Sammy leaves.

"We'll get permission from another victim, Lionel."

"Maybe we shouldn't, Scott. The victims are terrified."

"It's my daughter, Lionel."

Carlisle calls Endicott and Lukens into his office.

"Daryl Chapman's wife called," Carlisle says. "She wants you to come to the rehab hospital right away. She says her husband told her something. She says it's important."

Endicott and Lukens drive to the rehabilitation hospital where Chapman is a patient.

"I've already seen Chapman," Endicott says. "He has a young wife. She's being trained to take care of him at home once he's released. He's on a ventilator. He can't talk but can mouth words. I think he had something to say when I saw him. I just wasn't able to catch it."

They pull into the parking lot, enter the building. They walk down the hallway, enter Chapman's room, and greet Chapman's wife, Tricia.

"He's been excited ever since he heard you were coming," she says.

They stand over Chapman's bed. Chapman's thin, shrunken form lies beneath a sheet. His eyes are closed. His face is bony, like a skull wrapped in tissue. The rhythmic hiss of the ventilator sets up a resonance inside Endicott. For every breath forced into Chapman, something thumps inside Endicott.

"He's sleeping," Tricia says. "He goes in and out."

Chapman's eyelids float open. His eyes drift and settle on his wife.

"They're here, honey."

Chapman's thin lips move.

Endicott watches intently.

"Slow down, honey. Let these men ask you questions."

Chapman's lips go still.

"Can you describe the person who assaulted you?" Endicott asks.

Chapman's lips move, forming a stream of words.

Endicott makes out some of the words, but the full meaning escapes him until Chapman's wife translates.

"He's saying, 'I saw him at Tripler. He had a shoulder injury like mine.'"

"You saw him at Tripler?" Endicott asks.

Yes.

"He had a shoulder injury?"

Yes.

"The one who assaulted you?"

Yes.

"Can you describe him?"

They wait.

Then his lips move again.

I know his name.

"You know his name?"

Yes.

"What's his name?"

His lips move, but Endicott can't make out the name. He looks at Chapman's wife.

"Are you saying 'Otis Dietrich,' honey?"

Yes.

Chapman's eyes drift out of focus and his lids close.

Endicott asks Tricia to step out into the hallway with him and Lukens.

"You're good at reading lips," Endicott says to her.

"I solved it earlier," she says. "It took about a hundred guesses before I got Otis Dietrich. Then I called Carlisle."

"Go back in there and wait for us," Endicott says.

She goes inside the room.

"I wonder," Endicott says, "if Chapman's memory is intact. I'd hate for this Otis Dietrich, if there is such a person, to be just a bunch of misfiring synapses."

They go back into the room.

Daryl Chapman is alert now, mouthing the same name.

Otis Dietrich.

CHAPTER 22

The Extinction Event

The doorbell rings at Endicott's house and he goes to see who's there. The man standing on his front porch is wearing two clocks attached to golden chains, a big clock fastened to his belt, a smaller clock tucked into a vest pocket.

"Good evening," the man says. "Thank you for accommodating me at this late hour. As you know, we are in a bit of a fix."

The man points at his clocks. "A trifle noticeable, aren't they? They tell me they are for synchronization."

Endicott studies his visitor. The man has a rotund body, an unhurried manner, a voice reminiscent of Alfred Hitchcock's, and a face like an oil painting.

"Good evening," Endicott says. "Come in out of the night."

In the subdued light of the foyer, Endicott takes a covert look at his visitor. The man's skull is square, his nose and cheeks flat, his chest bulky, his waist a barrel. He is burnt bright red from the sun; walks with a clump on one side, as if something is wrong with a foot or shoe; and carries a battered old leather attaché case.

Endicott leads his visitor into the living room, where a jungle of potted plants greets them with an aroma of pure intoxication.

"Sit anywhere," Endicott says.

The man peers about and then selects a sofa to sit on.

Endicott eases into an easy chair across from him.

The man fixes Endicott with a gaze. "Are we alone?"

"Yes."

The man gazes around the room and then looks upward. "Endicott, your ceilings are magnificent. They soar to the sky."

Endicott smiles. "Yes, I know they do. I didn't catch your name when they called."

"Oh, I'm sorry. They're harried, of course. This business is erupting in ways we hadn't anticipated." His eyes continue to sail around the room. The gold links of his chains glint in the chandelier light.

"I bet they're busy," Endicott says. "Busy as bees."

"It's William, Endicott. That's my name. William Chills. A strange one, eh?"

Endicott nods. "I've heard stranger ones."

"There's no one else in the house?"

"No one."

"It's okay if there is. I'd just like to be informed."

"There's no one else here."

"We can start then." William unbuckles his attaché case, pulls out a notebook, and pages though it.

Sensing William needs a moment to prepare, Endicott rises from his easy chair and walks to the patio door. He pulls the drapes open, ties them back with a sash, and slides the glass door open. A breeze comes in through the screen. He soaks up the air and then notices a pair of eyes staring at him from outside.

His pulse jumps and he steps back. "Who's there?"

William is at his side in an instant. "It's Kat, my daughter," he says. "I told her to stay in the car. It's her week with me. Selma, my ex-wife, said I was not to leave her alone. You understand, of course."

"I understand."

"Can she come in? She's thirteen and incredibly curious about everything."

"Yes, she can come in." Endicott slides the screen door open, and a dark-haired girl in a black T-shirt, blue jeans, and red sneakers slips inside. She has a jagged cut under her left eye.

"Kat, this is Endicott."

"Glad to meet you, sir." She walks to Endicott and offers her hand.

Endicott takes her hand and shakes it. "I'm glad to meet you, Kat." Endicott feels uneasy looking at her cut. It needs medical attention.

He releases her hand.

Kat steps away from him and goes to the screen door to stare outside. It seems she wants to avoid her father.

"We can get that cut fixed," Endicott says, looking at Kat, and then at William.

"Yes, can we?" William says. "Lead the way, Endicott. I

trust you have a first-aid kit. Kat, where'd you get that cut? Did it happen in the car?"

"No. It happened here, on the grounds." She continues to stare out the screen.

"Were you sneaking around, acting furtive?"

"I was, Dad. I'm sorry. I should have stayed in the car."

"You should have heeded my warning."

"I know I should have."

They sit at the kitchen table, William swabbing Kat's wound with a sterile pad, Kat cringing, William opening a suture kit.

"I'm a medical doctor, Endicott," William says, "and as you can see, this is a wound that requires medical attention."

Endicott agrees. It's a terrible wound.

"I might need your assistance, Endicott. I might ask you to hold her down as I apply sutures."

"Okay, William," Endicott says. "I guess I can do that."

William looks into the suture kit. "Run us through it again, will you, Endicott? The extinction event? I've heard it before, but I need refreshing."

"We've all heard it before," Kat says. "Doesn't it make you sad?"

"It does," Endicott says.

"Please run us through it again, sir. For Dad and me."

Endicott nods. "I'll tell ye." He watches William select instruments from the suture kit.

"Somewhere amongst the swirl of recent memory there'd been an extinction event and the planet lived on in a mirror image, no one yet accustomed to the fact of being dead. Like a severed head retaining its last few seconds of consciousness, the earth lived on."

"Jesus, Endicott. Is there no other explanation?"

"There is no other explanation."

"Why isn't the media reporting it?"

"They're in denial."

"Media assholes are scared," Kat says.

William stares off in the distance. "It seems like we're still alive."

"Yes," Endicott says. "But the consciousness we possess is different. No one knows how long it will last."

"Endicott," Kat says, "can I inquire? What was your major in college?"

"I take it you're thinking of going to college but are undecided on a major?"

"Yes. I'm casting about."

"It was English, Kat. Long ago. I'm ashamed I ever went to college. I didn't learn much. I don't remember much."

He hated that school. Years later, he realized the only thing he learned was the depressing fact that most of the teachers were slimeballs. Everything of value he'd ever learned came from experience, not education. But he won't tell Kat that. He won't dissuade her from making the same mistakes he made, the same mistakes everyone makes: learning late the things you'd wished you'd learned sooner.

"Can I inquire, Endicott?" Kat asks. "What are your last thoughts? We can blink out anytime."

Endicott looks at her, and then at her father. William holds a needle in the jaws of a needle holder. Kat's eyes are focused on the needle.

"Okay, Kat," Endicott says, "if you want to know what my last thoughts are, I'll tell ye. I don't like what I see in you or reflected in myself. It starts in childhood. Everyone has a cage he or she must step into. To explore oneself, to see one's hidden dimensions, invites attack. All humans are predators at heart and enjoy feasting on their neighbor's or children's still-live flesh. I am guiltier than most. My wife left me, then my child. And now I am alone."

"Thank you for sharing that," Kat says. "I think I'll share my last thoughts, also, though they're not as complex. Will you suture me, Endicott? You're a quick study. Read the instructions. Can he, Dad? I'd rather you hold me down, not him."

William gives Endicott the instructions and then holds his daughter down.

Endicott reads the instructions, goes to the sink, scrubs his hands, goes back to the table, holds the suture needle in the jaws of the needle driver, and brings the edges of Kat's wound together. With a soft rotating motion, he pushes the needle through the midpoint of the wound, releases it, grabs it in the gap, and pulls it through. He pushes the needle through the other side of the wound and ties off the suture with a square knot.

While putting in this first suture, he almost got a sense of himself disappearing. It was such a strange thing to be doing, observing intimate body parts that one is not used to seeing, like looking into one's left ventricle or something. On impulse, he becomes like a bat swerving through the forest, navigating by echolocation, distancing himself from the event. It's someone else doing this, not him. He puts in sutures above and below the first one until the wound is held together, but not too tight, allowing room for further swelling. He's good at this, didn't know where he picked it up, the instruments tumbling artfully in his hands, fingers doing just exactly as they should, popping needle through flesh again and again, the pain of each pop bearing well—Kat hadn't uttered a sound.

Finished, he dabs blood from the needle holes, applies a thin layer of first-aid cream, and sticks on a sterile bandage.

"Replace the bandage every day," he tells Kat, "and re-move the sutures in seven days. How does it feel?"

"It feels like I've got this big thing under my eye."

"Get used to it."

"I guess it feels okay."

Endicott goes to the sink and scrubs his hands.

Kat and William come to the sink, also, and scrub their hands. Endicott watches them. They stand in the warm glow of the overhead light, a father and daughter, twin aches interspersed with a kiss of poison. The wound had been too deep for Endicott to probe and clean thoroughly; her father the doctor had to do that. But the sutures were something else. The sutures were everyman's work. But when would the work end? When would everything end?

They go to the living room and sit down, Kat beside her father on the sofa, Endicott across from them on his easy chair.

Endicott wants to tell William he's a good man and that he has a good daughter, but he keeps his silence.

❊   ❊   ❊

Kat and Endicott are sitting in the living room. Kat says, "Dad, you were out of it. So was I."

Endicott looks around, his mind dark, his world reduced to points of silence. A weasel with sharp little teeth is biting him all over.

"I feel woozy," he says.

"I feel woozy, too," Kat says.

"Map it, whenever you feel woozy."

"Map it. You've already told me that, Dad."

"Humor me. We need to review these things. We'll review them again and again. Map it. Promise?"

"I promise."

"Map it. Record where you were and what you were doing when you got woozy. Include the time. Always carry a journal and pen with you. Anything weird, write it down."

"I've experienced fear without apparent cause," Kat says.

"Write it down. Record the details. Also, search your memory for recent new friends, interests, and activities. We all have them, I believe, but the knowledge fades quickly. We need to know how they're changing us. Anything weird, map it."

"Dad, what if they're not changing us? What if they're just trying to keep us alive? Don't you recall the extinction event?"

"I recall it. But I question it."

"But things are different. There's this intruder that goes around."

"Kat, there is no intruder. The visitations are spawned by a technology of war run by the Department of Defense.

They can alter environments, insert sounds, and make you believe someone is with you."

He watches her curl up on the sofa and become thoughtful.

"Dad, why are you investigating the intrusions if there is no intruder?"

"Kat, there is no intruder, but there is danger of another sort. Our beliefs and independence, for one thing. They're being lost. It's my greatest concern."

Her eyes take on a narrow cast. She looks around the room.

Endicott looks around, also.

He stands.

"Kat, we need to leave the house for a while. It's not safe in here. We need to go for a walk."

They go outside, into the darkness, and peer around.

"Oh!" Kat jolts in alarm, and then races to the glow of a nearby streetlamp. Her father joins her.

"What's wrong, Kat?"

"I see wolf-shapes all around."

"It's your imagination."

"No, it's not. They're real."

"Come on," he says. "Let's go."

Cautiously, they walk through the neighborhood. A half hour later, they return home. Tired, they decide to turn in.

Kat, still frightened, creeps into Endicott's bedroom. He can't persuade her to leave. She lies on the floor.

He brings in a spare bed, pushes it against the wall, and she huddles there under the covers.

CHAPTER 23

Perform Your Role

In the darkened room, Rich Mauk slumps in his chair. The man in brown, Ted Howell, sits where Endicott sat, on the chair that looks like a bear rearing back on its haunches.

"Is there a predator?" Rich asks.

"Yes, but it's a sham. A human presence at the scene masks a field test of the technology."

"Why assault victims a second time?"

"By assaulting subjects a second time, they are setting up a sacrificial victim. The police cannot fail to arrive at a strategy of sitting over victims, waiting for the predator to show up again."

"A predator will show up then?"

"I misspoke. A sacrificial victim will show up."

"Would it do any good to search for surveillance cameras or microphones near these sites?"

"Don't bother looking for ordinary surveillance of the sites, either electronic or human. It's a technology that uses a far different method of surveillance. They can dial in any location on earth."

"Why are they doing this?"

"They're running the technology in public to fine-tune it preparatory to submerging it. They need an explanation for the strange events so they've created a predator. They'll permit the police to take the predator out at some point, but only after acquiring a degree of expertise they feel comfortable with. Then they'll stop the public run."

"So, they're setting someone up?"

"They're setting up a sacrificial victim."

"The control will go deeper then."

"It'll go deeper."

"What can I tell Scott Endicott?"

"Give him a device, a TV remote control or something. Tell him it brings down shields."

"Shields?"

"The technology creates shields in and around the attack environment."

"You think the shields will be brought down by the—"

"By the cadre controlling it? Yes."

"And then Endicott will be able to kill the predator?"

"He'll kill a scapegoat, an innocent."

"Endicott says the predator has taken his daughter away from him."

"It's pressure. They want Endicott as the triggerman."

"Is his daughter safe then?"

"That's an unknown. Endicott has to pull the trigger. The historical record demands it."

"I sent my wife and kids out of town to keep them safe."

"It won't do any good. Perform your role. That's the only thing that keeps them safe."

"What about you, Ted? What's your role?"

"Helping you and Endicott perform yours."

CHAPTER 24

Is Your Conscience Clean?

Kristen-Kate McCutchan is veiled in gauzelike sleep. The hours pass in deep, restful slumber. In predawn darkness, she feels an icy touch. It shocks her awake. She rolls out of bed, bounces across the floor, and freezes, her mouth dry.

There's a man in the room.

She feels the thump of her heart, feels her loins tighten. It's happening again. He's come here before. She doesn't know if he's real or not. She's given him a name: William Chills.

William Chills entered her bungalow yesterday. She felt his presence but did not see him. She slipped into her closet, closed the door, and listened. That's all she wanted to do: listen to him, not see him.

And now William Chills is in her room making noise as if he thinks he's all alone, so she tries to make herself as silent as possible, as small as possible, a little bead of moisture floating through the air, and hopes he will not see her.

Her closet has always been a sanctuary. But it's on the far side of her darkened room. How can she get there without drawing his attention? She thinks she knows a way.

She listens, and hears him breathe, and hears him walking near her bed. If she is to have any chance for survival, she must become like William Chills. She must become as stealthy as he.

She walks silently on bare feet toward him, but on an angle, bypassing him, heading for her closet. A navigation system has risen in her mind, and she is using it, avoiding obstacles, slipping through the room.

She stops in front of her closet door, reaches out and feels the brass knob in her hand. With catlike tread she slips into her closet and shuts the door.

She snuggles against the softness of her clothes and remains motionless. It's too dangerous to stand out in the open. Her mind is reeling with frightful images.

Day after day, William Chills has been coming to see her, teaching her strange things. Shut the world out, and I am here, he has told her.

Minutes tick by and she senses William Chills is gone. She slips from her closet. It's still early but she dresses for work and inspects her bungalow.

A few things need to be straightened up. William never leaves the place in major disarray. There are just odd bits of confusion. She straightens up and then eats breakfast.

Afterward, she looks out the front door and takes in the morning haze.

✳   ✳   ✳

Alvin spies Kristen-Kate standing in the doorway of her bungalow. He thinks she looks like a tropical flower in her purple and white outfit. He wonders if he'll get the chance to break her skull like he plans. He wants to leave her comatose, brain damaged, maybe even dead.

He sees her shrinking from view, the door closing. Moments later he sees her peering from behind a window blind. She has seen their approach.

"She saw us," Alvin says to Hector. "We lost the element of surprise."

"Don't worry, fuckboy."

"Why'd we come in from the street? Why didn't we come in from the alley like I said? Hector?"

"Alvin, stop being such a fuckboy. We're just here to scare the lady. She'll be sorry she fucked with your brother. Leave it to me, fuckboy."

"We're just going to scare her?"

"Right, fuckboy."

Alvin had told Hector what Kristen-Kate said to his brother Alphonso in the police station where she works as a counselor. Alphonso said she dissed him, and he couldn't fight back with all the cops around. He said she called him a fucking pussy, a fuck hole, a fuck puppet, an ass jockey, a bunghole, a queer bung, a cock robin, a wanker, and a fucktard. He said her voice sounded spooky, like it wasn't her speaking but someone else speaking through her. It was her, though.

Alvin told Hector about this and Hector said maybe Kristen-Kate just wanted to shake Alphonso up. But Alvin said even the cops in the police station were startled at what Kristen-Kate had said.

"You talk to her, Hector," Alvin says, "and I'll pick up a brick or something and smash her fucking skull. It's the only way to drive it home."

"You're right, fuckboy. Under normal circumstances it would be the only way to drive it home. But this is not normal circumstances. Trust me, fuckboy. You break her skull and someone you don't want to see will come looking for you."

"I don't believe you."

"It's not normal circumstances, fuckboy. I can feel it in my bones. We have to play it safe. We're just going to talk to the lady."

Alvin doesn't like how it's shaping up. He's known for a long time that a showdown with Hector was looming. He thinks Hector will call him fuckboy in front of Kristen-Kate. If he does, he'll have to kill Hector. He'll have to kill Kristen-Kate, too, as she'd be a witness.

"Hector, you don't even know what this lady does in that police station."

"She counsels people, fuckboy. She counsels troubled fucks like your brother so their conscience can come clean."

"How do you know?"

"I know, fuckboy. Trust me."

"Has she counseled you?"

"No, fuckboy."

"Is your conscience clean?"

"I don't have a conscience, fuckboy. Only fuckheads like you and Alphonso have a conscience."

Alvin does not believe that. He does not believe that at all. He thinks it's time for his small deceit.

"Hector, this lady said something about you."

Hector grabs a piece of Alvin's shirt, holds it knotted in his fist. "What did she say, fuckboy?"

"She was talking to Alphonso when she said it."

"What?"

"Alphonso said she called you a donkey fucker."

Steam rises off Hector. He snorts like a bull and releases Alvin's shirt. Alvin knows better than to say anything more.

Kristen-Kate sees them approach. She focuses on the subordinate; his emotions are running high. She sees the flushed face, the dark glare, the set jaw of an angry child. She shifts her focus to the dominant one and sees that he is a blunt instrument, like a .44 slug. There is an obvious conflict between them. The subordinate will have to be careful. The dominant one can destroy him in an instant. What do they want with her?

She retreats inside, shuts the door, locks it, and looks through a window blind.

They're closer. She recognizes Alphonso.

No, it's not Alphonso. It's someone who looks like Alphonso. Is he a brother of Alphonso's?

She's scared now, seeing this Alphonso lookalike. She mentally reviews her counseling sessions with Alphonso. Did she get through to him? She works in a police station counseling youths who've been courting disaster.

The two come up the walk.

Kristen-Kate senses danger for the Alphonso lookalike, but also danger for herself.

She wants William Chills.

What is she thinking? William Chills is a product of her overwrought imagination.

She scoots away from the window and picks up her cell phone from the living-room bureau.

She hears them on the stoop.

And then an extended silence.

Why aren't they knocking? Her heart is pounding, her whole body pulsing with fear.

She bolts toward the kitchen, turns and looks back at the door. Oh, I'm such a coward, she thinks, and punches 911.

With a crash, the door flies inward, the jamb in splinters.

❋ ❋ ❋

Time stands still for Kristen-Kate. She doesn't know what to do; nothing in her background has prepared her for this moment. She watches the dominant one. The blank emotional state he showed on the street is gone. He's fuming. What caused it? He's far more dangerous now. What can she do to deflect him?

Looking strange and animallike, he rushes her, pulls her off balance and throws her to the floor. She stuck out a hand to fend him off, but it was like pushing against a brick wall.

She stares up at him, paralyzed with fear and uncertainty. She fears a quick, brutal response if she fights back.

They dart from the room, the dominant one to stand guard on the stoop, the subordinate to search the bungalow. She hears the tramping of his feet. It's a small house; it won't take him long. In seconds, they'll both be back in the living room. She has no avenue of escape.

Her anger rises; she will defend herself. A strike to the eyes. *Yes! She can do that! She'll take their eyes out!* She visualizes her fingers as bloody weapons.

She eases to her feet, her mind giving her cautionary signals now.

Going for the eyes won't work unless …

She sees the phone in her hand, recalls she already punched 911. She puts it to her ear and hears the 911 operator ask for information.

"Help me," she whispers. "Someone broke in." She whispers her address.

… unless they're caught unawares.

She decides to lie on the floor and pretend she's helpless. When they help her up, she'll blind one of them and run.

She drops down.

They stampede back into the room. The subordinate moves in close, stutter-stepping like he's going to kick her in the head. Recognizing his deadly intentions, she screams into the open line.

"Help me!"

She raises her arms protectively as his foot whips through the air, and they take the brunt of the kick. The force knocks her across the floor. Her cell phone flies from her hands.

Pain drizzles and foams through her arms.

Piercing, numbing, icky pain.

A second kick smashes into her face, her arms offering only feeble protection. It stuns her.

Suffering intense pain, shrieking, she scrambles across the floor toward her cell phone, attempting to evade another attack by the subordinate, who is stutter-stepping toward her again.

She grabs her cell phone and screams into it.

"Help me!"

The dominant one rips the phone from her hands.

The subordinate closes in.

She wails, raises her arms, cringes.

Again, she takes the kick in her arms and face. Again, it knocks her across the floor. Briefly, she sees stars, then blackness.

Kristen-Kate awakens, her head swimming. She looks around. The room is lighter now, like she's in heaven. And then the room turns dark, like in a storm.

For a long while, she drifts in a land of broken color. When she comes out of it, she prepares for another kick, raising her wounded arms. She sees feet near her, doing stutter steps. She cringes. But the figure that kicks her is just a thing. Insubstantial. It whiffs air.

She eases to her feet, assesses her injuries. Her arms and face feel like they're in the fiery pits of hell.

She walks around the living room, her pain fragmenting

her mind. She knows she has fractured arms and a concussion. She knows she'll need medical attention.

She heads for the door and goes outside. She walks along the sidewalk and sees a strange sun.

Alvin no longer sees Kristen-Kate. He dismisses her from his mind; he thinks she's dead anyway. He's bedazzled, watching the room fill with shifting curtains of light. The light takes on the shape of a giant cathedral, with stained-glass windows, altars, candelabra, and wooden pews. People appear and sit in the pews. The people don't look like real people, but like animated puppets without the strings. The puppets begin to melt and drip into spine-chilling shapes. Like a slow dance in hell, demons and witches and half-human beasts become visible.

In this macabre menagerie, Alvin sees Hector. Hector is peering about, thin knives of light piercing his skull. Alvin has a strange kind of understanding: thin knives of light are piercing his skull, also.

Time seems to slow down.

Alvin sees several men in brown uniforms rush into the room. They slam Alvin and Hector to the floor, twist their arms behind their backs, and handcuff them.

The men yank Alvin and Hector to their feet and push them toward the door.

Alvin is standing on a road in a strange neighborhood, his hands shackled behind his back, a submachine gun pointed at him.

Hector is handcuffed a few feet away, on his knees, a man holding a handgun to the back of his head.

The area is full of strange colors. The rays of a strange sun slant through the sky. It feels unreal. At first Alvin thought he might be in heaven, but then he had a gut feeling about it and knew it wasn't heaven. It was L.A., but weird. Everything was weird. Sky and ground and buildings. Trees and everything.

Weird.

He looks at Hector.

"Call me fuckboy now!" Alvin shouts. "They're going to kill you then me! I'll kill you myself, motherfucker!"

Saying this makes Alvin feel better. Then the man guarding him rams the muzzle of his submachine gun into his gut, knocking his wind out.

Bent over in agony, Alvin hears a gunshot, and from the corner of his eye, sees Hector's lifeless body flop forward.

Alvin tries to run, but the man guarding him smashes him to the ground with the butt of his submachine gun, splitting his scalp open. Alvin is on the ground, feeling pain, terror, and the wetness of his blood.

Two men drag Hector's body away, and then walk over to Alvin, grab him, and drag him to the place of execution.

In his helplessness, Alvin sees Kristen-Kate standing near the executioner. I thought I killed her, he thinks. How many times do I have to kick her fucking head?

Behind him, the executioner takes aim.

Alvin starts crying.

The pistol spits a bullet, and Alvin dies.

✻　✻　✻

After being discharged from the hospital, Kristen-Kate is home, resting on her living-room couch.

She's nursing two fractured arms, a concussion, and numerous contusions. She's on a painkiller and an antibiotic.

On doctor's orders, she will take two weeks off from work.

During the debriefing, an Army officer told her that sensors planted in and around her bungalow sensed the threat posed by the two intruders and triggered a flood of protective shields.

He apologized for a malfunction that caused the shields to deploy late. He said the incident would be critiqued thoroughly and systems refined for future deployments.

He said if she hadn't taken spontaneous self-defense measures, i.e., raised her arms to ward off kicks to the head, she may well have been killed.

She walks to a window and looks out on the street. She doesn't know where the executions took place. It was probably nearby. She doesn't know every facet of the operation, but some things were evident.

The Army employed protective shields to lock in the target environment. They sent in commandos to capture the two criminals who assaulted her, and then they executed them.

Okay and hallelujah.

But she questions it. Executions like the ones she witnessed aren't legal.

The killings didn't happen in the heat of battle. It was not self-defense; the two criminals were in custody, under armed guard, and posed no further threat. It was cold-blooded murder. Normal soldiers would not do that.

Who are these people?

CHAPTER 25

'Tis a Dream I'm In

'Tis a dream I'm in, Cody Hobbs thinks. In the dream, Cody is a child, and he and his siblings are in a grassy field running to join their parents. He sees his littlest brother fall into a deep pit that opens right in front of him. No one knew the pit was there. His littlest brother falls a great distance and lands awkwardly on a concrete slab. And there he lies, in a bent and crushed position, unmoving, and Cody climbs down a ladder into the pit and stands over him and sees his brother's misshapen little body and screams for help.

But it wasn't Cody Hobbs's littlest brother who got hurt, it was Cody. Someone hurt him, hurt him bad. And he wasn't a child when it happened; he was an adult. And all he has now is memories of falling and landing hard and awkward on a big concrete slab, and there he lies, eyes closed, looking dead, his spine and shoulders twisted at grotesque angles, all hope gone from the horrified eyes of the onlookers who peer down at him.

They put Cody in an ambulance and took him to a hospital. He spent a long time in surgery, and then they wheeled him into the recovery room.

After two days, the dreams fade and Cody wakes in a private room where an icy hand touches him, and he flinches. The touch of a hand is enough to scare him now.

It is miserably hot in Southern California, but not in the air-conditioned hospital room where Cody Hobbs lies, fading in and out of consciousness. Cody's mind is as chilled as the air. The fall into the pit was a mental construct, something his mind needed at the time to make sense of events. Now something else is surfacing: memories of being attacked by a shadowy figure.

He senses someone in the room with him, a vague man-shape in the corner. He tries to sit up but cannot. A sphere of light hovers over him, and then lifts off and sails around the room, settling over the man-shape in the corner. The light in all its folly seems to be communicating something to him.

Cody's pain works its way up his right side—up his leg, up his torso—a fearsome pain so bad it's like a mortal enemy creeping upon him. And then he tells himself to stop being a baby, to grit it out. There are people who can't feel anything. He is disgusted with himself.

A nurse appears at his side, stands close and does something, but he can't see what it is. He believes he can engage in limited and purposeful movement now, so his hands go to his face, but she pulls them down, and he resents this. She is authority telling him he has no business learning what is wrong with him. But he obeys and keeps his hands at his sides.

And then he remembers more of the assault, and his mind clarifies an image for him: a cloaked figure of darkness streaked with dull orange light.

Pain assaults him again, and he cries out. He hears the nurse say something. She pushes a button on his IV line and says he will feel better now. And soon he does. The nurse leaves, leaving him with a button in his hand, a switch that controls the morphine drip.

She pointed out another button, one that would call her if he needed anything. She told him he would feel thirsty as he came more fully awake.

He sleeps. He wakes. He finds the button. Warily, he probes toward his face with his free hand, the other still on that precious button, and feels a tube. His hand follows the tube to his nostrils, where it's clipped in place. He is now conscious of a gentle buzz of air flowing into his nostrils from the tube.

He probes further and feels big, thick, rough-textured bandages on his face and skull. He feels something hard beneath his chin. He explores the object. It extends from his chin to his chest and from ear to ear, and does not yield to his touch. He realizes it's a neck brace.

He probes downward, reaching under the sheet, and under his gown, and feels big, thick, rough-textured bandages on his ribs and abdomen, and on his right hip and leg, extending too far down to explore fully.

He sighs, and tries to ease his head up a bit, but can't do it. His head explodes with the motion, so he eases back on the pillow. He tries to talk, but his voice comes out hoarse, and he can't do it.

He pushes the button to summon the nurse. He wants to ask her what happened to him. But he already knows. A cloaked figure of darkness attacked him. He feels lucky to be alive.

The man-shape in the corner stands and walks to Cody's bed, just as Cody pushes the morphine button, and the other button again to summon the nurse.

The man now looks distinct to Cody. He is tall, lanky, sandy haired. He has a mustache and wears a cream-colored suit and a blue tie. He leans over Cody's bed.

"What happened, Cody?"

Cody tries to speak but cannot.

"It's important, Cody. We need to know." He steps away. The nurse is walking into the room with a glass of water.

The man returns to the corner.

The nurse puts a straw in Cody's mouth and holds the water glass for him as he sips.

Cody tries to think. What did happen?

The nurse sets the water glass on a stand by Cody's bed and leaves the room.

The man walks to the door, closes it, and then walks to Cody's bed.

"What happened, Cody?"

"Who are you?" Cody asks, his voice a hoarse whisper.

"I'm a cop."

"So, you know about the spies?"

The cop eyes him curiously.

"Tell me about the spies, Cody."

Cody tells him about the spies, the danger they pose for society. "They're all over, checking on us."

The cop doesn't seem to be interested in the spies.

"Cody, try to remember the assault."

Cody tries to recall every detail. "Someone knocked on my door. A man broke in and took me down. I woke up tied to a chair. Dark shapes surrounded me and asked me questions. They didn't like what I revealed so they assaulted me."

"What did you reveal?"

Cody tries to shake his head but can't; his head is immobile. "I can't remember. Another part of me came out and revealed things the dark shapes didn't like. They asked me who my god was. I found I couldn't speak. They hurt me and I ended up crawling across the floor."

"Cody, the spies and dark shapes are illusions."

Cody feels his gut draw up as if he'd been punched.

"No, they aren't. They're real. Where's Jill? She can confirm it."

The cop studies him.

"Jill is in seclusion. What did you do to provoke the attack, Cody?"

"I-I don't remember."

The cop's eyes show impatience.

"Cody, there's someone who wants to see you. After him, there will be others."

The cop walks to the door, opens it, and sticks his head into the hallway. Moments later, a large man with a goatee comes into the room.

The man pulls a chair close to Cody's bed and takes a seat, his eyes floating into focus behind thick lenses.

"Hello, Cody. I'm Dr. Hecker. I'm a psychiatrist. With your permission, I'd like to hypnotize you."

A strange light entered the room with Dr. Hecker, and now bends its eyes to Cody and makes him shiver.

"Where's Jill?" Cody asks.

"She's dead."

The cop reacts instantly, wedging himself between Cody and Dr. Hecker. A chill rises in the room.

Dr. Hecker stands, raises a powerful arm and threatens to knock the cop out of the way.

"Oh, poof, Endicott. Don't be an ass. Cody would have found out soon enough."

Endicott sidles away. Another man enters the room and takes up a position behind Dr. Hecker.

Dr. Hecker refocuses his eyes on Cody, pulls out a notepad, and takes his seat.

"Cody, we have a real mystery here, one that's accelerating beyond our ability to comprehend."

Dr. Hecker glances at Endicott in the corner, and then returns his attention to Cody.

"Now, I would like you to relax. In a few minutes, another doctor will come in and administer a drug that will facilitate the recollection of memories. We have some forms for you to sign first."

The man standing behind Dr. Hecker produces a clipboard, stands over Cody, and points out clauses in a contract. His voice is formal, lawyer-sounding, and imprints on Cody's mind.

He reads a section of the contract that explains the legal and medical ramifications of the treatment Cody will receive.

Cody knows it's intentionally vague, but signs where the man tells him to sign.

The light in the room is now shining off Dr. Hecker's lenses, shining into Cody's eyes, and he is being captured in the metronome of Dr. Hecker's voice as another doctor enters and injects something into Cody's IV line.

Dr. Hecker gets up and struts about the room, his thick lenses spinning in the air.

"We must pause to gather our thoughts, Cody."

Back and forth Dr. Hecker goes, cutting wide swaths through the voluminous light.

"Are you seeing the light, Cody? It comes from the deepest pools within us."

Dr. Hecker's voice has intricate, tricky edges. It eddies in Cody's mind much as the light eddies in the room.

Dr. Hecker's aspect becomes thoughtful. He returns to Cody's bedside and settles into his chair.

"Cody, the shapes that sail among us are called light beings, for want of a better term. Sometimes we see them clearly. Sometimes we do not."

Cody feels a powerful sensation, as if drugs have swept into him. He no longer has a center. He is dispersed.

"Cody, we will now attempt to retrieve the memories that are most painful. We will try to discover what took place when Jill first entered your apartment."

"I-I don't think she was there at all."

"Cody, you have suffered trauma. Events are buried in you. We must discover what they are. I can tell from your expression when you feel pain. The memories, without filters, can harm you. I must do something more to prepare you for further discovery without pain. Do I have your permission to proceed?"

"Yes."

Cody no longer hears Dr. Hecker's voice. It seems like people are lurking. He wants them to go away. He wants ...

He hears a voice.

"Cody?" It's Jill's voice.

He hears his own voice, inflected in curious tones. "Jill, what am I supposed to do?"

"What do you want to do, Cody?"

"Cody, do you feel pain anymore?" Dr. Hecker asks.

Cody feels a pleasant sensation, as if he were floating around the room in the light.

"No," he says.

"Good. After a while, you will experience a return visit from Jill or the dark shapes or something or other that knocks on your door. I want to prepare you for this. Can I do that, Cody? Can I prepare you for this?"

Cody is swept with fear. He knows another part of him will come out, reveal secrets, and dance around the room with the dark shapes, and they will assault him again.

"Cody ..."

"Yes, you can prepare me."

CHAPTER 26

A Family Named McGinnis

Spiros is in the living room of a modest house in Van Nuys with a family named McGinnis. The room is surprisingly crowded. Glass and mahogany curio cabinets and display cases are everywhere, overflowing with the McGinnis's earthly treasures. A picture window looks on to a rock garden in the front yard. A pickup truck sits in the narrow driveway.

The couch the mother and daughter sit on sags like an old swayback mule. The cushions have a worn, faded look.

The mother makes odd little fists, folding her fingers over her thumbs and clenching them tightly. Worry lines furrow her brow. Her body leans forward as if she's about to launch off the couch.

The daughter, age eleven, has hair the same light-blond color as her mother's. They share the same fruity fragrance, the same chubby figures—the daughter's a magnitude less than her mother's.

Spiros hears thumping upstairs. The sound varies. The rhythm is sometimes like a musical beat. Whenever the thumping commences, the mother's face crumples and her fists grip even tighter.

Spiros senses various layers of emotion within her, things tightly packed and shelved. He wonders what emotions drove the McGinnis household before the accident, and what emotions reside within it now, with seven-year-old Kurt McGinnis's legs shorn off.

The mother's name is Rita. Her large breasts overflow her bra and blouse. In the midst of this darkening tempest, her display of flesh seems grotesque.

The father's name is Dwayne. He and the boy are upstairs, where the thumping is going on.

Rita looks worried and tense. Violet, the daughter, mimics her mother: a dusting of anxiety, hands forced into tight little fists, face crumpled, eyes pained.

Spiros sits across from Rita and Violet on an upholstered chair with a damaged spring. It continually threatens to poke him, bringing to mind images of being impaled. He stifles his sense of the absurd as his sphincter clutches convulsively.

It's not that he doesn't share their pain. He does. But he has to keep a distance. There's a monster in this household, and it's not allowed an outlet. He doesn't want it coming out the wrong way, irreparably harming someone.

Mother and daughter are like dewdrops suspended on a blade of grass, awaiting the explosion that will upset their equilibrium.

Spiros hears the thump, thump, thump of crutches upstairs.

"What's he doing?" Rita asks, harshness in her voice.

"He's teaching Kurt how to walk," Violet says, looking at her mother.

Rita gives a brief laugh. "Kurt learned how to walk in rehab. Dwayne can't teach that kid anything."

"Can you tell me about the accident?" Spiros asks.

"A car came up the street doing ninety," Rita says. "Kurt was on his bicycle. He didn't even see it."

"He landed in someone's yard," Violet says. "His bicycle landed there, too. He couldn't believe what had happened. He didn't know his legs were gone."

A violent flame of energy shoots down the stairs, harsh words from the father.

"My mom's got a college degree," Violet says in a rush, as if to draw attention away from the outburst. She looks at her mother with pride. "She graduated last spring. She's looking for a new job."

Rita nods, her mouth clenched, her body compressed, as if she were trying to crush something inside her.

"Dad never went to college," Violet says. "But he's smart. He says the reason our little boy lost his legs was because God was shooting smack at the time of the accident."

Rita slaps her daughter.

Violet slaps her mother.

"Mom, your God never helps anyone. We have to do this all by ourselves."

"You goddamn fucking kid!"

Spiros heads for the stairs.

* * *

He feels the creak of each step. Drawing closer, he hears the father's voice erupt. It sounds like he's berating the boy over something the boy couldn't help.

He walks down the hall and stands at the bedroom door.

He turns the knob and pushes the door open.

There's a hardwood floor, a small bed, a small boy in the bed, under a sheet. Two crutches and two prosthetic legs lie in a heap on the floor.

The father, Dwayne, stands by his son's bed. He's tall, sinewy, stone-faced. He turns and looks at Spiros.

Then he turns back to the boy. "You might as well stay in bed, then. You'll be in a wheelchair always, or in bed, and that will be your life."

The sun slanting through the window catches Dwayne McGinnis full force. Looming over his son, he seems almost demonic.

And then he shrinks away from Kurt's bed, eyes fallen, tightening down on whatever it was that came out of him.

Spiros walks to the closet, opens the door, sees the boy's clothes hanging from hangers, a wicker laundry basket on the floor, picture books and games on shelves. These are Kurt's earthly treasures.

He turns and looks at the pile of crutches and prosthetic limbs on the floor by the bed. He walks toward Dwayne.

"He crawled into bed," Dwayne says.

I was wrong, Spiros thinks. Kurt found it tough going, gave up, and crawled into bed. Spiros pulls the sheet back.

Kurt is wearing cutoff blue jeans. His stumps are encased in white prosthetic socks.

Spiros picks up the prosthetic legs. "Sit up, Kurt, and slide your legs over the edge of the bed."

Spiros gives the boy the limbs and watches him put them on.

Kurt holds his hands up and Dwayne pulls him upright.

Spiros hears a creaky floorboard. He turns and sees Rita and Violet standing in the doorway.

* * *

Kurt walks downstairs on his prosthetic legs, Dwayne in front steadying him, Rita and Violet behind.

It's a painstaking process. On the way down, Spiros asks the family if they've encountered any unusual phenomena, such as strange lights or sounds without a known source.

"We have," Rita says. "We keep journals."

The McGinnises sit in the living room: Kurt, Rita, and Violet on the sagging couch, Dwayne on a creaky wooden chair.

Again, Spiros sits on the upholstered chair with the broken spring.

The McGinnises' faces are wrung with fear, confusion, and worry. Spiros can't take that away from them. He can't reduce their burden.

"Has anyone been coming by?" Spiros asks. "Anyone you aren't sure of?"

Rita glances around, her eyes narrowing.

"We've had visitations," she says. She makes her odd little fists again, and her worry lines deepen.

"Visitations again?" Dwayne asks.

"Yes," Rita says. "While you're at work, Violet and I are in boot camp."

"Boot camp?"

"I hate it," Violet says. "The drill sergeant busts our asses."

"We do a lot of marching and calisthenics," Rita says, her body sagging. "The drill sergeant is a psycho."

Violet nods. "He's a psycho all right. When our bodies give out, he kicks our butts and drags us across the ground."

Dwayne grins. "So that's why the ton sisters have been losing weight. Thank the psycho for me."

Spiros asks Dwayne if he's had visitations.

Dwayne says he has but likes to keep them private. "I wouldn't mind watching my wife and daughter get their butts kicked, though," he says.

"Kurt, do you have a new friend?" Spiros asks.

Kurt stares at the floor, his lips pursed.

"He does," Violet says. "Tell him, Kurt."

In a wee voice Kurt says, "I have a helper, a man that comes to see me."

"Tell him who it is," Violet says.

"Woodsman," Kurt says.

Rita looks agitated. She's clamping down on herself, the skin around her eyes becoming red and crinkled.

"Kurt," Violet says, "can you help out around the house when Mom and I are in boot camp?"

"I can."

"You and Woodsman?"

"Uh, I think so."

"Can you tell Woodsman I'm having trouble with a teacher? The bitch thinks I'm stupid. She makes fun of me in class. Can you get Woodsman to do something about her?"

"Like what?" Kurt asks.

"Like bust her fucking ass."

Rita shows Spiros their journals.

He opens Dwayne's. Most of his entries have to do with Kurt and Woodsman. He opens Rita's. Most of her entries have to do with warding off Woodsman, whom she believes to be evil.

Spiros ponders the reality: Woodsman is a manifestation of the individual's own discipline and fortitude. He won't tell them that, though.

He senses the mother is a danger to her son. His trauma has cracked something open inside her.

Spiros leaves. He has others to see.

❊   ❊   ❊

Cheryl Toomey lives a few blocks from the McGinnises'. Spiros stopped there several days ago, but she was gone. He has to see her. It's getting urgent.

He drives to her house, rings the bell.

He peers through a window in the door, sees down a long corridor into the kitchen at the back of the house.

A dark shape flits across the corridor. It was there for just an instant.

He waits a minute and then rings the bell again.

Cheryl does not appear.

He walks around back and sees no one.

She's in there, he believes.

Suddenly, he's lost in a gray haze. Someone has a weapon focused on Cheryl's house. The world going gray is meant to confuse.

He navigates back to the front of the house, climbs the steps, rings the bell a third time, and waits.

Judging by the evidence, he thinks Cheryl has come under relentless attack.

If so, she has acquired a key piece of information, which she holds in utter ignorance. He will mine her for it.

He rings the bell a fourth time but there is no answer.

He walks away.

He'll have to breach the place later. He trusts she'll survive until he returns.

CHAPTER 27

Prevailing Beliefs and Attitudes

A portly young scientist named Matt Jefferson stands on an auditorium stage in Los Angeles and greets an audience of police officers. After introducing himself, he walks to a computer workstation at the side of the stage and flicks off the main auditorium lights. The only illumination now comes from safety lamps in the floor and walls.

Jefferson moves a mouse cursor and clicks on a folder containing U.S. Department of Defense classified videos. The videos will be displayed on a big-screen LED TV on the stage. He glances at the audience and takes a deep breath before speaking.

"I feel a rage building in me at the unwitting use we are being made of, but my rage dies quickly. I am not permitted a rage any more than General Dwight D. Eisenhower was permitted a rage during the events leading up to D-Day, June 6, 1944. We must set aside the ethical dilemma of sending men to their deaths and focus on national security. Eisenhower put millions of men to the task in that drama, and the present need is as great as the one he faced."

He pauses.

"We will now view a montage of eyewitness reports, victim statements, and prevailing beliefs and attitudes concerning the unusual circumstances we find ourselves in."

He moves the mouse cursor, clicks on a video link, and a man in his mid-forties appears on the big-screen TV. "This man has had a visitation," Jefferson says. "Listen closely."

"One evening my living room turned almost as dark as night. Nothing felt right. Nothing looked familiar. The air became impregnated with points of light, and I was held immobile in my chair. I thought I was done for when dark shapes appeared and performed surgery on me. I can't describe it. You might think I was hallucinating, but I wasn't. It happened."

The man on the screen pauses to rub his eyes.

"I got the feeling the ones doing this did not recognize my reality. To them, I was a blank, an energy form. I think they poured me into a new configuration, and presto, for a while I was a new person, living elsewhere, performing work for them. It's hard to remember. My memories are as dark as the room was."

"This is a textbook description," Jefferson says. "The next witness demonstrates a different level of understanding."

A young man appears on the screen.

"I had an adventure in another world with a young woman, and it was pretty neat. I know they'll come looking for me again if they need my particular energy."

Jefferson starts another video, and a middle-aged man appears.

"My living room got dark and shapes surrounded me. They

took me someplace and it was like an amusement park for a while. Then it wasn't fun anymore and I was suffering. When I came to, I discovered I had a lot of injuries. I only recall fragments. They block you somehow."

Jefferson switches to a new witness, a young woman.

"The experience is like waking from a dream that's just out of reach. But when you see blood on the floor and look in the mirror and see wounds on your face, you know it wasn't a dream."

A new witness appears, a middle-aged man.

"I only recall fragments, not the total experience. They mask the memory somehow. They manipulated my energy and then led me through a doorway. I knew I was going to be used in some drama they thought was magnificent but could possibly get me killed. I'm glad I had the experience, but I don't want them to come back. To them, I wasn't real."

A young man appears.

"I saw dead people standing around. Eventually, I realized I was dead, too. I did as I was told—killed some people in a war— then found myself back in my living room, injured in ways I can't describe. I don't want a second visit. It's unbearable."

Another young man appears.

"I felt a cloud all around me and I was swept away. I was crawling in the dirt and had my orders. A man was going to ride by on a horse and I was supposed to kill him. I had a military rifle in my hands and motive and hatred appropriate to the task. I was really into it and I'd have killed him sure enough but at the last moment a force prevented me from doing so."

A young woman appears on the screen.

"I walked out of my apartment with this guy and we weren't in L.A. anymore. It was wilderness and it was awesome until a bear

started stalking us and we had to climb a tree. *The bear left and we got down from the tree and had a picnic and the guy got fresh with me and that was that. I woke with an injured face. They always do something to your face. They're using us for something. I get the impression they consider us energy and that we don't occupy any higher status. We're for their fun and amusement."*

The parade of witnesses continues.

"I learned we are not real. We are things, constructs, and somehow they get us moving so we can perform for them."

"I learned we don't have identity except as blank energy forms. We're part of a big energy stratum that they mine."

"I'm injured. They disfigured me. I'm fed up with our culture. They never told us what we were. We aren't real. We're energy blanks that can be manipulated."

"Someone from another world came and got me. Their picture of us is much different than our picture of ourselves. We are below a threshold for them. They don't know we exist as viable beings. They see us as blanks they can shape into useful forms. When they're through with us they toss us back on the shelf."

"They configure us and use us for games or war. Millions of us are in their world at any given time getting killed or maimed. If we show up back here injured, you know they've done something to us over there."

"I had to attack someone over there. That makes it sound like I'm not a victim, but I am. The normal me wouldn't attack anyone. They come here and get us but I don't think they see us the way we see ourselves. To them, we're energy."

"I didn't mind it except for the injuries I received. I got a charge out of going over there and helping them. It also helped me in ways I can't explain."

"Dark shapes entered my house. They came to harvest me. We're energy in a blank state. They gather us as the need arises."

"I go there often but not of my own volition. My face is hurt. I experience chills all the time. Their big focus is on rites of passage for their young people. They steal us for that purpose and don't realize they're interfering with our lives."

The big-screen TV goes blank and the overhead lights turn on.

Jefferson paces the stage. He senses a need to explain something to the audience.

"Memories of events might be masks, so it's hard to assess the reality. In any case, someone is using us for a mysterious purpose, the work is dangerous, and we don't have a defense."

He pauses, and then asks them if they have any questions.

*   *   *

Endicott feels a shiver go up his spine, and then senses shivers throughout the room, as if his body were an antenna tuned to the shivers of others.

He glances around the room, and then looks at Jefferson, and sees that Jefferson's terrible eye is staring right at him. Something bursts inside Endicott, a memory. It lasts but a moment, and his shivering becomes a mosaic of fear filling his body. He can do nothing but shrink under the terrible eye of Jefferson's.

Endicott continues to shiver as he connects the mosaic of dots his brief memory explosion provided.

He thinks he is a god, and that Jefferson knows his terrible secret. A minute passes with Endicott in terror of being exposed, and then Jefferson shifts his terrible eye off him.

Endicott thinks a mosaic of control traceable to Jefferson exists, and that there is much that implicates Jefferson and others in massive crimes against humanity.

I am not one of the energy blanks, he thinks. I am a god, albeit weakened. I don't follow the law; I make it, or try to, and I am despised.

He wonders if he's going insane, or if he just needs more sleep like Lionel says. In any case, the conference with Matt Jefferson is over, and Endicott gets up and leaves.

❋ ❋ ❋

Back at police headquarters, Carlisle calls Endicott into his office. Endicott sees a man with Carlisle.

"Scott, this is Detective Mark Reese from Van Nuys. He'd like to go over some cases with you."

Endicott and Reese confer in the squad room.

"This is what I've encountered in Van Nuys," Reese says, peering over a mountain of case files. "The predator mesmerizes victims, uses suggestion to gain their trust, then tortures them. The predator pays repeat visits, and the torture gets worse. Victims have a tough time talking about the experience, as if the brain can't process what took place. Victims typically say the guy isn't human. Descriptions are fuzzy due to victims being in an altered state of consciousness during the attacks."

Reese pauses as other detectives crowd around.

"I think this guy comes from another world," Reese says.

Laughter erupts from the other detectives.

"I'm not kidding. This guy isn't human. Haven't you read the victims' statements."

"Don't feel bad," Endicott says. "I've started asking victims what they did in that other world."

More laughter erupts from the other detectives.

Then a grim-faced detective steps forward and asks, "What does this guy ask his victims?"

"It's almost like a job interview," Reese says. "He'll ask them if they can ride a horse and shoot a gun. He'll ask them what epoch they'd like to visit, what kind of dangerous animals and people they'd like to encounter."

"Epoch?" the detective says.

"Yes. It means age, era."

"Another world, huh?"

"Actually, it's many worlds. Alternate worlds."

The grim-faced detective turns to the others. "Don't laugh. I've been there."

Endicott and Reese are still in the squad room.

"We have to focus on a single predator and no alternate worlds," Endicott says. "That's the word from Carlisle."

"Is he crazy?" Reese asks.

"He might be. But that's irrelevant. What do we have?"

"A predator is going place to place torturing people for information. Later, victims can't talk and can't remember much anyway. No forced entry, no signs of struggle, no bind marks. I wonder, how does the predator get the drop on his victims?"

"Maybe he showers them with fairy dust," Endicott says.

"Maybe, but how is one person doing all this?"

"We don't need to know that. We have one predator and no alternate worlds. The word is we're close to identifying the predator."

"What if we catch more than one predator in the act?"

"We won't," Endicott says. "It's one predator. Everything we've seen can be done with technology. We don't need alternate worlds."

After going over several more Van Nuys cases, Reese opens a file and goes silent.

"What's the matter?" Endicott asks.

"There's a woman who isn't cooperating." Reese holds the file up.

"What's her name?"

"Cheryl Toomey. Her dentist called us; she didn't. The predator has visited her twice. On both occasions, he tortured her and removed a top front incisor. Her dentist said he replanted the teeth. Cheryl's eyes go tight every time I see her. She won't tell me anything."

"He's gone at her twice, huh?" Endicott takes the file from Reese, looks at it, then goes to make a copy.

"What else?" Endicott asks, upon returning from the photocopier.

"The guy sometimes plays cruel games with his victims. He sometimes seems unable to remember he has already seen them and has gotten certain information from them, sometimes openly, sometimes under duress. He seems to have a trick memory of sorts, according to some of the people who've been visited by him. I get the impression Cheryl Toomey might have a trick memory, too."

"She might hate cops," Endicott says, back at his desk, handing the original file to Reese, keeping the copy. "That could be why she's not cooperating."

"It could be."

"Why do you think she might have a trick memory?"

"Her mouth opened once when I questioned her, like on its own, and she dropped a name she didn't know I heard."

"What was it?"

"Spiros."

Endicott jolts upright.

"I checked it out," Reese says. "There was surveillance on a Stephen D. Spiros in Irvine. They dropped it after a Woodsman type of assault occurred while Spiros was bottled up at home."

CHAPTER 28

Rites of Passage

Kristen-Kate McCutchan feels a jolt as her horse, Lucky, pulls up near the canyon wall. She takes a moment to steady her nerves and then rises high in the saddle to scan the canyon's rim. Somehow, she must get up there. She feels it's too dangerous to backtrack out of the canyon. She can't shake the feeling she's being watched. She's felt it all morning, something piercing her right between the shoulder blades.

She guides the horse deeper into the canyon, searching for a way out. But it's futile. The rocky walls are too steep.

She tastes a big dollop of fear. She doesn't want to go back through the mouth of the canyon but knows she must. It's an ideal place for an ambush. Men might be waiting there, men she must avoid. But she can't stay in the canyon. It's a trap.

With nervous energy, she turns Lucky around and heads back the way she came. She maneuvers through a succession of narrow passages, bypassing towering rocks.

Every shadow casts a chill, every bend portends danger, but she makes it out of the canyon without incident.

She sees a gentle slope. It's the way she should have gone, but thought the canyon was a shortcut.

She urges Lucky upward. "Come on, Lucky, get us out of here." Lucky makes it to the top of the slope in a few swift bounds.

From this vantage point, she surveys the terrain, compares it with her map, and plots a new route, one she thinks will lead her safely to her destination.

She urges Lucky ahead.

The sun ticks higher.

She spies a man standing on the trail. He's caked with dust, his eyes watchful beneath the brim of his hat.

She slows Lucky as she draws near.

Without warning, the man whips a fistful of sharp grit into her face.

It stings her, and for a moment too much is happening all at once: the man lunging at her, Lucky rearing, her fear shooting skyward.

The man grabs Lucky's reins and yanks them from her hands. He's on a dead run, pulling Lucky off the trail.

Kristen-Kate seizes the saddle horn and grips it with all her might, afraid she'll fall off. She digs her heels into Lucky's flanks and the horse spurts ahead, colliding with the man.

The man scrambles out of the way, dropping the reins.

Kristen-Kate gathers in the reins, heads Lucky back to the trail, and resumes her journey.

She hits an area teeming with sagebrush and Joshua

trees, and wends her way through. Rounding a bend, she hears a deep, threatening growl.

An African lion is crouched in front of her. It's a full-grown male with a thick, dark mane.

Her hands jerk back on the reins. Her heart skips a beat.

Lucky is at a standstill, facing the lion.

Kristen-Kate is rock-still. Demon fear rises in her. Her heart slams around in her chest.

She watches the lion intently. Its eyes are on her and Lucky. It advances, emitting menacing growls.

She is barely able to breathe. Heat seems to have vaporized her brain.

She backs Lucky away, and then watches in amazement as the lion dashes into the brush.

She nudges Lucky ahead, hoping that if there's danger he'll sense it and refuse to go further.

As the horse negotiates the trail, Kristen-Kate watches for the lion. Not seeing it, she breathes easier.

She guides Lucky into a ravine and spurs him up the other side.

Deciding it's time for a rest, she dismounts and takes a drink of water from her canteen.

Refreshed, she takes a compass reading and studies her map. She thinks she's about where she should be at this time.

A large man on a black horse gallops up behind her. She thinks he was hiding back in the ravine. He doesn't look friendly.

"This is our land," he says. "You're trespassing."

Before she can respond, he reaches for Lucky's reins. She yanks the reins out of his grasp and leaps upon the horse.

He grabs for the reins again. She spurs the horse and gallops off, not looking back, the wind in her face.

Down the trail, she breathes a sigh of relief. What if she hadn't run? What would the man on the black horse have done?

It isn't his land. It's no-man's land. If he's that brazen, to claim this land as his, there's no telling what he might have done.

She studies her map again. She's supposed to follow a big circular route, not get too far off track, and manage her time so she's home for dinner.

Home's an old mining camp where she, the other trainees, and the training cadre have pitched tents.

She's at the terminus of her route, time to go home. But her gaze lingers. Ahead, off the prescribed trail, there's something dangerous going on, or so the training cadre have said.

They say there's a war going on over there, people pouring in to fight. They say there's lots of killing going on over there, the desert floor caked with blood.

They say there's a lot of interesting stuff going on over there, historical stuff. They're making it awful hard to follow orders.

The sky is so intense, the ground so stark, the horizon so inviting that Kristen-Kate decides to continue straight ahead, abandoning her circular route.

She rides until the light of day begins to dim. The trail has taken her to higher ground.

She strains to see, to hear. The broad plateau is rippled, and in the folds of land there are woods that flow like rivers flooding their banks. These rivers of trees are like blood oozing darkly from a ruined hand.

She follows a trail. Ponderosa pines close in. A man jumps onto the trail, waving his arms and yelling.

"My family has been wiped out! Help me!"

She draws alongside him, her mind conjuring up images of slaughter. "What happened?"

"I don't know. I came back from chopping wood and found my family dead."

Filled with dread, Kristen-Kate follows the man. They enter a campsite of tents. She dismounts and leads Lucky by the reins, her eyes searching everywhere. Caution guides her every step.

Horror-stricken, she sees that the tents are shredded. She sees bodies. Body pieces. Blood.

She tries to scream, but no sound comes out. Death is all around her. Fear permeates her.

She jumps onto Lucky and rides out of the camp. She rides until she is immersed in rocky woodlands and meadows. She hopes she is safe here.

She sits on a rock and ponders the situation. She has spent several weeks undergoing rites of passage in the Arizona wilderness, and this has been her worst experience yet. Honestly, she doesn't know what to think. Her mind is in fragments.

Judd and Sophie Wookey, cadre members, appear and help her pull the fragments together.

The three of them sit on the rock.

"Is our world truly being invaded?" Kristen-Kate asks.

"We can only assess the reality or unreality of an invasion through indirect means," Judd Wookey says. "When earth people speak of the invasion, it produces a shift of inner tides. Such is the pull this idea has on them. But does that make it a true idea?"

"I believe it does," Sophie Wookey says. "We are earth people, too. Our inner tides are our connection to our ancestors, to each other, to those of us yet unborn, an ocean that laps all shores. But inner tides do not always lead us to that which is good. They can also lead us into misery, fear, and superstition."

"If our world is being invaded," Judd Wookey says, "it is the greatest threat humans have ever faced: the possibility of becoming extinct at the hands of another species."

"We have seen much," Sophie Wookey says. "We have lived through the blackest of times, but this is overwhelming. Never before—through wars, persecutions, and the upheavals of nature—have we given up faith that good would prevail. But there might be no defeating this."

"Is there truly an invasion?" Judd Wookey asks. "Let us consider if, like a bubble, another world attaches to earth periodically and then skips away, and wherever it attaches, enemies pour in and kill us and maim us. Is that an invasion? Is that what's happening?"

"Dark clouds are over both worlds," Sophie Wookey says. "Think of the twisted minds, the fear, the ignorance, the hate. Blood flows like rivers, their own and our human blood."

"I don't think there's an invasion," Kristen-Kate says. "It's just minds gone fearful."

"But, Kristen-Kate," Sophie Wookey says, "the phenomenon of intersecting worlds is known intuitively by the elite members of all societies. Some even possess scientific or arcane knowledge of this. Elites have always shared knowledge of intersecting worlds with other elites, even from other worlds. I'm positive there is an invasion. Don't you think so, Judd?"

"Yes," Judd Wookey says. "There is an invasion and it's harming our world. The phenomenon we cherish, which we call rites of passage, is coming unraveled, leaving the depths and coming above ground, and before long the rabble will discover it and know what they truly are: puppets."

"Kristen-Kate," Sophie Wookey says, "long ago our society instituted rites of passage to ensure that certain young people recognize their leadership responsibility. Through the indirect means of our world, we believe the invaders are interfering with this process."

"I marvel," Kristen-Kate says, "that rabble cannot be given these sacred rites. Are they not human, also?"

"Truly, the rites do not work for them," Judd Wookey says. "The rabble gladly accept puppet status after the terror of the rites. The rites work only for us. The rites also serve to shove the phenomenon down and keep the rabble ignorant of their true roles. Chaos would result otherwise."

"Judd, is it true that I never encounter rabble during my rites?" Kristen-Kate asks.

"It is true."

"Then I will never understand rabble. I will never know what they are like."

"Are you forgetting? You live other lives in which you encounter rabble. We all do. Lives exist in teeming bubbles for all of us. Need I remind you of the essentials?"

"Remind me."

"Rabble believe in gods because they do not possess finer knowledge. When you hear talk of gods within a structure of belief, it is rabble."

"You will learn all things through indirect means," Sophie Wookey says. "In our world all things are indirect."

Kristen-Kate sighs. "But aren't the rites supposed to make me conscious of rabble, of all their wiles and malice?"

"The rites," Judd Wookey says, "are supposed to prepare you for leadership by making use of the phenomenon discovered in antiquity, the illusion of many worlds."

"Nothing is real in our world," Kristen-Kate says.

"Exactly," Sophie Wookey says. "Nothing is real. We know that. The rabble do not."

Kristen-Kate thinks there must be something that's real. She will try to poke a hole in all that the Wookeys have said.

It's night. A man named Snake enters a dim bar in a toxic section of an Arizona town and sits in a booth. There's an aura of danger in the bar, a ruckus of evil, everyone sizing up everyone else, loud, rough talk, jostling, shoving matches, an evil eye following you wherever you go.

An older man enters the bar. He spreads a story about being wronged by a woman and asks for help in extracting revenge. He draws interest from a rough crowd. Someone points out Snake.

The man approaches Snake, says his name is Hercules Jurgens. He offers Snake a job: help him bust up a girl's legs. Bust them up so bad she might lose them. Break her jaw, too. And knock her teeth out. He says they'll use baseball bats.

He hands Snake a photo of Kristen-Kate. Snake looks at it. The girl's about nineteen or so, a knockout.

"She deserves it," Hercules Jurgens says. "I'll pay you five hundred bucks. A thousand if she loses one or both legs."

The man says there's enough animosity toward her that suspicion will fall elsewhere.

Seems like Snake is used to these offers. He mulls it over, but there's no doubt he'll do it. He's just curious, is all. Why this girl? What's so god-awful important about her she needs her legs broken? He studies the photograph. Good-looking girl, but sometimes that's the worst kind.

They talk a while longer, and then leave. The man who's going to pay him drives. There are two baseball bats in the car. They talk about the woods; that's where the girl is, camping out. They discuss what they're going to do when they get there. They negotiate a little something extra, for which Snake needs a gun. Luckily, Snake has a gun on him.

✳   ✳   ✳

It's dark. Kristen-Kate and the Wookeys sit around the campfire. "Will rites of passage ever be allowed the rabble?" Kristen-Kate asks.

"The rabble will eventually receive watered-down versions," Judd Wookey says. "Its real power will be concealed, reserved for elites."

"But how come?"

"Rites harken back to the days of antiquity. If rabble got wind of it, they'd mistake the power of the rites for a god and start killing people. Unsophisticated rabble cannot be trusted with arcane knowledge."

"What we do," Sophie Wookey says, "during these rites speaks of something deep and mysterious in the human system. Until favored channels open for them, rabble have no use for this."

They hear sounds of footfalls through the trees, masked by the wind. Someone is moving toward them. Scared, they huddle closer to the fire. Kristen-Kate sees fear on the faces of Judd and Sophie, and this causes her to be even more frightened.

Who's out there? Who is moving their way?

Snake and Hercules Jurgens are in the woods, stalking the campers. The sound of wind masks their approach.

They rush the three who sit by the campfire, fight through an older couple to get at Kristen-Kate. But she's too quick for them and escapes into the brush. They turn on the older couple, use baseball bats to break their arms, crack their skulls. Howls of frenzied animals accompany their assault.

Finished with the old couple, they track Kristen-Kate through the brush. Snake prepares to do the extra deal. He takes out his gun. When they find her, Hercules Jurgens will prop the young woman up, and Snake will discharge a bullet into her spine. They will leave her to die a slow and agonizing death.

But something is slowly eclipsing Snake's world, bringing with it new shapes and sounds that dwell in his mind. A small, dim voice calls in his head. It's his mother's voice calling his name. *Stephen.* This wrenches him from his spell. He tackles Hercules Jurgens as he goes after the girl.

He sticks the photo of the girl in Jurgens's face, shines a light on it. "She's your daughter, Nat."

Nat McCutchan breaks from the spell and tries to gather Kristen-Kate in his arms. She's hysterical and won't let him touch her. Eventually, she calms down.

Snake knows he must sneak away before Kristen-Kate and Nat learn who he is. In their world, he is a wanted man.

In the emerging heat of dawn, Snake crawls from his hiding place in the brush. He watches the horizon, his eyes focused on the heat mirages that warp the air. Illusion, he thinks. It's all illusion. He whirls about.

The illusions grow. He sees glassy, fragile, shivering light.

And then he sees them. Wisps of light, human appearing, until you look closer. Until now he'd only heard of them, didn't know if they were real.

They saunter close, menacing him with their eyes.

He runs.

Exhausted, he slows, not daring to look back. The heat is insane. He collapses into shade beneath a tree. Timorously, he glances back. The light beings have vanished.

Sitting, shivering despite the heat, he removes his cap and runs his fingers through his hair. Strange verses begin to steal through his mind. They become hypnotic, and then terrifying.

Falling rain, catch a little with your brain.
If your skull's convex, fix it with a hammer hex.
Then bore a little hole so your brain can get full.
But get rid of that hair, can't have any there.
Now you're set, a cupped skull yet.
A hole in the center for rain to enter.
Now it rains on little brains.
As you ride those long, long cattle trains,
You'll feel the water log and chug.
As you pick up speed you'll scoot and bug
Off the earth in flapping flocks
And flying shoes and dropping socks
And you'll discover as you go
You're insane and so and so.

He stands and looks around. Desert brush stands witchy against the heat mirages. "Who's following me? Who's singing?" He sees no one.

He wonders what will happen to his world when the invaders control all planetary reality constructs. What will they be capable of orchestrating then?

He knows he must leave, wonders if he can find his pickup, wonders if he can find his way home.

CHAPTER 29

The Trickster

Spiros drives his pickup slowly through a Santa Monica residential neighborhood, studying the environment. Sky and ground seem strange. Objects sway, sunlight quivers. He's detecting the early, barely perceptible signs of another dimension impinging upon the earth plane. Another world moving in. Most people wouldn't notice.

He pulls to the curb and shuts off the engine. He climbs into the cargo bed, throws a canvas tarp off two tripod-mounted synchronized tracking cameras, and looks through the viewfinder.

As expected, he sees shimmering lines of demarcation—the boundaries between worlds. Then he sees something that's hard to believe. Something disturbing.

Cautiously, he steps back, shakes his head, and with the naked eye takes a look at the surroundings. Unaided, his eyes detect the subtle signs of an alien intrusion.

He puts his eyes back to the viewfinder. Transfixed, he watches as filaments of light assemble into human form and walk about. Light beings.

Watching them, he feels a cool sensation, like running water slowly spreading from his abdomen and collecting in his joints. It's like an ocean tide, or a siren song, from the new world that's intersecting with earth. It's a pleasant feeling and slowly abates.

He pulls his eyes away from the viewfinder.

Has the technology—his own brainchild—gone wild? Is it spawning new beings, new worlds? Or is it simply behaving as designed: producing illusions and altering perceptions?

He realizes time is running short. Whoever is running the technology—aliens or humans—will likely have a credible god step forth soon and make a proclamation. The world will change then. There will be a new master.

Cheryl Toomey is likely his last, best hope.

If the technology has mutilated her, like he suspects, she unwittingly possesses key information.

But twice he's stopped at her place, and twice she's been inaccessible.

There must be a way to get to her. A way to bridge the worlds.

He puts his eyes back to the viewfinder and searches the environment. He sees tendrils of light branching out all over, the new world sinking roots, establishing its shapes, colors, and shadows.

He throws the tarp over the cameras and fastens it down with padlocks.

He stands on the sidewalk and looks around. His eye is practiced—he detects about one percent of the transformation without aid of the cameras.

Warily, he walks down the sidewalk.

He sees an old lady sitting on her front porch, her face contorted, a dark presence hovering over her, constricting her heart. She's not aware of the cause of her pain. He thinks the dark presence will eventually kill her. There's nothing he can do about it. If he scared it off, it would return. It seems to get its power from something buried inside her.

He keeps walking. The evidence, witnessed over the last several months through synchronized tracking cameras, does not lie. Someone is altering earth-plane reality. Odd slices of life are continually being crafted and matched with harmonizing pieces until full, coherent dramas take shape.

It's nothing short of world-building.

But who is doing it?

A young brunette passes by, eyeing him. He recalls her name: Kristen-Kate. He's not surprised to see her again on the streets of Santa Monica. He remembers her from that night in King's Forest Restaurant.

In all likelihood, King's Forest was a stand-alone drama, detached from everything else. What was its purpose? It seemed to divert him from something.

He continues walking.

A pickup truck is pacing him on the street. He glances at it, then snaps his eyes forward. He doesn't know the consequences of looking at something like that. It's a pickup truck exactly like his. The man driving it is exactly like him. He won't risk another look.

Did Kristen-Kate's presence on the street open a doorway to a parallel world? It's not too hard to imagine Kristen-Kate as the local trickster personality.

In myth and legend, trickster personalities often lead people astray. Moreover, a trickster can serve as a bridge between worlds.

He thinks Kristen-Kate played the role of trickster at King's Forest, pulling him into a world of death masks, superfluidity, and counterfeit reality, and now plans on doing it again. Her appearance on the street foretells it.

What will the new world be like? He's determined that it will be a world of his choosing, not hers.

For now, he wants to try another gambit. He'll take the local trickster personality to see Cheryl Toomey, bridge the two worlds, and force her to give up the information that identifies the predator.

He'll snatch Kristen-Kate off the street.

But first he must see Otis Dietrich at the Hotel Marquesas and warn him about two threats: Woodsman and the trickster.

❄   ❄   ❄

Spiros enters the Hotel Marquesas and heads across the lobby to the desk.

"Hi," he says to the desk clerk, whose nametag identifies her as Rachelle Golden.

"Hi," she says back.

"I'm looking for Otis Dietrich. Is he here?"

She frowns and drifts to a computer. "One moment, please."

A moment passes as she does something on the computer. Then she looks at him. "Otis isn't here yet. Can I take a message?"

"I must see him. It's important."

She looks around. He can tell she's hesitant to give him information. She faces him. "He's due any moment."

Spiros's curiosity is piqued, and he studies her. She's wearing a burgundy outfit with a white kerchief. Her face is almond shaped, her eyes blue, her hair a light auburn, falling to her shoulders in tousled waves. Windblown locks fall across her forehead, offsetting her otherwise neat appearance.

Windblown locks?

Spiros takes a closer look at the drift of locks upon her forehead. They look normal now.

He places his hands on the counter and looks her in the eye. "I really must see Otis. When do you expect him?"

Her mouth opens as if to speak, but then closes as she does some thinking. Eventually, she responds. "I'm sorry. We can't give out that information."

Spiros looks around. The lobby is a place of pillars and red carpet. The desk is centrally located, a little fortress in the middle of things, with people walking all around.

He looks back at Rachelle. He senses her mind drift, and sees her body drift toward a phone.

He wonders if he should let her make the call or if he should stop her. He can stop her by clarifying his interest in seeing Otis. Or he can let her make the call and discover what happens next.

He smiles at Rachelle and she smiles back. That's all it took. She stops drifting toward the phone. She plants herself, her locks windblown again, the rest of her neatly in place.

"I'll wait here for Otis," Spiros says, and steps back.
Rachelle nods and goes back to work.

❊   ❊   ❊

Otis walks into the lobby of the Hotel Marquesas, wondering what kind of mask Rachelle will be wearing today, if she'll be her usual demeaning self, or if she'll be on the other end of her spectrum, a kinder, gentler Rachelle. In any case, it will be interesting.

He's thought of murdering her on more than one occasion. It's just a fantasy, but a very pleasant one.

He sees Rachelle at the desk. She's in a burgundy outfit, a white kerchief tied around her neck. The kerchief gives him an idea. Maybe he could strangle her with it. If he does it quickly, he could lower her body to the floor behind the desk, and no one would be the wiser. He would just step around her until he had time to dispose of her body in a more proper fashion.

It gives him joy to plot her murder. There's a skip in his step as he approaches the centrally located desk.

He sees a man standing at the desk talking to Rachelle.

The man is wearing a white shirt and dark slacks, just like Otis. He's about Otis's size. He has a receding hairline, just like Otis. He has a blunt jaw and blunt shoulders, just like Otis.

Otis halts.

He's seeing himself over there at the desk, a man just like him anyway. The same clothes. The same hair. The same face and body.

He blinks a few times and shakes his head. He looks again and then Rachelle is in the way.

Otis walks closer. Rachelle drifts out of the way, and Otis sees the man again. He's smiling at Rachelle.

The man's top front teeth are missing!

The sight of this man's missing teeth triggers intense fear in Otis. Fear that blasts his insides with dread. It's an unreasoning fear; he can't place it. And he keeps walking, right past the desk.

* * *

Spiros sees a young man walking toward the desk. He's tall and has blunt features. Rachelle looks that way, and then looks back at Spiros, her mouth in a frown.

She shakes her head.

Nope, not Otis, her expression says.

The young man walks past the desk, fades left, and vanishes into a corridor. Spiros thinks it was Otis and that Rachelle redirected him.

He looks closer at the environment. His trained eye discerns a line of demarcation. He thinks the Hotel Marquesas is partitioned off into two dimensional realities. He thinks Otis walked through a zero point and into another reality.

Spiros grabs Rachelle and pulls her to him.

"You're the trickster."

He pulls her over the top of the counter, holds her close, and looks into her eyes.

"I want you to help me."

"Okay," she whispers, and then purrs like a cat.

He walks her out the door. Minutes later, they are in Spiros's pickup heading for Van Nuys.

* * *

Cheryl is at her picture window gazing outside. She sees dozens of telescopic lenses suspended in the air, tucked within shifting layers of fog. They are all sizes: some huge, some tiny. They are alive, not mechanical, and seem to purr as they adjust focus.

The lenses and fog fade, and sepia-toned scenes from an earlier era appear. It looks like the Dust Bowl of the 1930s. She sees period buildings, cars, and people. Stark rural scenes form in rapid succession, most of them bleak views of churches and graveyards.

Cheryl has always felt an affinity for this period in American history, and for the people who lived through it. There was deep and widespread suffering.

The visions fade and she sees Spiros approaching her front door with a woman in a burgundy outfit and white kerchief.

No, not again! Cheryl runs to the hall closet, grabs her gun, and returns to the picture window.

She shoots at Spiros and the woman, the bullets punching through the glass.

Spiros and the woman are down. She backs away from the window, the gunfire ringing in her ears.

She collapses onto her living-room couch, the gun useless in her hand. She lets it drop to the floor.

What have I done? I've killed them! They're probably innocent!

Cheryl knows she has no charm, knows she's appealing only for her body, and maybe for her gumption, which only sprang upon her in recent times. But now they're stealing her gumption. And causing her to act impulsively.

These unreasoning murders ...

What will they do to her this time? More torture? Will they yank her teeth out again?

The torture is the worst. You can't breathe. You can't move. You're helpless. You feel like you're going to die.

That's when they get information from you. That's when another part of you comes out and reveals your secrets, or mysterious knowledge you didn't know you possessed.

Fog forms in the air.

She tenses and stares straight ahead. The room goes dark and she sees menacing shapes around her. She hears a voice but can't make out the words.

The words don't matter; she's learned that. What counts is the information they get from you when you think you're going to die.

She tries to move but finds she can't.

She's having trouble breathing. That's the key to the whole thing. They restrict your breathing. That's torture.

A frightening shape rushes at her, paralyzes her, robs her of her breath. She fights it, cries out, but with no air her voice is a silent shriek. She sinks away into a whirlpool of terror.

Moments later, her breathing is restored, and her terror fades. She tastes blood on her lips, sees blood on her blouse, on the couch, on the carpet.

✻ ✻ ✻

Spiros stands on Cheryl's front stoop, Rachelle in his arms. She's being friendly to him, but he knows there's a trickster in there, so he keeps a wary eye on her.

Fog is all around.

They hear gunshots. Star-shaped cracks appear in the picture window.

Spiros's heart lurches. He presses against the door.

Dimensional sightlines are suddenly visible. He sees Rachelle looking around.

She nuzzles him. "Don't worry. She saw us fall."

Spiros looks through a window in the door, sees down a long corridor into the kitchen at the back of the house.

He tries the knob. It's locked. He kicks the door in and rushes inside.

He runs into the living room and sees Cheryl slumped on a couch, two bloody incisors on the floor at her feet, a gun as well. Her eyes stare straight ahead.

Spiros watches her eyes and steps closer, Rachelle by his side.

"Cheryl, can you say 'Kiss the ...'?" he asks.

Cheryl squints at him, and then throws her head back and erupts in gales of laughter, blood spraying from her mouth.

Spiros steps back to avoid it.

"Kiss da ..." she says, her tongue hitting the gap where her teeth had been.

She explodes in laughter again.

Spiros asks his question again, and again he intentionally leaves a piece out.

"Can you say 'Kiss the ...'?"

Cheryl stares. It comes out in a bloody squall, her voice a deep rasp.

"Kiss da wolf."

CHAPTER 30

Sweet Grass, Juniper, and Sage

Otis is at work at the Hotel Marquesas, behind the desk with Rachelle. He tells her about the other world he's been visiting. The green world.

"Rachelle, the green world is my predominant world now."

"You can't be serious, Otis."

"I am serious. I spend most of my time there. It's like I'm on hiatus whenever I come here. Over there I have a heavy responsibility. I'm something of a dark angel."

"Uh ... what do dark angels do?"

"I better not say."

Rachelle makes like she's sprinkling magic dust on him.

"Otis, I think you need help. You're cracking up."

"Rachelle, the green world is real."

Again, she makes like she's sprinkling magic dust on him. He's relieved. Today, she's the kinder, gentler Rachelle.

✻ ✻ ✻

The next day, Otis drives to the San Bernardino Mountains and picks sweet grass in a high meadow. With the sun soaring higher, he drives to a lower elevation and picks juniper, and then to the desert and picks sage.

He stops on the way home and buys several earthenware pots and a box of wooden matches.

At home, he chops up the sweet grass, juniper, and sage and fills the earthenware pots with it.

The following day, he rents a circus tent, telling the owner he needs it to host a flea market.

He transports the circus tent to the mountains in a rental truck and sets it up in a meadow.

He spends the rest of the day inserting stout wooden poles into the ground inside the tent and attaching crossbeams across the tops of them to form an eight-foot-high corral-like structure that rings the inside of the tent.

Then he goes home to sleep.

He wakes in the morning and cruises the streets of L.A., looking for people who wish to take part in a spiritual journey.

He finds over a hundred eager seekers. He tells them to fast the next day and then come to the big grassy meadow in the mountains in the evening where they will find a circus tent.

He goes to a hardware store and buys several hundred feet of rope and a knife used to fillet fish.

He goes to a veterinarian supply store and buys a twelve-inch suture needle that's intended for use on cattle.

At a butcher shop, he buys a large quantity of bones, which are normally sold to dog owners. He takes the bones home and splinters them into long, sharp pieces with a hammer and chisel.

He stays up late that night, sleeps most of the next day, and then at 4:00 p.m. drives to the mountain meadow.

He disperses the earthenware pots throughout the tent and lights them. Slow fires send aromas of sweet grass, juniper, and sage into the air.

The spiritual seekers begin to arrive. Per instructions, they wait outside the tent, and Otis invites them in one by one.

The first participant is a man named Jerry.

"Hi, Jerry."

"Hi."

"Please come inside the tent."

Inside the tent, Otis instructs Jerry to kneel in front of an earthenware pot, which is casting off a burnt offering of sweet grass, juniper, and sage.

Otis stands off to the side and gives Jerry instructions on how to say thanks. Jerry says thanks in the prescribed manner.

With a lightning move, Otis grabs Jerry by the neck and applies enormous pressure to his carotid arteries until he blacks out.

Otis strips off Jerry's clothes, ties his hands behind his back, and binds his ankles.

He shoves the big suture needle through Jerry's shoulders between the clavicle and scapula on each side and threads a length of rope through.

He reaches into Jerry's mouth, pulls out his tongue, and shoves a long, sharp splinter of bone through it.

He drags Jerry to the back of the tent.

Using the rope he'd strung through Jerry's shoulders, he hangs Jerry from one of the eight-foot-high crossbeams.

Otis steps outside, invites the next participant in, and repeats the process.

In due course, more than a hundred men and women hang from the crossbeams, naked, bound, splinters of bone through their tongues.

Fires in earthenware pots burn inside the tent, sending sweet scents into the air.

Otis watches the strange tableau.

The flames cast stiletto-like shadows.

The air is thick with sweet grass, juniper, and sage.

With knife in hand, Otis walks to the first subject.

In the flickering firelight, he sinks the blade into the subject's chest, cutting deep into flesh.

He draws the knife down the torso, making a long incision.

He makes a parallel incision an inch away.

He cuts loose the intervening flesh, peeling it away top to bottom, letting it hang.

He cuts three more strips on this subject, on the meatier portions of the body, and then moves down the line.

Eventually, all participants are similarly filleted.

They are crying out, though they can't make much noise, as they have bones through their tongues.

Otis reflects upon their suffering.

Their suffering isn't just dim lights and savory smells and fasting and giving thanks; it's having one's flesh stripped from one's body; it's hanging from ropes inserted through bone and gristle; it's not being able to use one's tongue for expression; it's having to go deep inside oneself and touch something never before touched. He can't do that for them; they must do that for themselves. If they want an escape from the life that drove them here, they are on their own. He has given them an opportunity for self-reflection like nothing else in their society ever has.

See how easy it was. See how willing the victims were to place their trust in the hands of someone who promised them an easy path to salvation.

They do it all the time. They place themselves and their children in the hands of imbeciles.

They never take responsibility for their own lives; it's so easy to hand it over to another.

Where is their God? Is He riding to their rescue? Can galloping hoofbeats be heard?

Otis walks to a subject. The man's eyes are staring into unknown places. There is nothing to say to him.

Otis walks to another subject. There is nothing to say to this one, either.

He repeats the process with each of them and finds he has nothing to say to any of them.

Their spiritual journey must happen without a speech from Otis. He does not know what to tell them.

He's hung them up like cattle. What comes next?

Is this a mirror for their lives outside the tent? Are they cattle out there, also?

He hates to just leave them here. But what else can he do?

Has this done any good?

The fires grow dim.

Their cries end, they pass out, and a soul is nowhere to be seen.

Otis picks up a cell phone belonging to a subject, tries it out. It works.

He leaves the tent, gets into his car, and drives off.

A few miles down the road, he calls 911.

CHAPTER 31

Speak of the Devil

The phone rings in Endicott's bedroom. He wills peace and quiet to descend, but like a bad dream the sound persists. He turns on a lamp and answers with a sleepy, "Hello."

"Scott, the feds want your help on an investigation. They need you right away, tonight."

It's Carlisle. Endicott is instantly wide awake, his pulse jumping. "What's up?"

"Mass murder. In San Bernardino County. The feds say they need you. A car is on the way."

Endicott looks at the clock. It's 2:19 a.m. "I'll be ready in fifteen minutes."

"They said to dress casually and take an overnight bag."

"All right."

Carlisle hangs up.

Endicott turns on the television, surfs the news channels. There is no breaking news.

He dresses and packs a small suitcase.

He is certain of nothing. He feels a sense of dread as he hurries to the door.

Endicott stands in the open air watching the street. Moments later, a car pulls to the curb. Two men step out and identify themselves as FBI agents. Their names are Eriksson and Gillette. They check Endicott's badge and ID and tell him to get in back. Endicott gets in and buckles up.

Gillette gets behind the wheel and Eriksson takes the passenger seat in front. Eriksson tells Endicott it's a fast car. Why, Endicott thinks, does he feel it necessary to tell him that?

The vehicle pulls away from the curb with lights flashing. On the freeway, Gillette opens it up. It is indeed a fast car. The ride is unsettling.

Gillette exits the freeway near the city of San Bernardino and drives up a mountain road, headlights lancing through the darkness.

The road levels off and Endicott sees banks of powerful lights illuminating a circus tent in a meadow. People are prowling the lit-up areas, fanned out in a search. Farther out, helicopters are in the air, spotlights searching the ground.

Gillette pulls into a cordoned-off area and parks beside other official vehicles.

"More than a hundred people were murdered inside the tent," Eriksson says. "There were only two survivors."

"Someone skinned them alive," Gillette says.

Endicott feels himself inflate with a mixture of horrific fear and intrepid energy. He was not prepared for anything like this. He wants to do something right away. He is practically bounding out of his seat.

They leave the vehicle and go into the tent, where they witness bodies being photographed and swabbed for evidence.

The entire place is a crime scene. They are told where to step, where not to step. An hour later, they return to the FBI vehicle.

They watch as workers begin loading body bags into SUVs with darkened windows for transport to the county coroner's facility. In the powerful lights, the immense tent looks like a gray tombstone giving up the dead.

"Security tapes are being checked in the areas where these people were accosted," Gillette says. "When we ID the suspect, we'll furnish pictures to the media. We'll warn citizens and ask them for assistance in tracking down the person who carried out this attack."

"San Bernardino detectives have a working theory," Eriksson says. "Based on preliminary interviews with the two surviving victims, they believe a technology rendered victims unconscious, and then an unknown subject strung them up and tortured them."

Endicott feels a chilling numbness throughout his body. They're saying one person did all this.

Gillette's cell phone rings. He takes the call.

"We have a destination," he says. He starts the car, pulls out of the cordoned-off area, and heads down the mountain road.

They drive on a secondary highway into the Mojave Desert and enter a military base, where they pull into an underground parking garage.

An Army colonel escorts Endicott into the building, shows him to a cafeteria, and tells him to eat.

Afterward, the colonel shows him to a room that has a bed and an adjoining bathroom and tells him to get some sleep. He does not let him watch television.

＊　＊　＊

The following morning, the red numerals of a digital clock taunt Endicott's mind: 10:46 a.m. He is shocked at how late it is. He pries himself from bed. Why didn't they wake him? He dresses in the same clothes he wore the night before and leaves the room, his suitcase in hand.

He bumps into an Army sergeant in the hallway.

"Good morning, sir. I was just about to wake you. If you're ready, you can follow me."

They walk through a labyrinth of corridors and enter the cafeteria. About two-dozen people are scattered throughout the room, some in uniform, some in civilian clothes.

"Please find a table, sir. You can select from any of the serving lines. It's self-service at this time. Have a pleasant day."

Endicott walks to a table and sets his suitcase on a chair. He keeps an eye on it as he walks to a serving line.

He picks up a tray and plate, eyes the food, but has no appetite. His stomach does not feel good.

He wishes he could watch the news on TV. There are several TV screens mounted throughout the cafeteria, but all are dark, as they were last night. He wonders why.

"Americans are such curiosity seekers, you'd think they'd be watching television, but that's not the case. Makes you wonder."

Endicott turns toward the voice and sees a man walking

toward him. He's in his mid-forties, medium height, compact build. He's wearing a dark-green polo shirt and khaki trousers. He looks tough. He flows with catlike grace. In another life he could have been a swashbuckling cavalry officer or a lion tamer. He has a direct gaze and eyes that seem capable of grasping everything. His whole manner seems to want to cut to the chase.

"Mind if I join you for breakfast? Or is it brunch we are having?"

"Be my guest," Endicott says. "Brunch, I think, but I'm not very hungry. In fact, my stomach doesn't feel good."

"Stress?"

"Yes."

"Eat something, if you possibly can. Some fresh fruit, perhaps."

"I think I will," Endicott says. He goes through the line and selects strawberries, blueberries, and cantaloupe, and then adds two deviled eggs, toast, and coffee to his tray. His stomach is feeling better, and his appetite is returning.

"As for me," the man says, "I'll have a six-egg omelet; a stack of pancakes a foot high; maple syrup; two dozen slices of whole-grain toast with raspberry preserve; a whole cantaloupe, sliced; an orange, sliced; ten cups of coffee; twelve large boxes of raisin bran; and ten gallons of milk. That should hold me until dinner, Endicott."

"You're joking, sir," a young man in a white mess uniform says.

"That's true. I'm joking."

"You know my name," Endicott says.

"I knew there'd be an LAPD Detective Endicott here.

Since I recognized everyone else, by process of elimination, I figured it was you."

The man has piled his tray high with food. They walk to the table where Endicott left his suitcase on a chair. They set their trays on the table, pull out chairs, and sit.

"Do you have the tools of an assassin in there?" the man asks, motioning toward Endicott's suitcase.

"Not exactly." Endicott takes his suitcase off the chair and puts it on the floor beside him, positioning it against his leg. They begin to eat.

"You're guarding it as if it contained valuables."

"Just a change of clothes and some toiletries."

"Have you heard the phrase, 'make one's toilet'?"

"Yes."

"Most Americans would not understand it. They would see humor in it."

"True. It's not in our vernacular much."

"I think I know why they aren't letting us watch television."

"Why's that? And what's your name, by the way?"

"My name's Chester Manley."

"Glad to meet you, Chester. What do you do?"

Chester smiles. "That, I'm afraid, will have to remain unanswered."

"Okay. So why do you think they aren't letting us watch television, Chester?"

"I'm speculating, of course. The public at large is watching TV. We aren't. The government is afraid of panic, so the public is being given a watered-down version of the truth. I think they're afraid we might lose focus if we are surrounded by the same lies they're feeding ordinary citizens, don't you?"

"Good point."

"This sorry state of affairs needs to be corrected."

"Aren't you afraid of panic?"

"No, I am not. Oh, I believe there would be panic, but I simply do not care. We are lied to all the time, not just by government, but by every institution in the land. We are bombarded by falsehoods day and night. We tend to believe the falsehoods; the conditioning is pervasive and deep. Undeniably, our common identity depends on our shared ability to instantly embrace beliefs that are entirely irrational and false."

Chester falls silent as he works down the mountain of food on his plate. Between mouthfuls, he says, "Endicott, you're new at this game, but I'm an old hand. The people who command us are frightened, not just of our enemy, but of us. We need everyone fighting back this time. We can't do it if the public is misled."

Chester's eyes fix on something across the cafeteria. "Speak of the devil," he says.

Endicott's radar locks on. An Army officer and a young woman are walking their way. As they get closer, Endicott sees that the officer has four stars on each shoulder. The young woman is wearing a frilly white dress, and appears to be about eighteen or nineteen.

They stop beside Endicott and Chester.

"Let me introduce General Nathan McCutchan," Chester says, nodding toward the four-star. "That's his daughter you're staring at, Kristen-Kate."

✵   ✵   ✵

General McCutchan escorts Endicott and Kristen-Kate into a conference room. "Sit at the table," he says. "Give Chester and me twenty minutes."

Endicott and Kristen-Kate sit at the table.

The general leaves, closing the door.

A moment later, Kristen-Kate looks at Endicott. "They're acting pretty blasé about this, but they're really scared. Why are you here?"

"To assist in a criminal investigation."

"Wanna bet? They're discussing your situation out there right now."

"Oh?"

"Yeah." She leans toward him, as if wanting to speak in confidence. "Why do you think these alternate realities have sprung upon us?"

Endicott eyes her, his mind churning. He doesn't want to get into that with her.

"Did you know that Stephen D. Spiros is orchestrating all of this?" she asks.

He nods though he doesn't really know.

"Spiros keeps pulling me in," she says.

"Pulling you in?"

"Yes. He pulls me into alternate realities. It can be exhilarating at times, but also life-threatening. Afterward, I'm usually terrified. I've told my father about it. My father wants to kill him."

"Why would Spiros do that to you?"

"No one knows why. But it's obvious he has a plan for me. One of these times he's going to kill me."

She twitches in her seat, and nods as if encouraging him

to speak.

A minute goes by in silence, during which Endicott stares at the glossy surface of the table.

The door opens and Nat McCutchan and Chester Manley enter the conference room. The general asks Kristen-Kate to step outside. She does and shuts the door behind her.

Nat and Chester take seats across the table from Endicott.

"We know your plan," Chester says. "We have a source in LAPD. You and your partner are going to sit up over a victim named Cody Hobbs and wait for the predator to make a return visit."

Endicott nods.

"It's a good plan," Chester says. "It'll work. Shields will be disabled, allowing you to take the predator out. You don't have the option of making an arrest. Spiros wants a kill. It'll be the guy who's been committing the assaults LAPD has been investigating. By agreement with Spiros, it ends the chain of violence."

Endicott frowns. He knows he can't trust them. They left him alone with Kristen-Kate—or whoever she is—so she could trick him into revealing something. He didn't bite. They've been tagging Spiros without evidence. Now they're presenting a predator, also without evidence. An investigator needs to see evidence.

"Something else is on the table," Endicott says, "and it's more important than your little games."

"What's that?" Chester says.

"My daughter."

He sees them exchange looks.

"Your daughter?" General McCutchan says. "We know nothing of your daughter."

"I want her returned," Endicott says. "And she had better not be harmed."

Endicott sees the muscles of Chester's jaw tighten, and then a slight nod.

"You'll get her back," he says. "She'll be unharmed."

CHAPTER 32

A Terrible Presence

Jalaluddin Khan sits under the stars, a solitary figure whose mind chills and wanders, and then returns to the diminutive dancing flames before him. The log, burning more for illumination than heat, looks like a blackened flute with glowing fingers around it.

He lights his hashish pipe with a wick pulled from the edge of the fire, the wick glowing brightly and then flaring into eternity as he casts it into the darkness. The aroma of the cannabis pulls him into a mood far removed from the tranquil glow that meets his eyes.

A noise pierces the night—the creak of a door. He looks toward a mud-brick hut and sees Haji framed in the doorway. Haji watches him a moment, and then walks to the road.

Haji is going away for the night, but Jalaluddin Khan will see him again tomorrow. He resumes his meditations, his pipe laying contented wreaths about him. When it burns out, he sets it aside, lies on the ground, and falls asleep by the dwindling fire.

The next day, Jalaluddin Khan stands on a rugged footpath alongside a field bright with crops. Confused, he shields his eyes from the sun's glare. It has become difficult to see anything around him. This is a strange and new experience for him—in the blank slate of day, not being able to see. The bright flashes and confusion are oddly reminiscent of battles he has been in, though he does not expect to find the enemy here.

"The Americans are not here, are they?" he asks Haji, who stands nearby.

A strong wind hits the back of Jalaluddin Khan's neck and sends a shiver through him. And then an even stronger wind strikes him, accompanied by the image of a large bear that takes shape in his mind. The bear stands behind him and pours its powerful breath on him, letting it out through its sharp teeth.

He hears the sounds of this terrible presence behind him and his fear explodes into terror. He runs, or tries to.

He finds he cannot run; the earth seems to hold him fast. A circle of pain in his chest squeezes his heart, holds it in a powerful grip. The pain, seeking channels, runs to his arms, his throat, his face and head. He finds he cannot breathe except in shallow gasps. His mind grows dim and he collapses, words forming on his lips. Haji leans close to hear, adding another layer of suffocating misery with the powerful stench of his breath.

"Wind ... Bear ..."

Jalaluddin Khan's words whistle through his trembling lips in Pashto, his native tongue, and then he breathes no more.

Twelve American Special Forces soldiers rise from the terrain and creep around, keeping a wary eye.

After Haji informs him of Jalaluddin Khan's dying words, the Special Forces team leader transmits an encrypted message to the Pentagon via laptop computer and satellite uplink.

Wind. Bear.

The farm field is in northern Afghanistan.

There was no wind. No bear.

A weapons system rumored to be run from a secret military base in the Mojave Desert lured Jalaluddin Khan to this field and then triggered a drama shaped by fears lodged deep within the Afghan's psyche.

No one can know the full drama. Based on Jalaluddin Khan's panicked behavior and last words, experts in the Pentagon would be forming opinions as to the story that took shape.

The team leader sees a flash on his screen—a message from the Pentagon. He reads it. They have Jalaluddin Khan's death drama solved, somewhat.

He reads the first sentence: *Bear means Russians.* He reads the second sentence and feels a jolt.

He looks up, sees Haji standing a short distance away. The sun seems to do odd pirouettes around him, but otherwise he looks flesh and blood.

The team leader reads the full Pentagon report, which is only five sentences long.

There was no Haji, either.

The team leader draws his 9mm automatic and points it at Haji. "Who are you? I know you can speak English."

Haji takes a step away from the team leader, and keeps backing up.

The team leader knows the man is trying to escape, but he can't bring himself to pull the trigger.

"Tell me who you are."

Haji turns and runs across the field.

The team leader lets him go and makes a report to the Pentagon.

The Pentagon, acknowledging his report, reinforces earlier training.

The team leader calls his men together.

"Do not assume anything," he tells them. "Do not assume genuineness in anyone. Watch for anyone new. Watch for attempts at trickery. There is so much trickery inherent in this thing."

The men knew it. They'd been over it before.

CHAPTER 33

A Unique Signature

Spiros drives his pickup truck along a dirt trail in the Santa Ana Mountains. At a bend in the trail, adjacent to a succession of rugged hills, he parks, slings on a backpack, and walks to higher ground.

It's hot and he's perspiring freely by the time he reaches a dense thicket high on a hillside. He pushes through the thick growth, sees no one, hears only the wind.

He enters a small clearing, approaches a flat rock, kicks it, and waits. He kicks it again. Nothing stirs. He pulls an entrenching tool from his backpack and uses it to flip the rock over.

He digs down through the hard dirt and unearths a watertight metal box.

He brushes the dirt off the box, puts it in his backpack, and heads downhill.

He gets into his pickup, slips on latex gloves, opens the box, and removes a .44 caliber automatic, four boxes of ammo, and a Bowie knife.

The handgun, ammo, and knife are not traceable to him. He loads the gun and then slips it, the ammo, and the knife under the driver's seat.

He takes a sealed envelope from the box, opens it, and removes five official-looking documents. He glances through all of the documents, and then carefully examines just one of them. He already knew what was on the document but needed to verify it.

Wolf is Matt Jefferson.

He puts the documents back into the envelope and sets it aside.

He takes the gloves off, starts the engine, and drives back along the trail that brought him here.

Spiros drives to Matt Jefferson's house in Hesperia, a city in the Mojave Desert. He parks on the street and walks to the front door.

He knocks and waits, and feels the heat. The desert sun is a fiery devil in the clear blue sky. No one answers and he knocks again.

As he waits, he reviews a critical security measure.

Two years ago, he taught five U.S. military physicists how to run his technology, giving each a unique signature, telling each it was a required systems check, when it was actually a secret check on who was using the technology.

One of the five physicists was Matt Jefferson.

Jefferson was given Wolf. The other signatures were Lobo, Tarantula, Shakespeare, and Puck.

Only Matt Jefferson uses *Wolf* as a systems check.

Among the five, only Jefferson's version of the technology asks subjects if they can say *Kiss the Wolf.* A subject properly charmed, thinking his or her top front teeth gone, will say *Kiss da Wolf.*

In some cases, the subject's top front teeth will actually be gone, as the technology can torture for real or simulate it.

When Spiros heard Cheryl Toomey say *Kiss da Wolf,* he knew he would have to confirm that *Wolf* was Jefferson's signature by digging up the buried box and looking at the documents, as he did not know if his mind still held facts, or if he was the pawn of a treacherous faction of government that could plant any idea it wanted.

Spiros has his .44 automatic and his Bowie knife with him. He knocks on the door again. No one answers. He goes around back, breaks inside, and waits for Jefferson to return home.

❋　❋　❋

An hour later, Matt Jefferson pulls into his driveway. He walks to his front door, unlocks it, and steps inside.

He walks into the living room and sees a man sitting on an upholstered chair. The man appears indistinct against the sunlight filtering in through the drapes.

Jefferson takes a closer look. The man looks like Spiros.

Spiros holds a gun in one hand, a big knife in the other.

Jefferson sits on a couch facing him.

Spiros stands, walks toward Jefferson, and stops a few feet away.

A moment passes in silence.

"Spiros?" Jefferson asks.

The man nods.

This can't be, Jefferson thinks. He stands, looks behind him, and sees several bullet holes in the wall.

He can only imagine what happened.

When Spiros broke in, security sensors went wild, triggering another Jefferson to come home. That Jefferson had a conversation with Spiros after which Spiros aimed the gun at Jefferson's head and pulled the trigger several times.

Spiros should have left, happy. But he knew better. He'd shot a light being.

He waited for the real Jefferson to come home.

I am dead, Jefferson thinks. He's going to kill me.

Maybe he can finesse his way out.

"What can I do for you?" Jefferson asks, facing Spiros and remaining on his feet.

"Wolf is your signature," Spiros says.

Jefferson nods. "Whoever calibrates the technology uses Wolf as a systems check."

"No, it's your signature. It's unique to you. It's a security check, to see who's using the technology. Did you share it with anyone?"

"Uh, yes."

"Who did you share it with?"

"You don't have a right to know."

"You broke the secrecy agreement."

"We keep it within a tight circle. It would have been irresponsible to not share certain aspects of the technology.

If nothing else, we all take vacations. Someone has to run it in our absence. And if one of us should die ..."

"It wasn't supposed to get out like that."

"No, I don't suppose it was."

"How much was shared?"

"I'm not prepared to tell you."

Spiros starts circling him.

Jefferson's pulse leaps. He backs toward the entry.

"Look," Jefferson says, "I do field tests in Afghanistan. I work with the military on combat applications. That's all I do. There's another person I've entrusted. An associate."

They keep circling.

Too much, too much, Jefferson thinks. Sharp pains crawl through his chest. He feels like he's having a heart attack. His fear explodes, and he runs for the front door.

Spiros catches him, whacks him on the side of the neck with the barrel of his pistol.

The sudden surge in blood pressure from the blow shocks Jefferson's brain, and he goes limp and falls to the floor.

Spiros plunges his knife into Jefferson's ribs, tearing through his shirt and sticking flesh.

Jefferson shrieks.

Spiros pauses in his attack.

Jefferson looks down at his ribs, where blood soaks his shirt.

Spiros drags Jefferson back to the living room and throws him into a chair.

Jefferson sits slumped, his hands clamped to his wound.

Spiros sticks the point of his knife into the flesh beneath Jefferson's right eyeball.

"Tell me who else runs it," he says, "or I'll cut your eyeball out."

"I run it," Jefferson says, wheezing.

"Who else? You said you had an associate."

"I am Wolf!" Jefferson shouts, as if delirious. "I run it!"

Spiros pulls his knife away from Jefferson's eyeball and sticks him in the ribs again, drawing a second blood trail onto his shirt.

Jefferson hunches, shrieks. He looks at Spiros, his eyes struggling.

"Tell me who else runs it," Spiros says, "or I'll cut your head off." He raises his knife as if preparing to behead Jefferson.

Jefferson thrusts his hands up. "No, wait!"

With one swipe of the knife, Spiros cuts a swath through Jefferson's hands.

Making ghastly sounds, Jefferson whips a handkerchief out and presses it against his bleeding hands. Instantly, the white material is soaked with bright-red blood. Jefferson's eyes chase around the room as if looking for something bigger to press against his wounds.

"So, who's the associate?"

Words come violently from Jefferson. "There's a cloistered community in the San Bernardino Mountains! You can find him there!"

"Sounds like a trap."

Spiros whacks Jefferson in the face with the blunt edge of his knife.

Jefferson's head snaps back. He goes limp, turns dark, and bleeds from a fissure in his face.

He makes a gurgling sound and slips off the chair. He lies on the floor, bleeding from his face.

Spiros stands over him and watches the light fade from his eyes. He hunches closer.

"Who did you share the technology with? Who's running it in L.A.?"

Jefferson manages a croak.

Spiros leans closer.

"Who?"

Another croak.

And then a slow and halting voice issues from Jefferson. And Spiros strains to hear.

CHAPTER 34

The Monster

It's dark when Spiros drives his pickup out of Hesperia. Following Matt Jefferson's directions, he heads up a mountain road and encounters a community nestled in the hills. The homes are far apart, though not quite isolated from one another.

He locates the cabin Jefferson identified, drives past it, and parks in a stand of pine trees. He kills the headlights and shuts the engine off.

He watches the road from concealment. No one drives past. He gets out of the pickup and walks to the cabin, the moon breaking free from shuttering clouds, lighting his path.

The yard light is on. He stands among conifers and ferns, pine needles and dirt underfoot. He walks closer to the cabin. The windows are dark.

He stands in the pale glow cast by the yard light and knocks on the door. No one answers.

He dons latex gloves and pulls a lockpick from his pocket. He picks the lock, swings the door open, and steps inside.

He waits a couple of minutes in darkness, feeling the thump of his heart, and then pulls a flashlight from his belt and blazes a path through the rooms.

It's a large, well-kept cabin.

He finds the pictures where Jefferson said they would be, mounted on a wall in a bedroom: *Himself, Wini, Kristen-Kate, Kent, Cheryl, Otis, Rachelle, Jefferson.* Many others. A bond that stretches the imagination. A forever bubble.

Only lately had Jefferson been able to figure things out.

Spiros flicks the flashlight off and stands in the dark bedroom of the monster's cabin.

He walks into the living room. The glow from the yard light filters in through the curtains, giving everything a feeble quality. He sits on a wooden chair, sees shadows and shadings of shadows. A deck of wild cards.

He flicks his flashlight on and scans the room. The sharp corners of a low bureau jut into view. He flicks his flashlight off. And waits.

He hears a vehicle pull up on the crushed rock that serves as a driveway. He creeps to a window.

A lone individual, a white male, emerges from a sport utility vehicle and walks with purposeful strides to the front door of the cabin.

A key slips into the lock. The knob turns and the door opens. A draft of fresh air wafts into the room.

Spiros is standing beside the door, holding a sap. Nothing stands between him and the hand that reaches in for the light switch.

He sees a paw loom, and whacks it.

A sap is a springy device wrapped in rawhide, the business end being a lead weight. A loop at the end of the handle keeps it from flying out of your hand should you lose your grip.

Spiros didn't lose his grip.

The sap connected with the back of Chester Manley's right hand. Spiros thinks something broke, and it wasn't the sap.

Chester cries out in pain.

Spiros takes a step toward him and whacks him on the bridge of the nose.

Chester screams in agony, his hands flying to his nose.

Spiros aims again and saps him on the back of the neck.

Chester goes down, crying, "Jesus, God, motherfucker!"

There is one final sapping spot: a point on the side of the neck. A blow here carries a knockout jolt to the brain.

Chester is on his knees, his head to the floor, crying out his agony.

Spiros whacks him on the side of the neck.

Chester slumps—silent, motionless.

Spiros closes the cabin door, holds his breath, hears the steady *thump, thump* of his heart.

He pulls three coils of rope from his belt and hog-ties Chester.

He drags Chester to the bedroom.

He pulls a nylon stocking from his belt and puts it over his head. He whips a sheet off the bed and drapes it over the bedside lamp. He turns on the lamp and there is a dim light in the room.

He pulls a marble from his pocket and puts it in his mouth so his voice won't sound like his.

The sap is back in his pocket, ready for a quick draw if necessary.

He removes a hypodermic kit from a pouch, gets a syringe ready, and waits, watching blood ooze down Chester's face.

Time ticks.

Chester stirs.

Spiros walks to him, kneels, slaps him sharply across the face, one way and then the other. Chester's head flies back and forth.

He comes to, moaning softly.

Spiros slaps him again and then pinches his nostrils shut. He leans into him, his face inches from Chester's, stares into his eyes, the marble in his mouth, the stocking on his head.

He brings up the syringe.

Something like a light goes on in Chester's eyes, cutting through his sharp focus on his pain.

"Let's get one thing straight, buster," Spiros says. "I want you sane for this"—he shakes the syringe—"dialogue we're going to have. Savvy?"

Inside his blanket of misery, Chester nods.

"One drop of this and you'll slip away permanently. You comprehend?"

Chester nods again.

Spiros eases to his feet and backs away.

"Your name?"

"Chester Manley." His tongue is thick, the brain behind it addled by the repeated saps.

"Where do you live?"

"Hesperia."

"I'm told you come to this cabin for a purpose," Spiros says. "What is that purpose?"

Chester gives a muffled cry, apparently feeling an eruption of pain, and then replies. "This cabin and this village should not be."

Spiros feels a cold tingle upon his skin. "Go on."

"We monitor all the cabins," Chester says. "I'm assigned this one. It appears we are specimens in a strange zoological experiment."

Chester pauses, as if to put his thoughts in order, and then continues.

"It appears we are captives of a technology not of our making. To wit, we accept lines of demarcation, zero points, and alternate realities but know nothing about them. We accept beings that assist us or attack us. We know nothing of them, either. We have become violent, some of us exceedingly so. You come here, Spiros, and assault me as I enter the cabin, though I freely give this information to all who inquire."

His words shake Spiros, make a part of him that was asleep come awake.

He pulls the nylon stocking off his head, takes the marble from his mouth. He removes the sheet from the lamp, throwing more light into the room. He kneels and cuts the rope from Chester's wrists and ankles.

He goes into the living room and opens the front door. Air comes in through the screen door. He opens windows, and the curtains begin to sway. He turns on lights.

Chester trudges into the living room, his hands nursing his smashed nose. Spiros sees fear in his eyes, mixed with flickers of sheer terror.

They sit on chairs, facing each other.

"Tell me about yourself, Spiros."

He tells him about the Woodsman entity he created for the U.S. Air Force, the Pain-Shunt treatments he created at Quade Medical, the patients he counsels, the alternate worlds he tracks.

"You are Puck," Chester says.

"Puck?"

"Yes. Where do you live?"

"Irvine."

"Are there alternate worlds there?"

"Yes. They're all over, not just in Irvine."

"How can you tell?"

"I have equipment I use to monitor lines of demarcation and zero points. I routinely get reports from lucid people who say vast tracts of land are no longer around, as well as the people, buildings, and other things that occupied the land."

Chester looks away. Worry, or something, crosses his brow.

"I monitor the same things in Hesperia," he says. "My equipment likely differs from yours. I've identified five vast realms."

Chester rubs his forehead and then looks at Spiros.

"Are you familiar with Wolf, Lobo, Tarantula, Shakespeare, and Puck?" Chester asks.

An explosive shockwave strikes Spiros's core.

Chester continues, his eyes drifting.

"It seems these five realms are in competition to create a panoply of gods for a civilization not dissimilar from our own." His eyes stop their drift. "And we are likely the field test."

Spiros does not find his voice until after his mind has processed the information a good many ways. "Uh ... yes, I am familiar with them. Gods, huh?"

Spiros feels himself drop into a tighter spectrum, where he possesses greater knowledge.

"It'll be science, not a preacher," he says, "that will someday reveal our souls to us."

Chester watches him, and nods.

"I am Puck," Spiros says. "The scientific one. And Wolf and Tarantula have been flanking me all along. Shakespeare's realm is likely far and wide; certainly, it includes King's Forest. And where has Lobo been all this time? Was that him, or maybe her, at the Hotel Marquesas?"

He's identified Chester as part of the Wolf realm.

Wini as Tarantula. L.A. cops, also, as Tarantula.

Who else? Who runs the technology for Wolf in L.A.?

Chester is talking, and Spiros tunes him back in.

"Ordinary human awareness is like that of an animal poking its head up from a burrow," Chester says, "a prism through which nothing of a higher order is absorbed. It's time we had real gods guiding us."

"Who runs Wolf technology in L.A.?" Spiros asks.

"Hobbs ran it sometimes."

"Say again?"

"Cody Hobbs. He's a technician at the base. He aimed it at his apartment to impress some broad named Jill. The idiot almost got himself killed. We caught him and found out he'd been aiming it all over L.A."

"Hobbs? Give me an address."

"I'll give you an address, Puck. But realize that another realm is likely to win this competition. It'll probably be that imp Shakespeare. You are far too violent; the rest of us are on a higher plane. I suspect the eventual winner has already sunk below a critical threshold. When he takes over, we won't even know it."

"I'm violent? What do you call the attack on Kent?"

Chester does not respond, instead writes something on a piece of paper and hands it to Spiros.

Spiros takes the paper, sees that it's Cody Hobbs's address.

Anger creeps into Spiros's voice. "It was Wolf's signature attack. You fractured Kent's cervical spine. It wasn't Hobbs. It was you. Kent's dead; they pulled the plug. You did it to others, also."

"It was unfortunate. We wanted to find a way to hobble the population if necessary. Of course, it went wrong."

"You wanted to find a way to hobble the population?"

"Yes. It was part of the field test."

"What kind of a monster are you?"

"The kind that searches new paths. The kind that accepts new realities. Ultimately, we'd have found something that worked. We'd have done away with law enforcement, the courts, the penal system."

Spiros walks to the door, reaches for the light switches, pauses to glance at Chester.

Worry rides up Chester's face, then fear. His lips start working, but make no sound. The blood on them takes on an unhealthy sheen.

Spiros douses the lights.

"Wha-wha-what?" Chester sputters. The dark has thrown him off.

Spiros seizes him, hog-ties him again, Chester unable to put up much of a fight. He drags him toward the low bureau.

"What are you doing?" Chester's voice trembles.

Spiros flicks his flashlight on, sets it on the bureau. The light does a hoodoo dance across the wood grain.

Spiros grabs Chester. "When did you first realize I couldn't let you live?"

"No!" Chester explodes into rage.

Spiros swings Chester high.

"No!"

Spiros slams Chester face-first onto a sharp corner of the bureau, slams him a second time, a third time.

He drops him, flips him over, shines the flashlight on him. Chester's face is caved-in, a gore-fest.

Spiros checks his pulse.

He's alive.

He decides he'll leave him.

Spiros takes his rope, takes his flashlight and knife, takes whatever is his and leaves everything else. He'd worn gloves, so no prints.

He doesn't close the windows or door. He leaves the lights as they were when Chester became jelly. Dead off.

He leaves the cabin quietly and scuffs his shoes across the dirt yard.

He jogs down the road, comes into areas of waxy light as he passes residences.

He slips into his pickup and drives down the road. He feels the breeze through the open windows and luxuriates in the green sappy smells of conifers.

He drives to San Bernardino and pulls into Cody Hobbs's apartment complex. He parks as close to the front door as possible, kills the headlights and engine, and gets out.

He slips on gloves, carries his lock pick and his .44 automatic, and walks to the door.

CHAPTER 35

The Revolver Ritual

It's dark in Endicott's bedroom, except for a sliver of moonlight at the window. He stares at the slice of moon and feels a powerful compulsion to get his revolver, load it, and put it to his temple. He decides he will defy them—the sick ones who suck him into these dramas. In fact, he will mock them. He will load the gun but will not put it to his temple. He rises from bed, walks to the closet, pulls the revolver case off the shelf, and carries it back to his bed.

He loads a round into each cylinder and sets the revolver beside him.

He feels a slight give in their instructions. Are they backing off? Has he discovered something profound in resisting their orders?

Something makes him want to continue in this vein, to resist the revolver ritual completely.

And then a powerful urge takes him over and he grabs the gun and puts it to his temple and pulls the trigger, but his hand jerks and the bullet hits the wall.

He turns on a lamp and sees a bullet hole in the wall. The sound still rings in his ears.

Before his heart has time to settle, another powerful urge seizes him and he puts the revolver to his temple again and pulls the trigger.

Click.

This time his hand did not jerk. The gun misfired. Was it a bad cartridge?

An idea evolves in his mind. A world—its myths and legends—is taking shape around him. The revolver ritual, a test for Endicott, will now become a parable.

❋   ❋   ❋

It's morning. Endicott sits on his bed, takes the revolver out of its case, puts it to his temple, and pulls the trigger.

Click.

It's empty.

He puts the revolver back in its case and puts the case on the shelf in the closet.

He's done it again, another revolver ritual. He's done how many of them now? And at no time did he blow his brains out.

The gun has always been empty. *Though he did load it in the dream last night.*

He paces his bedroom. It's not yet time to go to work.

He doesn't want to go downstairs. No one is there.

Katrina doesn't come over anymore. He never sees Renee. All he has is his job and the revolver ritual.

He looks at the back of the room and sees a spidery shape. He keeps it in view and it vanishes.

They don't like attention. They prefer to hide below the visible world and influence events.

He knows he has been too passive. How can he defy them? He thinks of what he must do next. He and Lionel must sit up over Cody Hobbs, wait for the predator to show, and then blow him away.

He won't do it. He'll stay here. How's that?

They're looking at him now, the spidery shapes at the back of the room.

"I'm not going to do it," he says.

And now the spidery shapes are crawling out of the shadows and marching around him.

They tell him he has passed two tests thus far. They tell him if he passes a third, he can be their king. Then the spidery shapes crawl back into the shadows.

"But if I refuse?" He hears sounds of rapid movement in the shadows. The spidery shapes flock back to him.

Yes, you can refuse! But first you must escape into the un-known!

"Escape into the unknown?"

Yes, escape into the unknown!

"But isn't that dangerous?"

You must do it!

He must do it. He must follow their orders and escape into the unknown and then he will see Renee and Katrina again.

It's not enough for them to coerce him into performing. The decision to perform must come from the deepest levels of Endicott or it doesn't work. And if Endicott isn't up to it then someone else will be. Now he understands. He's in competition with others.

He sits on his bed and clears his mind and lets the spidery things crawl all over him and talk to him.

He knows he'll appear in some sacred text. What will his legacy be? Will they read about Endicott the Elder, Endicott the Vain, Endicott the Swine?

There is no answer yet. He shall go and do the right thing. He shall go and face the test.

He sits on his bed, his mind wound tight. It would be magnificent to be the spider god, to see all and know all and spin webs that ensnare people when they need to be ensnared.

But is that what he wants?

He would not be able to see Katrina and Renee again. They would be of a different order.

He thinks the spidery things will hurt him if he does not choose allegiance to them.

Will they hurt Katrina and Renee also?

He asks them.

"Will you hurt Katrina and Renee?"

He sees Katrina grow out of the wall and crawl toward him, Renee behind her. They crawl around him and then crawl back into the shadows and vanish.

The sight leaves Endicott empty and perplexed. He is like a candle in a world with no flame. How long does it take such a candle to die?

The idea doesn't seem strange anymore. He is sitting up over Cody Hobbs in Hobbs's apartment, his mind touching other places, as he and Lionel wait for the predator to make a return visit.

The predator always makes a return visit. Why didn't they grasp that long ago? Why didn't they sit up over a victim long ago? He knows the answer. The time was not right.

But now the time is right, and he has made his decision. He knows he cannot have his wife and child back if he accepts the mission to become the spider god *Tarantula*.

He wants Renee and Katrina to be a part of his life. He does not want to be the spider god and peer out over his realm in loneliness.

For this he knows he will be called Endicott the Traitor.

Or even worse.

They will read of him far and wide.

But he will have his old life back. And it will include Renee and Katrina.

He hears a sound, someone out in the hallway.

The place is mostly dark. Cody Hobbs is in a chair in the living room, Endicott on the balcony, Lionel in the kitchen.

Endicott listens. He thinks someone is trying to work a charm on the dwelling.

CHAPTER 36

Shifting Lines of Demarcation

Katrina flies awake in her bed, leans over, and turns on a lamp. The glow spreads over her like a fiery moth opening its wings. She cowers, half under the bedcovers. Then the bedcovers are swiped from her and she is laid bare in her pink pajamas.

A frigid hand strokes her cheek. A face looms.

Woodsman.

Moments ago, in her dreams, she was locked in combat with Woodsman over her father, losing the battle, losing her father.

And now Woodsman is in the bedroom with her.

He holds up a bloody nub, something fleshy, messy, and Katrina shivers at the sight of it, knowing it was freshly severed from someone's body. A nose? Could it be a nose?

"Dad?" She starts to rise. He was sleeping in the next bed. They'd been sharing the same bedroom for protection.

"Dad?"

She's about to scream, but a hand wraps over her mouth and pushes her down into the mattress.

Dad! Dad! Oh, what did he cut from you?

Woodsman releases his hand from Katrina's mouth.

"Hush," he says. "You must stop it, Katrina."

"Where's Dad?"

"Your father is a trickster."

"He's my dad. What did you do to my dad?"

Woodsman holds up the bloody nub.

And that is when Katrina realizes the front of her pink pajamas is covered with blood. Her own blood. And that the tip of her nose is missing.

"Your father bit it off," Woodsman says. "He went at you in your sleep."

"Ahhh ..." Her wail dies softly and tears spill down her cheeks. She raises her hands toward her face, holds them close to her wound, not wanting to touch anything.

"The gods are at war, Katrina," Woodsman says. "You must be strong."

Katrina collapses into whimpers, her mind going to pieces.

Woodsman shakes her. "You must stop it. There is trouble. Someone has diverted your father from his rightful task."

"Where is my dad?" She must go to her dad. "Oh. Help me get up. We must go to a hospital. My father—"

"Your father must be returned to his rightful task."

"What is that?"

Woodsman points to the shadows.

She looks into the shadows, feels a sharp intake of breath. Her hand flies to her mouth and she stifles a scream.

She sees her father deep in the shadows—with a gun, waiting to kill someone.

✳   ✳   ✳

Her mother is shaking her, and Katrina wakes. She finds that her nose is okay, and that she is not covered in blood.

"You were having a dream, Katrina," her mother says.

"A dream?"

"Yes."

"I saw Woodsman. He told me Dad was in trouble."

"Your father is at work, on a case. Don't worry. We'll be living with him again soon."

"He's at work this late?"

"Yes."

✳   ✳   ✳

Cody Hobbs feels confident he will be protected. Two cops are guarding him, one in the kitchen, the other on the balcony.

He felt totally vulnerable the last time the spies entered his apartment and assaulted him. That won't happen this time.

Will the spies come, though? He's been home from the hospital for two weeks now, still not healed, and he's been anticipating this moment. They say tonight, but how can they be certain? It's almost as if they were arranging it.

He's moving slowly. The dark shapes worked him over good. His body is a mass of puffy scar tissue. He's bruised all over.

Cody and Detective Lukens fix sandwiches in the kitchen and carry them to the balcony, offering one to Detective Endicott, who waits there.

They are talking about sailboats, standing on the balcony, and Cody thinks something is not quite right.

* * *

And now they are talking about Hawaii, standing on the balcony and having a blast while doing so, talking about how sailboats operate.

The night air is warm, a hint of wildfire in the air.

All three have decided they will retire to Hawaii someday.

"Did you know Hawaii is famous for whale hunting?" Cody says. "At least it used to be, in the nineteenth century."

Lukens retires to the kitchen to await the predator.

Cody and Endicott stay on the balcony.

Endicott is a big, rawboned man. He wears a cream-colored suit, a light-blue shirt, and a red tie. He's sandy haired and has a mustache. He drove a white sedan here and spends all his time surveying the area, maintaining a serious, contemplative air.

"Let's go to Hawaii after this is over," Cody says. "Bring your wife and daughter, too. What do you say?"

"I say you're nuts. Count yourself out."

* * *

Cody feels an urge to go to Hawaii. He wonders why. He doesn't even like Hawaii, except for whales and volcanoes, and you can get them elsewhere. Come to think of it, Hawaii is the best place to get them. It's great over there. What was he thinking?

"I'm going to phase out my existence," Cody says, "and move to Hawaii. That's the place to be. No more worries, no more cares. I'll go surfing, I'll go fishing, I'll go exploring."

"How will you pay for it?" Endicott asks.

Cody thinks. "That's the problem. I have no money beyond making ends meet. I need to solve that first, then I'll go to Hawaii and live the life I've always wanted to live."

They stand on the balcony and eat sandwiches off paper plates, a late supper. They talk of Hawaii, the whales and volcanoes. Also, the military; it has a big presence there.

"I knew a guy," Endicott says, "who was injured in Hawaii. He was bodysurfing and a wave threw him onto the beach. He broke his shoulder. He underwent a medical treatment and acquired a pain god. Do you know what a pain god is?"

"Yes. The spies told me."

"This guy could easily have fractured his cervical spine if he had landed differently on that beach. His pain god talked to him and convinced him he had to fracture other people's cervical spines or he'd revisit that wave with a different outcome. He's been fracturing cervical spines ever since to avoid that fate. Meanwhile, the guy's pain god orbits the new victims, expanding its realm."

"How does he get away with it?"

"He's good. He practices his moves."

"Jesus."

"That's not all. His pain god arranges little conspiracies

so he's never caught. Law enforcement has been told to back off or be under the same charm."

※　※　※

Cody sees a tall man on the balcony. He's wearing a dark baseball cap and glasses. He is thickset and has a watchful aspect.

The man turns sideways and looks in all directions and then goes back to watching Cody.

He has a blunt head and blunt shoulders and is long in body. He has short dark hair, a round face, and stands about six-four. He seems out of place but not threatening.

He's overdressed for the weather. Why's he wearing so many clothes? Cody wonders. It's too warm for all that. He even has a jacket on.

He seems concerned about something. It looks like he might approach Cody.

※　※　※

Cody and the tall man with blunt features are standing on the balcony talking about Hawaii.

"Did you know they used to hunt whales in Hawaiian waters?" Cody asks.

"Yes, long ago."

"Now the whales are just for tourists."

"I know."

"They have active volcanoes on the Big Island. The islands are still growing because of volcanic activity."

Cody feels something is not right. He leaves the balcony, steps into the living room, and sees the tall man there, also. He ambles through the other rooms looking for the two cops and finds no one.

He realizes the cops were never there.

He ambles back to the living room.

He stands his ground and the tall man comes at him fast.

Cody sidesteps him, gives him a shove, and then runs out of his apartment and heads down the hall.

Moments later, Cody observes the tall man leave his apartment, and he sneaks back inside.

Spiros senses shifting lines of demarcation in and around Cody's apartment building. It's an unstable environment. He can't get into the building. His lock pick won't work. He tried to shoot the lock, but his gun wouldn't fire. He is shut out. A zero point has shunted him aside.

A controlling force is aware of his presence and has redirected him.

He feels he must escape the target environment or encounter an unknown danger that might prove deadly. He searches for a seam, finds one, and slips out.

He locates his pickup and gets into it. He drives aimlessly through the streets; his only objective is to stay away from Cody's building. He feels like an animal lying up in a storm.

He thinks the game isn't over.

He thinks he'll get his chance. He thinks he'll play an integral role in the ascendance of a new god.

Otis knocks on Cody's door. A young man answers.

"Are you Cody Hobbs?"

"No."

The door closes.

Otis doesn't know what to think. It was Cody. Why'd he let him do that? Next time go after him—and make it fast.

Otis knocks on Cody's door again. Cody opens it and Otis rushes in with a fingertip pressed against Cody's forehead.

Cody backpedals and falls to the floor. He thrashes about as Otis kneels and keeps pressure on his forehead.

Cody goes still and Otis removes his fingertip from Cody's forehead. Cody is awake, his muscles paralyzed, his breathing shallow.

They told him Cody has old wounds. Make him bleed from old wounds, they said.

Otis strips off Cody's shoes and socks, shirt, trousers, and underwear, exposing his entire body.

He begins his examination. There's a massive network of scar tissue up and down Cody's body. He counts more than forty wounds, large and small.

He selects a wound that runs from Cody's right hip to his knee. It's a rough crease of scar tissue.

He rolls Cody onto his left side.

Otis takes a knife he uses for filleting fish and cuts the wound open along its entire length.

Blood seeps from the reopened wound and streams down Cody's legs and onto the carpet.

Otis selects another old wound, a ridge of scar tissue across Cody's chest, and reopens it, cutting as deep as possible without inflicting a mortal wound.

Cody is fully conscious but unable to make a sound or move.

Otis takes his time, cutting deep along each previous wound, but careful not to cut too deep.

He reopens all of Cody's old wounds.

Otis examines his handiwork and then takes his knife and widens the wounds, probing them to see if he can go deeper. He finds he can and makes the additional cuts.

When he is done, Cody is a mass of jellied flesh.

He puts Cody's clothes back on him and props him on his feet. Cody begins walking around the living room.

Cody sits on a chair, and Otis takes his knife and cuts off Cody's nose.

✳ ✳ ✳

Endicott and Lukens fire their guns at the predator, hit him multiple times, see him fall. Endicott goes to him, checks his carotid artery for a pulse.

The man is dead.

Endicott takes his cell phone out and calls it in.

"Scott, I feel a little woozy," Lukens says.

"Record it," Endicott says. "Whenever you feel woozy, record it. Anything weird, record it."

* * *

When Cody went to the door and opened it, he saw no one. He backed away and found himself on the floor, temporarily paralyzed.

He got up and walked around the living room and then sat on a chair.

He waited for the predator to pay another visit.

They say the predator always makes a return visit.

Cody was confident the two cops would protect him, the one on the balcony, the one in the kitchen.

He got up and checked on them. They weren't there. He looked in a mirror and screamed. *His nose was gone!*

There was nothing there but a blood-soaked void.

He tried to run to the phone but collapsed.

He tried to crawl across the floor but couldn't move.

His whole body was a mass of quivering flesh. He realized his tendons had been cut.

CHAPTER 37

The Heart of Human Darkness

As Spiros and Kristen-Kate acclimate themselves to Jelly Thompson, and to Africa, they learn that he is a man of fierce body and mind sinew. Like the African land itself rising out of the morning mist, Jelly emerges each day with an inner terrain that pours forth, enveloping them in its hypnotic contours. But on this, their third day of safari, Jelly has been like the mist itself, obscure rather than revealing. This morning a runner from an indigenous hunter-gatherer tribe stopped by camp with a message. Jelly has been in contemplative orbit since, worried but trying not to show it. His rifle has not left his side all day. And this, a picture-taking safari, where nary a shot is to be fired, except in extreme circumstances to save a human life.

❋　❋　❋

The truck thuds into a shallow dry pan and delivers a jolt to Spiros's injured left foot. In agony, he sits and muffles a cry. Kristen-Kate remains on her feet, her head poking out of the sunroof, scanning with binoculars. Maxwell, the black man at the wheel, laughs. He knows about Spiros's injury, the lack of a genesis, though Spiros has never mentioned it to him, and Jelly swears he hasn't told him, either. Maxwell's laugh is one of kindness—he is sharing Spiros's pain and wants to steal it away. Spiros removes his boot, rubs his heel and arch, soothing his pain, as Kristen-Kate takes her seat beside him for a brief rest.

It is evening, the sun a fiery red tempest on the horizon, the sky shifting in hues of pink and blue. The engine sings and the vehicle dances and the two Americans stand, poke their heads out of the sunroof, and scan the savanna with binoculars once again. They sway to the gentle rhythms as the modified Toyota Land Cruiser floats over the green swords of grass, aflame with fire from the setting sun.

"How many people in Africa are eaten by lions in a given year, Jelly?" Kristen-Kate asks. She lofts her voice to compete with a fish eagle whose macabre refrain streaks the air with tints and shades of dementia.

Jelly is sitting in the front passenger seat. He favors Kristen-Kate with a glance and a slight uplift of chin. "I couldn't begin to guess, love."

"Liar!" Quick as a cat, she swipes Jelly's bush hat from his head and waves it out the sunroof.

Jelly spins, reaches into the backseat, and grabs a handful of Kristen-Kate's khaki shorts. He gives a firm tug but she won't give up the hat. She waves it as high as she can in the open air, squealing with delight. Jelly tugs harder ... harder ...

Kristen-Kate's pants begin to slide down. She grabs her waistband and holds tight, making an awful mewling sound.

A tug of war ensues. Spiros watches as inch by inch the entirety of Kristen-Kate's velvety buttocks are exposed.

She gives Jelly his hat back and hoists her shorts, her face turning as red as the sunset.

Jelly puts his hat on and gazes at her. "You're trying to evoke the authority figure in me, aren't you, Kristen-Kate? I should put you over my knee. What do you think, Spiros? Her pants were conveniently off. Should I have put her over my knee?"

Spiros is shocked. Jelly is not like this. Arrogant, yes, but with a bit of humor cushioning it. Now, though there is humor in his tone, it borders on something savage.

"She got her reward, Jelly," Spiros says. "She lifted you out of your blue funk. No need to compensate her further."

Jelly roars with laughter.

Kristen-Kate smiles and nudges Spiros with her elbow, letting him know it's okay. But Spiros knows she is hurt. She will cry later, he thinks. He puts an arm around her, nuzzles her hair, sneaks a look into her eyes. She is crying now, a satiny tear on her cheek.

"Kristen-Kate," Jelly says, "Africa does not keep good account of its man-eating simbas. Keep in mind leopards do their man-eating chores, also. Crocs kill and eat more humans than do lions and leopards. Elephants and hippos kill humans but refuse to eat them. Snakes kill humans. Mosquitoes kill humans. Parasites, germs, and viruses all kill humans. Humans kill humans in wholesale numbers. And no one keeps track of the slaughter."

Like a witch floating out of the gloom, an acacia tree looms. All eyes in the truck scan the murky ground beneath it and then zoom to its wide-reaching branches, silhouetted in the dying embers of the sun. Something is draped on a branch.

"Leopard," Jelly says. Maxwell steers the Land Cruiser into a wide arc around the tree. Two luminous eyes lock on the truck.

Spiros and Kristen-Kate lift their cameras and snap pictures.

"She's got an impala up there with her," Jelly says.

"She?" Kristen-Kate says. "How can you tell in this light?"

"The pattern hits me, love."

"Spooky, Jelly," Kristen-Kate says with admiration.

"Sorry about your pants, love. Didn't realize my own strength. My mind has been a bit wandering today. Also, should have known you weren't wearing anything underneath."

"That's okay, Jelly. But next time, look. The pattern will hit you."

Jelly laughs. "She's quite a gal, Spiros. I envy you, old man."

Spiros relaxes and inhales the fresh scents that wash over him, his spirits lifting to fly with the tendrils of the coming night.

He and Kristen-Kate sit and tuck their cameras away. The truck resumes its journey, leaving the acacia-bound leopard behind.

Spiros recalls the runner who came by camp this morning inducing Jelly's funk.

"Jelly," Spiros says, "what did that man say to you this morning?"

"He said nothing."

And that is exactly what Spiros remembers. The man stood before Jelly, a silent melody. And Jelly only stared.

❊   ❊   ❊

"Garlic," Kristen-Kate says. "I was just thinking of garlic. And smelling it. And seeing it, like little sparkles in the air." She looks at Spiros, wonderment in her eyes. "You too?"

Spiros nods, to humor her. "It's dinner time, Kristen-Kate. That's why."

She wrinkles her nose at him. "I don't know, Spiros. I think it has something to do with vampires."

With Kristen-Kate setting the mood, little granules of garlic greet them as they sprinkle themselves into the twilight in northern Botswana. Halos of garlic and gasses from garlic—splinters of light and scintillating sniffs. The air is free and all its lights and all its smells lead them where they want to go.

"Come on, Jelly," Kristen-Kate says. "Tell us why you're so apprehensive. Is it vampires?"

He says nothing, so she makes as if to swipe his hat again, but he grabs her wrist and holds it tight.

"Kristen-Kate, my instinct, gathered from much experience on the African continent, tells me we have been in danger all day. The man stopping by this morning was mere confirmation."

He releases her wrist.

"Do you fear a lion attack?" she asks.

He laughs. "No, not lions. We are peering into the heart of human darkness, Kristen-Kate, and this heart, as dark as it is, hides an even darker heart beneath."

"I have an alternative explanation," Kristen-Kate says. "The whole world is a circle of garlic lights and garlic smells that keep the deadly ring of vampires out, but in Africa, and certain other places, vortices are allowed to exist, and no one knows why. In these places the usual rules don't apply."

Spiros only half listens to Kristen-Kate. She's being goofy again, to cheer them up. He dwells on Jelly's words. Is he talking about war? Spiros knows the dangers of war in Africa. Killing runs along ethnic and tribal lines. Rivers run red with blood as torrential currents wash bodies downstream.

"Jelly, is there a war brewing in Botswana? If so, we should seek safety now, rather than venture into further risk." He watches Kristen-Kate for signs of disapproval; she's always eager for adventure, but of the playful kind. He sees that her eyes are intent upon Jelly, hanging on his every word.

Jelly answers Spiros's concern. "No, Spiros. Not in Botswana. In Sierra Leone."

"Sierra Leone? Where's that?"

"Sierra Leone is a small country on the west coast of Africa, about three thousand miles north of Botswana. Freetown is the capital."

Something in Jelly's tone makes that distance miniscule in Spiros's mind. "What's going on there, Jelly?"

"A civil war, Spiros. Insurgents are running guns to replenish their wares. There's a grisly sideline to this war. Rebels with axes enter villages or Freetown itself, find defenseless men, women, and children, and hack their arms off. They make you watch as you wait your turn. You beg and you scream, but the rebels laugh at you. They've done it to thousands, earning Sierra Leone the distinction of having the world's highest number of amputees."

An icy chill digs at Spiros's bones. Kristen-Kate makes an awful mewling sound, dark and grim. The icy chill inside Spiros gives way to a simmering rage.

"Why such cruelty?" Kristen-Kate asks.

"You might ask why the victims are so meek," Jelly says. "I think I know the answer to that. To its disgrace, the human race abhors itself and teaches erroneous values, seeking grace from a supernatural source. All human societies teach their children meekness and obedience. To be a child raised as a strong entity within the family and culture is to be from another planet. Adult humans are mere children in bigger clothing. From this mess, cruelty rises and finds victims as easy as the sun finds daisies in a field."

The night is talking to them. Light from the sunken sun bleeds deep twilight into the sky, puts purple smudges on the faces of the high, wraithlike clouds. The clothing that covers the land might be the cloaks of vampires.

Something in the grass arrests their attention. Something long and slithery and catlike. The last burning embers of the sun are flying around and the first faint stars are beginning to flicker when Maxwell stops the truck.

"We shouldn't do this," Jelly says.

But they all pile out to chase the wounded animal.

"Spiros," Kristen-Kate calls, "tell us what this means from an evolutionary standpoint."

Her question throws him. He is momentarily unhinged. What does she mean? The rebels who chop people's arms off? This animal that's trying to hide? Or us, on our misguided mission out of the truck? He grabs at something and laughs with a sick hilarity as he shouts. "You're blood-thirsty, I'm bloodthirsty, we're all bloodthirsty."

"No, Spiros," Kristen-Kate says. "Nature demands scholarly reflection, and you're the scholar."

She's right. But he has no ability to reflect on anything right now; he is seized by the realization that Jelly has been shouting at him.

"No, Spiros, stay away from it!"

Spiros watches in horror as the hyena comes out of no-where and tears into the pregnant cheetah—not for the first time. Pieces of cheetah, the mother and newborns, lay littered across the grass. Mother was giving birth when the hyena first found her. Now she is being eaten alive.

"Shoot, Jelly, shoot!" Kristen-Kate yells. "Shoot the motherfucker!"

"No. Everybody, back in the truck," Jelly yells. They disobey, and stand and watch.

A long, wild squeal erupts. They see another hyena bounding through the grass. It pounces on the cheetah. The first hyena drives it off. Freed, the cheetah rises and hobbles away. Both of her hind legs have been bitten through to the bone and are flopping around useless. Slinking away on her rear stumps, she looks sloped-backed, like a long, looping hyena.

The two hyenas see their prey escaping. They cease their quarrel and drown the cheetah in a frenzy of snapping jaws.

"Everybody, back in the truck!" Jelly shouts. They run.

The evening is rapidly taking on a dark and furtive look as they pile back into the truck. Spiros sits in the backseat with Kristen-Kate as Maxwell eases the nimble Land Cruiser forward. Jelly sits in front, watching the darkening terrain, his rifle cradled in his arms.

"I want to kill something," Kristen-Kate says, and pounds her fists on the seatback near Jelly's shoulders.

"It's nature, child," Jelly says. "We can't interfere. You're a part of nature yourself, Kristen-Kate. When you fall in love with a man, do you want some third-party asshole with a rifle to come along and sort things out for you? Tonight, the cheetah and hyenas were meant for each other. Think of it as their wedding night. For now, it's the only morality we have."

Spiros shifts his weight to favor his left foot, which feels like fire on ice. He agrees with Jelly, though is stunned by the ferocity of the hyenas.

Then Puck arrives with a long, slender needle dipped in poison, and Spiros braces himself for the first of what will be many stabs into the deepest pits of pain.

Why did I take on this wound? For whom? And what multi-tude of sins does it represent?

His thoughts shock him. Before he can stop himself, he utters something bizarre.

"I'm becoming Jesus."

Everyone looks at him. He feels exposed; he feels as if he were floating across the face of the moon for the entire world to see.

"I'm confused," he says. Their eyes peer oddly at him. "Forgive me; it came out wrong." Their eyes glide away. Then Puck slides the needle into a new place deep inside his foot and Spiros yelps.

Puck draws his needle back a hairsbreadth, and with a claw as dark and dangerous as anything in Africa, pries open one of Spiros's eyes. Tears stain this eye. This eye and its brain see only dim halos. Puck draws his needle back another hairsbreadth, and Spiros's vision clears. Puck releases the eyelid and watches it flutter shut. He pries the other eye open. But this eye is no good.

He primes Spiros's good eye again. Peers out of this eye. Still good. He lets the eyelid slide shut. He experiments with his needle, repeatedly trying to see out of Spiros's other eye. But the other eye is still no good.

It is essential that this eye be made good. He goes to work on this eye, drawing his needle into ever more intricate areas of Spiros's left foot. The left foot is all he needs for this; it knows the whole person.

Where is that eye? He does not find it. Puck is not emotional. He does not curse the gods. The eye is there, but it will take time to locate. He probes Spiros's emotions, searching for related avenues. He finds something interesting.

If Spiros's eyeball were to be struck and blinded by his father's malevolent thumb, Spiros's reaction would be ...

And this branches to other centers. Puck probes them, but backs off, sensing unexplored dangers. He forgets the eye for now. He checks Spiros's temperature, blood pressure, pulse, and blood oxygen level. He listens to Spiros's heart and lungs. No signs of trouble.

But Spiros still sees out of one eye, and Puck wants them both. Spiros still controls his destiny, somewhat.

Puck does not curse the gods. He immediately begins a psychological war with Spiros, to seize total control, which is crucial to the cause.

* * *

For Spiros, a while back, everything disappeared over a distant rise. Shadows whispered to him. Now, as the truck halts and the engine is shut off, there is only silence.

He cracks an eye open. He knows the others in the Land Cruiser think he is still passed out. He looks up through the open sunroof. He wants to see a shooting star blaze across the heavens, for luck, but sees only barren purple sky. Then he hears Jelly's voice. And he closes his eye and listens.

"What's your assessment, Kristen-Kate?"

"I think he's being prepped to take on wounds, Jelly. Don't you?"

"Maxwell?"

"I agree with Kristen-Kate. He will take on wounds. He will be remarkable."

"I'm afraid I must disagree," Jelly says. "I think he is being prepped by Puck to be a warrior. I see that as crucial at this juncture. Taking on wounds must occupy a backseat."

"But he has already been taking on wounds," Kristen-Kate says.

"I know," Jelly says. "And if he consciously wants to, I'm sure he can continue to take on wounds, but I think Puck prefers he become a warrior."

"We must prove to the world that it is possible to take on the suffering of others," Maxwell says. "A Jesus therapy, if you will. That is what we need from Spiros."

"I understand your concerns, Maxwell, but it is Puck who decides, not us. I think Puck is setting Spiros on a warrior path. As evidence—"

"I was just going to ask you for evidence, Jelly," Kristen-Kate says.

Maxwell adds, "We already have evidence that Spiros will be a type of Jesus. He has said so himself."

"That Spiros will kill goes without saying," Kristen-Kate says. "All humans can be induced to kill. Puck isn't required for that. Taking on wounds, though, is highly specialized."

"Right you are, Kristen-Kate," Jelly says. "But you're forgetting what we're up against and what we need in the way of killing skills. Let me explain.

"Pretend all the evil people you've ever known are parading past this truck. Imagine them vividly. Stare into their eyes. See their nostrils flare. Hear their throats roar, their feet thunder. See the color of their skin, their hair, their eyes. Smell their rankness. All the evil people you have ever known. Pick the worst one and multiply that times a thousand and you'll have what we have out there now watching us."

"They're here?" Kristen-Kate says in alarm.

"They're here," Jelly says. "Now that you have imagined the evilest person you have ever known and have multiplied that times a thousand, you have what we have out there now watching us. Someone out there has an ax and wants to maim you for life.

"Now pretend you are a child of, say, twelve. A child encultured to be polite and obedient to adults. A child unaware of the dangers of the world. Unaware of the cruelty. A child who, when faced with human evil, will plead and beg and cry for mercy. A child who will be terrified. A child totally defenseless against strong men who wish to take off her arms.

"Now imagine you are one of these strong men, and you have an ax, and you see this child of twelve. You have every reason to believe that you will prevail, and that no harm will come to you as you chop her arms off.

"Now let us fool with this equation a bit. Imagine a monkey. A monkey of any age, any species, either sex. About twelve pounds of monkey, say. And you are a big strong man with an ax, and you are given a mission to go chop off this monkey's arms, and you have helpers with you who will hold this monkey down as you do the chopping.

"So, you see the monkey. And you are ignorant of monkeys. And you walk toward the monkey, your helpers at your side, your ax in your hand, seeing it as small and furry and weak. You are prepared to give it orders. You believe it will meekly obey. You believe it will break down and cry and open up your joy centers as you chop its arms off.

"But as you approach the monkey, suddenly you can no longer see from one of your eyes, and your whole face seems to be on your head sideways. You drop the ax and reach up with your hands, and with your mind spinning away, you try to assess the damage, and suddenly you realize you are a toothpick and that the monkey can break you.

"The monkey does break you. It snaps your neck. And you are dead. And your helpers are similarly disposed of, or have scattered to safer climes.

"Primates are an excellent choice for illustrating violence. The murder rate among apes tops that of humans. Our furry friends also excel in rape and torture. Don't let the bleeding hearts fool you. We humans are far less violent, far less dangerous, than our furry friends. Your standard African monkey would just as soon rip your eyes out as look at you. They hate people. They are strong. And quick. A small monkey is more than you can handle. You'll easily be walking around with your face on sideways.

"Now imagine this girl of twelve faced with these strong men, one of whom carries an ax. They start giving her orders. She's alone. They want her to come with them. She feels a little stress. This does not seem to be a normal situation.

"So, stressed now, and feeling endangered, this little girl experiences a biochemical change, and a little bit of the wild primate creeps into her. She is no longer easy prey.

She is no longer a polite, obedient child of planet earth. She is Empress DNA from outer space and she knows how to survive. Human muscle can be every bit as quick and strong as monkey muscle, given proper priming.

"Instinctively, she fears for her life, her limbs, her safety. She is now biochemically prepared to either scoot to a safe place or to rip their faces off and snap their necks. Her instincts will decide for her. In any case, the man with the ax loses. And, if he survives this encounter, the next time he is faced with the task of chopping off the arms of a twelve-year-old girl, he might take up another line of work."

"And they're out there?" Kristen-Kate asks.

"They're out there, summoned by Puck. This is Spiros's test. Your own as well. You, Maxwell, and Spiros are going for a walk. Some men are going to accost you. One of them will have an ax. The only thing that stands between the three of you and amputation will be Spiros. And Puck."

Kristen-Kate makes an awful mewling sound.

Maxwell joins in, making his own mewling sound, and then shouts, "No!"

Spiros cracks an eye open. Jelly has removed his .45 from its holster. "Out of the truck," Jelly says.

No one moves.

"Puck!" Jelly barks.

Spiros's hand jerks his door open. He steps out, hears the smack of Jelly's pistol against Maxwell's face. Maxwell yelps but is stunned into silence by another smack. Spiros walks around the truck, sees Jelly's door fly open, sees Jelly emerge, a cowed Maxwell in his grip.

Spiros watches Jelly yank Kristen-Kate's door open and

pull her out. She wails and collapses to the ground. Jelly reaches a hand inside her blouse and seizes a breast.

"Start walking, love, or you lose it." He points to the hills with his pistol.

Whimpering, she clutches his arm, pulls herself to her feet, and begins walking toward the hills, Jelly's hand still gripping her breast. Jelly walks beside her a few steps and then removes his hand from her breast. Brandishing his pistol, he motions Maxwell toward Kristen-Kate.

"Stay together," Jelly says. "Look smart, and everything will be just ducky."

Jelly walks behind them.

Spiros falls in beside Jelly. He looks at Kristen-Kate. It's hard to tell in the gloom, and from behind, but she seems to be drowning in tears.

"No candlelight dinner tonight, Kristen-Kate," Jelly says, holstering his .45. "And I had a hyena story to tell."

"Asshole," Kristen-Kate says, sniffling and wiping her tears. "I bet you'll tell it anyway."

Jelly chuckles, and then says, "A hyena's jaws are stronger than a lion's. If Spiros were conscious now, he'd give us a good evolutionary explanation for that."

Suddenly, words trip from Spiros, but they are not his own. They carry an icy resonance that chills him to his bones.

"Many things are known. They swim through the sky. They float through the depths. They leave stars and trace paths of fame. The art of life is written in the constellations above."

Hearing this voice spring from him, Spiros knows he is under possession by Puck, though the possession is not complete.

"Puck is here," Jelly says. "Spiros is gone. Great oration, Puck, old man."

"Jelly, you are the evil one," Kristen-Kate says. "I hate you. Bring Spiros back. He was becoming Jesus."

"Ah, Kristen-Kate, what would you rather have standing between you and a psychotic with an ax, Jesus or a monkey? I'll take a monkey any day. How about you, Maxwell? Jesus or a monkey?"

"A monkey, of course, Jelly," Maxwell says. "I only wanted Jesus to heal the afflicted. But if it's to be a fight, a monkey makes more sense."

"Now you're talking, Maxwell. Kristen-Kate?"

"All right, Jelly. A monkey does make sense now. Spiros?"

He hears her soft voice, senses she has turned her head to look at him. He hears the crunch of grass as they walk along, feels his feet touch earth, and he answers Jelly's call.

"Hyenas hunt but are primarily scavengers. When they find a carcass, it is usually just bones. Only hyenas with powerful jaws can crunch up bones and get nourishment. They alone survive to pass their genes along. Natural selection favors hyenas with powerful jaws. Lions' jaws don't have to be as strong as hyenas'."

"Excellent answer, Spiros, old man. I see you are still with us. You'd better leave soon and leave yourself to Puck, or Kristen-Kate and Maxwell are going to be amputated, yourself as well. What do you say, Spiros?"

"I—" he says. And with that, Spiros sinks away.

❊ ❊ ❊

Puck opens an eye and begins his battle plan. "Jelly," he says, "point out constellations in the heavens as we walk."

"Too light yet, Puck. And I can't say I'm familiar with constellations."

"Pretend. All of you pretend. Pretend as if your lives depend on it."

Jelly does, pointing out imaginary constellations in a sky that shows just a few faint stars. Maxwell and Kristen-Kate look up, pointing, and Jelly weaves a spell. They watch a constellation sail away. Watch it land. Watch it turn into a lion and vanish into the tangles of the night.

"Good, Jelly," Puck says, his voice loosening from its icy spell. "Continue this trickery periodically. Our enemies will soon be in hearing range."

They wander toward the hills, which look like an army of dark tents against the marginally lighter sky. Puck licks the darkness with his consciousness, throwing out mesmerizing shadows of himself as they near the skirmish line.

They reach the hills and travel upward through trees and thickets. Puck continues to probe the darkness, sending fragments of himself farther into the night.

Seven men from Sierra Leone sit in the hills above them. Each carries a pistol and machete. Some of them carry assault rifles. One of them carries an ax. They hear a voice. These men understand English well enough to know that the speaker is talking about the stars in the sky.

Puck allows Spiros to return for a while, to get a feel for the new consciousness, and then sends him away again.

Fully possessing Spiros now, Puck focuses his attention on Jelly, sending telepathic instructions.

Jelly's voice grows loud. "Jovial souls are we; we'll castrate the seven insurgents from Sierra Leone tonight, and name a constellation of seven stars in their memory; call it Eunuch."

Puck sends a portion of his consciousness snaking uphill, and delivers a vulgar translation to the enemy.

Seven enraged men from Sierra Leone begin a flanking maneuver downhill.

Puck brings Spiros back.

"You are Jesus, Spiros. And that is all you are. It is up to you to save your friends. If you feel inadequate, call me. Call Puck. And I will rescue the four of you. And I will castrate the seven and let them wander the hills. And I will stand with cloven hooves and insert myself as ruler of earth. Cheerio, Spiros."

Spiros's mind plunges into a petrifying sea of flowing, shifting shapes. A monstrous heartbeat enters him and two images cry forth: blood and a mirror broken to bits. A thought tethered far away grows closer: *I need a candle ...*

The rebels from Sierra Leone have Spiros, Kristen-Kate, Jelly, and Maxwell spread-eagled on the side of the hill, faces into the grass. They were swarmed over immediately when Puck left. Blazing torches stuck in the ground announce the demon faces around them.

From the corner of his eye, Spiros sees an ax rise above him. He thinks of blood, and of a mirror broken to bits, a mirror that reflects his face in a thousand shattered fragments.

Oh, pray, a mirror for me. But Spiros does not trust in God. So why should he pray? To him the Lord is an old man hard as flint with a mean little stick up his ass.

Puck, come quickly! There, it's done!

The ax comes down in a flash, and Spiros hears a spine-chilling scream.

What am I? Jesus? No, I am a candelabrum. An infinity of candles. And a truth comes to him. There is a power, and it has a multitude of faces, and each face glows, touching all with its wisdom. One face heals. Another face confronts.

The air whips into frenzied rhythms as the man's stump sprays blood. It's one of the men from Sierra Leone. He had been holding one of Spiros's arms out, gripping it at the wrist preparatory to amputation, but Spiros—possessed by Puck—wrapped his hand around the man's wrist and pulled his arm to him as the ax swooped down.

Spiros stands, holding the man's amputated arm by the hand. He tosses it aside. He sees the other six Sierra Leoneans standing in the heat of the blazing torches, their eyes on him, gaping in utter incomprehension.

He takes on their wounds. Since none of them have any wounds to speak of, Spiros feels hardly a twinge in his left foot. But six Sierra Leoneans are now bathed in the light of a compassion they have never known before. Some of them seem to be crying. Their weapons drop from their hands.

Spiros looks at the amputated man. He's cringing in the grass, curled up in fetus posture, holding his abbreviated arm as if it were an infant in swaddling clothes, his face a mixture of shock, disbelief, and rage. Several of his companions are looking his way, possibly trying to share their new-found, heart-strumming compassion with him, or maybe fearful he will draw his pistol and shoot them.

In any case, Spiros will not take on his wounds.

He turns his face upon his six disciples and takes on more of their wounds, reaching deeper into their psyches. His foot aches now. But the six stand with facial muscles twitching, their eyes expressing immeasurable gratitude.

Spiros looks at Jelly, Kristen-Kate, and Maxwell. They are in a tight cluster, standing downhill. All are safe. Jelly gives a cautious wave to Spiros, a tight smile on his face, a slight nod. *Well done.*

"Jelly," Spiros says, "all of you, take torches and go downhill. Wait for me there."

They pull up torches and leave.

Through the flickering light of the remaining torches, Puck becomes a liquid fire dance, electrifying as a butterfly in flight.

He walks to the amputated man, slips the man's knife from its sheath, and cuts away the man's clothing in swift flourishes.

With deft but powerful touches to the man's shoulders, head, and chest, Puck lays him on his back.

With the precision of a master butcher, he cuts off the man's genitals and tosses them into the gloom. He then helps the man to his feet.

As the man rises, the torches illuminate a river of blood gushing from between his legs, and for a moment the man from Sierra Leone looks as if he is giving birth to a hot, liquid fire.

Stabilizing the new eunuch on his feet, Puck hands him his knife and gives instructions. The man stares vacantly; he does not seem to understand English well, though English is the official language of Sierra Leone. Puck breaks into Krio, an English-based creole, understood by ninety-five percent of Sierra Leoneans, but still the man stands dumbly.

The sun, the moon, and the stars shine their light into mine eyes, Puck thinks; in fact, all of creation, the forest, the plain, and all its denizens shine their light to me—but not this dumb bastard. He recognizes this not so much as a language problem but as one of deep recalcitrance. Before long this mutilated fool will be even tougher to deal with.

Puck touches him further—head, chest, shoulders—inducing a deeper somnambulant trance, one more amenable to his control.

Using lots of gestures as he speaks, Puck says, "Look, old man, you'll have to use your teeth as your second hand. You'll have to hurry, but use all due diligence. You are in combat now. You are a surgeon, and you must save lives."

At last the man understands his mission. He accepts it gladly. He hurries to get his clothes on, and puts them on with great difficulty, being new to one-armedness. Puck watches patiently; this was not part of his instructions. But he waits.

Dressed, blood darkening the front of his trousers, the man walks toward Puck, carrying his knife at the ready, pointing his eyes around as if on combat patrol.

Puck touches him on the side of the head. The man stops and Puck turns his attention to the others.

The six bathed in the light of compassion will believe anything Puck tells them. Puck tells them they will enter the Kingdom of Heaven only if they are eunuchs. He tells them to remove their clothes and lie on their backs and assist their comrade as he does the cutting.

They remove their clothes and lie on their backs.

The one-armed man leans over the first disciple, and using his teeth and the knife, cuts off his genitals. He crawls down the line of believers and cuts off the genitals of each.

When he is finished, Puck commands all of them to stand.

"Wander ye through the hills until ye die," Puck says.

They begin to wander. Puck picks up a handgun, places the muzzle to the back of the amputated man's head, and pulls the trigger. The blast blows out a good portion of skull, but the amputated man still walks. Puck shoots him again and again until his head is just a superstructure of face and eyeballs. The man falls to the ground. Puck reloads and blows out the skulls of the other men. And they all fall to the ground.

The gunshots still resound through the hills as Spiros pulls a torch from the ground and heads downhill to join Jelly, Kristen-Kate, and Maxwell.

He sees flaming torches through the trees. The torches begin to display energetic motion. They are a convulsion, tearing place to place and leaping through the forest. He realizes they see his approach and know he is a soul on fire. They are afraid of him and are trying to hide.

Spiros continues walking downhill.

He rejoins Kristen-Kate, Maxwell, and Jelly, and they walk downhill in silence.

After a while, Jelly seems uneasy, and glances around. "Puck is trying to reenter you, Spiros, old man. You lost your nerve and cast him out. He is not happy about that. He will try again."

As they continue their journey downhill, Spiros sees a path propped obscenely open. There is nothing in their human lexicon to account for what happened tonight.

No one foresaw the coming of Puck.

Spiros, Kristen-Kate, Maxwell, and Jelly come together and stand in a tight circle, arms embracing, shock gathering around them like a flock of screeching birds pinching and pulling their flesh, eyes focused on the ground, illuminated by the torches they have stuck into the earth, the flames treading unruly over the things of the earth, ears hearing the crescendo of sound the night is suddenly filled with: the incredible piercing wails of disbelief that come to tortured minds.

They are speechless. They are mindless. They are a mass of huddling flesh, standing alone on the earth.

The forest becomes quiet.

Spiros raises his head and looks at Kristen-Kate, Maxwell, and Jelly, his arms still wrapped around them. Their heads remain bowed. They fear him. Lord knows why they have not deserted him. But he also senses they see him as their protector.

He steps away from them. They raise their heads and look at him.

"Kristen-Kate, Maxwell, Jelly," he says, "when something comes out of the mist, we give it shape and form and substance. We give it a face. We give it a voice. We give it a bush hat or whatever it needs. It is how we order our world. This will be no different."

Spiros looks away from them, tortured thoughts criss-crossing his mind. Was he adequate in explaining what took place tonight? No, he failed miserably. He did not explain anything. He has no voice.

But Puck does. And Spiros and the others hear something faint in the forest:

"In that backward time
Did a haunted sinner chime:
'It collides and collides in a mad ride.
Miles to tell in a whispering well,
A striking bell doth toll from your hell.'"

EPILOGUE

Contingency Plans

A cloaked figure of darkness enters a lecture hall and delivers a lecture for a class called *Preparation for Invasion.*

"What is it like for these nearly exhausted energy forms that still roam earth, mingled amongst the myths and gods and legends and histories and everything else we have created there through their participation? What are they like?

"What are these humans like?

"Let us take a look.

"They do not possess any higher knowledge of who they are or what they are about. They are energy blanks. They are invested with a modest consciousness of a type that makes it easy for us to intervene. They see themselves in a certain way, but it is not a true way. They are merely energy that roams about with a rider: a consciousness that forms an image of itself, which includes a history, myths, and gods.

"In order for us to make use of these blanks, we simply send an energy mass that has infinite power to absorb earth energy. We are taking nothing that is actually there. They think we are taking a face, but there never was a face; they just think there was.

"Usually, though, they have no idea what has happened. Some will, because consciousness forgets nothing—it's a matter of accessing it. Some will access the truth, but it won't be the real truth. They will get a partial truth, some of them. The partial truth is that they have been compromised in some fashion but don't know exactly what. They get a feeling, that's all.

"The real truth, the ultimate truth, is this: they are energy blanks. They walk around with a rider, a consciousness, a thing that gives them identity: their cultural history, their personal history, their form, their shape, their memories, their face.

"As we infuse them with new energy, which we must do periodically to run new dramas, they get a sense of change, yet it has happened to them many times in their long history. They would not exist if not for us, running our dramas there, within the energy they represent.

"They think they are doomed, but they have been through this many times before; it never ends.

"They are energy; consciousness is the true rider, the true self.

"This is just an energy drama, separate from real life, such as it is. We blend our energy with energy blanks that occupy earth, and we direct new dramas, which result in new histories, new myths, new gods, and eventually that one new god that will keep the rabble in their place: the god that serves all needs.

"What is it like for a human experiencing our arrival on earth? Is it important for us to know this? Yes, for it is the beginning of the new myths, the creation of the new gods, and ultimately of the one god that will be the master of all needs.

"We explore this next: the drama of one human being as we begin the new round of dramas. They think they're human; we know better. But they must be ignorant of their true selves in order for any of this to work.

"A man in a cabin is the first to encounter us. Not the first; there have been others, but he is the first to really get a feel for it. He is a philosopher, and through him we will get our name, which is light beings.

"He was sent to the cabin by a mysterious organization. He was given little information. He thinks something has changed, some new discovery or something, and he must help them break the news to the population.

"The man in the cabin runs out of food and coffee, and resupply is late. He undergoes sickness, caffeine withdrawal, and thereafter experiences a changed environment. It's changed because we have arrived in his immediate area. We have, of course, been operating elsewhere, or the man in the cabin wouldn't be there; there'd be no need for a philosopher to figure us out.

"Ultimately, these feeble energy forms on earth might figure themselves out, but still think they have an identity. Their alleged identity is just a mirror image of a narrow band of consciousness, soon to blank out after our dramas are done, when we have our new god. Then the energy forms on earth will continue to roam in the midst of the old dramas, histories, myths, and gods that form their blinkered existence.

"The man in the cabin wakes after his sickness is over and he is healthy again, and he goes outside and sees tracks, our tracks. He follows them and sees a black formless mass in the distance. The mass chases him back to the cabin. The man slams the door and bolts it.

"All these details must be focused on: life is not life without the details that give it authenticity.

"The man goes out the next day and sees more tracks. He comes to a conclusion. The black mass was looking for his face. He is correct. But he doesn't know the black mass is him now, and so we give him some knowledge, so he can do some writing, and begin our dramas.

"The man contacts the outside world with his radio, but that is not really his main way of communicating. His way is writing. He is writing our story, the beginning, giving warning. He is already one of us. Little does he know he was always one of us, an energy blank.

"We next see Vinnie and Greta Kincaid, a couple on their honeymoon in the same cabin as Todd Schwartz, our philosopher.

"How can this be? Well, it's because we have two worlds to play these games in. We have alternate worlds, so we can control better. This is not difficult; there are mirrors all over that reflect us all infinitely. Earth energy forms do not know this.

"We must ask questions. It is a good way to clarify.

"What happens when an alien life-form comes to earth and makes use of humans for a purpose? And the purpose is to create new dramas and a new god for this alien society. What happens when consciousness changes and no one knows why? What happens when humans acquire new memories, lose track of people and places they once knew, and begin doing new things with people they've never seen before?

"What happens when a philosopher claims earth is under invasion by strange beings called light beings? What happens when no one doubts him? What happens when people accept this?

"What happens when people come out of the wilderness changed? When no one is immune from this?

"What happens when a technology capable of mimicking an alien invasion appears?

"Dark times are upon earth as people report strange encounters with black, formless masses.

"The formless energy comes. It steals what it needs. It steals human faces. It steals human lives.

"The energy comes and wends deep into human society and acquires the shape and form of humans and begins the dramas that lead to a new history, new myths, and new gods.

"Our first new god will be a pain god. If you have pain, something will appear next to you. You will get used to it eventually, but first it will be disconcerting.

"Your pain god will take on some of your pain, but will also leave you with some of it. It will eventually manage your pain, relieving you of the worst symptoms, and giving you enough to remind you that you have a condition.

"What is the value of a pain god? It can make life livable for millions of people.

"A pain god, though, might make your pain worse if it has a reason to, for it is in control of you. It is your personal god. You cannot escape it.

"What happens when you begin to feel pain outside your body, when you begin to share consciousness with others, when you begin doing new things with people you've never seen before?

"What happens when you break your shoulder and you feel pain ten feet away from you?

"What happens when a ravenous animal in the forest chases you and you run into your cabin and bolt the door and hide from it and you discover the next morning that the animal has stolen your face and it likely has returned to civilization as you, and here you are, and you think you have a face; you look in the mirror and see a face but the more you look you realize you have no face and the more you keep looking the more you realize you never had a face at all and the more you keep looking you realize you are nothing more than an energy blank with a rider, which is a bit of consciousness that seems under the control of someone else, and the more you continue to look in the mirror you realize you likely have no identity at all; you are an energy blank; all people on earth are energy blanks; all of you are continually being used by the intelligence of another world in dramas that shape myths, histories, and gods.

"That is what you begin seeing when you look in the mirror long enough. You see all of history etched upon your face, all myths, all gods, all people, all ideas, all of it swirling within your own identity, which must mean you have no identity, and then you see your face again and you know what's lurking behind it but you are losing the memory and you realize something is happening to change all of earth's inhabitants.

"You look in the mirror or any reflective surface and you think you see another world moving in. You look around you and you think you see the same thing, fleetingly. You experience things outside of yourself, including pain. You begin to experiment with the new consciousness and realize you can blend with others, and they with you. You think of the possibilities and you believe you must inform others; you have a responsible position.

"You speak to others, and they report the same strange things, shadows on the edge of things, a new world moving in. You must be careful, though, because there might be another explanation. You are dealing with consciousness and it is tricky.

"You cannot avoid it. A new world is moving in. You are rapidly losing track of the changes. You must get others to record things so the old ways are not forgotten. You must break the news to the population. You employ an expert to do this.

"You realize you have employed one of them, an expert sent by that new world that is moving in.

"What happens when a new world moves in?

"You see shapes around you: black formless shapes. The shapes notice you and chase you. You lock yourself in and you think one of them has stolen something from you. It has stolen your face. It has stolen you.

"When something new appears, we give it a face, or whatever it needs. We cannot tolerate black formless masses in our midst. We must give them shape, a name, a face. We must identify it somehow.

"Life is no longer simple. Now we have two worlds in which we must live. Fortunately, we do not retain much memory of the other world. Through living in two worlds we gain empathy for others, but also toughness. We need to be tougher.

"We realize another civilization is intruding, and bringing us another world, and reflecting us in its world, for it is the only way.

"We believe we are dead. We believe we have been wiped out by a catastrophic event. We don't recall it. We can't, because we were wiped out at the time. A dead person can't recall what killed him. We don't recall the event that wiped us out, or altered us. Are we dead? We are different. What is the difference? We feel pain outside of us. We sense an entity close to us. There are such things as pain gods now. We didn't have them before, did we?

"There are other new things that we don't recall having before. But we are losing track of the changes. We can't even find writing that makes sense of the changes. It's all disappearing. We are disappearing, too, at least as we were before.

"We are different now. We have two worlds to live in. Before, we had one. We are learning to be tougher, and to have empathy. We have pain gods now that manage our pain. We have less pain, but more pain. We find ourselves missing sometimes, and reappearing, sometimes wounded.

We have unexplained wounds. We know we are being used by another civilization for something. We know we are energy blanks, shaped for war or for other dramas to serve an unknown world. We know they are searching for a new god, new dramas, new myths. We believe the purpose of earth is to serve this civilization as a training ground. We believe when they leave us alone, we dive into a swirl of old earth memories, myths, histories, and gods, until it's time again for us to be reshaped, reconfigured, into useful forms for the dramas of this other world.

"Is there another explanation? Yes. There could be a technology that controls consciousness, but we think it couldn't explain everything. We think there is a technology that controls environments, but a technology that drives all of this?

"We think it's another world moving in and rearranging us in some odd fashion for dramas, myths, histories, and gods.

"A new world is moving in. It causes us to have another identity. Each of us is two, now. It is difficult to live two lives, because we have memories trailing off, still dipped in that other world. We are learning new things. We aren't human. We are energy blanks. We are given shape and substance, a face, a voice, to play roles in dramas for another world.

"We all have many identities. We all live in more than one world. We all have other identities helping us, and harming us. Till now we didn't know this.

"New tableaus are around. They include new myths and new gods. They also include us. We discover we are each in another world, as well as in this one.

"A new round of activities is planned. We will each play a part. Some of us will play many parts. We will sacrifice ourselves and play roles that help another civilization create new myths and new gods. We do this willingly. We know nothing else but our duty. But some say there are memories of another way, another life, where we had choice. But that was a hard life, they say. This is so much easier, so much better, not having to choose. So, we sacrifice. We wake up with wounds we can't account for. We know we are being used in war by someone else. We see gods around us. Some of these gods help us; some of them are probably going to destroy us. What can we do? We are energy blanks used by another civilization. We don't have choice. We are in dramas, and in the dramas we have choice, but it's limited, contained within the boundaries of the dramas. We know nothing else.

"A new memory asserts itself: humans believe they are dead, victims of a mysterious catastrophe. No one remembers the event. Life goes on, but now we are each two people, some of us even more. It seems a mirror is being held up to us, and we each have another identity within the mirror.

"A mysterious predator is going around breaking people's necks. This predator does not want to kill his victims, but wants them kept alive on life support. He dials 911 and calls for an ambulance before he commits his assaults.

"What happens when a mysterious predator goes around torturing and mutilating victims and leaving them without adequate powers of speech or memory to tell of the events?

"What happens when a person has a suspicion of living another life and it's just outside memory, but not completely?

"What happens when a person wakes in a new environment, one not too different from what he is used to, but different enough for him to call on his two-way radio and report it to the people who put him in that environment in the first place? Is that what they expected, this change, and him reporting it? They were vague when they briefed him before sending him in. Now he must let them know of the change. He calls them and they don't seem too concerned. But by all rights, they should be. What, he wonders, is going on?

"What happens when a young woman leaves a secret facility at night and drives the back roads until she is safe at home where the hands do not reach her? In her half sleep she reviews her job as it was originally constituted: the tiny writing in her contract explained by a stern Army colonel. The Pentagon was developing ways of reformulating the perceptual processes of an enemy, to sink them. That was the purpose of the African training site, where she saw giants in cages, giants leaving cages. Where she saw crumpled forest and simulated executions that didn't seem like simulations. If anything should go awry there were contingency plans. She drifts asleep, thinking the contingency plans were now in effect."